HEGEMON REIGN
Shadows of Nemesis - Book One

S. J. Halls

Hegemon Reign

Copyright © 2024, S. J. Halls

First published, 2024
Minor revisions, July 2024 [Reprint 1]

All rights reserved. No part of this book may be reproduced in any form or by any electronic or mechanical means, including information storage and retrieval systems, without permission in writing from the author, except by a reviewer who may quote brief passages in a review or article. S. J. Halls asserts the moral right to be identified as the author of this work.

This is a work of fiction. Names, characters, places, and incidents either are the product of the author's imagination or are used fictitiously. Any resemblance to actual persons, living or dead, events, or locales is entirely coincidental.

Book cover image Copyright © S. J. Halls

ISBN: 9798884418523

Published by S. J. Halls (sjhalls.com)

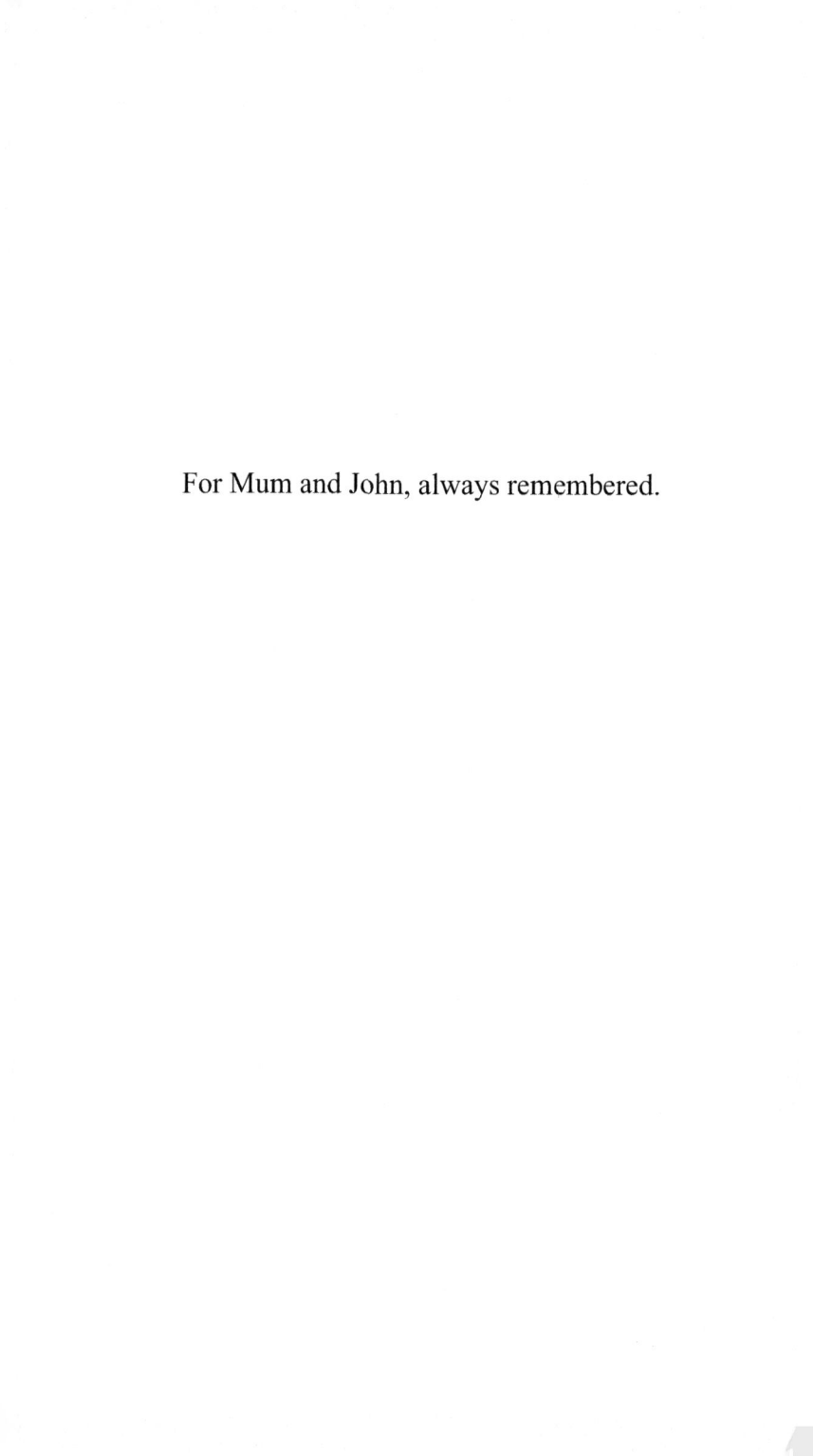

For Mum and John, always remembered.

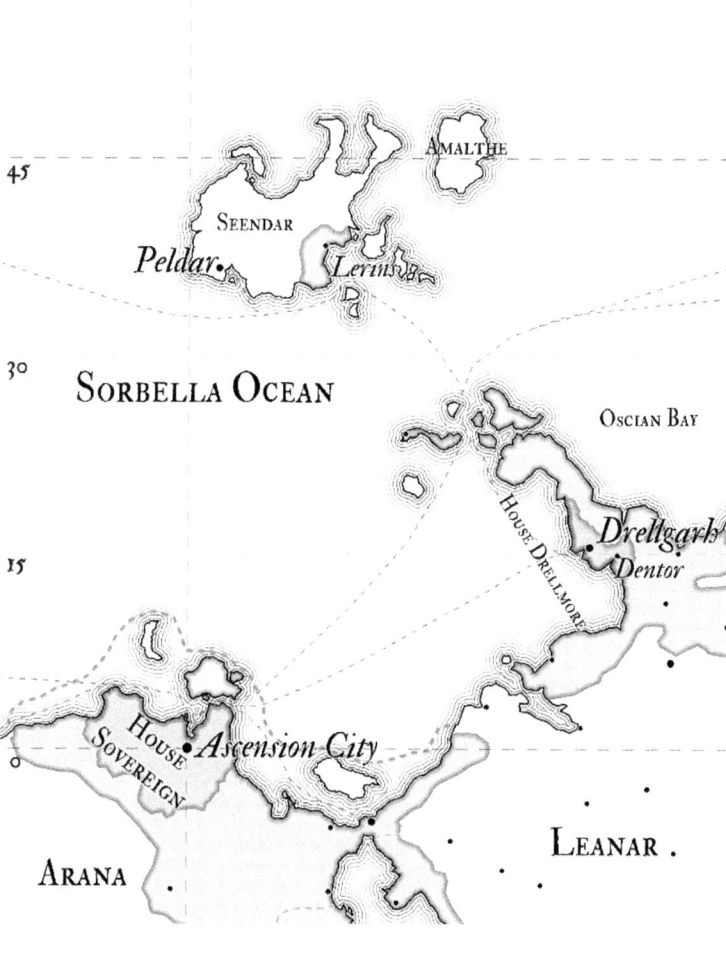

Sorbella Ocean region

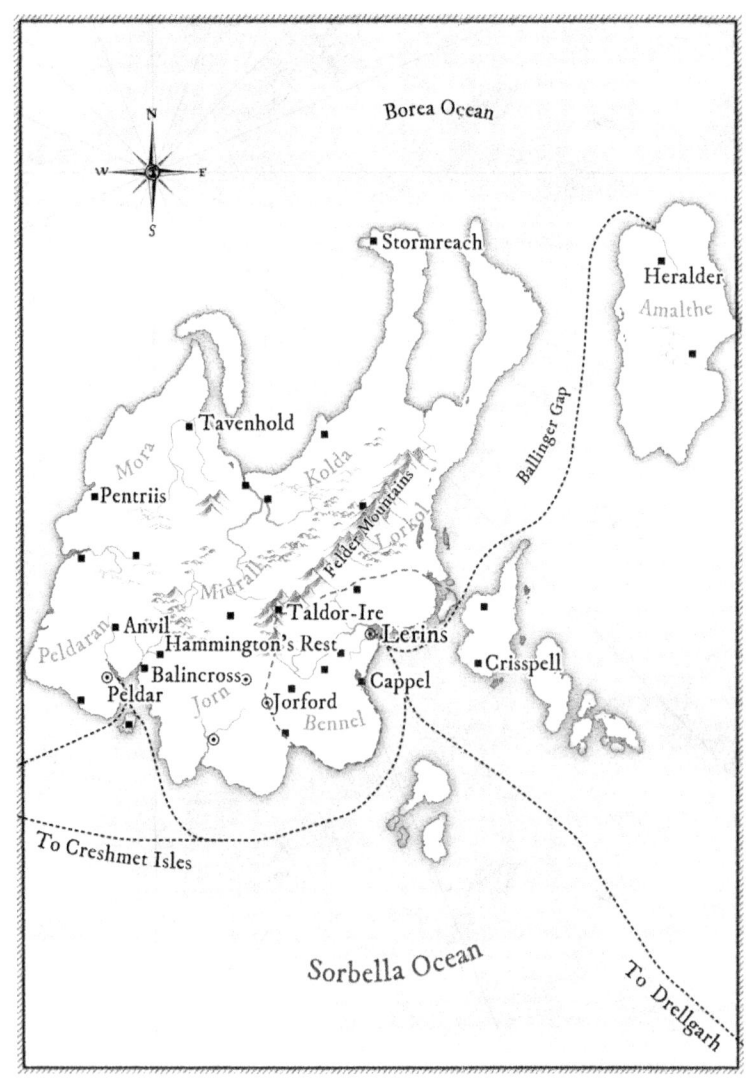

Map of Seendar islands

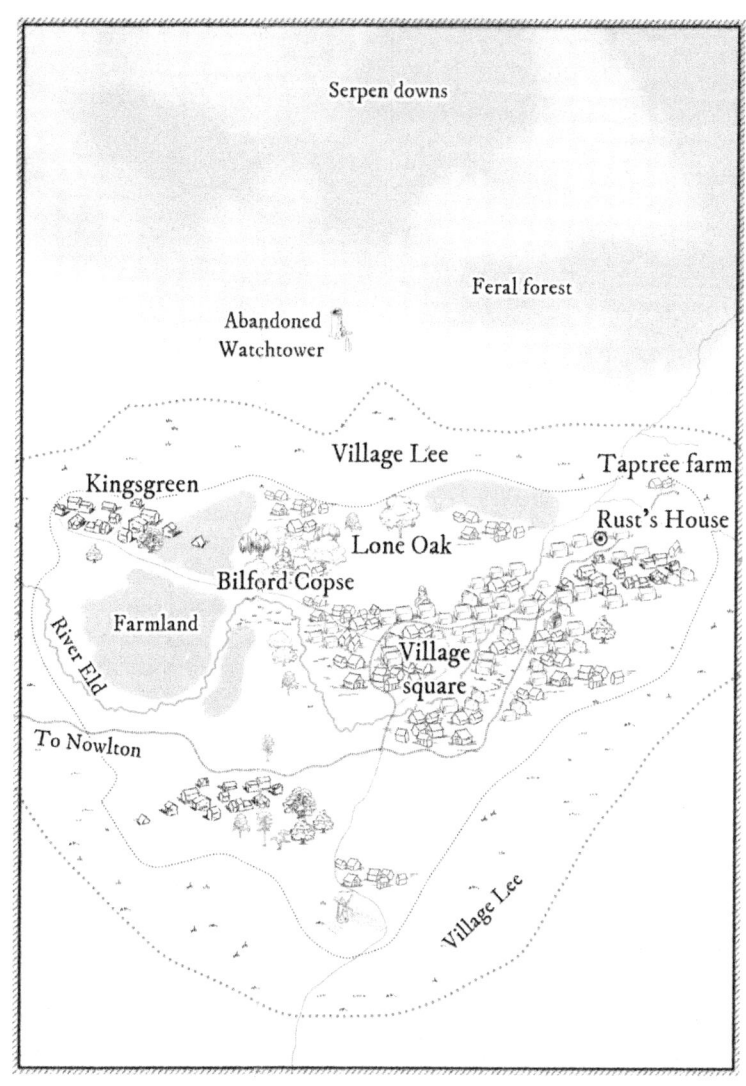

Hammington's Rest

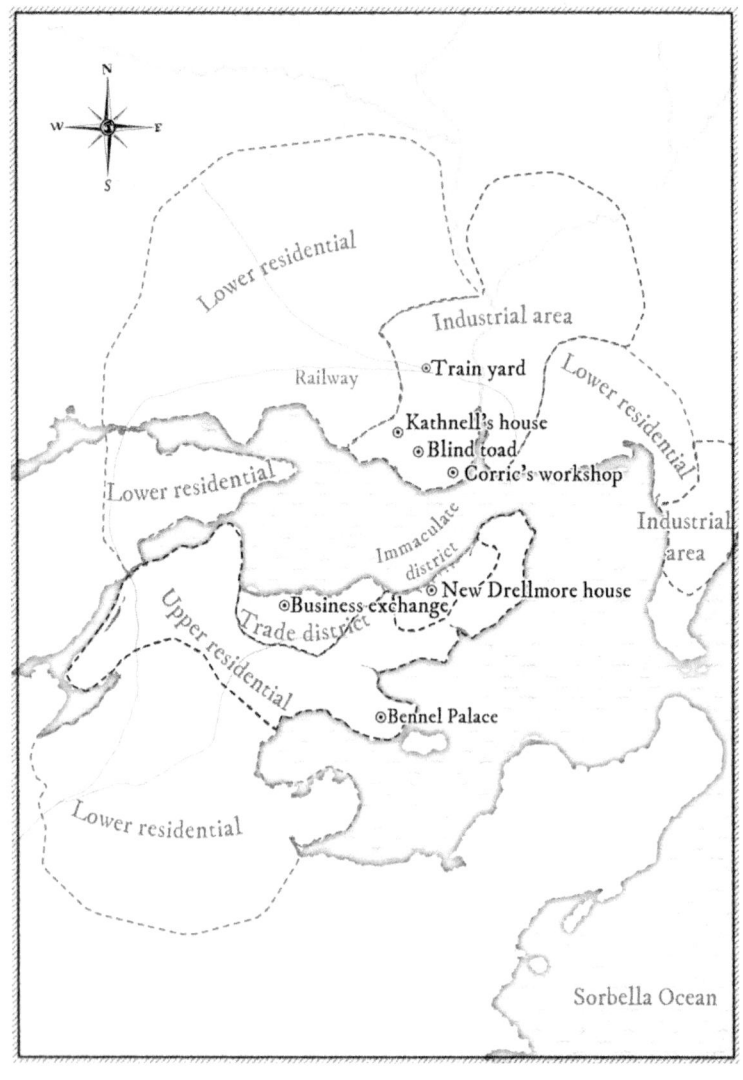

Map of Lerins City

Part One

What is a memory? Truth? Fiction?

I have memories. I remember. But, are they real, or something fabricated? Is there a difference? I'd like to think that the things I hold dear and cherish are mine. But can I really be sure?

Are they immutable or malleable? A series of singular moments strung together in a semi-coherent sequence. But does remembering alter the memory itself, so that it changes over time, becomes distorted, evolves? Do we amplify some portions and deaden the rest, to where it bears little resemblance to the actual moment?

Do the actual moments still exist in time? Locked for eternity, fixed and unchanged. Prisoner of the past. Forever existing, but no longer observable.

You'd think that after all this time I would know, but even at my ancient age, I do not.

I remember the person I was in life. Things I liked: the food, the places, the smells, the people. The sweet taste of a ripe strawberry plucked from hydroponics. A lover's smell. The intense cold of tasting vacuum. So long ago.

Before I died.

Before I became something different.

I suppose I can be surer of my memories after that point. Maybe those before are simply a fabrication constructed for my benefit. To ease me into this new extant state. Memories woven around a fiction of someone who didn't exist, or a pastiche from several.

Enough! Sometimes I bore myself with endless philosophy and internal debate. As they say, I will be what I will be.

My role in this story began long ago, under different skies. This isn't that story, although it is important to what came after.

This story begins much later.

We both thought we were doing the right thing. A clash of ideals.

Chapter 1

He dreamed The Long Dream. The world turned. The skies wheeled.

Ages past. Until, at last, the dreaming ended.

The Emperor awoke.

He perceived the wonders his children had achieved.

They hailed for all to look at what they were creating again.

And he knew that all would be lost.

For Nemesis would come once more.

Books of Maleth - Origins - Eight

Rust

Bright daylight above, deep darkness below, dividing the world in two.

Rust gasped for breath, clinging to the rope. The only thing preventing another plummet. Her feet scrabbled for purchase against the shaft. Sore palms, a harbinger of rope-burns yet to form. Her body had struck the wall hard during her brief fall. Her ribs burned, bruised at least, she thought. She felt tentatively around the pain of each new breath.

The descent into the ruin had been going well, until her foot slipped against the ancient stone, slick with moisture.

A shadow appeared in the square patch of daylight above. Indiril. Older than Rust by two years, and least six hands taller. A trait he shared with the rest of the tree-folk. Rust, by comparison was relatively short for a human, standing just fifteen hands high.

"You alright?" Indiril called, long hair hanging down around his face.

She replied with an indistinct croak. She spat dust and grit. Tasted blood.

"Rust?" Indiril called again, "Rust!?"

She gulped down air and the tightness in her chest lessened a little.

"I'm fine," she croaked. "Just the wind knocked out of me, tis' all."

"Did you fall far?"

She dabbed blood from a split lip. It wasn't too bad.

"No. I've hurt a couple of ribs, though. Nothing broken. I think."

"I knew this was a nax-headed idea. Dumb! Can you see the bottom?"

"Shit. Hold on."

Rust let her eyes adjust to the gloom. The bottom, still an indistinct shadow.

"I reckon it's another fifteen hands. Maybe twenty. Going to continue."

"Are you sure? We should go back," Indiril said.

"I'm fine. When I get down, I'll tell you."

"Shit. Sindar's teeth be bloody careful. What do I do if you fall?"

Rust smiled to herself. Indiril rarely swore. He was almost certainly praying to Sindar and the Divines in whom he put so much trust.

"Stop worrying! I'm fine."

Rust reached the bottom and lit her lamp with a match. The heavy scent of gelderbush oil filled her nose. She closed the glass cover, and the light strengthened and steadied. Both lamp and matches were from Uncle's store room. Taken without permission, of course. He knew nothing of what they were up to.

"I'm down. Going to look around," Rust said.

"Be quick, for the Divines' sake. We need to head back to the village. I promised I'd help uncle Beldar at the temple. With All Winnows Day coming, there's a lot to do, and…"

"Yeah, yeah," Rust cut him off.

Typical Indiril, always worrying about pleasing his family. Trying to get his father's approval.

In the lamplight, Rust could make out more details. A square shaft made from bright white stone, twenty hands in width. The floor made of the same stuff. Smooth to the touch, cold, damp, and slightly translucent. Similar to the packed snow you found in the village's cold-store.

Elderstone! It had to be. Relic of the long vanished Maleth. Some said these places were haunted by ghosts. This was the first one that Rust had seen up close. Unlike Indiril, she didn't believe in ghosts or haunted ruins. The reason he'd refused to descend.

Water dripped from above. It didn't pool on the floor. Instead, it vanished into the floor's surface. The place smelled damp. Wet soil and rotting vegetation. The air was cool. Cooler than it was at the surface. Cooler than it should be at the height of summer. Rust shivered.

Three corridors led off from the shaft. Two of them ended a few hands in, full of impacted soil and loose rocks. A pick, broom, bucket, and shovel lay just inside one.

The third corridor was clear, inclining downwards. It ended at an iron banded wooden door. Definitely NOT part of the ruin, she thought. Installed relatively recently. The wood was new, unblemished. She tried to open it. Locked. It would take over five people to force it open.

Rust reached into her pocket and withdrew a single iron key. The one Uncle kept hidden in a box at the back of the plantation tool-shed. She inserted it, and to her slight surprise, it unlocked with a faint click.

"The key worked!", Rust shouted.

"Shit. I really don't think this is a good idea!" Indiril's response echoed down the shaft.

Rust ignored him. He was prone to backing out just when things got interesting. This was the best thing they'd done in years! It reminded her of when they were children. Now, they were both on the cusp of adulthood. There wouldn't be many more opportunities like this.

They hadn't come upon the ruin by chance. It was a year ago when Uncle's activities had raised Rust's suspicions. Uncle had said he was going into Nowlton. Instead, Rust had spied him disappearing into the feral woods to the north. Nowlton was west, along the main road. There was nothing north of the village, except for an unbroken expanse of feral woodland. He'd returned later the same day. She'd seen him do it several more times since. Every few months. She'd never followed him the whole way.

Until last week.

As usual, he'd left Hammington's Rest and turned north,

across the lee that separated the village from the feral-lands and into the fields of creepgrass beyond. Up into the dark Spinewood. She'd been careful to keep out of sight. Years of Uncle's training were put to good use. He would be proud!

After a couple of hours, Uncle had stopped in the middle of a clearing on top of a hill. The crest marked by an unusually tall spindle oak. Unlike Lone Oak that grew on the village common, spindle oaks were twisted nightmares, all angles and spines. This one was huge, at least a hundred metres high.

They were deep within the feral. Even the summer hunting parties rarely came this far. Around the clearing, white Elderstone spires jutted from the soil, three meters high. Like white fingers reaching for the sky.

Rust squatted behind a feral bush, avoiding its venomous spines. A heavy rain started. Water ran through her hair. She wiped it from her eyes. She was quickly soaked. Somewhere nearby came the shrill cry of a cinder-crow. A sound terrifying to people unaccustomed to the feral. Not to her. She knew they were harmless vermin.

Uncle removed branches from the ground, lifted a wooden hatch, and secured a rope around a nearby white spire. The whole procedure: ordered, practised, familiar. He'd disappeared into the ground. He'd reappeared twenty minutes later and returned home.

The whole strange episode had raised many questions. Why did Uncle visit this place? What was hidden here? Why had he never mentioned this place?

Today, she was determined to find out.

She'd waited until Uncle left with the rest of the weekly caravan for Nowlton. A regular trip to buy supplies for their Taptree farm. He wouldn't be back until tomorrow.

Rust had spent the last week persuading Indiril to come with her. In the end, he'd relented. Rust wasn't sure if he wanted to go, or more likely, he'd agreed to come just to shut her up. Now he probably wished he hadn't agreed.

Rust hesitated, her hand gripping the door handle.

Sybelle

Sybelle Drellmore stepped into the carriage. The interior smelled of delicate perfume. Velvet seats, freshly cleaned in readiness for the journey. Gellid, their butler, closed the door behind her.

The driver issued commands. The carriage lurched. Wooden wheels rolling unevenly on the cobblestone courtyard. Sybelle let out a sigh. Her stomach was a tight ball.

"Try not to worry, Syb," her mother said. "Everything will be fine. Whatever happens. It will be all right. The saints will watch over you."

Mother always said inane things like that. Try not to worry! Everything will be fine. Saints this, saints that. Mother sat on the opposite bench. Despite Mother's smile, Sybelle could see the concern in her eyes.

Sybelle removed her aspect from her face and rubbed her eyes. She began biting her nails. A habit that started after her brother died. She often thought about him. The tiny scar above his right eye from when he'd hit his head on a tree. She tried not to let the memories go. Each month, they became hazier. She was terrified one day she would wake up and they would evaporate completely. Burned away like morning mist. She'd been sixteen when he'd died. She was seventeen now.

"Syb. Stop biting your nails. And put your aspect back on," Mother said. "It's disrespectful for an immaculate to be seen in public without it."

"Yes, Mother," Sybelle replied, re-fastening her porcelain aspect over her face. Her reply was overemphasised, bordering on sarcastic. She tried not to be like that. She hated how it sounded.

It was customary for every immaculate over the age of seventeen to wear an aspect in public. She still found its presence uncomfortable. A foreign object. Itchy. Sweaty. Mother insisted she would get accustomed to it in time. She hated it.

Her aspect was simple and covered only her forehead, painted the same colour as the velvet bench. The sea-blue of House Drellmore with four golden feathers denoting she was a member of the ruling Drellmore family. She tightened the leather straps that secured it to her face. The itch returned immediately.

Her mother's aspect covered her forehead, nose and eyebrows. Its golden feathers, larger, more elaborate. Still far simpler than the face covering, gem encrusted, and exquisitely designed aspects of the central family.

They passed through ornate gates and into the street. Sybelle tried to forget about the upcoming test that would decide her future. Or lack of it, she thought. She sighed again.

"And, for the blessing of our Emperor and his holy Saints, please stop sighing," Mother said.

"Yes, Mother," she replied.

Her mother frowned. Let her, Sybelle thought.

Sybelle looked at the world outside. Neat streets. Houses surrounded by stone high walls. Made from red-stone, quarried from mountains to the east. Balconies and red-tiled roofs. Cut lawns and neat rose gardens. Expensive. Exclusive. Typical Upper-Drellgarh. Home to the immaculate families that ruled House Drellmore. Many streets away lay Drellgarh Palace, from which Lord Sayond Drellmore VIII ruled. It sat prominently on a hill, visible from the entire city. Grey granite walls rising above the park. The embodiment of the House's wealth and power.

Sybelle had never set foot inside the palace. Mother had, many years ago. Their own home was on the lower edge of Upper-Drellgarh, where it gave way to the richer mundane-human houses beyond. Even though they were Drellmores, they were far from the line of succession. Still, their name carried weight. And with that, responsibility.

Sybelle fidgeted, worrying about the test. Out of the other window lay the human section of the city, the docks, and the deep blue of Maris Bay. It was hot, the midday sun shining from a cloudless summer sky. Sybelle slid the window down, breathing in the fresh breeze from the ocean.

The mundane-human part was far larger than the immaculate one. It spilled over the lower slopes of the hills that bordered the bay.

Sybelle wished she could walk through the lower city like a mundane. Free from responsibility. Free from worry. Master of her future. Without her aspect, she would look just like the mundanes. Darker skin maybe, but there were mundanes from elsewhere that had similar coloured skin. Most in House Drellmore were dark-skinned, but other immaculate families had fair skin. The ruling family of House Carthain had fair skin and golden hair. Remove the clothes and there wasn't much to tell immaculate and mundane apart. She could cut her long black hair. Cover it with a headscarf. Apart from the gift that ran in their blood, she didn't know why the immaculate were so special.

Smoke rose from industrial areas. The bay was full of ships of all shapes and sizes. Drellmore was a house of the ocean. Its navy was the best in the Hegemony, which by definition, made it one of the best in the World.

The great naval docks came into view. Two large warships were in dock. Sun glinting off polished metalwork. One more was leaving, powering through the calm waters, heading out into the Sorbella ocean. Water vapour billowed from stacks, hinting at the void-stone powered fury within.

As a child, she loved watching the void-ships. Her father would take her and her brother Belar down to the overlook. Watch them for hours. Now, the sight deepened Sybelle's black mood. It reminded her of the last time she had seen

Belar alive. Before he went to fight the bloody heretics, never to return.

It had been last summer. Almost a year to the day. There was no cool breeze that day. Air still, dry, and heavy. Dust hung suspended in the air. The seaward horizon was black. Distant thunderstorm clouds yet to break upon the land. There was an earthy smell in the air; of rain upon distant dry land. The heat reflected from the worn quayside.

It was always hot in Drellgarh during the summer, but it had been exceptionally hot that day.

They had gone down to the naval docks to see Belar off. He was twenty and had recently graduated from the Drellmore Army academy. He was dressed in a neat blue uniform, with a long cloak detailed in gold. A sword hung at his waist. Smart. Impeccable. His aspect covered his face from the nose up. Three bright green triangles denoted the rank of lieutenant. Just above, two gold triangles of the Jurament. The elite summoners of the Hegemony military.

The Jurament possessed the most powerful magical artefacts and weapons. The Hegemony military was the most advanced in the world, but it was the Jurament that was most respected. They selected only the best summoners. Belar had been exceptional.

Mother and Father had beamed with pride. Uncle Zarl congratulated Belar on being a fine example to them all. The docks teemed with activity to prepare for the fleet's departure. Sybelle was mesmerised. So many people, both human and immaculate. Carts loaded with weapons, provisions and personal effects.

The huge iron hulled warship towered over the dockside. Clouds of white water vapour rose from its stacks, venting unused energies from the massive void-stones within. Void-stones that could only be tamed by summoners.

She stared as a huge tracked vehicle had risen out of the water along a stone ramp. At least three metres high, and twice that length. The front was glass, water visible within.

A ceph conveyance!

The first she had seen up close. The massive blue tentacled bulk of a ceph matriarch moved within. It turned, and she looked into one of its dark eyes. A deep intelligence stared back.

The ceph were like squid, but much larger. Intelligent. Cunning. They were a valued part of the Hegemony. Markings on the conveyance denoted this one was from House Oceanis, the most powerful ceph house. Smaller forms moved within, attentive and submissive. Non-sentient males.

Several humans attended the conveyance. One was watching the ceph matriarch closely as it made a complex series of patterns with its tentacles, swirling from one shape to another. The human translated these into the common tongue for the benefit of the other humans. Sybelle wondered what they were discussing.

"… learn some ceph, Syb?"

"Eh?" Sybelle replied.

Belar laughed. He had been talking, but she'd been lost in her thoughts. The rest of her family were all smiling as well. She felt suddenly stupid. Felt the heat rising in her cheeks.

"I said, are you trying to learn some ceph?" Belar repeated.

"Oh, I was trying to work out what they were saying."

"Probably discussing the voyage. Did you know that most iron-hulls have at least one matriarch on board? They command the brood sisters and the males. Very useful they are, too."

"No. I didn't know that."

"Well, Syb. It's time. I need to be going. We'll be leaving in another hour, and I need to report in."

She threw herself at him. Gripped him tightly, burying her head into his chest. A series of sobs went through her. Belar laughed and said she was just sad that she wouldn't be able to get him into any more trouble. They had all laughed. It was a happy day, but tinged with sadness. Full of pride and hope for the future.

"I don't want you to go," she said. "It's dangerous."

"Hey, Syb. It's fine. I'll be gone for six months, a year at most. I know it seems like a long time, but it'll fly past. When I get back, I'll tell you all about the things I've seen."

"Might even bring you back a present from 'the other side of the world'," he said theatrically, sweeping his arm towards the horizon.

She laughed.

"Will you write?"

"Of course. But only if you promise to keep studying. One day, you might follow in my footsteps. The gift may be strong in you, too. Do you promise?" Belar said.

"I promise."

They had stood on the dockside and watched as the ships left port. It had been nighttime. Sybelle was exhausted. The storm had arrived and rain lashed down from swirling clouds. They took shelter in a nearby pavilion. Syb's mother had been smiling, but there was a weight behind her eyes.

That was the last time they had seen her brother. The heretics had killed him three months later. Somewhere in the deep feral jungle near House Bargolis, far away, thousands of miles to the East. No presents would ever arrive. No letters.

Instead, they had returned to the docks several weeks after to collect his ashes. They'd cremated his body already. She had overheard her father saying it was because his body had been mutilated and badly burned. Her mother sobbing. That conversation had seared itself into her mind. It still haunted her now.

The heretics had not only taken her brother from them; they had taken his dignity and her family's ability to bury him. The heretic rebellion had gone from being something they taught in school to a terrible reality. They'd stood in silence as Belar's ashes were handed over. Words of condolence said. They'd travelled back home in silence.

Father had scattered the ashes in the garden. Mother had wept. Sybelle had just stood. No tears, just numbness. A brief gust of wind had carried some ashes over the garden wall and away. Gone.

She'd realised then that her life was not her own. The immaculate had a responsibility and duty to rule the Earth. In the name of the glorious God-Emperor, whom had blessed them with the gifts that protected them all. The cost of those gifts was sometimes high.

Hatred had also flowered in her. It remained to this day. She often prayed to the Emperor for revenge against those that had killed him. Such prayers were bad, against the church's teachings, but it didn't stop her.

They arrived outside the College of Thaumaturgy. The carriage entered through iron gates hanging from giant stone pillars. The college spanned a vast area. Grand stone buildings separated by cultivated gardens and tree-lined avenues.

Hundreds of students walked through the grounds. Almost everyone inside the walls of the college grounds was immaculate. Any mundanes were closely supervised by the guilds.

She was here to undergo the Test of Attunement. It would determine if she was a gifted summoner. Every immaculate of her age had to take it. If she passed, she would be enrolled into the College and trained how to harness the gift.

If she didn't pass, she would continue to attend school until the end of summer, and then on to normal college for two years. There was no shame in it. Most immaculate didn't possess the gift.

Neither Mother nor Father had possessed the gift to a high enough level. But Belar had been exceptional. It happened sometimes. Just the right mix of bloodlines.

The weight of the test pushed down upon her. She'd thought of little else. She had a feeling that the future was an unchanging line, and she was a passive observer, waiting to see what fate had in store.

The carriage stopped outside a large building. A middle-aged man in white college robes was waiting for them outside. His aspect covered his forehead only.

"Miss Drellmore, would you follow me please?" he said.

A gigantic statue of the God-Emperor stood guard outside the entrance. Smooth, almost featureless face turned towards the sky. Arms raised in front. Water flowed from upturned palms into a pool of water beneath. Several students and academic staff prayed on mats in front.

Banners of the Hegemony houses hung on either side of the entrance. The Colleges of Thaumaturgy encompassed all the Hegemony, not just one House. Under them, all houses were equal.

There were four banners fewer than there used to be. Those belonging to the heretic houses were absent. Removed after the Schism twenty-eight years ago. At school they lectured about the Schism all the time. The history. The reason. During the Schism, Nemesis had sent the heretics to wreak havoc and spread chaos. The ancient enemy. Its temptations had seduced them. Only the wisdom of the immortal Emperor kept them safe. She sometimes wondered what it would be like if the Emperor wasn't there to protect them. It gave her nightmares.

There had been five heretic houses originally, but one of them, House Bargolis, had been defeated. The cost had been high for both sides. Now there were just four rebel houses. They still continued to cause trouble worldwide.

The corridors twisted and turned. They came to a square wooden panelled room with a large window giving splendid views of the college grounds and the city beyond.

"Please, take a seat. I will return shortly," the man said. "Help yourself to tea and a biscuit."

Sybelle chewed her nails again.

"Syb…," her mother said.

"Sorry, Mother."

Mother poured them both a cup of tea.

"And try not to worry."

Sybelle sipped the hot fragrant tea.

"What happens if I pass?"

"Then you will do our family a great honour."

They sat in silence for a few minutes. The same man that had greeted them returned.

"If you would like to step this way, Miss Drellmore?" he said.

She stood and followed. Her mother remained seated. She would have to do this next part alone. Her mother smiled and mouthed, *go, it will be fine*.

More corridors. The walls loomed over her. Her future would be decided in the next few minutes. Summoner, or career. Military, or civilian. Left, or right.

She was taken to a small room with three people wearing college robes sitting behind an ornate wooden desk. All immaculate. Each bore aspects denoting seniority within the college. The outer two people had aspects that covered the forehead, top of the nose and eyes. The woman in the middle, older by several decades, wore an aspect that covered most of her face from the forehead down. She smiled at Sybelle warmly. When she spoke, it was soft and friendly.

"Hello, Sybelle, I am High-Examiner Jeldar. Please take a seat." She said.

A High-Examiner! Sybelle swallowed. Mouth dry.

"Thank you, High-Examiner," she croaked as she sat.

Several closed wooden boxes sat on the desk in front of her.

"Now," Jeldar said, "try to relax. I know this is a very intimidating experience, but I promise we don't bite. Believe it or not, I was once on the other side of this very desk. A long time ago! I know how you are feeling."

The woman patted the desk with reverence.

"My colleagues are here to observe," she continued, "and will not talk during the test."

Jeldar's smile was sincere, warm, almost motherly.

Sybelle felt slightly more relaxed. Jeldar picked up one of the wooden boxes, and from it removed an intricately decorated metal disk about the size of her hand. Mounted in the centre was a large white gemstone, held in place by ornate clasps. A void-stone? It had to be.

"Could you please put your right hand on top of the disk and tell me if you feel anything?"

Sybelle did as instructed. Nothing. She concentrated. Still nothing.

"I can't feel anything," she said.

"Wait, a moment. Relax. Just breath. Concentrate on your hand. I will tell you when to stop."

Sybelle concentrated on her hand. There was nothing.

No, wait, there was something. A sensation in the middle of her palm.

"I can feel something. It's like warmth, moving towards my fingertips and into my wrist. Wait. It's changing. Now it feels like a wave of cold. Spreading outwards. It's odd. It feels like it is both hot and cold."

"That's excellent, Sybelle. You may remove your hand."

Next, Jeldar opened a smaller wooden box. Within were several silver rings set into a velvet liner. All inset with a single black gemstone. More void-stones. Jeldar picked a ring. To Sybelle, it looked the same as the others.

"Sybelle, please give me your left hand."

Jeldar placed the ring on Sybelle's index finger. Almost immediately, the gemstone glowed from within. A pale blueish white. Jeldar removed the ring and returned it to the box.

"That's excellent Sybelle. Thank you," Jeldar said.

The door opened, and the aide returned.

"Please come this way, Miss Drellmore." he said.

Sybelle was confused. Most of the boxes on the table remained closed. Was that it? She turned back to Jeldar. Again, she smiled at Sybelle?

"We are finished for now, Sybelle. We have performed the tests we need. All done. See, I told you it was nothing to worry about. Didn't hurt even the smallest bit, did it?"

"No, it's just, um, I was expecting more. Did I pass?"

"We will contact your family in the next few days and let you know our decision. Have a pleasant day, Sybelle."

"Thank you, High Examiner," Sybelle replied.

Sybelle rose from her chair and followed the aid. And that was it. It was over. She was awash with confusing and contradictory emotions. She had so wanted to fail the test. Passing meant certain enrolment and a lifetime of servitude to the Hegemony. A great honour, yes, but the thought had filled her with terror. One step along the terrible road her brother had walked.

Now she was almost certain she had failed. She would probably join her father's shipping business. A respectable role within a respectable company. Safe and gloriously normal. Surely this is what she wanted? Shouldn't she be happy? But there was an overwhelming sense of disappointment. She felt inexplicably angry. A feeling that she'd been robbed.

At first, she wasn't sure why. Then she realised. If she'd failed, she wouldn't become a summoner. She wouldn't be able to strike back at those that had taken Belar and had destroyed her innocence. Any slim chance of revenge would be taken from her.

Kathnell

The workshop was dim. Partly illuminated by gelder-bush oil lamps suspended from the ceiling. Normally, the windows would be open, allowing bright summer sunlight to fill the room.

Not today.

The place smelled the same as usual. A mix of rusty water, oil, lubricant, cloth, and iron. Today, it felt different. Hot. Stuffy. Pent up heat mixing with oil and other workshop chemicals. Smells she would normally find comforting. The benches, tools and books that were normally familiar, now cast dim shadows onto the wall. One of the two shadows on the far wall was hers, the other wasn't.

Kathnell Bilt's hands trembled. She held the valve seal tightly, trying to orient it. Calm down, you've got this. But, it was so damn dark. It was slowing her down. Time, she needed more time!

There was still much to get finished. The top valve body to be lifted in place. Bolts to be inserted and tightened. Pressure tests. More time. Droplets of sweat formed on her freckled forehead. She resisted the urge to remove her goggles and wipe them. She stuck the tip of her tongue out between her teeth, biting it gently. A habit her mother said she shared with her late father.

Just when she thought she had the orientation correct, the seal slipped and fell onto the floor. Nemesis' Teeth!

Behind her, the other shadow shifted.

Quickly, without thinking, she picked up the seal from the floor. Time seemed to fly past, each precious moment counted by an insistent ticking of the wall clock. She was sure it was speeding up.

She put the seal back in place on the lower half of the valve and held the upper part of the valve above. After lowering it into position, she realised her mistake. Idiot! In her haste, she had forgotten to inspect the seal and wipe it clean. It would surely by covered with dust and other crap from the floor, rendering the seal compromised. What use was the valve if it sprang leaks? She had probably failed the test with that last mistake.

Kathnell took a deep breath, wiping the sweat from her brow with the rough sleeve of her overalls. She checked the seal over in the dim light, wiping it with a clean cloth. Feeling the smooth surface underneath. Satisfied, she put it back into position and continued re-assembling the valve.

She quickly performed the other steps. Finally, pressure testing on the rig at the end of the workbench. The gauges went up, stabilised. Held.

The shadow on the far wall separated itself from the background. It reached towards the shuttered window. Dusty shafts of sunlight streamed in, briefly blinding her. She removed her goggles and brushed red hair away from her face.

The light revealed the contents of the workshop and illuminated the face of Corric. He looked serious. As usual. He glanced towards the old clock on the wall.

"Five whole minutes over, Miss Bilt," he said, wiping sweat from his balding head, "slower than last time by a good two minutes."

Kathnell sighed. She felt angry with herself. Dropping the seal had thrown her, and she'd panicked. She hadn't known that the test was to be performed in semi-darkness. If she had, maybe she could have practised more. Typical Corric, she thought, springing something like this on her at the last moment. Always expect the unexpected, he always liked to say. The engineer's first rule, he called it.

Corric was her mentor. She spent the best part of each week under his tutelage. Learning the ways of steam engineering from a master.

Kathnell had always had an interest in the steam that powered the Hegemony. As a child, she used to stare in wonder at the great clouds of vapour that rose from the powerhouses. The heat transported through pipes all across the city. Her father had also been an engineer within the Guild of Steam. He had sometimes taken her to see the machines up close. Officially, the Guild forbade such things, but many parents did it.

Once, when she was about eight, her dad had taken her to a powerhouse. She remembered the cavernous interior. Ornate roof arching high overhead. At its heart lay an enormous metal vessel. Banded by steel. Pipes of all sizes entered the vessel from all angles, some painted blue, others red. It looked like some kind of massive metallic heart, keeping the city alive. On one side, there was a glass panel. As she approached, she could feel the heat given off by the metal.

She glanced inside. A giant gemstone, at least twelve hands across, sat at the centre, cradled by a metal frame. It glowed a dull red. Around it, the water bubbled, swirled, and roiled. The first void-stone she had ever seen. They powered the Hegemony. Controlled and wielded by the immaculate. Her father explained this one was a heart-stone. One of the bigger types used to heat water for various purposes. This one was used to provide the power and heating to the Lerins Naval docks.

Others were used to provide heat and power to immaculate families located across the bay. Even the industrial areas and wider population benefited from heating and hot water. If not in individual homes, then from communal bath houses. Clean water pumped into every street. The Hegemon provided for its citizens and protectorates. At least that was according to the propaganda they liked to peddle.

Other, smaller stones burned with more intensity and powered the various magical artefacts and weapons that kept the immaculate and the Hegemony in power. Some stones released gasses. When placed in water, they could be seen bubbling away. They collected the gas and used it for a variety of purposes, including lifting the Hegemony's impressive airships.

Her father had died shortly after that visit. Killed by a Hegemony raid on an illegal rebel gathering whilst he'd been delivering a pump. Wrong place at the wrong time. Mum had blamed herself, saying that if she had only let him leave the house earlier, Dad would have made the delivery and been home before the Hegemon raid. Corric had been with them that day. He had always been a good family friend and colleague of her father's.

"It's my fault," her mum had kept saying between sobs, "if only I would have let him leave early. But I insisted he finish his breakfast."

Corric had tried repeatedly to calm her, insisting it wasn't her fault. Kathnell had quietly sat on the stairs to their two-bedroom tenement, winding her hair around her finger over and over. Almost like nothing in the world was wrong. Over and over, she wound it. Round and round.

They had cremated him two days later. Again, she had stood there as if nothing was wrong. It was only years later that she would grieve for her father. And with that grief came a hatred for their immaculate rulers. It seemed abhorrent that they could dispense their so-called justice without consideration for innocent bystanders.

He had been killed, not because he'd done anything wrong, but because he was human. A mundane. Another statistic ground under the wheels of the great immaculate machine.

With each passing year, she'd felt her father's presence grow. Like a shadow behind her. Asking her why. Why him? She felt him in the room now, just another shadow.

"Sorry, Corric," she said. "I panicked when I dropped the seal. Just couldn't make up the time. Shit!"

He held up a hand to silence her, but she could see from his face he wasn't angry. More amused.

"No, you couldn't. But, importantly, you were operating in different conditions than you were expecting. Yes, you dropped the seal, and yes, you put the seal in place without first checking it. But, and this is important, you realised the mistake quickly and took measures to rectify it. You did this without giving up, even though I suspect you knew the time was up.

"Being a steam engineer," he continued, "is just as much about how you approach a problem as it is about knowledge, diagrams, facts and formulas. Yes, you were slower, and made a few mistakes, but under the circumstances, it didn't go nearly as bad as you think it did."

He pointed to the valve on the test bench.

"Do we, or do we not, have a tested and fully working valve in front of us?" he said, smiling.

"We do," she replied with a smile of her own. She breathed out, the tension leaving her to be replaced with sudden tiredness.

"As I am always saying…" Corric said.

Here it comes, she thought.

"… expect the unexpected," he finished.

She stifled a laugh.

"Something amusing, Miss Bilt?"

"No, Corric," she replied.

"We often have to operate in conditions that we are not expecting. Today was no exception. But you need to improve your speed at this task, so we shall perform this test again soon. You're getting close to taking your journeyman exams, but you need to improve on some of the technical aspects."

The thought of her upcoming exams filled her with equal parts excitement and terror. Excitement at what she could do with her new qualification. Terror, because of how hard the exams were supposed to be. With it, she could seek employment in many of the guild affiliated steam engineering companies that operated throughout Lerins. Perhaps further still, in one of the immaculate houses across the ocean. From there, she could find ways of getting back at the Hegemony. Make the shadow proud.

Corric moved to the far wall and removed the last of the blinds. The shadows retreated. Corric picked up several leather-bound books and handed them to Kathnell.

"I have placed bookmarks at several points," he said. "They all concern themselves with the procedures required for entry into an immaculate facility or residence."

Corric must have seen her face drop. His face turned serious.

"This is precisely the type of reaction that worries me." Corric said, "Being a member of the Guild of Steam is not all tinkering with pipes, valves, pumps, and elbow joints. There are procedures to be followed. You have an aptitude for the technical Kathnell, but the guild is a stickler for details. Procedures! Sometimes I don't think you take those aspects seriously enough. A bit too much like your father, to be honest. You will do none of us any good if you get arrested for accidentally bumping into an immaculate just because you failed to follow the correct procedure. Some of them take their segregation from us VERY seriously.

"And," he continued, "you must stop your nonsense of questioning the designs in the guild books. They are the law. It is not our place to question them, no matter how sensible your query might sound to you."

"You have to admit, though," Kathnell said, "some designs could be improved. You must have noticed it. Like with the KL-5 pump, with just a few tweaks to the impeller housing you could easily…"

"Enough Kathnell," Corric said. "We have been over this many times before. If the wrong ears were present, that sort of comment could get you fired, or worse. The designs are The Designs. You are better off accepting it now, or maybe seek another mentor!"

"Sorry, Corric," she replied. Smile gone.

Corric seldom got this annoyed, but when he did, it shamed her. Since her father's death, she had looked up to Corric. He wasn't a replacement father, but more like an uncle. More family than teacher.

"It's all right. Now, I'm going to be away bidding on a new job for the next few days. It's across the bay in the immaculate quarter. Money could be good. I doubt anything significant is going to happen until I get back. If it does, ol' Blemshot next door will deal with it."

Corric cocked his head toward the neighbouring workshop.

"Buy him a honey-snowcake from the bakery, and he'll help," he continued. "I want you to take these books and READ the pages that I have bookmarked. A good portion of the exam will be on this kind of thing and I don't want word getting round that my apprentice doesn't know the difference between a request for access and a request for entry."

Corric gazed out of the window for a few seconds, thinking.

"I will be back on Mandalsday, but will probably have a lot of paperwork to do. It's All Winnows Day the day after that, so I expect you'll be drunk with the rest of 'em. So take the books, read them, and come back to work on Anyasday."

Kathnell placed the books in her bag and headed into the humid air. She left the workshop behind and walked down the alley towards the main street. Packed full of shops and industrial units. Blacksmiths, pipe makers, foundries, tanneries, cloth makers, and carpenters. Various smells from the street mixed with that of stinking mud wafting up from the nearby docks. She was used to it.

It was approaching evening. Many of the workers from the surrounding workshops were heading home for the day.

Lerins sprawled around a large natural bay where two large rivers met. The northern shores of the bay, where

Kathnell lived and worked, were home to the industrial areas, and various docks and wharfs. The southern part of the city, on the other side of the bay, was composed mostly of the business areas, along with a significant immaculate enclave belonging to House Drellmore.

Even from here, Kathnell could see the gleaming houses of the immaculate quarter. Beyond them, sitting on top of a rocky hill, stood the palace of Bennel. The place from which the Queen of Bennel ruled her people.

Everyone knew the queen didn't have any genuine power. Bennel was just a protectorate of House Drellmore. The Queen was just their human puppet. A very rich and powerful one maybe, but still a puppet.

Fucking immaculate and their Hegemon, Kathnell thought. She'd like nothing better than to see their empire in ruins. Wipe that superior look off their fucking faces. Get them back for killing her father.

Kathnell turned away from the dockside and headed towards home.

Rust

The handle turned easily, and the door swung outwards. Deep darkness beyond. The corridor continued to slope downwards. Rust entered, lamp outstretched.

The ceiling lit up. The corridor went instantly from darkness to something approaching daylight. She jumped, nearly dropping the lamp. Her heart thumped. She raised her knife. This wasn't like the flickering glow of her oil lamp. This was pure white. Unwavering. It seemed to pour from the walls and ceiling itself.

She stood frozen to the spot. Maybe Indiril was right! She should be away from this forbidden place. Evil magic! Like in the stories about the Maleth. Stories she had, until a few moments ago, dismissed as fantasy. She remained rooted, torn between leaving and finding out why Uncle kept coming here.

Get a grip, she thought! This is an Elderuin. You've heard about things like this, nothing to worry about. If she retreated, the questions would remain unanswered.

"What's that light?!" Indiril shouted.

"Not sure. It's coming from the walls. Magic, I guess."

"Maleth magic?" Indiril said, voice raised in pitch.

"Stop worrying. Uncle has been down here, so nothing to worry about," Rust replied, sounding more confident than she felt.

"Just be quick!"

The corridor extended for another three metres, widening to become a small room. The far side ended, once again, in a pile of earth. Blocked. However, it was the contents that held Rust's attention. Wooden benches on either side. Shelves above. Slowly, with the knife readied, she stepped inside. Nothing happened. No ghosts. No demons.

Of course not! Indiril would have probably fainted by now. She set the lamp down on a bench.

Various items were arranged on the shelves and benches. Tidy. Most of them were perfectly ordinary. Ropes, torches, lanterns, oil, blankets, preserves. The typical stuff of a remote tracking or hunting lodge. Things she was used to working with. Other items were unmistakably weapons; knives, swords, and a couple of ornate crossbows.

The crossbows sat on one bench. These weren't normal wooden crossbows used by the locals. These were ornate. Fashioned from polished metal and a black material. The trigger looked complex. Utterly unlike the crude wooden triggers she was used to. Hegemon technology! Its lightness surprised her. Quarter the weight of a wooden one. She ran her hands across its smooth surface.

What in Sindar's name was Uncle doing with Hegemon crossbows?

Rust had only ever seen the Hegemony once. About five years ago. She and Uncle had travelled to Balincross to advertise his tracking business. Uncle was one of the better game trackers in Peldaran. Certainly the best locally. Rich people from Peldaran, or even other countries, would come to the feral highlands to hunt big game. Bapnax, or if they paid enough, Basilisk.

Balincross, lay about fifty kilometres to the west of their village, Hammington's Rest. Nowlton was much closer, but a fifth of the size. The guild had offices in Nowlton, but you had to go to Balincross for the richer clients.

They had been walking along one of the busy streets near the city centre. Unfamiliar smells, sounds and sights of the city had assailed her. Rich spices. Unfamiliar food. Tobacco smoke. Languages she didn't understand. Dialects and accents, confusing.

There were tree-folk and a few of the insect-like t'kelikt. She'd even seen some cold-giants, ten hands taller than everyone else, striding through the crowd. Pale faced. Unlike the tree-people, who were tall and thin, the cold-giants were just BIGGER. They had been laughing with a group of humans.

Rust was used to seeing a few t'kelikt in Hammington's Rest, but there were many more here. She could hear their weird clicking and whistling speech through the crowd. Forelimbs waving as they spoke.

She kept walking into people. Constantly apologising as she went. She asked Uncle how so many people could all live together. He laughed and said Balincross was just a small city, and that some cities were ten times as big. Rust's mind had reeled. Ten times!

They passed into a cobbled market. People, shoulder to shoulder. Uncle told her to stay close. Sellers shouted offers. People haggled over goods. It seemed you could buy anything. Shoes, clothes, silks, animals, weapons, food, medicine. Anything.

She was in love. The place was amazing! Once she was old enough, she would leave Hammington's Rest and head for the city. She'd always wanted to leave Hammington's Rest. Some locals didn't like her because she was part Nothari. Her dark skin and hair inherited from her Nothari mother. This was somewhere she could go unnoticed.

Then a group of Hegemony had walked past. The locals ignored them. Uncle explained they were here to trade and she shouldn't stare.

Most of them were human. Dressed in neat armour with swords hanging from the waist, and crossbows slung across their backs. Their armour was emblazoned with the symbol of a wolf. The symbol of house Drellmore, the closest Hegemony house.

Those in the group's centre had been different. Dressed in long ornate cloaks, with fine embroidered tunics detailed in brilliant blue and gold. The immaculate. Rulers of the Hegemony. The only people on Earth still able to wield the old magic. Each wore a mask covering some, or all, of the face, partly obscuring their dark skin. Their black hair was oiled and plaited. These were the chosen. Sacred rulers of the Earth. Children of the immortal God Emperor. They had moved out of sight, swallowed by the bustling crowd.

Rust asked Uncle about them. He'd been reluctant at first, but on the long carriage ride back home, gave in to Rust's pestering.

He told her the masks they wore were called *aspects*. The colour, size, and decoration of the aspect denoted the wearer's place in the Hegemon society. He told her underneath the masks they looked just like everyone else, but to say so was blasphemy.

She remembered sitting in the cramped confines of their carriage, uncomfortable seats forgotten, transfixed by the details. The Hegemony controlled vast areas of the Earth. From the frozen poles to the warm jungles of the equator. They ruled through diplomacy, trade, religion, and military might. Actual open warfare with the Hegemony was rare. They possessed weapons and artefacts of legendary abilities. The old magic.

He waved his hands enthusiastically as he explained. Rust's imagination spun with tales of flying ships, giant iron-golems, and warrior knights that could defeat entire armies of normal men single-handed. She wasn't sure how much Uncle was embellishing the stories. She didn't care.

The nearest controlled Hegemony territory was the Kingdom of Bennel, just over six-hundred kilometres to the east.

Uncle said, what the Hegemony didn't rule directly was not worth controlling. Apparently The "Great" Kingdom of Peldaran, where they lived, wasn't worth controlling.

Rust hefted the crossbow off the bench. Far lighter than the local wooden ones. It balanced effortlessly in her hands. It had a wolf symbol on the side. House Drellmore.

A small leather-bound book lay next to the crossbow. Charred along one edge. Rust thumbed through it, but it was in a language she didn't understand. It was printed, rather than handwritten. Rare.

A fine, hand sized, polished wooden box sat in the middle of the other bench.

To its left, a glass display box contained a life-size wooden head. The head itself was featureless, just an elaborate stand for the item placed on it. A metallic head band, or circlet. A piece of Jewellery maybe, although she'd seen nothing like it. A bit like the jewellery Divinists wore at their weddings.

Intrigued, she opened the glass display box and looked closer at the metallic head band within. The centrepiece was a featureless flat silver disk, like a smooth silver coin. It sat centred on the forehead, surrounded by ornate silver and gold metalwork. From this, three elegant silver arms reached three quarters of the way round to the back of the head, securing it in place. Two at the sides, one over the top. It must be worth a considerable value.

Rust picked it off the wooden head and turned it over. The disk in the centre was strange, the back covered in a dull black material. It felt slightly sticky, like warm wax.

It was a shame there wasn't a mirror in the room. It would look good on her. No reason not to try it on, though. Indiril would be screaming at her to put it back. But he wasn't here.

She carefully lowered it onto her head. The disk came into contact with her forehead.

Coldness seeped into her skull, like snow on her forehead. Cold, but somehow warm at the same time. It felt unnerving. She went to take it off, but stopped halfway. A voice. Little more than a whisper. Behind her!

She wheeled round, half expecting to see Indiril. Nobody. She was sure she'd heard a voice! Like someone whispering. But there was only the room and the corridor beyond. Empty and silent.

Rust listened more intently, unable to shake a sensation of whispered voices just out of earshot. Faint. Distant. Not one, but several faint voices. Maybe Uncle had followed them here and was even now lecturing Indiril. Maybe Indiril's father was with them. They were going to be in severe trouble this time. Possibly as much as the time they had nearly burned the tracking lodge down. How would she explain this?

No. The voices seemed to come from inside the room. Always behind her, just over her shoulder.

She shivered. These strange voices seemed, paradoxically, both very distant and strangely close. They were devoid of any meaning. Just babble.

The more Rust concentrated, the clearer the whispers became. She was almost sure she could make out words, but no true meaning.

She took off the circlet and put it down on the bench. As she let go, its arms folded themselves up until the whole thing was smaller than her palm. Strange magic.

What was Uncle doing with this stuff?

She turned to the polished wooden box. It looked old, and possibly valuable. Rosewood maybe? Carved with swirls and patterns. She'd seen similar boxes in the Nowlton jewellers. Inside the box, a pocket-watch and golden ring lay on a bed of red velvet. The ring was a simple gold band with no noticeable markings. A wedding ring! The watch was finely engraved with images depicting scenes of sailing ships. Rust had seen a pocket-watch once in a shop window in Balincross. The price tag had made her wince. Six month's wages at least. Gripping the watch in both hands, Rust brought it up to eye level to get a better look.

The room spun. Pain shot through her eyes, sharp and needle like. She gasped, as much from surprise as from the pain. After the briefest moment, the pain relented. A shimmering encroached on the periphery of her vision. She blinked, but it remained. For a couple of seconds, it sat at the edges of her vision, then it rushed inwards.

Rust lurched back towards the doorway and tried to drop the watch. She couldn't let go! Her hands remained firmly clasped around it. The strange shimmering increased. She blinked again. She wanted to wipe her eyes. The shimmering was turning sky blue and dissolving away.

The room faded out, replaced with something else.

No, somewhere else.

She was no longer inside the old room. Suspended in absolute blackness. Unable to move. Looking down, she couldn't see her body. It just wasn't there. She felt her heart thumping in her chest. Sweat rolling down her head. Bile rose in her throat. She desperately tried to wake up from this strange, paralysing dream. The blackness remained.

Not total blackness. Stars. All around. Like the clearest, blackest of nights. She could pick out the constellations she knew. There! The Crow, the Anvil, the Goat. A faint blue disk off towards one side. She was sure it wasn't there a moment ago. It rushed towards her, ballooning. As it approached, she could make out swirls of white overlaid on top of emerald green, yellow, and blue. It was the Earth! Seen from far above. Her stomach turned over.

Before she could adjust to this strange new perspective, the blackness vanished.

It was daylight. The sun glared down from an almost cloudless sky. The only cloud in sight streamed from the top of a nearby mountain. One of a pair of mountains rising from a dry landscape. Rust heard two words, repeated in a whisper, "Cloud-maker… Cloud-maker…". It too faded.

New, confusing images rushed at her. Nighttime. Grey sky. Stars glimpsed through gaps in fast-moving clouds. Running through the streets of a strange city. Water pouring from the sky. Gurgling drains. Cobblestone streets. A man that looked like Uncle, but wasn't. Too young.

People running. Panic. White flashes, like lightning. People screamed. Behind them a vast white tower reached up to the sky, piercing the scudding clouds. It seemed to rise and rise, impossibly high.

Running. Running. Strange black figures behind them, dancing, leaving death in their wake. A panic and terrible fear that wasn't her own.

She felt increasingly ill. She needed to wake up from this dark nightmare.

Must wake up!

Must get away!

The confusing images wrapped a terrible cloak around her mind.

Chapter 2

Consider the following diagram. Pipework entering the manifold should be terminated next to Position B. Terminations at this junction should be perpendicular to the ascending steam pipe.

The length of piping between A and B should not exceed 5 SIU. Bend radius of pipe C should not exceed 2 SIU within the limits of the casing.

Any wilful failure by a guild member to adhere to rules 3 through 9 will be marked as a minor transgression and should be reported to a guild master. Wilful failure to report is itself a transgression.

Books of Prescription. Books of Steam. Book IV. Chapter 9

Sybelle

Sybelle sat quietly as the city rumbled past outside. She rubbed her left hand and thought back to the test. The weird sensations of hot and cold. Her hand reddened from the constant rubbing.

It was all over so quick. She wasn't sure how she felt about it. Mother sat opposite. Sybelle didn't feel like talking, so they sat in silence.

The coach swayed on the uneven road surface. The roads were busier than earlier; offices emptying for the evening. The machinery of empire stepping down a gear until tomorrow.

Mother turned to her.

"So, Syb," she said, breaking the silence. "How did it go? I thought I would give you a couple of minutes to tell me yourself. We'll be home soon and I'd like to know before we meet with Father."

Sybelle started rubbing her hand again.

"I'm sorry, Mother," she said. "I failed."

"Tell me what happened," Mother said. "And, don't worry!"

"There were loads of boxes and things on the table. They only used two of them. That was it."

"Go on," Mother prompted.

"The first test was strange. The examiner told me to place my hand on to a metal disk with a gem in the middle. I think it was a void-stone! Asked me if I could feel anything. There was nothing at first. Then there was this weird feeling. Like it was hot, but also cold at the same time. It reminded me of the ice game I used to play with Belar. You know, when we used to put our hands between two ice blocks in the cold cellar and see who could last longest?"

Mother remained silent.

"It was like that, but without the pain and with heat as well," she continued. "Like I say, it was strange. Then, they got me to try on a ring with another void-stone. It glowed blue. That was it. They didn't use any of the other boxes. I guess they didn't see any point if I'd failed."

"You didn't fail, Syb," Mother said.

"Sorry?" Sybelle said.

"I said you didn't fail," Mother continued. "They didn't need to do the other tests because you had a powerful reaction to the first two. They work downwards."

Sybelle sat back. The swaying seemed to intensify. It was so hot. Nausea crept into her gut. She opened the window and sucked in air.

"What do you mean?" Sybelle stammered.

Mother was smiling, but she blinked away what looked like tears.

"Your reaction to the first test was strong, so they skipped many of the intermediate steps. The ring they chose was one of the harder ones to activate. That you did so with little effort means that you have a potent ability. Maybe more powerful than your brother."

Just moments ago, she had been resigning herself to a dull life. College. A responsible career. Do her bit for the Hegemony. Married off to another powerful family. Have children. No special powers. No revenge. Mundane normality.

The world shifted. The future changed.

Distantly, she could hear her mother say she was proud of her. That everything would be all right. Sybelle wasn't really listening. Mother continued to blink away tears. Were they tears of joy? Pride? Sadness? Maybe it was all three.

Sybelle looked out of the carriage window, trying not to let the swaying overwhelm her stomach. Two quick tests had decided the course of her life. The long line of her future immutably drawn out ahead of her.

Gellid was waiting for them as the carriage pulled up.

He, too, was immaculate. Most of the higher house staff were. They employed humans in the kitchens and elsewhere behind the scenes, but senior staff were almost always immaculate. It was the way. Lesser immaculate families would have fully mundane staff. Families closer to the centre of power had entirely immaculate staff. No mundane kitchen staff and housekeepers for them. Their own home had areas that only the human staff entered. The places for preparing food and washing clothes.

"Please come this way, Miss Drellmore," he said. "I've had a bath prepared in your rooms."

"Thank you, Gellid," Sybelle said.

"Lady Drellmore," Gellid said. "Master Drellmore-Carntellis has returned home and wishes to speak with you in the library."

"Of course, Gellid," she said.

"Go ahead, Syb," Mother said. "Have your bath. When you are finished, join us for supper. I believe we have partridge tonight."

"Yes, Mother," Sybelle said.

The water was hot and faintly scented. It helped relieve some of the tension in her neck and shoulders. She lay in the bath and relived the day. The test, the thought of failure and the realisation that she had passed. She was a summoner! Holder of the secret gift. Mother had said she was possibly equal to Belar. Maybe stronger.

The sound of raised voices drifted down the hallway. Mother and Father.

Sybelle dried herself with the towels provided, each scented with roses and lavender. After dressing, she tip-toed down the corridor towards the closed library door. She pressed her ear up against it.

"It will only be for a while, Welyne. I will be back in a couple of months," Father said.

"A couple of months? Emperor save us, Bartain. Do you know where we have been today? Your daughter's test!"

"I know. I know. But this is important. The order has come directly from Lord Drellmore himself. They need me."

"Important! Your daughter is important, Bartain. SHE needs you."

"Hey, that's not fair, Wel. You know my family means everything to me, but I can't just ignore an order from Lord Drellmore."

"I'm sorry, Bartain. It looks like Sybelle might be on par with Belar. I think she might even be more powerful."

Behind Sybelle, someone cleared their throat. Sybelle started. Heart jumping. She spun round. Gellid stood silently a few metres away.

"Miss Drellmore, once you have finished checking the door for rotworm, supper is about to be served."

"Yes, of course," she stammered. She turned and headed for the dining room.

During dinner, Father congratulated her on passing her test and said he was very proud. He said that he was sure she would make an excellent pupil at the College and couldn't wait to tell his colleagues about it.

He said he had to go away for a while. Lord Drellmore had commissioned his shipping company to transport some important equipment to the Bennel, which lay across the Sorbella Ocean, far to the north-west of House Drellmore. Equipment vital to the fight against the heretics and their pathetic rebellion. He needed to oversee the shipments personally. It was an important job and a great honour. Blah. Blah.

Father talked like he was in control, but Sybelle knew he had little choice. Just like she had no choice. What the Hegemony said, you did. Very few had any actual control, she thought. All puppets. Cogs in a machine. Controlled by rules, traditions, procedure, and government. Dancing to the

distant whims of more powerful masters.

Rust

A dank smell of moist earth. Her back was wet. Someone was tapping her gently on the face. They called her name. Rust sat up abruptly. Eyes wide open. She paused for a moment, blinking, looking around.

She was still in the Elderuin, sitting at the bottom of the shaft. Indiril stood over her. Wide eyed. Nostrils flared. Like a startled felder-cow.

"Rust! Thank the Divines. I've been trying to wake you for over an hour!" Indiril said.

"An hour? I was just in there," Rust said, motioning the direction from which she'd come; the door to the room now shut.

"What happened?"

"I'm not sure," she said. "The last I remember was having a really weird dream."

She was still gripping the watch in one hand. In the other, she clutched the folded up circlet.

"Dream?"

"Not really a dream. It was weird, and happened when I picked up this watch."

Indiril looked sceptically at the watch in Rust's hand.

"Well, you gave me a real fright," he said. "I was waiting up top. I heard you screaming. There was a banging noise. Like a door slamming. The next thing I see is you at the bottom of the shaft trying to climb like an idiot plague-nester. I tried calling to you, but you just kept trying to climb the walls. All the time you kept talking nonsense."

"Nonsense?"

"Stuff about escaping. Weird crap."

Snippets of what she'd seen came back. The strange city.

Running away. Flashes and bangs. It was fuzzy, like trying to remember a dream. She shook her head.

"I don't really remember much."

"Then you just sat down and went to sleep," he said. "I had to come down. Been trying to wake you for ages. It's getting towards dusk! Deldrooks already started chirping. We need to be going back!"

Shit. She looked up at the square of darkening blue sky. She could hear the deldrooks from here, so the sun must have set. Being this deep in the feral was not somewhere you wanted to be once dark. There were spit vipers, or worse, basilisks. Rust stood. She shoved the watch and the circlet into her backpack.

They trudged on through the feral. It was darker by the minute. This time of year it would be true-dark soon, without the dim red light of Old-Red to see by.

They went the same way back they had come. In the dim light, it was treacherous. They avoided the denser pockets of feral. Darker green than tame-land plants, with a blueish, almost sickly, hue. They had to watch their step to avoid being impaled by poisonous thorns. Tripping was a real possibility, especially as the darkness was closing in.

They barely spoke a word to each other. Somewhere close by, a cinder-crow shrieked, probably alarmed at their passing. It flew off, screeching loudly. Four leathery wings, long tail, and four dull red eyes.

Finally, in the valley below, the oil lamps of the village came into view. Closer, Rust could make out the silhouette of the old Dolonde ruins rising above the feral. The Dolonde had ruled this area hundreds of years ago. All that remained of their empire were a few stone ruins, overrun by the relentless march of the feral. The Nothari Empire had overthrown the Dolonde, but that too had since fallen. Consigned to history. Rust's mother was Nothari, but had died, along with her father, in an attack on their trade caravan when she was only a year old.

She now lived with her father's brother on the edge of the village. Although the Nothari Empire had faded from glory hundreds of years ago, some people in this region still had a distrust of the Nothari. A minor border war three decades ago hadn't helped. Small-minded people.

Rust had come under verbal abuse from some older people in the village, sometimes even at school. At least when Uncle wasn't around. Few wanted to anger him.

They were the same people that also distrusted the tree-people. Indiril and Rust had been close friends for years, united by the village's distrust. Rust was nearly eighteen years old. Indiril had turned eighteen last month.

Uncle always told her that such narrow-mindedness was as old as humanity. He always became animated when talking about history and culture. He said that if you looked closely at the past, you could see the future.

When she talked about moving to the city, so she could see more of the world, he invariably became defensive. A source of many arguments. The arguments were even worse when she discussed joining the army. The word was that Peldaran may soon join their ally Jorn in the war against Bennel. She had considered joining up. Uncle had outright forbidden it.

Her spirits lifted upon seeing the ruins and village beyond. They were nearly home!

As they headed down-slope, the thick feral vegetation gradually began thinning out. Beyond the ruins, the feral woods gave way to a creepgrass plain. Tall, slender spines swaying in the breeze.

Beyond the creepgrass lay the lee, the border that separated civilisation from the feral. A wide margin around the village kept clear of feral vegetation by the villagers. Without it, the feral would eventually consume the village. First, creepgrass would take root, followed inevitably by larger plants. Just like the Dalonde ruins and, more recently, the ruins of Waywich. A reminder of the fate that welcomed failed villages this far from the centre of civilisation.

The lee around Hammington's Rest was well maintained, like countless other villages and towns the world over. In some areas of the Earth, the tame lands could extend for hundreds, or thousands, of kilometres. Entire countries, free of the feral. Out here, near the edge of the Kingdom of Peldaran, maintaining the lee was an unending battle.

"So, tell me what you found again," Indiril said. Talkative once more now that the village was visible.

"As I said, I found the strange circlet and the pocket watch. Here…"

She offered the pocket watch to him. He reached out one of his long thin arms and took it, slender fingers turning it this way and that.

"It looks odd. Not sure why. Looks expensive," he said. "What on earth was your uncle doing with it?"

"No idea."

"Going to ask him?"

"You kidding? What do you think he would say *Oh, thanks for asking? Sure, I'll tell you everything you need to know.* He'd go mad if he ever found out where we've been. I mean, he's kept the thing secret this whole time. That's the last thing I'm gonna do for Sindar's sake. There are Hegemon crossbows down there too. I mean, why's he got those? And swords. And Divine knows what in the other boxes."

"Do you think it has something to do with the rebellion? You know the heretics?"

"Don't be nax-headed, Indiril," she said. "What would Uncle have to do with the rebellion?"

"I dunno. It's just a bit odd. Dad says that the heretics are still causing the Hegemony a lot of trouble. Especially in the southern continents."

Rust glared back. Indiril changed the subject.

"Aren't you worried he's going to find out that his things are gone?" he said.

"Not really. He doesn't visit the place that often. Maybe twice a year. I'll take them back before then. Just want to look over them before I do."

"If you're sure," Indiril said, stopping to look at the watch. "And you say that when you grabbed it, you had some kind of *spooky vision*?"

He motioned with his hands, clearly still sceptical. Making fun of her. Rust snatched the watch back.

"If you don't believe me, that's fine. But I am telling you the truth."

Indiril held his hands up, palms towards him, fingers splayed. The tree-people sign for an apology.

"Sorry," he said. "It just seems a bit, you know, farfetched."

He paused for a breath.

"OK, what exactly did you see?" he asked.

Rust told him again what she could remember.

"The details are really hazy. It's like waking from a dream, things only half remembered. You know what I mean. It seemed more detailed at the time."

"Hmm. That tower sounds familiar," Indiril said. "It's like the White Citadel. Maybe you've seen pictures of it or something."

Rust had heard of the White Citadel, the legendary Elderstone tower at the heart of Ascension City. Home to the God-Emperor and capital of the Hegemony. The legend was that the Maleth had built the citadel to reach the heavens to talk to Nemesis. The forbidden god. Before the God-Emperor had saved them. Uncle had told her about it all, but had said it as was all fedlershit. When pressed, he'd never elaborated.

She was pretty sure she'd seen no pictures of the White Citadel.

They passed by the ruins and entered the creepgrass fields. They were headed for a series of low mounds that stood out against the brighter western horizon. Now that she thought about it, Rust couldn't ever remember mounds here.

"And you've had no visions since?" Indiril asked.

"No, it doesn't seem to do anything now. I wonder if it

is... Shit! Stop!"

Rust put an arm in front of Indiril to stop his progress. She squatted down, pulling Indiril with her.

"What are you doing..."

"Shhhh. Look," Rust whispered. She pointed towards the low mounds she had spotted a few moments ago. One of them was moving.

Bapnax. Four of them. No, there were more off to the left. Ten at least. A family group resting for the night in the creepgrass. They seldom came this close to the village, but it wasn't unheard of. They were big. Six metres long and about three high. They weren't outwardly hostile. They were, however, pretty dumb, and easily startled.

The herd was blocking their progress towards the village. One of them raised its long reptilian head, sniffing the air. It snorted once. They could go round, but it would take ages. No time. It was getting too dark.

Of course, Rust thought, the tunnels.

Rust tapped Indiril on the shoulder and pointed back to the Dolonde ruins. There was an old Dolonde tunnel connecting the ruins to a watch tower closer to the village. Hunting parties used it when going into the feral. Of course, they didn't have any real practical value, but one of the primary sources of income for Hammington's Rest was entertaining wealthy hunting parties from the city in search of adventure. What better way to start an adventure than going through a creepy old tunnel? Uncle said the rich folk loved that sort of crap.

They doubled back and headed for the tunnel entrance.

Rust held the lamp in front of her, lighting their way.

"Show me that watch again?" Indiril said.

"Now? Why?"

"Something about it has been bothering me. I couldn't work out what it was till now."

Rust handed the watch back to Indiril. He looked at the face with a puzzled expression.

"I knew it!" he said.

"What?"

"Look," Indiril said, pointing to the face. "It has twelve positions, rather than the normal ten? Why, for the Divines, would you make a watch with twelve hours? There are only twenty hours in a day, not twenty-four."

Rust couldn't make anything out of it, either. Odd.

Just one more question to add to her list.

Kathnell

Kathnell walked away from the docks. The streets became less ordered. Stone roads gave way to worn cobbles and then clay. There was seldom need for heavy traffic access to these parts of the city.

She headed roughly for home, taking a familiar detour towards the Blind Toad. I really ought to go home, she thought. Study the books Corric gave her. No, one quick pint of ale would be fine.

The houses became closely packed. The rule in this part of town was the closer you could build them, the more rent you got per square hand.

It wasn't the poorest part of the city. Far from it. That lay further to the north, filled with unskilled workers and the unemployed. The very poorest in Lerins. Many that migrated from the countryside ended up there. Drawn by the promise of work. Sadly, they often found the reality of city life wasn't as they imagined. Circumstances quickly pushed those that failed to adapt towards the forgotten northern margins. The Rat Cage, they called it. There was no clean running water there, despite what Hegemony propaganda said.

In recent years, the influx of migrants had spiked. People fleeing Bennel's absurd war with Jorn. The crime in the area had increased. It threatened to spill into the surrounding districts. Last month, the city had responded with heavy-handed marshals. Violence had erupted on the streets. The poor and desperate pushed to their limits. They had killed a city marshal. In the end, House Drellmore had sent in a couple of their fearsome knights. More violence. Several innocent people had died. Trampled in a rush to escape. It all played out with the inevitability of a cheap theatre play. Anti-Hegemony action and sabotage had increased. Rumours that the rebellion was again at work within the city. Any fool could predict it would only get worse.

The entire area was simmering, just on the cusp of boiling over. Desperate people under pressure. Like steam. Kathnell tried to avoid the area if she could help it. She could handle herself in a fight, but didn't go looking for trouble.

Kathnell pushed her way inside the Blind Toad. The oak door creaked.

Already busy. Musicians with piped instruments and drums were seated along the back wall. People laughed. Drink orders shouted. Give it another hour and it would be packed to the rafters. Then, you'd be lucky to hear yourself think.

Kathnell waved to the landlord Pelter and made her way towards an unoccupied table at the back. She sat and pulled a book out of her bag.

The Blind Toad's wooden walls had been a familiar haunt of engineers for hundreds of years. Generations of engineers fluxed around it. They drank there when they were apprentices, and on the day of their retirement. A bastion of comfort for the hardworking.

An Alchemists Guild apothecary bordered the pub on one side, and a working clothes tailor on the other. Both, now shut for the day.

Pelter walked over and placed an earthenware pitcher of frothy taptree beer on the table. He stooped, head brushing the rafters. Pelter was a big man, twenty hands high, at least. Over two metres of muscle! She was sure he was part cold-giant. An accusation he vehemently denied. People seldom caused trouble when he was around.

"Cheers," she said. She tipped the pitcher back and took a big gulp of the dark brown liquid. "Erchh, this stuff you peddle doesn't get any sweeter with maturing."

"Hah. You're welcome to try somewhere else, Kath," he replied, smiling. "I hear the Porill Rat is selling beer cheap."

Marshals had recently raided the Porill Rat for harbouring political criminals. It had few customers now. It was another reminder that the ills in the northern city were spreading into this area.

"How's ol' Corric doing? Still makin' you read those damn books?"

Pelter used to work with Corric when they were younger. Pelter had also known her father, but would always change the subject when she quizzed him about it.

"Same as ever. You know, he's Corric! Gonna be working over in Stonie-Town for a few days, so's given me some light reading."

They often referred to the immaculate as stonies, stone faces, or stones, because of the stupid porcelain masks they wore. A supposed symbol and reminder to the lowly humans of how superior they were. Arrogant fuckers.

"He never was one for having days off. I guess he's working through the Winnow's Day celebrations."

She nodded.

"As you say, he's Corric," he laughed. "You coming down?"

"Sure," she said.

He turned to walk back to the bar and then paused.

"Oh, and Kathnell. Don't forget, you still owe me for twelve pints from last week."

"Shit, sorry. I forgot."

"Just make sure you pay me before you leave. Or Roz."

Kathnell glanced across the pub to where Roz was standing, laughing with one of the other patrons. Her long plaited black hair hanging down her back. She was a good ten years older than Kathnell and had worked in the pub for years. Roz turned away from the customer and headed back towards the bar. Saint's teeth she looked good. That arse!

"Kath?" Pelter said, smiling.

"Eh? Oh yeah, of course," she replied. "I'll pay before I

leave tonight."

Pelter walked back towards the bar, still smiling.

An hour, and several pints later, Kathnell was bordering on drunk. No admit it, she thought, she was drunk.

Impossibly, the noise level had increased. Punters sang tunelessly along with the musicians. She wasn't sure they were all singing the same song. She joined in.

She had tried to read what Corric had given her, but just couldn't concentrate. Something about pressure release valves. Her mind wandered to the Hegemony void-trains. An obsession she'd had since she was a child. The big military ones had boilers heated by void-stones. They could reach speeds over one hundred and fifty kilometres an hour. One hundred and fifty! She felt she knew them by heart already, even though she'd never set foot in one. When Corric wasn't around, she'd read everything she could on them. She was never really sure why he had technical books on them stashed at the back of his storage room. Surely illegal. She was always careful to put them back afterwards.

A few years ago you were lucky to see one void-train a year. Now, with the war, they were common. There was usually at least one void-train in the city train yard. She often took a walk to have a look at them. Big bastards, two stories high. She would love to work on something like that one day. Of course, only the best, most loyal subjects were allowed. She'd have to study hard. Get recognised. Years of loyal servitude. Then, maybe she could get a job on one.

It would also put her in a great place to get back at the Hegemon. Somehow. Make her father proud. Get back at those that had killed him. As usual, her plan lacked detail. Drunk-dreaming, she called it. That state when anything seemed like a good idea.

She tried to read the book again. Diagrams, charts. All prescribed methods. Rigid. No leeway for improvement. No improvisations. Do this, then that. Her mind wandered again.

Why were the designs in the books so fixed? Surely it would be better for everyone that when they found an improvement, it was incorporated into future designs. But no, the guild insisted that the same designs be used. Year after bloody year. Questioning the designs could see you fired, or worse, labelled as a heretic. It made little sense to her. Nobody ever talked about it. Corric always shut down any such discussions.

It was like this stupid war with Jorn. For years the relationship with Jorn had been good, but two years ago, Bennel had declared war on Jorn over its refusal to hand over parts of the Felder Mountains. Everyone knew that House Drellmore had made the actual decision to go to war. Bennel, the obliging dog. Thousands of Bennel soldiers had died.

What the Hegemony wanted, they got. Everyone else was just meat for the machine. It made her angry. It really was time to be going home, but one more drink would be fine. She raised her hand and motioned Roz over to bring her another pint.

Things got hazy. Kathnell stood in a side alley, head spinning, wiping puke away from her mouth. The place stank of piss, her own puke, blocked drains, and river mud. She puked again.

The light from the oil lamps in the main street barely penetrated the gloom. Best not to linger here too long.

If only she had more self-control over the amount she drank. She remembered having another couple of drinks and then going to leave and settling her outstanding tab with Roz.

Then, shit! Oh no!

She'd made a pass at Roz. Again! Saint's bloody arse! A hazy recollection of leaning across the bar and trying to kiss Roz. Roz had pulled away laughing, saying she thought it was about time that Kathnell went home. Others around her had laughed as well.

She'd had made yet ANOTHER fool of herself. Stupid! Saint's-rotted-eyes she needed to have more control over herself. Her drinking was becoming a problem. Even Pelter lectured her about it, and it was his beer!

There was rubbish strewn around the alleyway. Kathnell noticed a printed piece of paper, recognising the emblem on the top. A broken horizontal length of chain with a hammer above it, an anvil below. She picked it up. A flyer printed by the group that called themselves Liberation. Everyone else just called them the rebellion. The Hegemony called them heretics.

Kathnell had seen their flyers before. They'd even been a couple posted inside the pub. Pelter was always quick to remove them. Didn't want the attention they would bring. Strictly no politics inside the pub. He said it was best not to get involved.

The heretics hadn't existed a few decades ago. They appeared out of nowhere, and if you believed the stories, turned several loyal Hegemony houses against their masters almost overnight. There were stories of madness within the rebel houses' central families. Massive battles between once friendly armies. Assassinations. Even one of the ceph houses had turned against the Hegemon. There was even talk of an assault against Ascension City itself in a failed plot to kill the Emperor. Could you even kill a God, she thought?

The Hegemon tried their best to quash any such rumours.

She read the flyer.

The Hegemony is a lie.
   The God Emperor is a lie.
   The rule is a lie.
   Their control, a lie.
   Their supremacy, a lie.
   Their guilds, a lie.
   They dominate through fear.

Break the lies that bind like chains.
Unshackle your hands. Your feet. Your mind.
Lift your gaze up. Away from the ground and towards the sky.
Liberation for all!
Liberation for all!

She went to throw the flyer away. Instead, she folded it, placed it in her bag, and headed towards home.

Trelt

Trelt Vellorson stood by the large window in his office and marvelled at Ascension City below. Capital of the immaculate Hegemony. It never ceased to amaze him. Even after all these long years.

His offices occupied a full floor of the Aurumill headquarters. The Aurumill was not talked about openly. Not quite a secret. Not quite common knowledge. Somewhere in the grey middle. Carefully maintaining just the right mix of myth, legend, and fact to ensure they were feared and respected equally.

Outwardly, the Hegemony ruled through vast economic power, cultural export, technical supremacy, and overwhelming military might. However, it was the Aurumill that were the eyes, ears, and sometimes hands of the Emperor. Its web of seers and agents spread far and wide. Listening. Manipulating. Quietly. Softly. Sometimes, not so softly. Far better to control like that than by wasting lives in pointless wars.

Trelt was the current leader of the Aurumill. His conviction, that without the Aurumill, the world would fall back to chaos. Humanity's ancient enemies would resurface. Enemies from both within and without. They would welcome Nemesis back again. All would be lost.

Even here, in the heart of Ascension City, at the heart of the immaculate world, the population was preparing for All Winnows Day. The annual celebration of the eternal fight against the feral. Looking towards the horizon, he imagined the vast feral jungle that surrounded them. Ever present, always seeking a way to reclaim the cities of humanity.

The ancient spire of The White Citadel dominated the

skyline. It towered over the city, tapering like a funnel as it went. A kilometre wide at its base. Top lost in haze, many kilometres above. The pure white elderstone shone brightly in the sunlight. Millennia of weathering and dirt had failed to dull it. A series of platforms stuck out from the spire at various altitudes, each one festooned with buildings. Attached to one platform was the vast bulk of a Hegemony airship belonging to House Lunarith.

The lower part of the citadel featured several enormous archways. Each, a half a kilometre high, exposing the hollow core within. At its centre, surrounded by lush gardens and parks, lay the Imperial Palace, governed by the immortal God-Emperor. The absolute, and literal, centre of the great Hegemon Empire.

The White Citadel itself lay at the centre of the immaculate district, the largest concentration of immaculate on the planet. Beyond it lay the larger bulk of the city. Home to the rest of the population. Distant docklands and factories to the east were shrouded in the haze of industry. The vast Everwill River snaked through the eastern city, filled with vessels of all sizes. Trade from all corners of the world.

Trelt's office walls were lined with bookcases, shelves, and maps. One wall was filled with maps of every nation in the world, highlighting political hot spots. Points of interest. People of note. Influencers. Those on the ascendant. Those falling from power.

The building was old. Built over six hundred years ago by the former occupants of Ascension City. Even back then, the White Citadel had stood at the centre. Ancient. A timeless sentinel, constructed by the Emperor and his kin before his millennia long sleep. Before the dreaming.

For nearly thirty years, the biggest threat to the Hegemony had been from those that now called themselves Liberation. Twenty-eight long years since The Heretic and her followers had caused a schism within the Hegemony. The Emperor had warned of their coming. But even he, with all his powers, hadn't predicted the way they would attack.

There were individuals in powerful positions within the Hegemony that the Emperor could influence directly. Chancellors, politicians, church leaders, governors, advisors. The Ascended. Through them, the Emperor could secretly watch, manipulate, and guide the houses of the Hegemon. Hardly anyone knew about the Ascended.

In an audacious attack on the White Citadel, the heretics had severed the link between the Emperor and many Ascended. The plan had largely failed, but the chaos it caused had been awesome. The Schism. They were still trying to pick up the pieces now.

The Heretic herself was long dead. But Liberation remained. Three immaculate houses, and one ceph house, still under their control. Trelt pursued them with fanatical zeal. He knew them well, for he had once been amongst their number. Before the Emperor had saved him and shown him the true path.

A whistle from the speaking tube beside his desk startled Trelt from his reverie. He turned the top towards him.

"Yes," he said.

Trelt listened to the reply.

"Thank you," Trelt said. "Please send him in."

A few seconds later, there came a knock at the door.

"Please, come in," Trelt said.

The door opened. An overweight, immaculate man entered. Dressed in a many layered grey suit. The colours of House Lunarith. His aspect covered most of his upper face and nose. Gemstones denoting an ambassador of high rank. Grey feathers representing House Lunarith family surrounded them. Trelt himself didn't wear an aspect. He never did. He wasn't immaculate. He was different.

"Wonderful," Trelt said. "Ambassador Delrain. Please come in. Take a seat. Tell me, was your journey pleasant? I know the streets are hectic in preparation for tomorrow's celebrations."

"Yes, quite pleasant. Thank you," Delrain replied. The man sat in the chair opposite Trelt.

"Would you like a drink? I've just received a shipment of a twelve-year-old Whisky from Ventarso. Lovely stuff."

"Thank you, that would be nice."

Trelt poured two glasses and offered one to Delrain.

"Biscuit?" Trelt said, motioning to a plate of biscuits on his desk.

"No, I'm fine, thank you."

"Oh, go on. Freshly baked this morning. They are rather good."

The man reached shakily for a biscuit.

Trelt walked back towards the window and gazed once more out across the city. He stood in silence. He sniffed the dark liquor, savouring the rich earthy aroma.

In the western sky, Trelt made out the tiny red speck of Old Red. Just setting. It glowed like a burning ember. This time of year, it rose before the sun and added enough light to read by in the early hours. It would continue rising earlier and earlier until it rose when the sun set. At that point, for a few weeks during the month of Redcrown, the world would not know true nighttime. Every year, on queue, the plants of the feral would begin their annual sporing, filling the air with sickly sweet spores. It would play hell with Trelt's allergies.

Months later, during the month of Spinsilk, ripe seed pods would pop, sending thread-like seeds into the air. Drifting on the wind. Settling. Taking root. Of course, the seeds wouldn't reach them here, but at the fringes of civilisation, they were a real problem. All Winnows Day was an annual celebration of the removal of the resulting saplings. Keeping the feral at bay.

Delrain shifted in his seat.

"You know, some people say that All Winnows Day is a waste of time this far away from the Feral," Trelt said. "I think it is a healthy reminder. Don't you agree?"

"Um," Delrain hesitated, "I'm not sure I follow you, Lord Vellorson."

"I mean, that the celebrations are a reminder, a symbol,

of our eternal struggle. Even this far from the Feral, we should remain vigilant to forces that would see our downfall. It is a time for plucking the feral saplings from the soil before they become established. Before they corrupt all we have accomplished. Of course, it would take many years for them to overrun our cities and towns, but it is always good to nip these things in the bud, as they say. Don't you think?"

"Yes," Delrain replied, "I suppose you are right. I've never thought about it that way."

"No, I don't suppose you have," Trelt said, turning away from the window.

"So, Delrain, have you got anything to report on the location of the missing weapon shipments from Requiem?"

"Unfortunately, we still haven't been able to trace the shipments. We have continued to investigate the issue with the utmost priority. I have been in touch with our seers today and they report we are continuing to search the dock areas."

"You know, Delrain, this is all very unfortunate. This is the second shipment of weapons that have gone missing from the House Lunarith docks in the last month. I hear that last month a further two shipments went missing as well, although a good amount of effort went into making sure the records of those remained quiet."

"Um. Well, I'm not sure I know anything about those," Delrain replied, "but I will make enquiries as soon as I get back to my office."

Delrain shifted around in his seat again.

"Not to worry, Delrain, I know this is very awkward for you, especially when someone so close to the family is implicated."

The colour drained from the part of Delrain's face visible beneath his aspect. He slumped into his chair.

"Oh, dear saints! How long have you known?"

"We've known for sometime Delrain. We know all about Lord Lunarith's cousin Daratt, and his dealings with the heretics. The secret meetings. The weapon shipments.

Everything. I had just hoped you would have the honesty to tell me in person. This is all rather embarrassing."

"How did you find out?"

"We've had an asset working within Requiem for the past month. It's amazing how much she has found out. Very illuminating."

"We have tried to stop him, Lord Vellorson. You must believe me! It appears he has become entangled with some disagreeable people and is being blackmailed. We were only trying to protect the family. If news got out that Lord Lunarith's cousin was dealing with the heretics, it could do the house a lot of damage."

"You have my sincere sympathies Delrain, I know you were just trying to protect the family. Family is important. I am afraid things have got messy and we've had to take direct action. Even now, our mutual problem is being dealt with. There will be no more missing shipments."

Delrain sat speechless in his chair.

"I've always liked you, Delrain, and considered you trustworthy. I admit I am a little disappointed that you didn't mention this to me when you had the chance. Now, enough of this. Depressing stuff. How are your wife and family?"

Delrain didn't answer.

"Missing home I expect," Trelt continued. "Although I hear your wife enjoys many of the finer things on offer in Ascension City. I would imagine that without your substantial ambassadorial income, it would be hard to continue such a privileged life. I wonder what your children would end up doing if they didn't have the benefits of such a stable family life?"

Delrain sank lower into his chair.

"Please make sure that you inform me of any further developments, Delrain." Trelt said. "That will be all."

Delrain rose unsteadily from the chair and headed for the door. Trelt disliked violence and veiled threats. Nasty stuff. It always made him feel sullied. But he would do anything to keep humanity safe.

If everyone knew the stakes, they would too.

Peasant girl

The young woman entered the dusty warehouse office, unsteadily carrying a tray filled with glasses of alcohol. She tried not to draw attention to herself.

The other people in the room were arguing. She pretended not to notice. Best not to be nosy. None of your business. Just set the drinks down quietly, then wait for further instructions by the door.

She was small and looked about twenty. Unclean black hair hung limply around her shoulders, partly obscuring her freckled light-brown face. She walked with a limp, probably due to some childhood affliction. Common in this area of Requiem. Especially since the troubles. Poverty and crime. Hard times.

The room was mostly bare, apart from a few chairs, some largely empty bookcases, and a wooden desk. The place smelled faintly of piss, the odour wafting in from the tannery across the road. Crates lay stacked against one wall. Contents covered with dirty sheets. Almost certainly containing some kind of contraband, she thought. None of her business.

A threadbare rug lay on the floor, only partly covering dirty wooden floorboards. A single grimy window gave views out across the rooftops of lower Requiem, capital of House Lunarith. Grey clouds and unseasonable drizzle.

On the back wall, a large wooden fronted clock ticked out the time. Tick. Tick. Tick.

A man sat behind a large wooden desk. Dressed in an ill fitting blue suit. His considerable bulk filled the chair, a mixture of fat and dangerous muscle. The man played idly with a small knife. Tossing it from hand to hand. Carl. The girls' current employer. He was a thug. But you had to count your blessings; she was lucky to have a job.

Two other men stood behind him, swords barely concealed beneath leather overcoats. Bodyguards. Another two stood at the back of the room. A man and a woman.

Carl scratched his thinning grey hair. He spoke calmly and quietly.

"No, no, no," he said. "As I have stated before, my dear Daratt, we have already agreed on a price. You have done very well out of our little arrangement. I thought we had an understanding."

The girl limped over to the desk and placed the tray of drinks down on it. Her hands unsteady, shaking; the liquid contents threatening to spill. She glanced at the other man as she turned away. Immaculate. Out of place in this dive. Smartly dressed in the grey colours of House Lunarith. Lapels and long coat detailed in gold stripes. His aspect belonged to the ruling family of House Lunarith itself. Even though this was Requiem, the capital of House Lunarith, it was unusual for someone of his standing to visit this area of the city. And on his own. She kept her eyes low, not wanting to show disrespect for her masters. Just be part of the background, she thought.

"How dare you speak to me in that tone," the immaculate man spat. "I have only raised the prices as a necessity. It is difficult to get the weapons out of the dock area without significant bribes being made. It is essential that nobody within my family finds out. Security has increased since the last shipment went missing, and I've had to increase the bribes to match the level of danger. I am just passing this cost on! You have no right to challenge me in this way!"

The guards behind the desk moved hands to the hilts of their swords.

The servant girl scurried back to her place by the door.

"Oh dear," Carl said, smiling, "I am very sorry that your costs have had to go up, but I don't see how this is my problem. We agreed on a price, and that is the price I will pay. I'm afraid you should have thought about all of this before entering this deal. Anyway, aren't you forgetting our little insurance policy?"

Carl casually opened a folder on his desk and leafed through the contents within. He picked up what looked like a photograph. Held it up. Photographic cameras and the equipment to process the pictures were the playthings of the wealthy. From her position, she couldn't quite see the details of the photograph. It featured a man and a woman in a state of undress. She blushed and lowered her eyes. Looked at her feet again. Carl showed it to one bodyguard standing behind the desk. The man laughed, winking at Darrat.

"Give that to me!" Darrat shouted, darting forward and attempted to snatch the photograph from Carl's hands.

Carl pulled the photograph away. Simultaneously, the female bodyguard behind Darrat rushed up behind him, slamming his head down onto the desk. His aspect cracked and half fell off. The man emitted a shriek. The bodyguard jerked him back upright by his neatly oiled black hair. Her other arm now holding a nasty-looking knife to his throat.

Apart from the ticking of the clock, the room was silent.

Carl rose to his feet. Smile gone.

"Let me get this straight, Darrat. You are in no position to change the terms of our agreement. It would be a shame if the envelope's contents fell into the hands of your cousin. I would rather that not happen. Believe me when I say that I am under just as much pressure as you. I am just the middleman. My employers would be very disappointed if the shipments ended. Not the sort of people that take disappointment well. It is in both our best interests that the current arrangement is maintained. Until I am told otherwise, the contents of this envelope will remain safely within my protection."

Carl nodded to the female bodyguard, and she released her grip. Her knife remained a few inches from his exposed neck. All eyes were on Darrat.

The man stammered.

"Sorry, you have something to say?" Carl said.

Then, unexpectedly, the bodyguard standing at the back of the room emitted a gurgling, choking sound.

The others turned to look. He raised a hand to his neck, from which the hilt of a knife now protruded. Blood spurted from between his fingers. The man's legs buckled, and he started falling towards the floor.

The clocked ticked. An instant passed.

Blurred movement by the doorway. Where the limping servant girl had stood just moments before, now stood a black-skinned abomination. It wore the same clothes as the girl, but its skin was jet black. It glistened like oil. Nose and mouth the barest of features. Smoothed out. Eyes black on black. The occupants of the room were only now registering what they were seeing. Mouths agape.

The wounded guard still hadn't hit the floor.

Tick.

The thing moved with impossible speed, appearing behind Carl. An arm flashed out. White blade. Its movement, a barely perceived blur. Carl's head was suddenly separate from his body. It arced through the air. Trailing blood.

Tick.

Darrat reeled backwards. Away from this unearthly horror. The other guards drawing weapons. The injured guard finally hit the floor.

Tick.

The thing wheeled around. Blurred movement. Towards the two guards behind Carl. They lifted swords. Trying to strike. One guard was airborne; an inhumanly strong kick administered to his midriff. A sound of breaking bone and tearing flesh.

Carl's severed head hit the floor. It rolled towards the back of the room.

Tick.

The other guard brought down a sword towards where the

thing was standing. The sword hit it squarely across the back, glancing off as if it had hit metal. The momentum of the sword continued uselessly down onto the floor.

Tick.

The airborne guard hit the back wall with a loud crunch. Lifeless body slumping to the floor.

Tick.

The thing twisted around to face the guard that had struck it. It punched upwards, striking the guard squarely in the face. A sickening crunch of splintered bone. The guard was dead before he hit the floor.

Darrat continued to reel backwards. Whimpering. He tripped and stumbled on the first fallen guard. The guard still clutching at the knife embedded in his neck. Life gurgled away through bloody fingers.

The last female guard had backed into the wall and was fumbling for the door handle. Eyes wide.

Darrat landed on his back. He scrambled away backwards. Feet wheeling. Towards the doorway. Panic. The thing advanced.

Tick.

"Please. Please. I beg you. Leave me alone," Darrat Lunarith said.

"Not today Darrat Lunarith," the thing said in a pleasant, feminine voice. "But know that the Emperor forgives you for your transgressions. Please accept his blessing. For he protects us all."

Then it was on him. A black hand over his face. Lightning danced between its fingers. Darrat slumped, lifeless.

Tick.

Vidyana Baylali, elite Aurumill agent, stood.

By the saints, her back hurt! One guard had struck her squarely with a sword. Her kavach armour had deflected most of the blow, but some had got through. It hurt. A lot.

Tick.

The terrified female guard opened the door and ran out into the hallway.

She summoned the gift of the dragon blood once more. The world around her slowed. She felt its power. Her muscles and tendons stiffened. For a few more moments, she would be much more than human. Swift and deadly. The holy gifts she had been given by the Emperor summoned once more to work. Such terrible power came at a heavy physical price. She would pay that debt in due course. Would spend hours shivering, muscles in spasm, wracked by cramps and sickness. But that was not for now. Now, she had to finish her job. Penance would have to wait for later.

She whispered to her shade. The strange second voice at the back of her mind. Always watchful. Always alert. Her own personal little demon. She whispered to it with her thoughts.

[Status?]

[You have suffered trauma to the ribs on your back. Mainly bruising, with some minor fractures], the thing replied.

[Give me pain relief], she said.

[I do not recommend administering pain blocking whilst you have dragon blood in effect. It could cause further tissue damage.]

[Do it.]

[I comply. Blockers are now in effect.]

The pain in her back stopped. It was just gone. She bolted for the open doorway. In the hallway, the female guard was running headlong toward the exit. To Vidyana, the figure was laughably slow. Vidyana picked up a vase from the nearby table and hurled it at the fleeing figure. The vase impacted the back of the guard's head at lethal speed. It shattered. The woman continued to run forward for a few paces before impacting the closed door. She crumpled in a heap. Blood started pooling around her head.

The oily blackness of Vidyana's kavach armour flowed away from her face, exposing her dirty servant features once more.

There was a scream from behind Vidyana. She turned to

see another woman standing at the other end of the hallway. Heldar. Another innocent servant working for the beast, Carl. They must have sent Heldar on some errand. Damn!

Vidyana rushed forward and grappled Heldar around the neck. Lightning danced between her fingers again. Not a lethal dose. The woman struggled for a few seconds before slumping unconscious to the ground. The boxes she carried scattering across the floor.

This complicates matters, Vidyana thought.

Vidyana carried the unconscious woman back to the room and laid her on a couch. She willed her shade to return her to normal. In reply, it whispered additional warnings about torn muscles. For the moment, she ignored it.

First, the good news. The targets were dead. The evidence secured. Letting the last guard leave the room had been a sloppy error. One caused by being awake for too many long hours, using her gifts too much.

The bad news; the unconscious Heldar.

Vidyana was the pinnacle of Aurumill agents. Best of the best. Ruthless, deadly, and smart. All she did was in the Emperor's name. The things she'd done during her servitude would make her a monster to some. However, she knew what she did was driven not by greed, hate, lust, or any other of the raw emotions that led people to sin. Her work was a necessity. Pure. Holding back the tide of chaos that threatened to turn the world to cinder. Vidyana was many things, but she was not a reckless murderer of innocents. She thought through her options.

Vidyana had got the job working in this warehouse about a month ago. Disguised as a girl from the poorer districts. Unlikely to get a job anywhere else. Just the sort of person who Carl could exploit. He had been the key to uncovering the missing shipments. The man thought he was more important to the heretics than he actually was. Too much bragging. Too many loose words in local pubs. It had proved his downfall. Amateur. Typical small time crime-lord with delusions of grandeur. The rest had been simple detective work. The local rebel cell identified. Members tagged and followed. Her group had already taken care of the local cell. At this very moment, their main hideaway was a collapsing, smouldering ruin. The chief rebel leaders, dead.

The downside was that the remaining Heretics would now be more careful than ever. It didn't matter. The message the attack sent was clear.

Vidyana worked directly for Trelt. A man she regarded as her mentor. The heretics had killed her mother and father when she was very young.

Using the Aurumill's globe spanning network of seers, she had been in contact with him for the past month. Feeding back what she had uncovered. Sordid detail, by sordid detail. Last night, she had received the kill order.

Vidyana looked down at the unconscious woman. Decision made. She would take the woman back to the Aurumill office. Once there, she would administer Silver Dew. The substance would flow through the woman's mind and destroy any memories of the last twenty hours. The Aurumill would leave her at her home, confused but otherwise safe.

Vidyana whispered to her shade, commanding it to raise the sensitivity of her hearing. She focused on the surrounding sounds. Tuning them out, one by one. The unconscious woman, breathing slow and shallow. Water running down a drain on the wall outside. People across the street arguing about late rent. Numerous beasts of burden in the surrounding streets. A distant train. Nothing to indicate an alarm had been raised. Nobody else in the building.

She willed her kavach armour to withdraw. Under her clothes, its oily blackness retreated from her arms, legs, and body. It flowed back, like liquid, towards her back, where it sank into two vertical ridges on either side of her spine. The only sign of their presence, hidden beneath her clothes.

Vidyana went to the folder on the desk and looked at the contents. There was nothing in this one that wasn't in the copy she'd destroyed earlier. Just photographs of Darrat with his mistress. In the wrong circles, they would cause a lot of embarrassment. She was not in any doubt that once Darrat had stopped being useful to the heretics, the pictures would have been released, anyway. The heretics had been spreading chaos in House Lunarith since they had been pushed out of neighbouring House Bargolis eighteen years ago. House Bargolis had been one of the rebel houses infiltrated by the heretics during the Schism. Although they had been defeated and their leaders removed, the area was rife with heretic cells. Sabotage and terrorism.

Vidyana went from corpse to corpse, placing their arms gently across their chest. Last, she went to Darrat, gently removed his cracked aspect, and placed a white cloth across his eyes.

She knelt in the middle of the room, head down, and prayed.

"Thank you Emperor, for guiding our way. Your wisdom is our strength. Through the Holy Four, you watch over us."

She crossed her arms across her chest.

"For they are the flesh you have sent us. Avatar of the Earth, I give to you the green grass, watch over our lands and their peoples. Avatar of the Air, I give to you the night, watch over our skies and the voids beyond. Avatar of the Water, I give to you my tears, watch over our seas and the depths beneath. Avatar of Balance, I give you my blood, guide our decisions and bring to us your wisdom."

She uncrossed her arms.

"Bless the saints, for granting me their inspiration, for their way lights the path. Your sacrifice is our strength."

She stood, picked the woman up, and headed for the window. She carried the woman onto the steep second story rooftop. Rain fell in sheets, making the rooftops slippery. Even with her gifts, she would have to watch her step.

Vidyana reached into her pocket and withdrew a small golden ball about the size of an apple, etched faintly with lines. She held it in her hand and whispered to it. The etched lines glowed red. Vidyana tossed it through the open window. With the woman over her shoulder, she jumped across the narrow street onto the rooftop of another warehouse.

The room opposite glowed bright orange from within. The light flickered. Within a few seconds, it was almost too bright to look at. Steam rose from the wet roof. A deep humming rose in volume. The air crackled, smelling of ozone. Flames started appearing around the window. Roof tiles cracked and fell inwards. Shafts of bright light shooting upwards through the holes. There was a deafening crack and a bright flash.

Where the room had been moments before, there was nothing. Just a perfectly spherical void, ten metres across. Bodies and evidence all gone. Flames leapt from the edges of the void where the room had been.

The device floated in the middle of the void, reflecting flames from its now mirror-like surface.

Vidyana held out her hand. The device floated across to her and she plucked it from the air.

Using the rooftops, she headed deeper into the city; the woman slung over her shoulder.

Chapter 3

The work before him was vast. Too much for one man. Too much, even for a god. His strength would not be enough. He wept for the world.

The watcher would come again. Nemesis. It would return to chaos.

Yes, too much for one god.

But, through his tears, an idea took shape.

Books of Maleth - Origins - Twelve

Rust

Lone Oak had stood sentry over Hammington's Rest for centuries. Empires had risen and fallen since it had been a sapling. It stood resolutely in the middle of the village green, on top of the hill at the heart of Hammington's Rest. The first thing you saw when returning from nearby villages.

There had been an older village here before, long in the past, belonging to the Delonde empire, but it had long fallen into ruin. It's stones reused by the current village.

Since that time, the village had grown and extended down the slopes and into the valley below, pushing back the feral as it went. Now, the area around Lone Oak hill was clear once again.

Rust lay with her back against the tree's trunk. She gazed down the hill, to the village beyond. Apart from an occasional trip to nearby towns, Rust realised she'd spent her entire life within the confines of that view.

Beyond the lee, the feral stretched on, unbroken, towards the distant horizon. Rust could just make out a grey smudge lying towards the horizon. Nowlton, the nearest town. Otherwise, Hammington's Rest was a tiny island in a vast feral sea.

She took a swig from a wooden cup full of honey tea. The refreshing liquid, welcome in the midday heat. Today was All Winnows Eve, a day for celebration and thanksgiving. Tomorrow would be All Winnows Day. The villagers would head out into the lee to remove any feral plants that had taken root since the great seeding during the month of Spinsilk. This year's seeding had been strong. The air had been full of floating seeds, many floating deep into the village. A result, they said, of a mild winter. Usually, the winnowing would be complete in a day. However, during poor years, it would take over three days to complete. Judging by the amount of feral saplings she'd pulled up in their own garden, she suspected it was going to be 'one of those years'.

She shielded her eyes against the glare of the sun. A shimmering haze rose a few feet into the air above the freshly cut grass of the common. It was filled with hundreds of people. Almost the entire population of the village. They had erected several marquees. Various stalls and games were dotted around, all competing for the attention of the villagers. The sweet smell of mown grass mixed with the sour-sweet scent of taptree beer from a nearby tent.

Uncle would be at work inside, persuading villagers to try his own brew. He'd maintained a taptree farm in the village for years, a sideline to his main tracking business. It kept them busy during the off season. This was the first year he had brewed the beer himself. In previous years, he had sold the raw taptree sap to a brewer in Nowlton. Taptree sap was one of the few useful feral plant products. Most of the other plants were poisonous. Uncle's beer wasn't too bad, if the repeat visits to the tent by some locals were any sign. Either that or it was because Uncle was selling it cheap as a tanner. She'd tried some herself. It was pretty good.

All Winnows Day was timed to make the winnowing as easy as possible. Earlier in the year, the feral saplings would be too small to pull up without breaking and leaving behind viable roots. Others would be missed. Later in the year, the plants would be too big. A pain in the arse to remove without digging.

Until the job was finished, the village green would host a communal gathering. Everyone would bring food and drink, which they would share with the rest of the village. A reminder that only as a community could they keep the feral at bay. It was also a chance to discuss local matters. Basically, it was just an excuse for gossiping and spreading rumours.

Earlier, an argument had taken place outside Uncle's tent. The argument had been about the war between Jorn and Bennel. Peldaran was in an alliance with Jorn. Bennel was just a proxy for the Hegemony. If Peldaran honoured their alliance with Jorn, they would not only be going to war with Bennel, but with the Hegemony too. Since that time, indecision and argument had paralysed the Peldaran government. An impossible choice between honour and self preservation.

That didn't stop pro-alliance people volunteering to fight for Jorn. The argument had broken out between the local butcher and the baker. The butcher had been drumming up volunteers to fight for Jorn. To invite a war with the Hegemony would be suicide, according to the baker. They were good friends, but cheap alcohol had brought things to a head. Emotions on the subject ran deep.

Uncle had split them up, sending them both off to cool off. It had drawn a crowd of gawping villages. They dispersed with a mixture of tutting, muttering, and laughing. They'd be talking about it for weeks. Small-minded village mentality, she thought.

Rust thought the butcher had made some good points. They were Jorn's ally. Bennel was the clear aggressor. Let the Peldaran government bicker and stall. It wouldn't stop people from joining up. She'd shared her views with Uncle several times. He shut any such conversations down. He said war wasn't the glamorous thing she thought it was. How would he know?

Tomorrow the winnowing would start. Rust was now old enough to fully take part in the winnowing. Last year had been her first, but she knew then everyone had been easy on her. This year, she suspected they would not treat her so gently.

Sindar's teeth it was hot. She wiped sweat from her forehead. She picked up a stone from the pile next to her and hurled it at the target rock lying about twenty hands away. The stone bounced on the grass and landed a couple of hands from the rock. She threw another.

There was a familiar clicking noise to her left. Rust turned to see TwoClicks waving with a forelimb from a nearby group of t'kelikt adults. Odd things, the t'kelikt. They were like six limbed insects, about the size of a human adult. They walked on their four hind limbs. Each arm-like forelimb ending in six dexterous digits. Unlike insects, they only had one body segment to which all six limbs were attached. The upper surfaces of their legs and body were covered with thick fur. The fur was almost entirely a greyish blue, except for striped patterns of various colours. A small round head sat toward the upper front of the torso, six red eyes constantly on the move, scanning.

There were several of them living in Hammington's Rest, including the juvenile TwoClicks. Rust wouldn't call it a friend. Their society and customs seemed too alien to her. But, TwoClicks sometimes joined her and Indiril for games. As a result, Rust could understand a little of the t'kelikt language. A weird mix of clicking, whistling and arm gestures. TwoClicks was just the name the humans had given it, because of the sound its native name made. In recent years, as they had all grown, Rust and Indiril seemed to have less and less in common with their insectoid friend.

Rust waved back and returned her attention to throwing stones at the rock. The latest one hit the rock. Yes!

"Not a bad shot, short-legs," a voice from behind her said.

She turned to see Indiril jogging up behind her. Indiril had just come second in a sprinting race. Not a surprise given that he was a tree-person. Silvar were always good at anything that involved running.

"Hey, Indi," she said. "Great job on coming second!"

He took a few seconds to get his breath back.

"Thanks. I nearly tripped on the last lap. I expect that would have got a laugh from some," he said.

Assholes. She would always have that in common with Indiril. Outsiders. Nothari girl and silvar boy. Indiril plonked himself down and picked up her cup of honey-tea.

"Do you mind?" he asked. He took a swig.

"No, go ahead," she said, smiling.

He took a couple more swigs of HER drink. He looked around, making sure that nobody was close.

"So," he said, "you had any more thoughts about what you are going to do with the objects? You really think they're safe?"

"Yes, Indiril. How many more times? I've put them under the house in our old den. In a wooden box. They are safe."

Indiril nodded. Frowning.

"Don't worry!" Rust said. "I've not touched them since."

"Good. That's good."

"I've been thinking about them. I'm thinking I might try them again, you know, to see what happens. To see if I can get any more visions."

Indiril stood.

"No, you mustn't. I don't think that's a good idea," he said. "I've been thinking about it too, and the more I do, the more I think those things are terrible balance."

"Don't start all that Divinist balance crap again, Indiril."

"It's not crap, Rust. Those things are bad. They are just wrong. The watch makes little sense. Why does it have twelve hours? I tell you, bad balance. Very bad."

"I don't know, Indi, but I want to find out. Don't you?"

"No! We should take them back. Before something bad happens."

Indiril started pacing.

"Oh, come on Indi. Don't be so bloody dramatic. I want to work out why Uncle had them. Maybe he found them years ago and didn't know what to do with them, so he hid them. That would make sense. Aren't you just a little curious about finding out?"

"I'm not curious, I'm scared."

"Scared? What for? It's quite exciting, I think."

"Exciting?" Indiril said, voice raising. "Why are you always going on about excitement?"

Rust looked up at him. He was shaking.

"Hey, hey, Indiril, I'm sorry. I'm sure there is nothing to worry about."

"Are you sure you've never seen a picture of the White Citadel?"

"No, I told you. Why?"

Indiril took a book from his bag and handed it to her.

"Look at this page and tell me if it reminds you of anything?"

The page featured a large hand drawn picture, annotated with silvar text she couldn't read. It didn't matter. The picture was of an enormously tall tower sticking up from the centre of a vast city.

"It's what you saw, isn't it?" Indiril asked.

Rust stared at the page. She'd heard of the White Citadel, who hadn't, but had never seen a picture. But even if she had, she wouldn't have remembered all the details. Although the vision had been brief, disjointed and confusing, she was sure this was what she'd seen.

Maybe Indiril was right, and the objects weren't just a curiosity, but represented something real. Something potentially dangerous.

"Isn't it?" Indiril asked again.

"Yes... it's the same," she replied.

"I don't like it. Not only do you get a vision, but you get one about the very heart of the Hegemony. A place that you assure me you've never seen a picture of. It's bad balance! Evil magic."

Rust didn't respond. Doubt displaced her previous confidence.

"I want you to promise me," Indiril said, "that you'll take those objects back to where you found them."

Indiril was probably right. Some things were best left alone. Uncle would have good reasons to keep them hidden. However, if it was something Uncle was involved in, shouldn't she know about it? She was sure that one of the people in the vision had looked like Uncle. She couldn't simply give up and return them without finding out. Even just a little more. Could she?

"Let me think about it, Indi."

"But-", he said

"I said, let me think about it."

"Hmph. Just promise me not to use them again, or I'll tell father."

"You've got no right to, Indiril."

"I mean it," he said. "I really think they are dangerous. Soul thieves, maybe. Or worse. Promise me."

"Soul thieves? No such thing."

"Promise me."

"Alright!" she said at last, "I promise."

She tried not to meet his gaze.

Vidyana

Vidyana had moved quietly across dark rooftops slick with rain. Footsteps light, despite the weight of the woman on her back. She avoided busy streets where possible, crammed full of people out celebrating All Winnows Eve. An unnecessary risk.

The street below was like countless others. It stood at the boundary between the human districts, the docks, and the more affluent trade and immaculate areas. The street wouldn't look out of place in any other Hegemony city the world over. The usual mix of shops, merchants, pubs, and the like. They all liked to think they had their own cultures, their own individual customs. She'd seen enough to know differently. They were all the same when you dug beneath the surface.

Oil lamps cast long shadows. The crowds had thinned, but there were still too many people to wander around calmly with someone over your shoulder.

Her destination was the red sandstone church across the street. Candles and lamps shone through elaborate stain glassed windows, bathing the neighbouring buildings in multicoloured light. Square, with a tower rising from each corner. Each tower honouring one of the Emperor's holy four. A central dome surmounted by a tall spire. A single lamp at its pinnacle representing the enteral light of the Emperor. A lone priest moved about within the central tower, invisible to normal, ungifted eyes.

There was a balcony facing her. Slightly below her level. About thirty hands away, she judged, fronted by a low stone wall. Three metres... It was quite the leap, especially carrying the unconscious woman, even with her gifts. She whispered to her protesting shade. Felt power course through her.

She jumped. A moment of weightlessness. As she landed, pain flared through her left ankle, piercing through the pain blockers her shade had already administered. Sharp, electric, intense. Her leg gave way. She stumbled, but did not go down. Muscle and tendons stressed almost beyond coping point. She gasped and swore under her breath.

[Please do something about this pain,] she whispered to her shade.

[Increasing the amount of pain relief would violate safety limits,] it replied.

She knew how to sweet talk it into compliance. Over the years, she'd learned phrases and commands that it couldn't ignore. Her ever vigilant, ever alert, guardian. It had saved her many times. If she ever lost it, she would never feel quite the same. A piece of her would be missing.

[Warning acknowledged. I permit you to violate safe limits. User authorisation given. Comply.]

No reply. The pain lessened almost immediately. It sulked if she disobeyed it too much. She had done so frequently over the last few days and would probably have to suffer prolonged periods of silence. Passive aggression. It would get over itself, eventually. It always did.

[Whilst you're at it, begin readjusting my facial web back to normal]

[Of course, master]

Yep, definitely pissed it off.

It would take a couple of days for the skin and tissues of her face to return to their normal darker pigments and features. The changes were subtle, a skin tone here, a tightening of tissue there. Just another gift the Emperor granted her. A rare one. One that had made all the difference. Nothing better for disguise than actually being able to change your face. After the transition, her face would itch maddeningly for several days. Adding another small torture to the list.

She emerged through doors on to a balcony overlooking the nave below. Oil lamps suspended on long chains hung from the domed ceiling. There were candles around the altar at the end. Shadows flickered and moved.

Vidyana laid the woman down on the red carpet and checked her gag and binds. Still out cold.

She avoided everyone on her way to the central altar. Most were seated in the aisles. Praying silently or reading from the scriptures. A priest talked to an elderly man. His voice was soft. The man wept quietly. Vidyana had seen that look before. Bereavement. The priest offered words of comfort and blessings. She, too, would say a prayer for this unknown man. Another walked through the aisles, blessing people as she went.

Vidyana picked a candle from a small wooden box, lit it from another and placed it alongside. The altar featured a marble statue of the Emperor. His face was almost featureless, arms held up in front of him, palms up, welcoming. He was surrounded by four smaller statues facing outwards. All reflected in the mirror-smooth pool of water that surrounded them.

Vidyana glanced at her face reflected on its surface. A face not quite her own. She'd miss the freckles. Saints, she hadn't realised how dirty she was. Hair everywhere. Soot and grime.

Kneeling, she prayed, seeking blessings and the wisdom of the Emperor.

She headed towards an area at the back of the nave concealed by heavy red curtains. Inside, she pulled a lever next to an iron-banded door. Heavy bolts being withdrawn. The door opened outwards, exposing a narrow corridor and a stone stairway leading down. Inside stood a man dressed in the red and white robes of a high priest.

"Welcome back Captain Baylali." he said, motioning towards the stone staircase.

She descended.

Another man waited at the bottom, dressed smartly in a linen shirt, trousers, and overcoat. Each item of clothing was a different pastel colour. Typical for an immaculate office worker. He wouldn't look out-of-place in any immaculate institution. Pale skin, dark brown hair plaited and coiled. Long beard, flecked with white.

"Woah - By the saints, Vid, you look like felder dung," he said.

"Thanks, Kaylaris, I love you too," she replied, smiling.

The man laughed.

"Smell as bad too," he said.

She'd worked with him for years. Although she reported directly to Trelt, she respected Kaylaris' opinion. They worked well together. He was a good lay as well.

They entered a large stone walled room. There were several others present, all dressed in similar nondescript clothes. Most were seated at wooden desks. At the far end of the room, a group was having a discussion around a table, upon which a map of the city lay.

In another corner, a woman sat with her arms folded across her lap. She wore the same style of clothing as the rest. Her white aspect featuring a single black stripe running down the middle, with a silver-coloured metal circlet around her head. Her eyes were closed, deep in concentration. A seer.

"So, what's the status?" Kaylaris asked.

"I have dealt with both targets. The evidence has been destroyed. I used the null-eater."

"Great job. Any complications?"

"An unexpected one."

"Oh?"

"I didn't have time to sweep the building before everyone arrived. Bloody Carl came to the warehouse early. Had to go with it. As a result, there was an innocent woman in the building."

"I see. Don't let it worry you. We knew there was a risk of innocent collateral death."

"No, you don't understand. I pacified her. She isn't dead."

"I see. What have you done with her?"

"She's upstairs, on the balcony. Bound and gagged. I brought her here. We can administer silver-dew, wipe the last day's memories, then return her to her district."

"Shit, Vidyana. You know how expensive that stuff is. It's supposed to be for informants. We only have a limited supply. We'll have to requisition more from Ascension City afterwards."

"I know, I know. What did you expect me to do, kill her?"

Kaylaris left the question hanging.

"Well, I didn't," Vidyana said.

"Fine. Fine. I'll send someone up to deal with her and get her sent back. Anything else?"

"I used my gifts heavily. I'm heading for a massive downer over the next few days. My shade tells me I have several torn muscles, severe toxin build up resulting in mild liver damage, and some broken ribs. It's annoyed with me."

"Alright, I'll get the physician to give you a look. You know we don't have a heal-coffin here, so you'll have to ride the worst of it out, I'm afraid."

"Yeah, I figured that," Vidyana said.

They called them heal-coffins, but the proper name was a restoraleum. Another powerful magical relic from the ancient days. They were legendarily rare, but could vastly speed up healing. Could even grow stuff back. The Aurumill had several. Vidyana would have been dead many times over without their miraculous help. But not here. Not in this city.

"You mind if I use the dorm here for a few days whilst I crash?"

"Of course. Go get yourself cleaned up. It smells like you could do with a bath."

"What if something else needs taking care of?"

"We've got things covered. We're keeping our ears out for any other heretic movements within the city."

He nodded towards the seated woman in the corner.

"Our seers are listening for heretics whispering on the seer web. They wouldn't normally be so bold as to use their own seers this close to the city, but our actions have caused a bit of a stir. We've got other people under observation. We're expecting several to bolt. All under control."

"Thanks Kaylaris."

"No, thank you. This last week has been a great success. I think this time we've broken the backbone of the heretics in this city. This could be a turning point to purge their filth from the entire region."

She smiled.

"All in a humble week's work," she said.

Vidyana walked through a door at the back of the room and headed for the dormitory. And the promise of a hot bath.

Kathnell

Kathnell was out of breath when she arrived at work. Her head felt worse than it had when she'd woke. It had been a hell of a All Winnows Day party. She should have gone home much earlier. She was late.

Maybe Corric would come in late today, she thought. He had been away for a few days. He may still be at home working on the new job.

She turned the handle to the workshop, hoping that it was still locked. The handle turned smoothly. Nemesis wept! Here goes, she thought, and entered quietly.

Corric was sitting at his desk. Some plans spread across its worn surface, ruler and pencil in his hands. He turned around as Kathnell entered.

"Well, well, look what washed up at the docks this morning," he said.

He appraised her with mild disgust.

Kathnell went to speak, trying to get her breath back from the jog. Bile rose. She swallowed. All she could do was cough.

"Don't tell me, the Winnow's Day celebrations spilled over into yesterday. You overslept and are about to issue a finely crafted and sincere apology."

Corric rose and walked over to the fire. Black iron teapot suspended above it. Wisps of steam rose from the spout.

"I'm... ahem. I'm so sorry, Corric. Mum didn't wake me. She thought I had today off."

"Oh, so it's your poor mum's fault now, is it? Did she also force you to drink a gallon of ale as well? Or at least I'm assuming it was a gallon based on the colour of your face."

"I really am sorry, Corric."

Corric poured some tea into two mugs and handed one to her.

"Yes, I am sure you are," he replied with more warmth than she expected. "It's a good job I'm in a good mood. I've had some great news. It will also surprise you to learn that me and your father engaged in similar revelry when we were younger."

The hot tea tasted good.

"What's the good news?" Kathnell asked.

"We won that contract I went to view last week. It's a good'un. Couple of months' of work, at least. Immaculate quarter. Good margins."

"That's great news."

"It'll also mean that you'll probably have to work weekends for a while. Tight schedule, you see. We'll do well from the pay."

"That's great!"

"If we don't fugger-it-up, that is. There is a lot to be done."

"What's the job?"

"Installing new heating systems into a series of houses. There are some immaculate families moving in, one is coming over from Drellgarh. A Drellmore! As you know, space is at a premium in the area, so they are converting some old diplomatic residences that belonged to a ceph matriarch and her brood."

Corric walked back to his desk and stood over it. There was a schematic, and a map with lines and notes pencilled on it.

"Its down on the wharf side. Looks out across the bay. Magnificent views, as you'd expect. The structural work has already been done. Now they want the hot water system linked up to the main district boiler."

He pointed to the house on the map and then moved his finger across a couple of streets to another square building.

"There is a void-boiler located here that supplies hot

water and heating to most of the lower half of the immaculate quarter. The house used to be connected to it, but the pipes haven't been maintained for years. They'll all need replacing. New radiators, taps, pipes, fittings. The whole brag-nut. As I say, a lot of work."

He turned to her.

"Did you read those books I gave you?" he asked.

"Yes, I've got them here," she said. She reached round and plonked the books down on the table. Between two books, the edge of another piece of paper stuck out, a corner covered in mud.

The flyer from the alley! Kathnell froze.

Corric idly reached for the paper and pulled it out. His face darkened as he scanned it, cheeks flushing red.

"What in the thousand hells is this?"

"I.. Um. I..", Kathnell stuttered.

"I asked you a Nemesis damned question!" he shouted.

"I forgot I even had it; I found it in an alley."

"Do you realise how dangerous this is? If they caught you with this, you'll be in a whole whale-gut of trouble, Kathnell. I can't believe you brought this to my workshop! If they find it here, we'll BOTH be in trouble. They've hung people for less. Get yourself strung up if you want to, but in all the hell's name, don't bring me into it. Are you that stupid? Well, are you?"

She'd never seen Corric this angry. However, she didn't like being called stupid.

"It's only a leaflet! Some of the stuff they say makes sense!", she shot back, "What I've been saying about the guild plans not changing for years. They seem to say the same thing. It makes sense."

"Makes sense?! Mark my words Kathnell, the rebellion are a lot of things, but foremost they are trouble. I've had dealings with them in the past. They are not to be trusted. All wormy words and smoke. You might think the Hegemony is bad. Who can blame you after what happened to your father, but this Liberation lot ain't no better. Just two sides of the same wheel. When it turns, it's people like you and me that get crushed under it."

He looked out the window.

"Tell me," he said. "How do you expect to work on those precious void-trains you keep on about if you are in prison? Not even that, if there is even so much as a whiff of the rebellion about you, the Hegemon won't let you within two kilometres of a train."

There was a knock at the door. Corric crunched the paper up and threw it into the fire. It immediately caught and burned.

The door knocked again. Corric turned to Kathnell and motioned her to be silent.

"Keep your eyes down, girl! And only speak when spoken to. You understand?"

She nodded.

He opened the door. Five people stood outside. Four dressed in the grey robes of the steam engineering guild. She recognised a couple of them. In the middle of the group stood a Stonie woman, forehead, nose, eyes and upper cheeks covered by her aspect. Long white cloak, with black lines. Cream coloured skin. She held a wooden walking stick with an ornate brass top, which she was about to use again to knock. She paused as the door opened.

Kathnell had seen immaculate before, but not one so high ranking. Had certainly never talked to one of them. Panic ran through her. Had they found out about the flyer? Tracked her here somehow?

"Mr Corric," the stonie said, "Please forgive this unexpected visit. May we come in?"

Corric bowed. Kept his head low.

"Of course, Master Acadrill. It's wonderful to see you again. Please come in."

Kathnell kept her eyes lowered so as not to offend the immaculate woman. She wasn't about to get herself into more trouble. The thought that she may have endangered Corric made her feel suddenly even more sick.

The immaculate woman's golden hair was almost down to her waist, neatly plaited into long strands. Each strand decorated with intricate gold bands and beads. Corric motioned to Kathnell.

"This is my apprentice, Miss Kathnell Bilt."

The woman nodded without comment. She glanced around the workshop and turned back to Corric.

"I'm afraid we are going to have to advance our timetable, Mr Corric," she said. "A family is arriving earlier than we had thought. A man married to one of the Drellmore family. Not the central family, but still Drellmore. He is on orders from Lord Drellmore himself. He will arrive here in less than two weeks. It is essential that the main part of his house be up and running before his arrival. Forget the other houses for now. He will come on his own first, but we expect his family may join him at some point. This means we will need to start work this week. I want you to tell me how much you can do by then."

"Yes, Master Acadrill," Corric said.

"I don't expect miracles, Mr Corric. I would rather know what is possible now, rather than finding out in a few weeks. We will make extra funds and personnel available if required. If something isn't possible, say so. Do you have any questions?"

"No, Master Acadrill."

"Good, if you have questions, please send them to Krelton," she said, nodding towards one of the four men that had accompanied her. The woman turned and left, followed by three of the others. The fourth man, Krelton, stopped in the doorway. He smiled at Corric.

"Don't cock this one up, Corric," he said.

"I'll try not to Krel. Who is this Drellmore fellow moving in early?"

"No idea. Works for a shipping company. He's moving in to house number two, so that's the one you need to concentrate on. If there's anything you need, let me know. Get the plans sent to me as soon as possible."

With that, Krelton left as well, leaving Corric and Kathnell alone. Corric breathed out.

"Saint's arse that was close," Corric said.

He turned to Kathnell.

"Now, do you see why having things like that leaflet is dangerous? If Acadrill had entered without knocking, which being an immaculate, she has every right to do, we would have been for the chop. Can't you understand that, Kathnell?"

"Yes, Corric. I am truly sorry. I didn't think about it."

"Clearly. You seem to have done an awful lot of apologising the last few days. Just like your father, you're a magnet for trouble. Impulsive. Reckless. I know you think I am overprotective, but I promised your father that if anything should ever happen to him, I would watch out for you and your mother."

His voice caught, and he turned away from her.

"Now the mallet has hit the manure with this job, we are going to be working long hours. No more talk about rebels. I mean it Kathnell. This has to stop. Now I need to re-arrange the plan for this new timetable. This will take a good few hours. Whilst I'm doing that, you can make a full inventory of the items on this list and note anything we are short of."

"Yes, Corric," Kathnell said, taking the list from him.

Kathnell spent the rest of the day going through the list. She couldn't stop thinking about the conversation. What did he mean he had dealings with the rebellion before? She was certain that he hadn't meant to blurt that out. She knew that he and her father were close. That they had been friends. He had watched over her as she'd grown, but she knew nothing about any promise he had made to her father.

She wondered if she should ask him about it, but didn't think he would respond to any more questions. She was sure that it had only slipped because he'd been angry. She didn't want to upset him again.

However, there was clearly more to Corric's past than she had known.

Rust

Rust pushed the barrel upright, and slumped against its side. The last one, thankfully. Twenty-four of them in total! All pushed from the barn to the end of the road. Each one, heavy with tap tree sap.

As expected, the winnowing this year had been difficult. Five days! The worst one in thirty-five years, they said. Her back ached. All over now; life had returned to a mundane normal.

It would be hunting season soon. The rich folk would start flowing in from the cities.

This morning Uncle had woken her early, and they had rolled a couple of dozen barrels down to the roadside to be collected by the brewer from Nowlton. Uncle had tried his own brew this year, but still most of their income came from Uncle's hunting and tracking business. He was good. She had plans to be as good, if not better. The taptree farm was really just for the off season.

Rust wiped sweat from her brow. The sun beat down from another cloudless sky.

"Thirsty work, eh?" Uncle said, approaching.

He held out a hand and pulled her up.

"Yeah, I'm exhausted."

Uncle smiled. Rust realised she was at eye level with him. When did that happen? She was so used to looking up to Uncle all her life. It must have crept up on her like a basilisk, finger-width by finger-width.

"Well, that's it for today. I'm going to go into the village to meet the brewer on the way up. Then I've got a load of other stuff down there to prepare for the hunting season, so won't be back till after supper. You've earned a few hours off."

"Thanks, Uncle."

Her uncle turned to her and looked suddenly serious.

"You know, Rust, I'm very proud of you don't you?"

She wasn't used to such language from him and didn't quite know how to respond. Her uncle held up a hand, smiling.

"It's alright, you don't have to answer. I just wanted to say it, that's all. And I think your parents would have been proud too."

"Thanks…"

"Right, it's about time I got going. See you later," he said.

Without another word, he headed off down the road.

The rest of the day spread out before her. She knew exactly what she was going to do. Indiril was right, the objects were too much of a risk. Best to be rid of them.

Rust entered the old den under the house, sandwiched between the dirt and the floorboards above. She'd spent many a childhood hour inside. There was barely enough room to turn. It seemed to have shrunk since she was younger.

She crawled to the back and brushed some loose soil away, exposing a wooden cigarette box. She opened it. The objects. It was the first time she'd looked at them since she'd stashed them. Her resolve faltered. All the questions came flooding back. She'd promised Indiril she wouldn't use them again. Promised she would take them back.

Her fingers brushed over the watch. There was the merest tingling sensation. A feeling, just on the edge of perception. Surely it would do no harm if she tried them again. Just once. Then she would take them back as promised.

She picked up the watch, preparing herself this time. At first, nothing happened. She held it in both hands as she'd done before and brought it up to eye level. Her vision swam.

Night. Stars on deep blue, glimpsed through gaps in

scudding clouds. Running through the streets of a strange city. Rain poured from the sky like a waterfall. An unfamiliar word entered her mind. "Monsoon". She didn't know what it meant. The streets ran with water, gurgling and swirling down drains. Sensing someone to her left, she turned and looked into the face of Uncle. It was him, but not him. Younger. Hair brown, rather than grey. His face screwed in concentration, exertion, and something else. Fear. He was pointing to something in front.

There was a bright flash followed by a boom. Thunder? Rust turned and looked behind them. Seen though flashes rising in the distance, a white tower of unimaginable size rose, piercing the clouds, disappearing into darkness. "The White Citadel". Other people were with them. All fleeing in the same direction.

Another bright flash and boom. Not lightning. Rust saw the city street cast into stark contrast. Figures in pursuit, glimpsed in white light. Armoured figures wielding crossbows. One figure held a long staff. Aimed it towards them. A bright white line of fire erupted from it, accompanied by a boom.

This was the source of the light. Not lightning. One of the people fleeing burst into flame and fell screaming. Other figures were in pursuit. Dressed in black. Skin like oil. Moving at impossible speeds. They sliced into the fleeing people. Almost like dancing. Rust experienced a mortal fear that was not her own. A feeling of bottomless sadness.

She was walking up a slope. The ground was dry and cracked, mostly barren. Rock and sand. She could smell the dust. Occasional feral plants clung to rocks, or hid in shady crevices. Squat bulbous things. Covered in spines. Another strange word, "Feral-Cacti". She glanced up at the cloudless sky. Could feel the heat bouncing off the baked ground.

Ahead, the slope steepened towards distant twin mountains. She knew she was headed for the taller of the two. A single cloud stretched back from its peak. It streamed away, to be torn into shreds by the wind. Two words kept repeating themselves "Cloud-maker, cloud-maker…"

Time skipped. She was no longer on the lower slopes. Now she was heading towards a dark cleft in an almost vertical slab of rock that towered high overhead.

The vision skipped. She was in a dark cavern. The only light came from behind. In front of her lay an enormous white egg, at least six metres long and four high. She ran her hand along its smooth surface. The hand belonged to a woman. She felt love for the thing. A connection.

The vision faded. The world returned to normal and she put the watch down. She felt lightheaded and her pulse raced. The visions were largely the same as she had seen before, but this time they were much more vivid. It left her feeling giddy. She felt exhilarated, almost drunk.

What about the circlet? If the watch was more vivid, what would she get from it this time? She had to find out. Rust picked up the circlet, it unfolded itself and she placed it over her head. As before, there was a strange tingling and coldness. A feeling of connection.

Distant whispering. Voices far away, indistinct, like a summer breeze blowing over dry creepgrass.

This time, rather than being one mass of distant voices, Rust could concentrate on each one. Singling them out. As she did so, each became momentarily clearer, bordering on understandable. Not just a sensation of whispering, either. There was something else overlaid on top. A feeling of space. Like she was centred in a dark void. The voices like star-like wisps, small and impossibly distant. Some, so remote she could barely perceive them. She tried to understand them, never quite managing it.

Then a new wisp appeared. It seemed to stretch towards her. This one was different. Whilst the others had somehow seemed human, this one was odd. Artificial. She wasn't afraid of it. Somehow, she knew it wasn't to be feared. It whispered to her. Fragments and suggestions of words on the edge of understanding. It sounded like a warning. She strained harder, trying to get more meaning. It desperately wanted to tell her something.

A new wisp appeared. It grew rapidly in brightness, eclipsing all the others. She felt like it was staring at her. It was impossible to look away. It reached towards her, increasing in intensity as it came. The other wisps vanished, including the friendly one. Now it was just her and this new one. An infinite void beyond.

A voice entered her mind. Clear. Sharp. Almost painful.

[Who are you?], it commanded.

Rust tried to break away. A feeling like a hundred needles penetrating her skull.

[WHO ARE YOU?]

[I am Rustari... Rustari Parra], she gasped.

The words spilled from her. She hadn't meant to answer. She shook her head and tried to break free of this strange interrogation.

[WHERE ARE YOU?]

She tried to resist the question. Once more, she felt the answers slipping out like her mind was being wrung out like a wet cloth. The light grew brighter. No, not light, more a sensation of brightness. It blossomed inside her. She felt her body go rigid. Tasted blood in her mouth.

[Hammington's Rest]
[WHERE?]
[Hammington's Rest, Peldaran]
[SPEAK]

Other things spilled out. The brightness intensified further. It was like being forced to look at the sun. Surely, she would go blind! She told it of the secret place they had found. How she had found the strange circlet. She just couldn't stop.

She tried to regain control of her thoughts. Forcing herself away from the thing. Instead, it pulled her closer. The pressure in her skull increased. The pain became unbearable. Surely her head would burst!

She tried to scream. She told it of the watch with twelve numbers and the visions.

I must get out! Must make it stop! STOP!

Abruptly, the wisp was gone and she was back under the house. She'd been thrashing about. Her clothes and hair all covered in dust. The ground was gouged where she's been clawing at it. One of her fingernails was split, blood running down her finger. She'd bitten her tongue.

She ripped the crown from her head. It folded itself up as it had done before.

Sweat poured from her. The space beneath the house felt suddenly much smaller. Closing in like it was going to crush her! She scrabbled to the exit and flopped onto the grass.

Her face felt sore. She reached up and realised she'd scratched her own face.

Sindar's teeth! What was that? She was no longer doubtful of Indiril's words. These things were bad. Bad magic. Bad balance. Forbidden.

Unsteadily, she rose to her feet, and went in search of Indiril. They would put them back where they found them. Today! Before something bad happened. If they set off now, there was plenty of time to be back before Uncle returned.

No sense in letting Indiril know what had just happened. He would only lecture her on how he'd been right all long. Annoyingly, he was seldom wrong.

Chapter 4

Seek not to hide your sins.
   Nemesis watches. Nemesis waits. Witness to all.

Unknown Author. Ventarso circa 400 BSC

Trelt

More documents. Endless things to sign. Trelt Vellorson scanned through yet another page of text. The wall clock ticked away the hours. Ticked away his life.

It seemed his job was an endless procession of paperwork. The more stable the government, the more paperwork. Until eventually, it all collapsed under the sheer weight of bureaucracy. He was certain it was some kind of universal law. With order came paperwork. A ridiculous theory he often shared with the Emperor, who in return was perpetually amused by Trelt's observations.

Trelt had witnessed many things, had endured many things, during his long lifetime. Most would think most of them were the ravings of a lunatic. But, as the ancient saying went, truth was often stranger than fiction.

There was a rap at the door.

Odd. His aide should have announced any visitors.

"Lord Vellorson," his aide said from the other side of the door, "I have an urgent message that I am to deliver in person."

"Come," he said.

His aid entered and handed Trelt an envelope. Sealed with the crest of the Order of Divination. The organisation that controlled the seers.

"Please forgive my intrusion, Lord Vellorson," his aide said. "A runner arrived with this note. He told me to hand it to you immediately and not to engage in conversation with anyone else, or to use the speaking tubes. The runner was most insistent."

Trelt frowned.

"Of course. You did the right thing. Thank you. You may

leave."

Trelt waited until the door had closed. The note was brief. It stated that it was of extreme importance that Trelt came at once to the Grand Seers' office and speak to no one en route. It was signed by Idaris Carthain, the Grand Thaumaturge himself. He'd known Idaris for years. Not someone prone to unnecessary drama. He burned the letter in the fireplace and when every part was cinder, he grabbed his coat and left.

Trelt arrived by carriage outside the Divination Order building. The red sandstone building dated from the time of the Red Star Ascendancy, nearly seven hundred years ago. The time just before the Emperor returned from his long dreaming. A time before the dawn of the Hegemony.

The building's surfaces bore the scars of centuries long exposure to the elements. Worn down by time. Details smoothed, edges rounded, slave to entropy. The carved faces of forgotten heroes, once detailed, now barely sketches.

The building lay in the shadow of the White Citadel, two thousand years older. It had not altered in all the long centuries since its creation. Unblemished by wind, rain, or time.

Idaris was pacing by the window. The man's dark face was almost entirely covered by his aspect. It was adorned with several large gemstones, denoting his impressive rank and stature. His grey-white hair, usually neatly tied, was a chaotic mess. As usual, the office smelled faintly of incense. Idaris claimed it helped him think.

A woman dressed in white robes sat quietly in one corner. Her aspect covering the upper part of her face and head. A vertical black stripe ran from top to bottom. A coin shaped hole in the aspect's forehead, exposing the skin underneath. A seer.

"Lord Vellorson, thanks for coming so soon," Idaris said.

"What's this about, Idaris?"

"Forgive me the question. Does anyone know about your visit here or the contents of the letter?"

"Nobody."

"Good. There has been an incident involving lost artefacts belonging to The Heretic."

The Heretic? Simona? This WAS unexpected. Especially after all this time. She'd been dead for over fifteen years. Trelt had been expecting many things, news of war, news of an unexpected assassination, but not something to do with his old colleague Simona.

"Go on," he prompted.

Idaris indicated the female seer seated in the corner.

"This is Amara. She is one of my best seers."

Trelt nodded at the woman, who stood and bowed.

"It is an honour to meet you, Lord Vellorson," she said.

"Likewise," he said.

"Please Amara," Idaris said. "Tell Lord Vellorson what you told me."

"A few days ago, a seer reported he had detected an unsanctioned seer web. This was not so surprising, the heretics use unsanctioned webs all the time. However, my seer said that this web was different, with a signature shape they had not experienced before. Possibly a new one. They also noticed that the user was strong but erratic. Obviously gifted, but without proper training. He located the user to somewhere in the northern hemisphere. Possibly around Ventarso, Creshmet or Seendar. I logged it, but I'll admit it didn't seem that important. Most likely some new rebel trainee, or a seldom used rebel web."

The woman stopped, as if unsure of going on.

"Please continue," Trelt said.

"About an hour ago, the same seer encountered the same presence. Only this time, the connection was much stronger, more attuned with the web. He immediately alerted me and I entered the Whispering. I sensed the other almost straight away, strong but with little control. They were broadcasting their location with no concern or self-awareness. They were also freely sending the signature of their web, which seemed especially naïve. No attempt to block or obfuscate. No usual tricks deployed. Definitely someone with no training, or indeed direction. It was a signature I didn't recognise. It had a very distinct shape, unlike any I had seen before."

Each seer web in existence had a unique signature. Experienced seers could sense it like a shape. The shape was unique to each web, written into them when they were forged. It could be obfuscated with the proper training. Neither the Hegemon nor the heretics would ever let someone use a seer web without weeks of mental training beforehand.

"It was at this point that I made contact," Amara continued. "The other accepted the connection almost straight away, and I could easily dominate them. The initial feelings I got were of a female, around seventeen to twenty-five years old. I'll admit I was shocked by the power of their connection, given the obvious lack of training. I discovered the girl is called Rustari Parra and is from a village called Hammington's Rest in the Kingdom of Peldaran, on Seendar. Had to look the place up. It's small. Income mainly from agriculture and hunting. Mixture of ethnic Seendar and mainland populations. They speak imperial standard. Pretty unremarkable place."

"After they disconnected, I immediately went to look up the signature shapes in the known web index. I couldn't find it, so I reported it immediately to Idaris, as I believed it may be one of the lost seer webs."

"I was sceptical at first," Idaris said. "I mean, one of the lost webs hasn't turned up for many years, but Amara was insistent she had not been mistaken. So, we went to check the Lost Codex. Amara quickly identified the signature. It was for the seer web belonging to The Heretic herself."

Trelt stood, letting the news sink in. There were only a few seer webs left in existence. None had been forged since the Schism. They were now a fixed and extremely valuable commodity. Simona's seer web had gone missing after she had been killed fifteen years ago. They had thought it destroyed, along with the demon-bitch Valtha.

"And you are certain the signature was a match?" Trelt asked.

"I am certain," Amara replied. "The girl was broadcasting it strongly, and it was a distinctive shape, like a double spiral. I recognised it immediately. It was definitely the same device."

"I concur," Idaris said, "As per protocol, I made Amara draw the shape before I opened the Lost Codex. What she drew was an almost exact match. Amara has had no prior access to the Codex. It is the same device."

Trelt thought for a few moments before turning to Amara.

"Thank you, Amara," he said. "You may leave, but do not speak of this to anyone but myself and Idaris."

Amara nodded.

"Of course, Lord Vellorson," she said and left the room.

Trelt waited for her footsteps to recede.

"That wasn't all of it," Idaris said.

Trelt nodded for him to continue.

"This Rustari made vague statements about touching a pocket watch and getting visions from it."

Visions? A memory-well? Maybe Simona's? If so, there was no telling what secrets it contained.

"I take it you haven't reported this to anyone else?" Trelt asked.

"No, the only people that know are the three of us. There was quite a stir in the seers' office, but Amara quashed it when she didn't recognise the signature."

"And she can be trusted?"

"Yes, absolutely. She was my personal student and many think she'll make Grand Thaumaturge one day. There is one more thing."

"Oh?"

"Did you know that Simona's, er... The Heretic's, seer web, was gen-locked?"

Most seer webs could be used by any attuned immaculate with the correct summoning skills. However, some were locked to an individual bloodline, useless to anyone outside the immediate family. It meant this Rustari must be related to Simona.

"I know. Which has it's own disturbing implications," Trelt replied. "I want you and Amara to keep a watch for this Rustari Parra to see if she surfaces again. I want to keep this quiet for now."

"Of course, Lord Vellorson."

"Have you informed the Emperor?"

"No, I thought it would be best to leave that to you."

Trelt

The White Citadel loomed over the carriage. The carriage fell into its shadow. The White Citadel was almost impossibly big. Far beyond the ability of any current world power to even conceive of constructing, including the Hegemony.

Elderstone, they called it. A relic of ages long past. Trelt was one of the few that knew of its original purpose. The foundation for a ladder that had stretched all the way into the heavens. Most alive today couldn't even imagine such a thing.

At that very moment, there would be thousands of people working on, and inside, the massive structure.

Trelt pressed his head against the carriage window and looked up. On a clear day you could see to the top of the tower, kilometres above. Today, the tower vanished into the base of dark grey clouds.

Nobody could work above a certain height. Not even the hardy t'kelikt. The air was too thin to be breathed. Nobody had been that high for millennia. Except maybe for one of the Emperor's own avatars.

The whole citadel was surrounded by a ring made from the same material, suspended on massive pillars a couple of hundred metres above the surrounding city. Its upper surface was covered with stone buildings, much later additions. About a third of the ring had collapsed, long in the past. The resulting blocks of elderstone were too massive to clear away. They had become part of the city, absorbed into its flesh.

Except for the citadel itself, the rest of the city was made from conventional materials. Stone, brick, tile and wood.

It was raining again. The city was used to it. The warm rain of the equator. Culverts, and well maintained drains carried the surface water away, towards the great Everwill river.

The rain ceased as Trelt's carriage passed into the interior of the White Citadel through one of the vast half kilometre high archways. They travelled through shaded parklands, headed for the Imperial Palace at the centre.

The archways let in enough light to support the gardens. Occasionally, rain-bearing clouds would be low enough to enter the actual structure and bring water to the gardens. The rest of the water was provided by complex artificial irrigation.

The carriage arrived outside the Palace. A massive stone structure several stories high. The Palace would have been impressive in any other setting. Under the Citadel, it looked modest.

He left the carriage and walked towards the great hall. Inside were hundreds of elite Imperial Guard, all standing to attention. They bowed in unison as he entered.

Seated at the centre of the hall, on four identical stone thrones, sat the Holy Four. Avatars, and physical manifestations, of the immortal Emperor. Human sized, thin, and almost featureless. Faces reduced to almost sketch-like simplicity. Indentations where eyes should be. Small nose. Their skin was an almost translucent white, like porcelain. They sat motionless. Each dressed in robes, identical apart from their colour. Green, black, blue and grey.

Trelt ignored them and headed for the back of the hall. All four avatars turned their heads slightly as he passed. The Emperor watching him pass with eight eyes.

At the far end of the hall, Trelt passed through an archway guarded by eight impressive knights. Each stood over two and a half metres tall. Their sentinel armour hummed with hidden power. One spoke, her voice projected through the smooth, eyeless helm.

"Welcome Lord Vellorson."

Few were allowed this far into the Palace. Fewer still were allowed into the Oracle. A small octagonal room, clad in varnished oak panelling. A black and white marbled tiled floor. It smelled of polish. In the centre, steps led up to a platform with a marble pedestal. On this sat a golden sphere about the size of a human head. Two hand shaped indentations adorned its upper surface.

Where would the Emperor be today, he wondered?

He placed his hands on the indentations.

Rolling green countryside. It stretched off towards an horizon that seemed impossibly distant. Four suns of various colours gave each tree multi-hued shadows.

Birdsong. Blackbirds! The distant call of an eagle. He tried to spot it, but couldn't. Lost somewhere in the endless sky.

He smiled. He knew this scene well. A pastiche of many places.

Trelt walked along a weaving gravel path towards a small stone cottage. The front of the cottage was partly obscured in honeysuckle as if trying to consume the dwelling one frond at a time. It crowded around the windows and door. A balance between chaos and control.

An old man knelt near the rough wooden front door, dressed in the simple clothes of a peasant. He tended to some roses with a pair of rusty secateurs. The old man hummed tunelessly.

The old man rose and waved as Trelt approached.

"Ah, Trelt. What pleasure!" the man said. "Care for some tea?"

Trelt smiled back at the Emperor.

"I'd love some Alexi," Trelt replied. The man hated being called the Emperor.

Trelt sat at the kitchen table drinking his tea. On the other side sat Alexi. The Immortal Emperor.

The most powerful entity in the world was currently brushing biscuit crumbs from his thick, white beard. They scattered on a floor already covered with dust and other detritus. Several chickens pecked amongst the grime, seeking discarded morsels.

Trelt knew this cottage wasn't really there. Neither were the chickens. He knew they were all inside a place of Alexi's own creation. That, in some way, they were actually within the mind of Alexi himself.

There were many places that Trelt had been to in this strange realm. Endless deserts, dark forests, windswept tundra... Mostly, the places he had visited were relatively ordinary, but others were extraordinary.

Once, he had visited a place that consisted solely of floating islands in an infinite void. Like fragments of a shattered world. The ruins of some long-lost civilisation scattered about. Dry, dead vegetation. Skeletons underfoot. A single huge red sun shone from an utterly black sky. No stars had been visible.

Alexi favoured some realms more than others. This cottage was one of the more popular ones. He changed his appearance as much as the scenery. Sometimes appearing as a peasant, as he did now. Sometimes a rich merchant, or many other professions.

Trelt often wondered where these realms ended, and Alexi began. Maybe they were the same thing. He wasn't an expert on such things. He had learned not to think about it too much.

Trelt had spent the last half an hour recounting recent events. Alexi listened without interruption. Alexi picked up another biscuit and crunched into it, adding more crumbs to his beard and floor. He finished that one and reached for another.

"And you are sure that the seer web belonged to Simona?" Alexi said at last.

"Yes, the signature was the same. I checked it myself."

"And the memory-well. Do you think it is hers?"

"It is impossible to say for certain, but if it is, it may contain very useful information."

"Hmm. This complicates things. If we are to assume that this Rustari Parra is blood related to Simona, then it most logically means that she is Simona's daughter. No other explanation would make sense. We always suspected she had become intimate with someone within the Hegemon. What are you planning to do?"

"I am going to visit the place myself."

"You must act quickly, Trelt. Whilst I do not doubt you have everything under control, word will surely get out eventually. We cannot allow the heretics to gain access to this young woman before we do. If she has access to Simona's seer web, then this watch might be Simona's personal memory-well."

"I've contacted the West Wind. They will collect Vidyana from Requiem and we will proceed to Peldaran. I have already sent word."

"You realise this will cause us significant political problems?"

"I do," Trelt said, "but I can see no other way. We will travel via Bennel. I want to be swift, but not so swift as to have every head turning. We should be there in about eight days."

The Hegemony was currently engaged in a proxy war between Bennel, that they controlled, and the neighbouring kingdom of Jorn. Alexi required access to an important Elderuin site within Jorn called Taldor-Ire, one that Jorn had not been prepared to give up. Despite several very lucrative trade deals.

Peldaran was an ally of Jorn, but had as-yet not committed forces to support its neighbour. War with the Hegemony would not be wise, proxy or not. Trelt knew that Peldaran wasn't stupid, but sending Hegemon forces to Hammington's Rest would almost certainly tip balance in favour of Peldaran joining the war. Some lines just couldn't be crossed. It wouldn't affect the ultimate outcome, but it would add to the death toll, something both he and Alexi were keen to avoid.

Alexi munched on another biscuit.

"So be it," Alexi said. "Your appraisal is accurate. We need to act. There is no other choice."

"Yes, Alexi. I will see that it is done."

They both stood.

"Be careful, my friend," Alexi said. "I feel we are entering a new phase. Things dormant for over fifteen years are on the move once again."

Vidyana

Vidyana awoke to the sound of someone knocking at the door.

She'd spend the last week recovering from her injuries and the comedown from using her gifts. Violent shivering. Sweating. Insomnia. Cramps. It had been an unpleasant experience. It always was.

Layered on top was the incessant itch of her facial features returning to normal. She hated that more than the pain. Like something crawling under her skin. She was halfway back to normal, neither herself nor the stranger she had been.

Her shade had been her constant companion throughout the ordeal, keeping her informed of progress, coaxing her back to health. Yesterday, she had felt well enough to go back to her rented apartment. She wanted to be alone with her penance.

The knock at the door came again.

She summoned the dragon blood. Time shifted. She focused. The minute details. A shadow underneath the door. One person. Others could be hiding, out of sight. No obvious sounds of anyone else. Background noises normal. She cast her senses wider. The normal sounds of the street outside. Conversations. Traffic. Nothing out of order. She shifted back to normal speed.

"Who is it?"

"It's Kaylaris," came the reply. "Let me in."

A brief pause, and then, "It's important."

Kaylaris? Aurumill agents wouldn't normally visit each other. Sure, she'd rolled around with him a few times, but it had always been somewhere neutral. An inn or hotel.

Normal contact would be via the facility, a seer, or courier. It must be important.

"I was having a bloody kip," she said, opening the door. "Couldn't this have waited till I got back to the office?"

She was naked, but didn't care. Kaylaris moved past her, not waiting to be invited in. He ignored her nudity.

"We just received a message from Ascension City. From Lord Vellorson."

"So?"

"The instructions were brief. You are to leave immediately and travel alone by fast coach to Solace, where you are to board the West Wind and await further instructions. Couldn't wait for you to come back to the 'office'. Hence this early morning wake up call."

The West Wind was one of the primary airships of the central Imperial Airforce. An impressive craft, crewed by equally impressive special forces. Three hundred metres from tip to tail. The embodiment of Hegemony superiority and might. Sleek, fast, powerful. The unofficial flagship of the Aurumill. It was currently engaged in anti-rebellion operations a few thousand miles to the east of Lunarith.

"The West Wind is travelling to Solace?" she asked.

"Yes. It's already en-route."

That the West Wind had been ordered away from its assignment, and that she had been summoned to meet it, could only mean one thing. Trouble.

"Fuck," she said.

Chapter 5

Look now at your hubris.
   Your devices cast into ruin.
   Peoples scattered. Histories lost.
   Reaped by Nemesis. Judgement cast.
   Look, and lament.

Books of Maleth - Lamentations - Twenty one

Welyne

The reading room clock chimed. Welyne Drellmore glanced up from her book. Ten o'clock; midday.

Sybelle sat quietly at the desk by the window, catching up on the homework that she had been set. The oak desk was old, two hundred years at least. A rare heirloom from the richer part of the Drellmore family. Probably their only possession that had ever gone remotely near the central family. The wealth of the great Drellmore family tree diluted to a single table by the time it got to their little twig.

It had been over a week since the trial at the College of Thaumaturgy. A week of worry. Welyne knew what the outcome would be. Sybelle would be summoned and invited to join the College. Just a matter of time before the letter arrived. Any day now.

It had been the same with Belar. He had proven to be exceptional. He had joined the Jurament, an elite wing of the military.

Just as they had planned! They finally had someone in the Jurament. With a possible future promotion to the Aurumill itself.

But plans go wrong. He'd joined, never to return. A part of Welyne, the motherly part, now feared the same for Sybelle. However, they still needed someone like her. For the cause.

A wave of guilt washed over her. She pushed it away. Always, that twin emotion of personal needs versus the greater good. It made her feel guilty every time. This was her daughter, not some faceless pawn!

Welyne sighed. Sybelle looked up for a moment, but quickly went back to writing.

No, this WAS a great opportunity. Sybelle would be told the truth and would join the cause. She'd be hard to convince. She was stubborn. Just, Welyne realised, like her.

Amid this, her husband Bartain had been summoned to the kingdom of Bennel. Bartain had asked them to go too, but for the time being, they remained in Drellgarh. She would have to face the coming days alone. Still, she had faced worse in the past.

Her marriage to Bartain had been planned for the greater good. He had been selected before they'd even met. Secret tests had projected their children would be strong summoners. A plan she had been fully complicit in. It was merely fortunate that in time she'd grown to actually love him. He was a good man. The perfect father for both their children. He, of course, knew nothing.

There was a tap at the door. Gellid entered, carrying an envelope.

"Excuse me, Lady Drellmore, but we have received a letter addressed to you."

"Thank you, Gellid."

She recognised the writing immediately. Zarl. Her cousin. A Sleeper. Like her.

"Hello Wel. Just thought I'd let you know I'm in town. Wondered if you were interested in catching up on old times. I'm staying at the Fell Cow for the next few days. Drop by. Z."

Cryptic, but she understood the hidden meaning. A chill ran up her spine. Things, long dormant, were awakening. *Catching up on old times.*

She placed her book carefully back on the bookshelf, controlling the trembling in her hands.

"Syb, I've just got to pop out for a while."

"Yes, Mother."

Welyne picked up her aspect and fixed it in place, adjusting it in the mirror over the fireplace.

"If you get stuck, ask Gellid for help. He's good with mathematics."

Welyne arrived outside the Fell Cow. The building stood on the border between the immaculate and human business quarters. Straddling both worlds. You couldn't really call it a public house. Or rather, people did, but the immaculate patrons would turn their nose up at the term. They called it a social parlour. It was a pub. A place where immaculate and human mixed without drawing much attention. Countless contracts, deals, proposals and offers were arranged within. Almost all of them, legal.

She hadn't been to the place for… By the saints, nearly seventeen years! Not long after, Syb had been born.

Welyne paused, momentarily frozen in the street. It wasn't the place she feared, but a time. Memories of a different life. Of secrets buried in the past. She walked in with a confidence she didn't feel. The place was filled with people, immaculate and human alike. Divided by culture, united by wealth and power.

Zarl was sitting in a cubicle towards the back. Welyne recognised him immediately from his white beard. It almost seemed to be an extension of his aspect. Zarl stood and smiled. Just two good friends, seeing each other. Nothing out of the ordinary at all. She smiled and waved back.

Welyne put down her tea. They'd retired to a rented side room for more privacy.

"So, what's this all about Zarl?" Welyne prompted.

"I got word that something was happening within the seers. Of course I couldn't get close, but I have a Sleeper working in the seers office. Been there for years. Good ears to have. Don't ask me any more. You know how it is…"

"Go on," she prompted.

"The contact says there was quite a stir a few days ago. Someone from Seendar had made contact. Girl, by the sounds of it. Untrained. Not just amateur, but COMPLETELY untrained. No warding. No mental discipline techniques. Entered the Whispering twice.

Rumour in the office was that the seer web wasn't one they recognised. Put their best seer on it too, right powerful one. She didn't recognise it either. Had to consult the High Thaumaturge himself."

"So? It could have been anybody's. There are still many missing webs. Could be just someone who'd found a new one."

"Ah well, here's the thing. My contact called in a few favours and got this. Projected it to my seer here in Drellgarh."

Zarl produced a piece of paper with a crude sketch. Some wavy lines, like a double spiral. Welyne recognised it immediately. The sketch hit her like a hammer blow. No mistaking the outline.

"Look familiar?"

"Yes, it's Simona's signature. How is this even possible, Zarl?"

"Now that's where it gets less believable. I thought it was destroyed. Never found out what happened to Harrod. Maybe he's had it this whole time. He wouldn't be able to use it, though. But that's not the end."

"Oh?"

"Apparently Ascension City went kind of crazy after that. Seers' office went into lockdown. That's what alerted me. My Sleeper contact knew something was up. Also, got word that one of their airships has been called back to Ascension City. Rumour is they will be headed for Lerins in Bennel. They've got the seers' office locked down pretty tight, but I'm pretty certain that this girl has gone quiet again. Just two broadcasts and then silence."

"And you think they are going after her?"

"It would make sense. A seer web belonging to Simona appears on the scene after sixteen years? Also, one that could only be used by her immediate family? They were probably thinking what you are thinking."

Simona didn't have any living relatives they knew of. However, she had been a recluse in her last couple of years.

Unless...

"Oh shit," Welyne said. "You think this girl is her daughter?"

"That would be about it, I'd reckon."

"The father?"

"I think you have your own suspicions about that, Wel. Probably the same as mine."

"Yeah. Shit. What do you think they'll do?"

"Capture her. Take her back to Lerins. She must be on Seendar somewhere. It's what I'd do."

"Why Lerins? Why not take her back to Ascension City?"

"I think they'll try to keep this one under wraps. Would arouse too much suspicion in Ascension City. Too many eyes for even Vellorson to keep in check."

"And what has this to do with me, Zarl?" she asked, already half sure of the answer.

"Some of it, I think you've already guessed. Oh, and your husband, Bartain, of course. I hear he has just gone to Lerins and you've been invited to go?"

"I'm waiting for a few weeks until they get the new house sorted out. Also, Sybelle is waiting to hear from the College. Had her test last week. Looks like she's a summoner."

"She is? That's fantastic news! We could do with another summoner after what happened to... Oh shit, sorry, Wel. I forget sometimes."

"It's alright, Zarl. Belar knew the risks when he signed up. Anyway, I think you were about to ask me to travel to Lerins?"

"Yeah... That's pretty much it. It's a great opportunity. Your husband's summons is the perfect cover. Couldn't have hoped for better timing! Would be good if you could get there as soon as possible. Tell your husband you miss him terribly, blah, blah, blah. Get established. You might even get there before the airship if you take a clipper. I'm not expecting miracles, Wel, but would be good to find out whatever we can. I will join you in a week or so. Couple of things I need to sort out this end first."

"Do I have any say in this?"
"Of course! You always have a say, Wel."
"Felder dung."
"Your words, not mine."

She sighed. The past was never as far away as you thought.

What would happen if the girl was Simona's daughter? What would happen if she fell into the hands of Alexi and his puppets? What had happened to Valtha? To Harrod?

Of course, this could all be a waste of time. Or a trap. Something to draw them out. However, there was the possibility that it was true. Wasn't that what they'd been waiting for all this time?

"Alright. I'll get my affairs sorted. We'll leave by fast clipper as soon as possible. It would do Syb good to get away from Drellgarh for a while. The bloody College will have to wait."

"Be careful, Wel. Tensions are high in the area. I'm not sure exactly where the girl is, but Bennel is engaged in a war with its neighbours. Of course, House Drellmore is behind the war, but haven't taken an active role. Yet. The bloody rebels have been causing trouble in Lerins too."

"Yeah, Bartain said as much. They take advantage of trouble. Like belderflies to a corpse."

"I doubt they will have got wind of anything, and I hope it stays that way. Them getting hold of the girl may not be much better than if Alexi does. Two faces of the same bloody coin if you ask me."

Kathnell

Kathnell tugged on the pipe. She tried pushing.

"Shitting-bloody-saints!"

The Nemesis damned thing was stuck. She wiped stinging sweat from her eyes using the back of her sleeve. A sleeve covered in grit. It scratched her as she drew it across her face. She threw her wrench down. It splashed in the water around her feet, sending rank warm water up into her face.

"Shit! Shit! Shit!"

The humidity was almost unbearable. Summer heat combined with hot-water pipes and fetid water. Working in enclosed spaces with sweat dripping down her face always made her irritable. She found the feeling uniquely unpleasant. The only illumination came from a single oil lamp. Her eyes hurt.

She was working beneath the main house, beneath the service rooms, in a brick corridor under the main kitchens. The servants' service rooms formed a hidden core to the building. If those were the heart of the building, then Kathnell must be in the bowels. Certainly smelled like it.

There was just one immaculate in residence. Some stuck up fellow from Drellgarh. She hadn't seen him, but Corric said he wasn't a bad one; for a stonie. Apparently, he was married to an actual Drellmore. Kathnell bet she was a right asshole. Had to be, given the name.

The job had been going well, until they'd received word that the owner's family, the Drellmore woman, and her daughter, had decided to visit earlier than expected. Bloody typical. Deadlines of weeks had transformed into days. Priorities re-written. Forget about the heating; it was summer. Concentrate on the hot water and kitchens. The decorators were in an equal amount of panic.

Nemesis knew what time it was. No clock down here, and definitely no windows.

Kathnell had been routing new copper piping through the wall. She was tired, hot, and irritable. In an attempt to rush, she had put too much pressure on the pipe and it was now stuck. The last hour, a total waste of time.

"You okay? Heard splashing and swearing." Corric's voice came from above.

"Yeah, got a pipe stuck. Kinked, it I think."

"I'll come down."

"Yep, stuck as tight as a tarn-beetle's arse. Not going any further. Have to pull it back through, straighten it up. Might even have to get another piece if it's creased. That's gonna cost."

"Sorry, Corric."

"Don't you worry about that now. The hours we are working, the pressure we are under, mistakes are bound to happen. If it makes you feel any better, I dropped my tool belt into the old ceph water tank this morning. Got to get a new one. I'll pick the old one up when we drain it. Don't know about you, but I'm knackered."

He sat on the wooden bench they'd both been standing on.

"Yeah," she said. "Doesn't help that we can't get access to the main house during the daytime."

"I know it's a pain, but that's just the way it is. It's not permitted for engineering work to be carried out within the outer house whilst the immaculate fellow is in residence. We need the correct authorisation. I've asked for it, but it hasn't come through. Until then, we have a set time when we can work in the immaculate areas of the house."

"It's just one guy, and you said he was alright."

"He's not bad." Corric said, "Spoken to him a couple of times, and I suspect he would let us work in the house whilst he was about. Unfortunately, that decision is not up to him either. We are bound by the rules of the guild. Which is why we are working these bloody awful shifts."

"The master is away tomorrow," Corric continued. "So, we'll have access to the bathroom. Should save us time and you'll get a look at how the other half live. You'll also have time to see the pile of paperwork on his desk. Might give you some sympathy for the poor bastard."

"Not likely."

Corric stood and slapped her on the back.

"Right-o, let's get back to work. If we get this sorted, there's a chance we can get to the pub before it closes. Last ferry doesn't leave for another couple of hours."

"Yeah, don't fancy kipping down here again."

Sybelle

The place was a hell-stinking mess. Half emptied boxes and random detritus lay in the hallways. From somewhere down below came banging and muffled sounds of workers.

A few days ago, she'd been mentally preparing for being whisked away by the College. Then, Mother had received the strange note, and the day after they were packing to leave. Mother had made vague comments about sorting the College out later. Another decision thrust onto her with no say so. Mother had insisted that the trip would be good for her.

Off to this saints forsaken wormery.

Sybelle lay on her bed and listened to the sounds of construction below her. How was she supposed to get any rest with that racket?

Her sickness from the journey was subsiding, but the smell of river mud clung to the inside of her nostrils.

The clipper they had crossed the ocean in had been small. Tossed around like a toy boat in a bath. Sybelle got little chance to sample the apparently excellent food. Instead, she'd spent most of the voyage staring at a spot on the cabin ceiling, swallowing sips of water, and trying not to be ill.

It had been raining when they had arrived at the port. A thunderstorm that had rolled in from the ocean. The summer heat causing tendrils of vapour to rise from hot cobblestones. The dockside they arrived at was reserved for immaculate vessels. It hadn't stopped the smell.

The ferry journey over to the immaculate quarter on the other side of the bay had been marginally better. Once clear of the docks, she got her first good look at their destination.

An area located halfway along a peninsula jutting out into the bay. White villas and buildings, unmistakably immaculate in style. They clustered around the waterfront, where several private yachts were moored. Beyond, the ground rose steeply, packed with more immaculate residences. In the distance, sitting on top of a rocky outcrop, sat Bennel palace.

She had pointed it all out to Mother, but Mother had been more interested in a dark smudge in the sky out to sea. Sybelle recognised it as an Hegemony airship. A big one. Sybelle had seen them before, but Mother had gawped at it like a child.

Father met them at a private jetty close to the new house. All smiles and hugs. Surprised and delighted to see them in equal measure. He'd only received word they were on the way over a couple of days ago. He apologised that the place was still undergoing building work. The hammer blow had fallen when he casually announced that hot water wouldn't be connected for a couple more days. Just great! Father had quickly changed the subject.

He'd pointed with enthusiasm to the house, explaining that it was once part of a ceph ambassador's residence. The house was big, maybe bigger than their home back in Drellgarh. Apart from the noises from beneath, and the clutter of half empty boxes, the place didn't look too bad.

The only places off limits were the balcony overlooking the waterfront and the inner service areas. Apparently, the balcony was dangerous. Looked fine to her.

The servants' areas were far larger than would be needed by their family. The house staff her father had introduced to them had looked lost in the space. The new kitchen was still being prepared, so the staff were using a temporary kitchen across the corridor. She hoped there weren't any rats.

Sybelle sighed and rose from the bed. It was about time she got ready for the evening.

Tomorrow, her parents would host a small party for some

of the new neighbours and her father's colleagues. Father said it would be a great opportunity to meet new people. It sounded more like an opportunity to be bored rigid.

Father had even half joked that there would be some eligible young men there. Well, if the College failed, at least she could be married off to some wealthy idiot so she could pump out babies like a good little Drellmore. It was nightmare inducing.

She sighed again and fell back onto the bed.

Chapter 6

The Emperor was just one amongst them.

He listened to the sound too, heard it's music.

In it he heard whispers. And in the whispers, he heard doom.

Books of Maleth - Origins - Three

Rust

Rust struck the finger sized metal pipe with a wooden hammer, forcing it a little further into the Taptree's trunk.

Getting close to wild taptrees was dangerous. Their trunks covered in thousands of long and exceptionally sharp spines. Each translucent tip was filled with toxic resin. A common defence mechanism for feral flora.

She'd once been stabbed in the shoulder during a careless moment pruning a tree. The pain was both sudden and intense. Her shoulder had been swollen for days afterwards. Typically, Uncle had laughed. Said it would teach her to be more careful. She hadn't made the mistake since.

There were tales of people running at full speed into a wild taptree and dying, the toxin too much for their body to handle. These trees were safe, though. The trunk of each one was pruned clear to three metres high. Above that was the usual spiny nightmare.

A droplet of sap formed on the end of the pipe. Rust connected a thin cane tube to the metal pipe and attached the other end to a larger cane tube that passed nearby. That was, in turn, connected to a web of pipes that snaked through the plantation, funnelling taptree sap downslope to waiting barrels.

She stepped back, satisfied.

The sun would set soon. The sky was already turning pink. Uncle had gone into the village but would be back by early evening. He'd left a list of things to do. Just sweeping the house left and she could rest.

Rust gathered her tools. She stopped, aware of a low droning, just at the edge of her hearing. Then it was gone, replaced by normal evening sounds. Cinder crows screeching. Village dogs barking. The distant lowing of bapnax. Probably just a swarm of sicklids, she thought. She hoped they stayed away from the village. Hated the bloody things. A bit early in the season, though.

Rust had almost finished sweeping when she heard the noise again. Louder this time. It came and went in waves. There was a pulsing quality to it. What in Sindar was it? Definitely not sicklids.

She looked out of the window, but couldn't see anything. There were raised voices coming from outside. The door burst open and Uncle rushed it. His face, pale.

"What's that noise?" Rust asked.

He ignored her and ran in to his bedroom. He returned and stuffed something into a small cloth bag. He pushed past her as if she wasn't there. He headed back towards the door, then stopped.

"Stay indoors! Do not go outside!" he said.

The first beginnings of fear went through her.

"What's going on?" Rust asked.

"I said, stay indoors and do not go outside. Pack your bags as if we are going on a hunting trip. DO NOT go outside. If I am not back in half an hour, open this. Don't open it until then."

He handed Rust a sealed envelope.

"What's going on?" Rust repeated, voice higher in pitch.

"Stay here. I mean it."

With that, he was gone, leaving her alone in the house.

She stood, broom in hand, staring at the door. Rust approached the front door and looked out, but Uncle was already out of sight. She pushed the letter into her pocket.

The droning noise grew louder; felt as well as heard. Dust fell from the rafters above. Down the street, towards the village centre, a group of people were staring towards the East. Towards something behind Rust's house. Rust rushed towards the back of the house and looked out.

Something impossible hung low in the sky. A dark

shadow. A long sleek cylinder, hundreds of metres long. Mostly black, with golden coloured designs painted onto the sides. An golden emblem, like a huge flaming bird, covered it's front. Underneath, a long bulge went from fore to aft, covered in windows and hatches. Large pods with propellers clustered around the exterior. Most pods had a single propeller, but others had more. Each hummed its own note. Wisps of vapour escaped from vents along the thing's side, trailing behind it.

It was approaching the village rapidly.

Sindar's Teeth! A Hegemony airship! She was sure of it. She'd never seen one before, but had heard of them. What she'd imagined fell well short of this monstrosity.

Several large, red, four-winged beasts circled underneath it. Wyverns! Each one had a single t'kelikt rider.

Some pods on one side of the airship flipped over to face forward. The pitch of the noise changed. The airship turned, slowing as it passed overhead and out of sight.

Rust ran to the front of the house and opened the front door once again. The thing continued to slow as it approached the village centre. As she watched, long threads descended from its underbelly. Tiny little black motes began descending the threads. With horror, Rust realised they were soldiers.

Then something much larger fell from it. Shaped like a human, but many tens of hands high. It landed out of sight over the rooftops with a crunch. A tremor passed through her feet.

People were shouting now. Some screams. A plume of dust rose where the thing had landed.

Rust just stood, mouth open, feet rooted to the spot.

There was an new noise. A wailing. Odd. Artificial. A voice boomed across the village.

"BY ORDER OF THE HEGEMONY. EVERYONE IN HAMMINGTON'S REST IS TO CONGREGATE IN THE VILLAGE MARKETPLACE. FAILURE TO COMPLY WILL BE DEALT WITH HARSHLY. DO NOT

ATTEMPT TO FLEE. DO NOT STAY IN YOUR HOME…"

Hammington's Rest was being invaded! By the Hegemony!

The list of demands continued. She shut the door and lent against it, panting. What were they here for? What did they want? Why Hammington's Rest?

Was this connected to her? To the things she'd found? She'd put the whole thing out of her mind since they'd returned the objects last week. Didn't want to think about that strange conversation she'd had with someone, or something. But now, less than two weeks later, Hammington's Rest was under attack by the Hegemony.

Nonsense! There had to be some rational explanation that didn't involve her. As Uncle was fond of pointing out, not everything in this universe revolved around Rustari Parra. No, it had to be coincidence.

Uncle would know what to do. His instructions had been clear. She went to her room and started packing, stuffing items into her backpack. After she finished, she went to the pantry and hid.

And waited.

Sybelle

The party was worse than she had feared. They'd been introduced to the new neighbours. The usual inane mix of pointless small talk. It was like a play. Try to show an interest in what they did, where they came from, the names of their children. That's wonderful! How interesting! Amazing! Really? Tell me more.

Most of the other immaculate were strutting around in their best clothing. All of them wearing aspects. Long gowns and multi-layered suits made from the finest materials. Trying to outdo each other with bright colours and intricate embroidered patterns. She overheard one woman bragging that her cape was Algardran Silk. How it was spun from a symbiotic moth larvae that only inhabited a particular feral tree on Ventarso. Apparently, very expensive.

There were a few mundanes too; representatives of Bennel Palace. Rich by mundane standards, yes, but with no actual power. They didn't seem to mind. Rich humans always seemed to get fat, more so than the immaculate ever did. She'd always wondered why.

Sybelle had spent the last hour smiling as she was introduced to everyone. Smile. Yes, pleased to meet you. Smile. Yes, I'm very excited to be here. Smile. No, I haven't been to the palace yet. Smile. Yes, we've settled in fine, thank you. Smile. Her face ached from all the forced smiling. Her cheeks itched where her aspect touched her skin. She desperately wanted to take it off.

Still, it wasn't all terrible. The wine that had been selected was great. Mother had some skills, at least. Sybelle grabbed another glass from the table where they were all arranged in neat rows.

Mother had told her to go easy on the wine. What did she care? She'd been odd these last few days. Distracted. Even this afternoon, Mother had sent a handwritten letter by courier. She'd waited until Father wasn't around. What was that about? More secrets.

Mother looked out of the window towards Bennel palace where, until earlier yesterday, the airship had been moored. It had approached the city the same afternoon they had arrived. An impressive sight, yes. But Mother had regarded it with a scrutiny it didn't deserve. It was gone now, but Mother kept glancing to where it had been.

Sybelle put the empty glass down and grabbed another one. She headed over to where Father was talking to a group of people. She vaguely remembered being introduced to them earlier. People that Father worked with. More than likely they had turned up simply because he was married to an actual Drellmore.

Sybelle's parents had married young, Mother's Drellmore name spliced with a rich business family. Of course, it was partly arranged. It happened if you were part of the ruling families, or part of an important business family. Sybelle didn't doubt that they loved each other. It was obvious whenever they were together.

Marriages like that didn't always work out the same way. Sybelle's cousin was married to an idiot. She had little choice in the matter, either. They'd moved to another city in House Drellmore. Sybelle hardly ever saw her any more. She didn't think they were happy together from the snippets she'd overheard from Mother. She dreaded the same thing one day.

She loitered in the background for a few minutes, but the conversation was intolerably boring. Shipments, transit times, complications with inland travel, mud, trains, overheads. The sun was just setting. The sky cast into red hues. You couldn't see much from the window as it was facing the wrong way.

Maybe the balcony afforded a better view. It was off limits, but surely a quick look wouldn't be dangerous. She needed some fresh air, anyway. Get away from this nonsense for a few minutes.

A loop of wire had been tied to the door handles. A sign fixed loosely in place. *Danger. Do not open. No access.* She easily untied it with one hand and stepped out into the evening air.

It was still warm, but a breeze travelled in from the bay and ocean beyond. What a fantastic view, she thought. She took off her aspect, letting the air touch her skin.

The sun was setting behind her, over the rooftops of the immaculate district and the more affluent human areas beyond. The bay glowed red in the evening sunset. In many ways, it was like Drellgarh, a city built around a large bay.

I wonder if you can see the palace from here, she thought. It took her a few seconds to get her bearings. The palace would be on the other side of the house from the balcony. Opposite the bay, up the hill.

If she got closer to the edge of the balcony she might be able to get a better look. She walked towards the edge.

Rust

Rust sat at the back of the pantry, staring at the door. This was stupid, she thought. I can't just sit here whilst divine-knows-what is going on outside.

But, Uncle had asked her to stay put. To stay hidden. He didn't know what she'd done! Finding the objects. The strange conversation she'd had when she'd put on the circlet. The visions of someone else's memories. The person, or thing, that Rust had communicated with had asked her specific questions. Who she was? Where was she? She'd felt compelled to answer. The words just poured from her. And now, the Hegemony was here in Hammington's Rest! Surely, none of this was a coincidence.

If they were here for her, it wouldn't take them long to find her cowering at the back of the pantry.

She should have told Uncle straight away. But fear and pride had kept her quiet. Instead, she'd pretended the whole thing hadn't happened. She'd promised Indiril never to mention them again. Indiril didn't even know she'd used them again. No, don't blame Indiril for your silence, she thought. The objects had terrified her more than she liked to admit.

And now this. Sindar!

Rust stood, grabbed her backpack, and headed for the door. Maybe she could undo this mess. At least find out what was going on. Anything was better than cowering like a terrified shrew. She opened the front door a fraction and peered out.

There were three Hegemony soldiers in the street. Two of them were like the ones she had seen in Balincross. Armed with swords and shields. Crossbows slung across their backs.

The third figure was enormous, completely covered from head to toe in blue armour. Not a single bit of skin was visible. It stood at least twenty-five hands high. When it moved, there was a whirring noise. Each footfall thudded with an impressive heaviness. It was armed with a metal staff in one hand and a metal shield in the other. A bloody Hegemon knight.

The staff was ornate, covered in gold and silver snakes. It flared out at one end like a torch. Rust had seen something like it before in the vision she'd had of the tower. Figures pursuing them through the streets. Heavy rain. Red flashes. White fire lancing through the darkness. Loud booming like nearby thunder. The fire tracing back to strange staves, just like this one.

Her heart thumped in her chest.

A few seconds later, the group passed out of sight round the corner. She checked the other direction. It looked clear. She stepped out into the street. Keeping low, she sprinted across the street and into the bushes on the other side. In her mind, she traced out a route that would take her near to the village marketplace without being spotted.

The few people she saw were being escorted at sword point towards the village centre. Wyverns circled overhead. As she was halfway down one street, she glimpsed movement on the roofline. She glanced up to see several t'kelikt, armour plating covering their spider-like limbs and central abdomen, forelimbs ending in blades. T'kelikt were strong normally, but these looked like they could tear you apart if they wanted. She edged closer to the wall. They moved quickly from rooftop to rooftop, leaping the distance between houses with ease. Where the gap was too great, they jumped down, then clambered back up onto the next house. Two of them were heading in her direction.

She rolled under a nearby shrub. Their armoured limbs clattered against the roof tiles. They stopped just above her, clicking and whistling to each other. Then, they vaulted the gap and onto the next house. Only once she was sure they were gone did she dare continue.

Further towards the village, she saw the butcher swearing at a couple of Hegemony soldiers. Finally, the man had a proper target for his anger. The soldiers stood impassively for a few seconds before one knocked him to the ground with the butt of his crossbow. They roughly bound his hands and shoved him along the road toward the village centre, blood trickling from his nose.

Her training as Uncle's apprentice came to the fore. Line of sight. Stealth. Shadows and light. She was sure that without it, she would have already been captured. What worked for tracking feral game, worked for Hegemony soldiers as well, it seemed. Even the six-legged kind.

The airship hung motionless above the village centre. Every bone in her body wanted to flee in the other direction. To run away from this new, terrible reality. It was only thoughts of Uncle that kept her moving. With each step, the guilt of not telling him what she'd done grew more acute. It was still possible this had nothing to do with her.

Every few minutes, the airship emitted a loud wailing noise like some demented feral beast, followed by a voice that echoed around the valley.

"THIS VILLAGE IS NOW UNDER TEMPORARY HEGEMON CONTROL. ALL RESIDENTS ARE ORDERED TO REPORT TO THE VILLAGE CENTRE. PERSONS FAILING TO DO SO WILL BE DETAINED AND ARRESTED BY ORDER OF THE HOLY EMPEROR."

She continued to move stealthily through the village.

On a couple of occasions, she had to duck into side streets to avoid more soldiers. Human and t'kelikt alike. They had started kicking in doors. Forcibly removing anyone they found.

Rust found a riverbank spot thick with reeds and a view of

the village square on the other side. It had plenty of ground cover if she needed to retreat without being seen. She didn't want to get much closer for fear of being spotted by the airship or the wyverns. She parted the reeds and peered through.

Most of the villagers were present. Rounded up like feldercows. A mixture of worried, puzzled, and angry expressions. She saw Indiril and his family on the far side. As far as she could see, Uncle wasn't there.

There were at least thirty soldiers. Six of them were Knights, whirring and humming, hinting at the strange powers contained within.

Beyond them stood something out of a nightmare. A human shaped metal figure at six metres high. A giant suit of armour without occupant. There were gaps in its armour through which she could see daylight. It must be the thing that Rust had seen fall from the airship. It had the same flaming bird emblem painted on its chest. In one hand it held a bone white sword, itself at least two metres long. The other arm ended in a massive clawed fist. The figure turned at the waist, as if searching the crowd for trouble with its almost featureless face. As it twisted, giant pistons and rods moved within, like metallic guts. A bloody golem! Uncle had told her about them, but she'd always thought they were another of his tall tales.

The ruins of the tailor's shop lay crushed beneath it. Roof collapsed, walls fallen outward. Rust guessed it still stood where it had fallen. She hoped the tailor hadn't been inside.

At the centre of the village square, an older man dressed in black and gold was standing next to a petite younger woman. She studied the crowd with absolute concentration. She had dark skin and black hair. The older man, much paler with greying brown hair. Oddly, neither wore aspects. Rust guessed they were in charge.

The man spoke.

"Please cooperate fully and nobody needs to get hurt," the man said. "We are here for a young woman called

Rustari Parra. Anyone knowing the whereabouts of this individual must inform us immediately."

A murmur went up from the crowd. Rust sat heavily. Her head spun. She felt sick. The world receded. It felt like she was in a dream. Until that moment, she hadn't been sure of their intentions. There was always that chance that it had all been a coincidence. That they were here for some other unconnected reason. But no, there was no doubt, they were after her.

She must get away. Away from this place.

The murmuring from the crowd intensified, accompanied by a few shocked gasps. Rust peered through the vegetation again. The far side of the crowd parted and one of the Knights entered, pushing a man in front of it, hands bound. Uncle! He was pushed roughly towards the centre. Blood stained his face from a cut above his eye.

"Found this one creeping around the village's edge. Knocked out one soldier," the Knight said, forcing Uncle to his knees.

The older man approached Uncle.

"Harrod Dar'Ellis! It's been a while," the man said.

"Trelt. Thought you'd be dead by now. Alexi must treat his dogs well. Guess he's still handing out plenty of treats and titbits?"

"Still quick with the tongue, I see. Not that it matters. I am surprised to see you, Harrod. I was expecting to find many things, but I'll admit you weren't one of them... Oh, you thought I was here for you? So vain. No, I'm here for the young woman. Rustari."

"Fuck you, Vellorson!"

"We'll see about..."

The next few moments passed in an incomprehensible blur. Half way through Trelt's sentence, Uncle rose and shoved something into the guts of the knight. Blue sparks flashed from the impact with a cracking noise. The knight froze and started toppling backwards, blue sparks continuing to crackle around its torso. Uncle rushed forwards, towards the man he'd called Trelt. The woman next to Trelt became an impossible blur of motion, almost too quick to see. The man, Trelt, was airborne, pushed violently away from Uncle by the woman. She was already turning back to face Uncle.

There was a bright flash. Brighter than the sun.

For a moment, Rust was blinded. Green and blue afterimages. She fell backwards as a violent hot wind slammed into her, punching the air from her lungs. A deafening noise. Small bits of flying debris peppered her face. Shredded vegetation, grit, and muddy water from the river.

She lay stunned, ears ringing. Her face stung. She blinked away tears. Gradually, her hearing returned. Wailing, screaming and shouting. The vegetation that had been hiding her was flattened. She quickly rolled to one side.

The far riverbank was ablaze. Nearly everyone in the village centre had been knocked over. Soldiers and villages alike. Some villagers were screaming in fear, pain, or both. Some rose and fled back into the village. Indiril and his family among them.

Where Uncle had stood just moments before was now a blasted crater four metres across. Of Uncle, there was no sign. The man named Trelt lay sprawled on the ground, cape smouldering. Unconscious or dead. One of his arms lay a few metres away. Dark red fluid seeping into the ground.

A strange black figure lay close by, clothes on fire. Like a statue made from oil. It, too, was motionless.

The soldiers were regaining control, but people were already fleeing. Dispersing into the streets. Knights stomped off after them. The giant metal figure started walking after them as well. A man in long robes held a golden gloved hand out in front of him. White fire erupted from it, stabbing out over the heads of the fleeing populace, accompanied by a cracking noise.

The oily-black figure stirred.

Rust watched it all with a detached fascination. Uncle is

dead, she thought!

The black figure rose onto one arm.

Uncle is dead.

The black figure stood. Burning clothes falling away.

Move, Rust thought, for Sindar's sake, you must move! She pushed away from the riverbank and ran back up the hill, keeping low. Back towards her house. Towards home.

No, stupid. Not the house. That was an idiot-nester decision. It will not take them long to find out where you live. Where then? Think dammit.

Rust stopped. They are not after me, she thought. They are after the objects. Maybe she should give herself up. Tell them where they are. Then this whole thing might be over. Go back to how it was. Before...

Uncle is dead!

Whatever happened now, there could be no going back. The world had changed, never to go back to how it had been before. Whatever the Hegemony was here for, whatever the objects are, Uncle had died to protect them. To protect her. She would go back to the elderuin and retrieve them.

And what then?

That decision was for later. One thing at a time.

Rust reached the northern edge of the village, keeping low through Uncle's plantation. The sun was setting, and it was getting dark in the trees. She went to the back of the tool shed to get the little box with the iron key. Thank Sindar! The key, still safe inside. She allowed herself to exhale. She stuffed the key and a length of rope into her backpack.

It would be dangerous in the feral this time of night, but not as dangerous as staying in the village. Rust stood between two dangers. The wild untamed feral to the north, and the Hegemon to the south.

She glanced towards the village. Search lights had appeared on the giant airship and were sweeping the village. Lit torches could be seen throughout the village. From somewhere fairly close by, she was sure she could hear the scuttling sound of t'kelikt.

No turning back now, she thought.

After she reached the ruin, she could retrieve the objects and plan on what to do next. She headed off north along the brook that would take her into the feral.

Vidyana

[Emergency automated response. Pain relief and stimulants have been administered.]

Vidyana rose on one arm, blinking away bright after images. She pieced the last few seconds together. The gathering, the capture of Harrod, and the explosion.

Her clothes were on fire. She ignored them; her body covering kavach armour would protect her.

They had come for Rustari Parra, but had found the traitor Harrod Dar'Ellis instead. She knew him by reputation only. He had been one of The Heretic's closest advisers. He'd been there when her parents had been killed. Someone like Harrod Dar'Ellis wouldn't let himself be captured. He must have had something in his mouth. A hollow-shell, by the looks of the damage. The stupid knight should have searched the man. The knight had paid for her mistake. Her ancient sentinel armour ripped open, exposing what was left of the woman within.

The true loss was the armour itself. Another priceless artefact ruined. Lost, never to be replaced. Forged in the days of magic, before the Emperor returned from his long dream. The suit of armour had been handed down, from knight to knight, hundreds of times. Nothing like them could be constructed now. The places that forged them long dismantled and destroyed. That was the price of stopping the return of Nemesis.

Muffled shouts and screams.

[I have detected moderate ear damage and am boosting receptors.]

Sounds sharpened.

Trelt lay face down in the soil. His arm lay several feet

away. Blood soaked the ground around the tattered remnants of his shoulder. He stirred. She tried to get up, but her legs weren't responding. Her shade nagged about nerve shock. She crawled over to him. He rolled onto his back and blinked up at her.

"Don't worry about me," he said. "Find the girl!"

"You are my priority. By blood, by order, and by duty."

"Forget your oaths for the time being. My shade has regulated the blood loss. Others can attend to me. I will go back to the airship. They have a restoraleum on board. I'll be fine."

Blood still leaked from Trelt's tattered shoulder, but it had slowed. He was right, his shade would protect him for now. Vidyana scanned the surroundings. People were fleeing in all directions, but Hegemony soldiers were getting things back under control. She shrugged off the remnants of her clothing.

"I will await the clerics first," she said.

"No, your top priority now is to find this Rustari Parra. She must not be allowed to escape. Harrod being here only confirms my suspicions. Go!"

It hadn't taken long for Vidyana to find the girl's house. Several villagers had been more than willing to tell her. The houses were abysmal. Wooden. No glass windows, only shuttered holes. She hated villages like this. All dust, shit food, shit drink, and bugger all to do in the evenings.

The house was full of the trappings of a rural hunting business. Made sense, someone working with The Heretic would have the relevant skills. Two knights patrolled outside, just in case someone was there and fled. The girl was gone, of course. Things scattered about in her room and pantry. Signs of hasty packing.

It was doubtful Harrod and the girl had expected their arrival, otherwise they would have been long gone. The airship then was probably their first warning. She pieced it together.

The airship had appeared. Harrod had gone into town and had told the girl to pack. And go where? A nearby town? They would pick her up in the next few days. But Vidyana couldn't leave it to chance. She needed more intelligence. She should find people close to Harrod. Close to the girl. She needed to be quick; the evening was darkening by the minute.

"Will someone get me some new clothes!" she called to the knights.

More questioning led her to the home of a wealthy Silvar family. Rustari and the son were close. By most accounts, inseparable. The house was more luxurious than the girl's. Well, for this region at least. It was built in the middle of an orchard. A domed structure, two stories high. Wooden, but ornately carved and decorated in the way the tree people tended to. All curves, with hardly any straight lines.

It was surrounded by a lush garden. Well tended vines and fruit bushes climbed the outside, blurring the lines between house and garden. Vidyana's senses detected the scents from various flowers. Her shade identified them as roses and lilac. Thanks, she thought, very useful.

There were sounds of raised voices within. Vidyana motioned for the knights to stop and walked up to the front door alone. She listened.

"What else aren't you telling me, Indiril?" a woman said.

"Nothing, mother, I promise," someone sobbed.

"So you've kept all this secret. All this time. And now this! Sindar be blessed, Indiril, you should have told us."

"Sorry."

"Sorry! People are dead, Indiril, and you only think it's worth mentioning this trip and the stuff you found now?"

"Hey," said a man, "don't be so hard on him, Melwis. He didn't know this was going to happen. It's not his fault. It's that bloody Parra girl."

The woman sighed.

"I always knew there was something odd about that

Harrod," the woman said. "He always seemed—"

Vidyana opened the door. Everyone within froze. The three she had heard, plus a fourth man. An old silver man dressed in the green robes of a divinist priest. They were clustered round a table. Two adults, a teenage boy, and the old priest. The mother caught mid rant.

"This all sounds wonderfully fascinating," Vidyana said. "Tell me more about this little trip. And the stuff you found."

Chapter 7

Consider how much of the Earth is covered by feral, and how tiny the tame lands of our races really are.

Surrounded on all sides, forever under threat of being consumed by the great untameable feral. The "Great Hegemon" is in reality a pitiful patchwork of scraps scattered far and wide.

Then ask yourself; Who are the real masters of this Earth?

Part of a Liberation leaflet, circulated Ventarso, 671 SC

Rust

The throbbing in Rust's left leg intensified. The pain that began in her calf now pulsed into her thigh. She stopped again and rolled up her trouser leg. The puncture wound looked angry, red swelling radiating outwards for several finger widths. She removed some mashed-gillroot from her backpack and rubbed some more of the foul smelling paste into the wound.

After stumbling in the dark several times, her luck had finally run out about half an hour ago. Tripped by the tangle of dense feral undergrowth, she'd fallen and had been rewarded with a spine-sting from some nemesis-dammed-plant. In the dim light, she didn't know what plant it was.

Sindar! She should have been travelling slower, she thought. Rushing headlong in the dark was a sure way to wind up maimed. Or even dead. It was something that Uncle always lectured her about.

Uncle...

She still couldn't believe he was dead. She tried to put it out of her mind and concentrated on getting to the elderuin. Eventually, something would remind her and she was transported back to the explosion.

"Fuck!" she sobbed.

She breathed deeply and willed herself calm. It was all her fault. Uncle had always said she was impulsive. That it would get her killed. But it hadn't. He was the one that was dead. Because of her. Now she was on the run for reasons she still didn't fully understand. Another sob escaped her. I need to get myself back under control, she thought.

The gillroot started working. It didn't stop the throbbing, but at it lessened the pain enough to continue. Time to get moving again.

She reached the summit of a low hill. It was dark now, but the twin moons still gave a small amount of dim, colourless illumination. If she had calculated her distance correctly, it should be... There! The hill. The silhouette of a tall spindle oak. Black against the deep blue-black sky.

Sindar, thank you! She didn't believe in the Divinist way, or any of the crap from the Imperial church either. Uncle said they were clueless at best, liars at worst. Put a prayer now couldn't hurt, she thought.

The village was to the south, hidden now by kilometres of dense feral. She didn't expect to see anything, so was surprised to see a single beam of light shining through the thick forest. Several kilometres back. Halfway up the opposite hillside. The beam swept around. Another identical beam appeared next to it.

They looked a bit like the lensed lamps that shepherds used. Maybe oil lamps? No, the colour was wrong. These glowed blue, not the yellow-white of gelderbush oil lamps. They started moving downslope.

Her heart thudded in her chest. Not directly towards her, but in roughly the same direction. They had to be looking for the elderuin. What else was there out here? She guessed she had at least an hour's head start on them. Maybe longer if they were unfamiliar with the terrain. Still plenty of time to get to the ruin, grab the objects and leave.

The only people who knew the location of the elderuin were Uncle and Indiril. Please no, not Indiril. She hadn't stopped to think about him since she'd fled. Sindar, she prayed, let nothing happen to Indiril!

Her head swam, filled with images of her best friend. Possibly her only friend. She had been holding herself together by focusing on getting to the elderuin. But now, she was filled with a deep dread. She'd hadn't thought twice about anyone else since she'd fled. Now Indiril was probably in danger too. She had brought this mess not only into her life, but Indiril's and everyone else's in Hammington's Rest. People were most likely dead because of her. People she knew. She thought back to the butcher and his bloody nose. What would happen to them all?

It all hit her like a hammer. She started sobbing uncontrollably. None of this makes any damn sense!

The distant lights blinked out, leaving the distant hillside in darkness once more. Alone, surrounded by darkness and the soft noises of the feral. A cinder crow shrieked nearby, shattering the silence.

The noise galvanised her. The distant light must surely mean the others were heading for the ruin. She still had a good head start on them. Best to keep low, just in case they'd sent out wyverns as well.

As she went to move, her knee froze solid. Shit. The gillroot had helped a little, but there was only so much it could do. It would get worse before it got better. Thank the divines, it had only been a single spine. Gritting her teeth against the pain, she limped onwards. Towards the distant hill with the tall spindle oak.

Kathnell

Kathnell tightened the valve fitting, putting just the right amount of torque on the wrench to satisfy herself it was secure.

Her eyes were sore. Her back and shoulders ached. A whole day spent installing pipes and valves in the area next to the dockside. The sun had set. A welcome breeze blew in from the ocean. The hot day had left her unpleasantly sweaty. The cool air blew across her damp shirt, cooling her skin.

A couple of hours ago, the stonie owners had started having a party. Obviously trying to impress the new neighbours, she thought. Fucking stonies and their stupid egos. You could feed her entire street for a year with the money this little evening would cost.

She could hear them above. Talking. Laughing. The music they played. Not the raw sing-a-long stuff they played at the Blind Toad. No, this was played on pianos and sitars, accompanied by brass wind instruments. Refined, they called it. That wasn't a word she would use. It sounded sharp and made her ears hurt.

The smell of spices wafted down from the kitchens. She tried to imagine the sumptuous food and drink they were serving. Her stomach rumbled at the thought. Bastards, the lot of them.

Kathnell stood back from the valve and checked everything for the last time. If this worked, she could check it off her list and catch the ferry back. Go for a quick drink and then go home. She turned the valve one quarter and eyed the pressure gauge installed above it.

A brief judder, then nothing. Shit.

She turned it back to off and checked everything again.

Turned the valve. Still nothing.

Might be the gauge, she thought. She tapped the faceplate, making sure it wasn't stuck. The needle stayed still. Zero pressure.

She traced the path of the pipes in her mind, up the wall, over the edge, under the conduit, into the recess, and into the isolator. Oh shit, she thought, the bloody isolation valve!

Yesterday, they had been on the balcony above. She remembered Corric reminding her to open the isolation valve before she started this morning. Before the stonies party started. In all the thousand hells! The guild rules prevented her from entering the building now. She would have to start early tomorrow and turn the bloody thing on, before they were kicked out of the house by the bloody "rules".

The isolation valve wasn't far, she thought. Just in the recess at the back of the balcony above her. She could use the vines that clung to the wall to climb up. Not too far to climb, she thought. She was unlikely to run into anyone. They were all too busy getting drunk. The balcony was off limits because the railing at the edge wasn't complete. Too dangerous for poor-little-stonies!

The party was at the other end of the building anyway, and it was getting dark. She could climb up, open the valve, and be back down in under two minutes. Nobody would know.

Kathnell pressed into the narrow recess at the back of the balcony, positioned against the back wall of the house. Once their work was complete, the recess would be insulated and hidden behind something suitably ornate. She turned the valve.

The balcony door swung open. A young immaculate woman came out, dressed in a deep red gown. Kathnell stiffened. If she was caught here, she would be in big trouble. She was far enough into the recess to be in shadow.

Kathnell tried to shrink further back into the shadows.

The young woman took off her stone mask and leaned against the wall. Shit, she would be in even worse trouble if she was caught spying on an immaculate without their aspect. Strictly taboo. Just stay still and wait for the stonie to go back inside. She'll go away in a moment.

One minute. Two. The bloody girl just stood there looking out across the bay, occasionally taking a sip from a wineglass. Kathnell could tell from the way she moved that the stonie girl was drunk.

She was no expert on stonies, but guessed they were about her age, maybe a little younger. She was quite short, even for a stonie, and had the same aloof look and fine bone structure they all did. Dark skin, with black plaited hair spilling down her back. Pretty too.

The stonie pushed away from the wall and headed towards the balcony's edge. If she turned around now, she would surely see Kathnell.

Right on queue, the girl turned around as if to look at something behind the house. Kathnell tried to edge deeper into the recess. She dropped her wrench. It fell to the slabbed floor with a clunk.

The girl looked right at her and gasped, stepping backwards towards the balcony edge. As she did so, the heel of the stonie's shoe caught in a gap between two slabs, twisting her ankle to one side. The girl yelped, stumbled sideways, and disappeared over the edge.

For a second, Kathnell just stood there with her mouth open. Then, she sprang forwards, sprinting the short distance between the recess and the edge, half expecting to see the girl sprawled out on the courtyard below. Instead, the stonie was hanging a few feet down, holding onto the vines with one hand, stone mask and wineglass lying shattered on the ground below. Her feet wheeled frantically against the stonework, desperately trying to seek purchase. At Kathnell's appearance, the stonie whimpered and her legs thrashed faster. Eyes large.

"Please, don't hurt me," the stonie said.

That wasn't the reaction Kathnell had been expecting. *What the bloody hell were you doing in my house*, or *please help me*. Kathnell squatted down and extended her arm over the edge.

"Here, grab my hand."

The girl continued to thrash. Kathnell heard a cracking noise to her left. Vines, pulling free from the masonry under the strain.

"Shit! Stop thrashing about like a bloody beached fish and give me your hand. Now! The vines won't hold much longer."

The girl reached up and grasped Kathnell's outstretched arm. Kathnell hauled the girl upwards. It was harder than she'd expected; the effort straining her muscles. The girl was petite but still weighed a good amount. After a few long seconds, the stonie got some purchase with her feet, easing the burden.

There were a few moments when Kathnell thought the girl was going to slip, but inch by inch, she pulled her up.

They both lay panting on the balcony. Kathnell's arms and back burned from the exertion.

"Shit, that was close," the stonie said, rising on one elbow and looking at Kathnell. Kathnell rolled over and sat upright, looking at the girl.

"I thought you'd fallen for certain."

"So did I. Good job about the vines! They were supposed to have been pruned back yesterday. Thank you for pulling me up, but do you mind explaining why you were sneaking around on the balcony of my father's new house? Who the fuck are you?!"

Reality flooded back in. How was Kathnell going to explain this one? This was potentially career-ending stuff. The sort of thing Corric had always warned her about. Don't mix with the stonies. Not without the correct forms and ass-kissing first.

"I'm... sorry," Kathnell blurted, "I was just here to fix some of the heating pipes. I know I shouldn't have come onto the balcony, but, but I thought it had been cordoned off. I... I didn't think anyone would come out. Party going on. Your party I guess. Looks nice. It was a stupid mistake. I'm so sorry. Please. I just thought I could... you know... just come up and... Sorry."

You're babbling, Kathnell thought.

"I thought it would only take a few minutes," her mouth continued. "Poor decision. I know, I know I should have asked permission, but it was late and I wasn't thinking straight. I didn't mean to scare you, it's just. Well. I am sorry."

For the saint's sake, Kathnell just shut up, she thought.

"Please don't tell your parents I'm here. I am only an apprentice. I'll do anything to keep my job..."

The stonie girl was laughing. Kathnell stopped.

"And I thought you were a gutter thief," the stonie said, voice slurred. "Come to check out the new arrivals. Easy pickings."

"Hey! I'm not a thief, just an engineer's apprentice from across the bay. Anyway, just because I'm not one of you a lot doesn't mean that I'm a crook!"

The girl paused for a few moments.

"Don't worry, I will not tell my parents. I shouldn't be out here, anyway. Just trying to get away from this nemesis awful party. By the way, my name is Sybelle."

"Um.. Kathnell," she replied.

It was fully dark now. She was sure it had still been light a couple of moments ago. They must have been talking for an hour at least. Sitting together on the edge of the balcony, facing towards the bay.

"So that's when Mother came here," Sybelle said. "I didn't even get a say in it."

The glow from the setting sun had long vanished. She could barely make out Sybelle's features in the dim light.

The only illumination from the twin crescent moons, and the feeble lights of the city. Both moons hung low in the sky to the east. Balthar was little more than a dot. Chandra, big and white, pockmarked with dark seas and craters. The dark expanse of Lerins bay reflected the lights of the northern districts.

She had never spoken more than ten words to a stonie before. Indeed, to do so would have been absurd. Don't mix with stonies. Never talk to stonies. Never look at stonies. The rules.

However, it was the stonie girl that did most of the talking. Kathnell just needed to keep the girl sweet so she wouldn't tell her parents and get Kathnell into a thousand hells' worth of trouble.

It was obvious that Sybelle had little contact with people like Kathnell, either. The girl told her about her move out to Lerins from Drellgarh. She babbled as much as Kathnell. Possibly the drink. The girl didn't know anybody here. Sybelle told her about feeling that she was trapped by family and circumstance. About her mother and how much she controlled her life. She said that she wasn't supposed to talk to "mundanes" like her unless they were staff. Guess that is a gate that is locked in both directions, Kathnell thought.

In return, Kathnell explained that the conditions for many in Lerins were tough, and had got much worse since the war started. Sybelle seemed genuinely interested in Kathnell's life. They were as different as you could get. There was a part of Kathnell that wanted to punch the girl in the face, a fist for all the injustices that the immaculate had inflicted on her family.

What she should have done, ages ago, was go home. But there was something about this girl that intrigued her. It was not something she had expected from a stonie brat from Drellgarh. A bloody Drellmore no less! Maybe it was because something in the girl stirred dangerous thoughts and equally dangerous sensations in her gut. Maybe it was just because she was so nemesis-dammed pretty. All fine features and a perfect smile.

Kathnell snapped herself out of it. She needed to leave soon, otherwise she would miss the last ferry back to the other side.

"Something wrong?" Sybelle asked.

"Oh, no, it's just that I am going to have to go. I don't know what time it is and I don't want to miss the last ferry."

"I see. Thank you again for helping me earlier."

"You're welcome. I was hardly going to let you fall. Us 'mundanes' aren't all monsters, you know. And not ALL of us are thieves."

Sybelle laughed. Kathnell liked the sound. It was very much time she was leaving. Kathnell stood.

"Thank you for agreeing not to tell your parents. You falling was partly my fault."

"Wait. I have enjoyed our conversation tonight. I've learned a lot about you, about this city. Could I speak to you again? There is so much more I want to find out. Mother will not tell me anything. I hate it here."

Kathnell wasn't sure that would be a good idea. Conversing with the stonie girl in the first place had been a mistake. Deliberately seeing her again would be plain stupid. Reckless even. She could imagine what Corric would say. Best to just make her apologies and leave. Tell her it has been nice to meet you, thank you very much, but now it's time to go our separate ways.

"Of course!," Kathnell said. "I'll be working in the rooms behind the old kitchen the day after tomorrow. When the clock chimes seventeen, knock twice on the iron door at the back. I'll be waiting."

"Great!" Sybelle replied.

Rust

Rust sat at the bottom of the shaft, lungs burning from exertion. The pain from her leg had lessened, but her knee was still stiff, almost solid. It made everything an effort. Getting down had been a painful and frustrating experience. She wasn't looking forward to ascending again.

Pale moonlight shone from above, barely illuminating the walls. Beyond them, deep darkness.

Rust didn't have a lamp. Fleeing using a lamp to see would have been a bad idea. She hadn't thought far enough ahead to remember that these first corridors would be pitch dark. Dammit! I need to get my head in order, she thought. Uncle always said that you should think first, act second. Out here in the feral, panic was a killer.

She took a few deep breaths and rose. This needed to be quick. There hadn't been any more lights in the forest and she'd stopped to listen on a couple of occasions. The wind was in the right direction to carry any sounds to her. But she'd heard nothing, apart from the usual sounds of the nocturnal feral. Maybe her pursuers had got lost. That was a distinct possibility if they were following directions from Indiril.

She limped down the corridor, feeling along the walls. She touched the rough surface of the wooden door. Finally. Her hands searched out the lock. There!

A noise from back towards the shaft stopped her. She froze, listening intently. This was it, she thought. This was the moment they found her.

The small patch of light at the bottom of the shaft dimmed. A shadow of something above. She had failed. Uncle was dead and now they had found her and the objects.

Damn, they had got here quickly. She had thought they would at least be another hour.

There was a scratching noise and what sounded like feral grass being ripped up. It took her a few moments to work out what it was. The sound of grass being eaten. There was a snort, and the shadow disappeared. Rust breathed out. Just some dumb feral animal sniffing round the entrance. Felderhogg, maybe. They were jumpy creatures. If the Hegemony were nearby, the thing would have fled. Its mere presence meant that they weren't here. Yet.

The door opened. Just like before, the ceiling lit up with diffuse white light.

She quickly retrieved the odd crown and the pocket watch. She picked up a Hegemon crossbow, some bolts, a fire making kit, a few bandages, and one of the short swords.

The letter! She'd forgotten all about it since she'd stuffed it into her pocket. The bright light afforded her a brief opportunity to read it.

"Rust,

I am sorry for what I am about to tell you. I am even more sorry for my silence all these years. Everything I have done, I did to protect you. I loved your mother and father very much. They were the closest thing to a family I had.

If you are reading this, then it probably means that I am dead, and the past has finally caught up with us. I am not sure what the circumstances will be when reading this, but it is likely that people will be after you, and you must hasten.

I've been a coward. I promised your mother that I would tell you everything when you were old enough, but I have been putting it off for years. I always felt that if I didn't tell you, then I could protect you from it all. Instead, all I do is rewrite this bloody letter every year.

I have looked after you like I promised your parents. What started as devotion to them has transformed into genuine love.

I am not your real uncle. You are not part Nothari. The truth is more complex, too complex to put in this simple letter. Even now, I cannot bring myself to tell you everything. Sometimes, the truth is worth forgetting.

What I can tell you is your mother was an exceptional woman and an equally outstanding leader. I would have followed her anywhere. It was her dying wish that I protect you and keep you safe.

I am truly sorry that I can't tell you anymore than that. I know you will find that hard to take. It breaks me to think of the pain this letter will cause, but you must try to move on. Leave the past behind. These problems shouldn't be yours to bear.

Whether or not to tell you has been a struggle I have wrestled with for years.

I can understand if you are angry with me. I am willing to die knowing that my love for you has grown stronger than my promise to your mother.

I have hidden a hundred Peldaran crowns under the plantation shed in a wooden box. In the far corner, under the pipe crate. Take them and head to Nowlton. Avoid the main road. Stick to the feral. Use all the skills I have taught you. It is likely that people will be after you. I am not sure who they will be. They might be Hegemony, they might be others claiming to be friends. Trust no one. Keep moving. Especially for the first couple of days. You will be tired. You will want to rest, but it is important that you keep going.

Once in Nowlton, go to the Imperial Bank and hand them the attached cheque."

Rust looked at the cheque. It was for five hundred Peldaran crowns. More money than she had ever seen. A year's wage. Two maybe. Of course, the hundred coins in the shed were useless to her now. She wasn't about to go back to Hammington's Rest to get them. She continued to read.

The letter told Rust to get a job in Balincross. It gave her the address of someone that would put a roof over her head for a couple of months. Someone from uncle's past that wouldn't ask questions. The letter told her to forget all about her previous life. To seek a new one and never look back.

It ended with another apology from her uncle. And an instruction to destroy the letter.

"Again, I am truly sorry for everything. Please forgive me. Love, Uncle Harrod."

That was it.

No mention of the ruins. Nothing about the secret hiding place or the objects. Nothing. No answers. Just vague comments about her mother and father. Nothing tangible, nothing useful.

She didn't know what she had been expecting. Some details about Uncle's past, maybe. How he had come into possession of the objects. Why he had hidden them away. Something.

A noise from above. Snuffling and munching. The creature was back. A warning to get moving.

There would be time to digest the letter later. To read it again before destroying it. Now she must move. She would skirt around to the north and then head West, towards Nowlton. Best to stick to the feral, but keep the main road in sight. A few day's trek. Food and water would be a problem for most people. Nearly all feral plants were inedible, but she knew which scant few plants afforded at least a bit of nourishment and moisture. Not enough to sustain her for weeks, but enough to get her to Nowlton.

She hurried back along the tunnel towards the shaft.

Vidyana

Vidyana pulled her hand away from the smooth white wall. It glowed from within. A pure uniform light. Elderstone.

No great surprise, there were old Maleth elderuins scattered everywhere. This one still had some of the ancient magic coursing through it. Rare. A perfect place to stash something of value. Most cultures shunned them as being cursed, especially one that shone with ancient magical light.

The place was deserted now, but someone had been here recently. The room was illuminated when they arrived. With no one around, it would soon have returned to darkness.

Feral grass fragments lay strewn in the corridor. Fresh, still plump, some crushed by boots. A heavy wooden door left unlocked and open. On one shelf there were several Hegemon crossbows. A vacant space showed where one more had been, its outline sketched by the absence of dust. A wooden box lay upturned on the worktop, open and empty. A torn corner of an envelope lay on the floor.

She pieced it together. The young woman had come. By the looks of it alone. She had taken the objects. Then, maybe she had stopped to read something before leaving. In a hurry, too. Recently. Maybe just a few minutes ago.

It was likely that the young woman knew she was being followed. She'd probably seen the lights from the two knights that accompanied her. The bloody idiots had lit them up when some local feral beast had shot off into the forest. Twin head mounted beams of light striking out into the forest. It would have been obvious to anyone for kilometres! Idiots.

She'd quickly told them to turn them off, but the damage

had probably been done. Not that the knights were stealthy. They whirred and crashed through the feral undergrowth, breaking plants as they went. Maybe bringing them had been a mistake. Too late now.

Vidyana examined the other shelves and their contents. She picked up a knife marked with the same insignia as the crossbows on the wall. The wolf's head of House Drellmore.

Vidyana used her heightened senses, looking for anything else that could give her any clues. Nothing.

[Let me see heat]

Her vision changed. Colours became skewed. Shifted. Reddened. Now she could see colours invisible to most. There was a vague hint of warmth on the floor. Fading even as she watched.

The two knights stood either side of the tree boy. He sat on a log, glaring at Vidyana. His eyes burned with defiance. She couldn't blame him. The boy had been reluctant to tell Vidyana about this place. Loyalty to his friend had stayed his tongue. He'd only been persuaded after Vidyana had broken a couple of his father's fingers, and convinced him the next blow would be fatal. She'd have done it too, before moving onto the mother. Anything to protect the Hegemony from heretics.

She didn't enjoy what she did, but the Hegemony came first. More souls were at stake than were present in this pissy little village. Lord Vellorson seemed agitated in a way she hadn't seen before. It made her uneasy.

A third person stood next to the knights, a slight man with a shaven head. A seer.

"Send a message to Lord Vellorson. Tell him that the young woman was here recently, but has fled into the feral again. I am going to pursue."

The seer nodded and closed his eyes. He stood motionless for a nearly a minute, then opened his eyes again.

"Lord Vellorson instructs you to make sure Rustari Parra

doesn't escape. Lord Vellorson has been taken back to the West Wind and will shortly be put into the restoraleum. He expects he will be unable to issue further orders for at least a couple of days. He also said to bring her back alive."

That Trelt was going into the restoraleum so soon meant that his injuries were serious. Obvious really; a missing arm would count as serious. Hopefully, if the damage to the limb wasn't too bad, the restoraleum would knit his arm back into place. If not, he would have to wait until they got back to civilisation to have another grown.

"Tell Lord Vellorson that I shall pursue the target alone," Vidyana said. "I will send the knights and yourself back to town as planned. Ask Lord Vellorson to send troops out into the feral and along the roads towards the nearby towns, but avoid going into the towns themselves. I will be back in touch."

Again, the seer closed his eyes and became motionless.

"Master Vellorson acknowledges your request and wishes you happy hunting."

She turned to the nearest knight.

"Take the tree-runt and go back into town. Make as much noise as you like. Use your lights as much as you feel like."

"Yes sir," one of the knights said.

The knight reached down and yanked the tree-boy to his feet. The tall teen struggled against its grip for a few moments but soon realised the action was pointless. The four of them moved off, the knight shoving the tree-boy forward.

Vidyana moved towards the tree line. When she was sure that she was out of sight, she extended her kavach armour. Its blackness emerged from the two vertical slits on either side of her spine. She felt it flowing outward across her skin. It was an odd sensation, almost like a warm tickle. Almost pleasure. An intimate embrace by something ancient and powerful. It flowed across her, covering every inch in its warm protection. Hands, eyes, nostrils, fingers, ears.

She stripped out of her clothes. She felt the wind on her

skin as if the kavach armour wasn't even there. Felt the soil between her toes.

She moved around the perimeter of the clearing. Ghostly silent. Senses attuned, looking for signs of where the young woman had exited the clearing. Warm patches highlighted the hiding places of various feral animals. Wrong size, wrong shape.

There. A tiny rise in warmth against the background. Quietly, she moved over for a closer look. A small patch of crushed plants. Light human footstep tracks. The tracks were faint, well hidden; in just the right places to avoid obvious marks. Rustari Parra obviously had some skills in tracking.

Vidyana smiled. This might actually be fun, she thought.

Chapter 8

This specimen was found in the Tangletharn, just south of Libraris. It had killed some livestock and a villager. It was hunted and killed by House Bargolis rangers.

Although this Rakshash measures over four metres long, it is a juvenile. Adult Rakshash can grow to over seven metres long. They can still be found in the deep Tangletharn.

They do not normally enter populated areas. This one is thought to have been displaced from its home by rival females.

Rakshash (The forest demon). Killed 602SC
Inscription under specimen in Altaris Museum.

Rust

Rust had fled from the elderuin just minutes before the others had arrived. She'd spied them walking up the hill towards the summit. Two of the terrifying knights, and three other figures hard to make out in the gloom. One of them was taller than the rest, thinner. Indiril?

For a moment, she considered giving herself up. She was tired and confused. Her leg hurt. It could all be over. Just give herself up. Just walk towards them, arms held up in surrender.

But something had stopped her; the vision of Uncle running headlong towards the strangers and erupting in blinding, sacrificial light. A sacrifice for reasons she still couldn't fathom. With the memory came resolute defiance. She gripped the letter and limped onwards. Further into the darkness of the feral.

Rust headed north, then west. Once, she had spied the distant village through a gap between the trees. Everything looked normal, save for the giant black silhouette suspended above the village. Even from this distance, the airship looked impossibly vast. A symbol for powers immensely greater than herself. She hurried on, trying to put as much distance between herself and the horrors of the day. She continued west, roughly towards Nowlton.

On the next hilltop, she could look down into the valley. The main road towards Nowlton would usually be empty at this time of night. Tonight, it was studded with lights. Some wavered like torches and lamps. Others were a bright blueish-white. Elsewhere, she spied an occasional white light from within the feral itself.

She'd carried on through the night. With each step, the

pain in her leg returned, bit by bit.

The events of the day and the contents of the letter played on her mind. She found herself re-living the confrontation in the village centre for what seemed like the hundredth time. The memory repeated over and over on a loop. Had she put everyone in danger? The whole village? What about Indiril? He'd be alright wouldn't he? Dammit, Indiril, why did you lead the Hegemony to the ruin! No, it wasn't his fault, she thought, it was hers. It was all her fault. She'd put them all in danger and got Uncle killed.

"Uncle! Why didn't he tell me any of this earlier," she sobbed.

No sooner had she settled on one emotion, another rose to replace it. She mumbled to herself incoherently. It was difficult to concentrate on tracking skills. She desperately tried to keep the signs of her flight as hidden as possible. But, Sindar's eyes, she was so exhausted.

It would be dawn soon. In the next valley, she spied some decrepit Dolonde ruins on the border between the feral wood and a creepgrass plain that descended towards the road. Maybe from the ruins she could catch her breath for a moment and tend to her leg.

She found the ruins overgrown by feral plants. The walls long collapsed. Only a few bits of wall reached more than a few hands into the air. She'd tried to climb over, but the stiffness in her leg stopped her.

There was a crunching noise behind her. The sounds of splintering wood. She spun around. Several bapnax stood on the edge of the feral wood, noisily eating leaves from the low-hanging branches.

Maybe she just needed to rest for a few minutes, wait until the bapnax had gone. Just let her leg recover a bit.

Morning sun warmed Rust's face. It was nice. She teetered on the edge of wakefulness. One foot in a new day, the other in the comforting embrace of sleep. A light breeze brought with it the musty scent of dry creepgrass. Their long fronds rustling.

Another noise. Voices.

Momentarily confused, she tried to remember where she was. Why was she asleep outside, and not back at home? Was she away on a hunt? She blinked her eyes open.

Rust

Rust blinked away sunlight through watery eyes. Crow's eyes. How long had she been asleep? The sun was many hands above the horizon.

Her leg was still stiff, but was much better than it had been in the night.

Voices. Far off. Someone laughing.

She peered over the wall. To the south, she saw several figures walking across the creepgrass plain between her and the road. About half a kilometre away. Hegemon soldiers. Five of them. Sindar's fucking arms! They were moving towards the ruins. The sound of general chatter. It seemed relaxed, so she guessed they didn't know she was there.

There was no way she could get past them across the creepgrass.

Then she heard other voices, this time coming from behind her. Louder. Closer.

She went to the other wall and peered over. Here, the woodland was patchy but gave way to thicker vegetation up-slope. A group of Hegemon soldiers were exiting a thicker patch of woodland. They, too, were heading straight for the ruins.

One of them waved directly at her. She froze, thinking that she had been spotted, but realised the soldier was just waving to the other group. The soldier stopped and performed a series of hand gestures that ended with them pointing off towards the west. Some kind of silent code. The trackers used similar techniques when hunting game. The closer group continued down-slope towards the ruins. Towards her. They would be here in a couple of minutes.

Directly in front, a low gully began a dozen metres away

from the ruins and snaked up into the tree line. Part of it held up by a low wall, its purpose lost to time along with its builders. If she kept low, maybe she could use it to get out? No, there was no way she could make the distance between the ruins and the gully without being spotted.

Fuck.

Maybe she could hide within the structure. Pull some debris over herself. Rust looked around, desperately trying to figure a way out.

Off to the left, about a hundred metres away, she spotted the group of bapnax she heard the in the night. They were probably out of sight from both groups of soldiers around a low rise. They were alert and looking around, wary of the noise from the soldiers. Stupid outsiders, didn't they realise bapnax were dangerous if startled? With that thought came an idea.

She unslung the crossbow and studied it. She'd used wooden crossbows before when game hunting, but nothing exactly like this. She cocked it and slid one of the smooth bolts into the guide slot. She hefted it up and lined up on a bapnax on the far side of the group. It was facing towards the soldiers, long snout sniffing the air. The beast was larger than the rest. Almost certainly the bull. Perfect. She pulled the trigger. The bolt whistled away. It sailed straight over the bull. Shit, these things are powerful!

Rust checked to see if the soldiers had noticed either the bapnax or the bolt. No, they were oblivious to both. She needed to be quick.

She reloaded the crossbow and lined up again. This time she aimed a little lower, more sure of the crossbow's capabilities. Fired. The bolt was perfectly aimed. It struck the beast on its hind flank. The creature let out a terrifyingly loud cry.

There was no way a single crossbow bolt would do any significant injury to an adult bapnax. But maiming or killing the thing wasn't her plan. When startled, bapnax would do two things. Shout and run. Normally, they would rush away from what they perceived was the greatest threat. Often hunting parties would perform this exact trick to push herds into an ambush. Hit a beast at the back of the group with an arrow or bolt and it would invariably run off in the opposite direction, the rest of the herd predictably in tow.

The bapnax immediately bolted. Towards the approaching soldiers. The rest of the herd rose in unison and fled after it, each adding their own alarm call to those of the startled bull. The soldiers stopped, and were staring back up the slope towards the noise of the approaching bapnax, still out of sight over the crest. They had no clue what was going on.

Then the bapnax must have come into view. The soldiers ran. The bapnax spotted the soldiers and adjusted their course to avoid them.

Rust moved. She vaulted over the wall, and keeping low, ran towards the gully. Once in its shadow, she kept low and continued to flee along it. She tripped, stumbled, and went down on her injured knee. A searing jolt of pain shot through her body. She cried out. The crossbow spun away along the dusty ground. The pain momentarily paralysed her.

Move, she thought, you'll be found if you stay here. Through gritted teeth, she scrambled back to her feet, grabbed the crossbow, and limped away as quickly as she could.

When she got to the edge of the feral wood, she lay on the ground next to a swinderspine bush. She distanced herself from its ugly arm length spines. Worse than taptrees. She didn't need to be messing about with those things.

Only now, when she was back in the relative safety of the feral wood, did she dare look back. She could see the dust kicked up by the stampeding bapnax. They were heading off across the creepgrass plain, still blowing fury and alarm. The soldiers stood, staring after the rapidly receding spectacle. After a few moments, they turned around and continued downslope towards the ruins. Laughter and swearing.

Rust turned to leave.

Another soldier appeared. This one was much closer. Twenty metres away at most. The soldier was looking straight at her. Shit. The soldier had already raised his crossbow and was aiming directly at Rust.

Rust rolled to the left. With a thunk, a crossbow bolt struck the soil where her head had been just a second ago. The soldier was now running at full speed towards her. Sword raised. His crossbow now discarded.

"Hey, stop!" the soldier shouted.

Rust grabbed her crossbow, braced it against a nearby tree with her good leg, and cocked it. The soldier continued his charge. Rust slid a bolt into the crossbow. Aimed. Only now did the soldier notice the crossbow in Rust's hand. He dodged as she fired. The bolt missed the soldier by less than a hand. The soldier was close now, just a couple of seconds away. Too close for another shot.

Rust rolled back towards the swinderspine. She wrenched a spine off it and held it out in front of her as the soldier approached. He swung the sword towards her. She dodged, shoving the sharp spine into the man's leg. The man shouted some obscenity and quickly swatted it away. Rust scrambled to her feet and moved away from him. He pursued; the sword raised for another attack. Then the sword fell from his grip. He stopped, shaking his head, staggered and fell silently out of sight behind some feral bushes.

Rust sprinted blindly into the feral woodland. Trying to put as much distance between herself and the downed soldier. Was the soldier dead? Hunters used swinderspine toxin to fashion arrows. Capable of bringing down even the larger game if enough toxin was used.

Had she just killed someone? Actually killed another person? The thought made her feel sick. No time to think of that now, she thought. Just keep moving. She blundered onwards.

Some time later, she slumped into a ditch. Her left hand

was bleeding badly from a deep cut. She must have got it when she fell over. She wrapped it in a makeshift bandage. Her knee pounded painfully in time with her pulse.

She looked around, but couldn't see anyone in pursuit. Satisfied that she wasn't being followed, she limped deeper into the feral.

Sybelle

The clock on the landing struck seventeen. Sybelle got out of bed and quietly padded over to the door. All quiet. She tip-toed out onto the landing.

Lamplight flickered from a gap under the library door. The sound of Mother and Father talking. She crept to the door at the back of the landing that separated the private part of the house from the domestic innards. She lit her lamp and went downstairs, using the service stairwell. The new kitchen was nearly complete and would be operational in a couple of days. She ignored it and went into the old kitchen. The place was almost bare now, its contents transferred to the new one.

The domestic staff had left for the day. Unlike the house back in Drellgarh, this one had no permanent members of staff. It made the place feel cold and deserted.

Sybelle tip-toed across the old kitchen. The white tiles were cold against her bare feet. This wasn't the first time she'd come here at night, but this time she wasn't after cakes and buns. She crept past the larder and approached the iron door at the far end. She listened, but couldn't hear anything. Like she'd been told, she knocked three times and waited.

Silence.

Maybe the human had been lying. Maybe she was, even now, down in some grotty human pub laughing about Sybelle to her friends. Laughing about the stupid, gullible, immaculate girl. The thought filled her with a weird sense of betrayal. She'd never talked to a mundane her own age before. Sure, she'd commanded human servants, but had never taken the time to actually talk to them. It just wasn't something you did.

Kathnell hadn't been at all like she had imagined. The girl was smart and knowledgeable. There was an odd envy as well. Kathnell had the run of the city. Could go into all the places that, as an immaculate, Sybelle couldn't. Whatever the reasons, Sybelle had thought of little else for the last couple of days.

The noise of the lock turning made her jump. With a clunk, the door swung inwards. On the far side, illuminated by an oil lamp, stood Kathnell. Sybelle's pulse quickened. Kathnell looked down at Sybelle's legs.

"Shite girl, you got not a damned thing on your feet!"

Sybelle looked down at her uselessly bare feet.

"Oh, I, umm," Sybelle stammered. She felt stupid. Felt her cheeks flush.

"Wait here a mo," Kathnell said, and disappeared back down the corridor.

Why hadn't she worn anything on her feet? She was used to padding around the warm carpeted interior of the house. She just hadn't thought about it.

A few seconds later, Kathnell returned with some work boots. She handed them to Sybelle. They were rough. The soles covered in oily grime. They smelled like month old cheese.

Kathnell was grinning. Sybelle realised she was scrunching her own face up in disgust. Kathnell's eyes glinted in the lamplight. Was it amusement? Sybelle felt her cheeks redden further. Blessed saints! Not wanting to look even more stupid, she sat on a chair and quickly put the boots on. They were rougher on the inside than on the outside. She thought it best not to mention it.

"Ready?" Kathnell asked.

"What for?"

"Thought you might like a tour of the innards. It's your house, after all. And I know this spot where you can look right across the bay. Fabulous view. Eat my lunch there most days."

"Right, yeah. That sounds great. Is it safe?"

Kathnell smiled and headed off. Sybelle watched her receding for a few moments. Kathnell turned and looked back over her shoulder, smiling.

"You coming, or not?"

"Oh… Yes," Sybelle stammered and headed after Kathnell.

Why had she suddenly turned into a blithering imbecile?

They passed down the long corridor and round a bend to the right. The decor changed from white stone walls and tiled floor, to basic grey masonry and slabs. Various heavy wooden and metal doors led off from the corridor.

"Did you know your house was much bigger once?" Kathnell asked.

"Yes, I think so. Father said it belonged to a ceph or something."

"That's right. Most of the street belonged to the same ceph family organisation. A ceph matriarch owned the whole thing. You hear what happened, though?"

"No, what?"

Kathnell went to the second door on the right and opened it. They went through and then down a narrow circular metal staircase.

"Apparently, her daughters turned on her and killed her. Ripped her to shreds with their own tentacles! Just like that! Then they killed each other, fighting over ownership of the organisation. The whole place fell into ruin. The ceph just abandoned it. Apparently, it's not uncommon for weak matriarchs to be overthrown by their daughters. However, It IS unusual for the daughters to turn on each other afterwards. Nobody is sure what happened, but the rest of the family is said to have disappeared. Many think the whole family was killed by their own society for going rogue."

Sybelle thought about ceph killing each other. She felt sick.

"That's awful."

Kathnell shrugged.

"I suppose so. To us, yes, but the ceph are different. Not the same minds. More different than you and me are from each other."

At the bottom of the stairwell, they emerged from a door halfway along another corridor. This one was larger. Wider, with a high arched ceiling. Pipes hung from the roof and disappeared into the gloom. Kathnell pointed down the corridor to the left.

"That way leads to your neighbour's house."

"That seems a little insecure. Can we get in?"

"Thinking of snooping? Go and try. Can't get in there," she said, thumbing toward their neighbour's. "It's all locked up and protected by several big iron doors. Tight as a saints arse."

Sybelle had never heard anyone being so casually disrespectful to the Holy Church. She didn't know whether to be amused or angered.

"Oh. I had no intention of snooping. I was just asking, that's all."

"If you say so," Kathnell laughed, "Anyway, once everything's finished, this whole place will be locked down and bricked up."

Kathnell turned round and headed off to the right. Sybelle followed.

"Down this way is where the ceph lived. Much more work needs to be done down here. Still full of ceph tanks and all the gubbins. Be awhile before it's ready for the sto… ahem… immaculate."

They came to a large metal door with a small round window set into it. Darkness beyond. Under the window was a large round wheel, which Kathnell began turning.

"This leads to one of the ceph tanks. It's empty now, but was once full of water."

Sybelle scanned around. The air was warmer and more humid than she was expecting.

"I didn't know any of this was down here."

"Why would you? Most of your kind stick to the nice bits. Bet you're the first stonie to come down here in ages. Maybe ever."

"Stonie?"

"Shit, sorry, that just slipped out. Um, I meant you know. Er, your people... immaculate."

Sybelle hadn't heard the term before.

"What's it mean? Stonie?"

Now it was Kathnell's turn to blush.

"Well, it's just a, you know, a name we give to your people. Because of those masks you wear. Stone face. Stonie. What do you call them again?"

"Aspects," Sybelle said, laughing at Kathnell's discomfort.

After a few moments, Kathnell joined in.

"Guess neither of us are used to this," Sybelle said.

"No, guess not," Kathnell said, pulling the door open. Heavy hinges creaked.

They went through into a cavernous room with a high vaulted ceiling. The place was at least twenty metres across. They stood on a balcony that went round the edge of the entire space. Beneath them, about eight metres down, was the bottom. Sybelle could just make out white tiles showing through a hand's worth of water. At the bottom, two large semi-circular archways led away from the space into darkness.

"This was all flooded a couple of weeks ago. Half way to the top. We had to drain it. We are below the water level here. Shutters at the top are for letting in light. All seized shut. Rusted to the worst thousand hells."

They were headed for another door on the far side. Sybelle wiped her brow with her sleeve.

"It's hot down here," she said.

"You should try working here."

After spinning another wheel, they went through the other door.

On the other side, Kathnell pointed to a load of dials and

some valves.

"These control the water for the tank. It can be pumped out using steam pressure, which is off at the moment. Don't touch any of this, especially that one," she said, pointing to a large valve handle painted red.

"Why?"

"Cuz it will flood the whole place in under a minute. If either of these doors are left open, you'll be flooded right up to the stairwell. It's easier to let water in than it is to pump it out again."

Kathnell didn't wait for a reply and headed off again.

They went through a couple more corridors, up some more stairs, and then through a metal door that led onto the quayside. Kathnell opened it with a key.

The view from the quayside really was lovely. A few hands below their feet, little waves lapped gently against the old stonework. The moons cast long shadows across the bay.

Around them, the ground rose steeply out of the water. Villas, and other residences clinging tightly to the slope. Street level was at least six metres above their heads.

The area was secluded and tucked away round a corner from the house. Sybelle couldn't even see their house from where they sat. The place was surrounded by stone walls of other private residences.

Kathnell explained there were tunnels below the waterline that the ceph would have used to move in and out of the house. Disused and closed off now. She pointed out where drainage culverts directed rain water from the streets above into the quay. Using them, you could come up in any number of other streets. She said that sometimes she used them as shortcuts. Sybelle did not know that there were all these spaces under the city. She supposed it was probably the same back in Drellgarh, tunnels and culverts. A whole other city beneath the city she knew.

Kathnell opened a bag that she had left on the quayside and removed a couple of bottles. She offered one to Sybelle.

"Beer?" Kathnell said.

Sybelle hadn't tasted beer before. Not wanting to look stupid, she grabbed the bottle and took a swig. Sybelle wasn't sure she liked the taste. It was harsh and earthy. She drank it anyway.

Then, just like the other night, they simply sat and talked.

Kathnell told Sybelle more about her life, where she came from. Sybelle was fascinated by the freedom that Kathnell seemed to have, the places she could visit. Kathnell had talked at length about the area she lived and worked in. The pubs and shops. It all sounded so vibrant. So alive! Not like the sanitised and protected world Sybelle lived in.

"Your district sounds so nice," Sybelle said.

"Don't be too quick to think where I come from is all roses and herbs," Kathnell said. "It might sound great to you, but for most people, it's a real shit-stained struggle."

"You don't make it sound too bad."

"It's different if you can retreat somewhere when you're tired. There are many people in my district that have desperate lives. Born into poverty with little or no hope of ever getting out. It's got worse with the war. There are people where I live that would literally 'kill' to live somewhere like this."

Kathnell swept her arms round at the surrounding houses.

"But," she continued, "they know that no matter how hard they try, they would never be, could never be, like you."

She sounded bitter.

"Stonies seldom come down into the poorer areas. I mean, why would they, unless it is after whores or other vices?"

Kathnell stopped and looked away from Sybelle. Sybelle didn't know what to say. They both sat in silence.

Kathnell's words stung. It wasn't so much what she said, but what it represented. It was clear to Sybelle how dimly some of the human population viewed the immaculate. In

Drellgarh, she always had the impression that the immaculate were respected and looked up to. Maybe it was because Lerins was further away from the Hegemony than her home city, where the Hegemony had a tighter grip. Or maybe she had spent her entire life living a fantasy.

"Show me," Sybelle said.

"Show you what?" Kathnell asked, cocking her head to look at Sybelle.

"Where you live, your district, your pub."

"You bloody crazy? Beer must av' gone stale and addled your brain."

"Probably, but that changes nothing. I want to see it."

Kathnell sat back silently for a good minute, before seeming to decide.

"You really sure?"

"Yes."

"Alright, meet me here in three nights from tonight. About this time. Here is the key that will let you through that door, and the one into your kitchen," she said. Pointing back to the door they had come through.

"Won't you need it?"

"It's fine. We have a spare. Don't worry about what you dress in. I'll bring some clothes you can wear. Can't have you walking around looking like that. You'll get us both lynched."

Chapter 9

Landfall to Spinsilk to Hiemfast,
   Lastkeep to Redset to Darkspin,
   Grassrise to Winnowill to Southdark,
   Longsun to Shadowfall to Yieldenlight,
   Redclimb to Redcrown to Gatherfall,
   Vaultwitch to Brittlemass to Northdark,

List of calendar months, Hegemon standard calendar

Rust

Rust lay amongst dense feral scrub overlooking Nowlton. Downslope, the vegetation thinned out to become an expanse of creepgrass, finally giving way to the town's Lee. Like the one surrounding Hammington's Rest, only much larger. There was no abrupt edge between the sickly blue-greens of the creepgrass and tame-grass of the Lee, just a gradual blending of the two.

It all looked and sounded like just another ordinary day. No sign of troops, or indeed, any sign of the Hegemony. It was still early, the Sun just a couple of hands above the cloudless horizon. The ground, already warm against her belly. It was going to be another hot one; she thought.

The town was already awakening. Faint sounds, waxing and waning on the breeze. Dogs barking. The rhythmic banging of metal, probably from one of the town's many blacksmiths. The occasional acrid smell of industry.

There was little traffic on the roads into town. Just the usual early morning mix of horse or feldercow drawn coaches and wagons. Trades bound for the market. She waited another couple of hours to be sure.

She'd spent the last couple of days hiking through dense feral wilderness. There had been little opportunity to rest. She'd only managed three or four hours of sleep each night. Fatigue had made her careless. Concentrating on anything had become difficult.

There had been a couple of occasions when she'd stumbled, once narrowly avoiding another nasty looking feral plant by a hand's width. Her leg had improved and was little more than a dull ache now. She didn't want to go through all that again.

At first, it had been necessary to hide from frequent Hegemon patrols and circling wyverns. She put everything Uncle had taught her to use. All those days spent tracking and hunting. In hindsight, it was obvious Uncle had been preparing her the whole time. The countless lessons. What was good to eat and what to avoid. The ground to avoid detection. The flora that were easily damaged, and therefore easy to track through. How to find water that didn't make you sick. Uncle was the best tracker in the region.

'Had' been the best, she remembered. The thought came like another slap.

She was tired, but at least she wasn't dying somewhere, wracked by poison cramps and an unquenchable thirst. It just made her think of Uncle all the more. With it came all the guilt and sorrow.

Yesterday, Rust stopped at a fast-flowing stream. She'd taken a few moments to rip Uncle's letter into pieces and bury them in the mud at the water's edge.

By the end of the second day, the signs of Hegemon activity had dwindled and finally ceased altogether. Since then, nothing. No sign of troops, Hegemon, wyvern, or airship.

She'd waited long enough.

Judging by the sun, it was nearing midday. No sign of any Hegemon activity all morning. Whatever search activities they were performing were obviously limited to a few kilometres around Hammington's Rest. They clearly hadn't ventured this far.

The biggest challenge would be getting across the Lee. It was a good two hundred metres across. Wide and open. Impossible to cross without detection. She could run across, but if there was anyone watching, they would surely spot her. No, it was better to use the road. Cross the lee where it was narrower and join the rest of the traffic. Hide in plain sight.

She circled around until she was within a few hundred metres of a road into town, and waited for a large group of feldercow carts to pass. Traders from another village or town. As they passed, she looked to make sure that she didn't recognise anyone. She stepped out and started walking parallel to the road. After a few minutes, she joined it, walking a few metres behind the last cart, trying to look as inconspicuous as possible. Just one more visitor walking into town.

A few minutes later, she entered the town without incident, and headed immediately towards the bank. No sense in staying around longer than necessary.

What was she going to do then? Hire a carriage to Balincross, like her uncle's letter had advised? No, probably better to take an indirect route.

The streets were busy, but not excessively so. The usual mix of travellers, locals and traders. She passed the open door of a baker's shop. The smell of freshly baked bread made her mouth water. Time to eat later. For now, it was best to keep moving.

The sooner she retrieved the money and got out of the town, the better. If the Hegemony were looking for her, they wouldn't constrain their search to Hammington's Rest forever. Eventually, they would come looking here. They could arrive days, hours, even minutes, from now.

Nowlton wasn't a big town, but it was an important hub for the communities that lived this far from the central tame lands. It had a variety of shops, inns, merchants and minor industry. It was the largest congregation of humanity this side of Balincross, a further forty kilometres west.

On one street corner, she walked by a group of people and a t'kelikt talking. She had almost passed them when she heard Hammington's Rest mentioned. Pretending to look in an ironmonger's window, she stopped to listen. It didn't take long to confirm her fears. The Hegemony hadn't physically reached Nowlton yet, but word had. There was talk that this was a prelude to a full scale Hegemony invasion of Peldaran. Fast runners had already been sent to Balincross, and the militia were being mobilised from the nearby towns and villages.

One of the people, an older woman, said there were eyewitness accounts of Hegemon forces looking for someone, that one villager had blown themselves up with forbidden magic.

On the surface, the town had seemed normal. Today, just like any other. But this conversation was proof that news was spreading out from Hammington's Rest like ripples on a pond. Rust couldn't help but think that she was the pebble that had created the splash.

Crossing the town quickly, avoiding the main roads, she continued towards the bank.

As she rounded the last corner, she caught a glimpse of movement behind her. Like a black shadow. Rust wheeled around. Someone, or rather something, stood motionless in the street about ten metres away. A silhouette of a naked woman, night black from head to foot. Even the thing's eyes were black. A demon of nightmare. Old tales of dread Nemesis made real. She'd seen this figure before, back in Hammington's Rest when Uncle had died.

Rust stepped backwards, away from the apparition.

The figure spoke.

"Not one more step, Rustari Parra. I have no desire to hurt you, but won't hesitate to do so if you don't cooperate. Fully."

Rust turned and ran.

A blur of motion. The figure appeared in front of her.

It thrust a hand towards her chest. Small sparks, like lightning, danced between its outstretched finger tips. A moment of intense pain, replaced almost immediately by total numbness. No, not just numbness, the total lack of any sensation. She tried to move. Nothing. It was like her body had ceased to exist.

She tried to shout, but all that came out was a pathetic swallowing noise. With no control over her limbs, she collapsed backward onto the ground.

Rust stared unblinking into the cloudless sky. Even that slight movement had been robbed from her. The face of the demon appeared above her. It smiled, and as it spoke, blackness flowed away from its eyes and mouth, exposing the dark-skinned face of a young immaculate woman. Large green eyes looked amused and her smile mischievous.

"Why doesn't anyone ever listen to me? I mean, just for fucking once, it would be nice to do things without all the drama."

She reached towards Rust with an outstretched hand, lightning dancing between her fingers.

Sybelle

Sybelle told her parents she'd been tired and gone to bed early. After waiting a while, she slipped into the old kitchen, down through the under-house, and outside. Kathnell was waiting on the quayside, just as she'd promised. She had been worried Kathnell wouldn't be there, so when she spotted her, Sybelle had felt relieved and more than a little excited.

Kathnell produced some clothes from her bag. A long flowing brown shirt and baggy trousers. A yellow cowl covered the head, hiding most of the face.

"What's this?" Sybelle asked.

"It's a Helmara trader's dress. The city gets a lot of them come into port. They run a lot of the trader ships from the Creshmet isles. Won't turn any heads."

Sybelle wasn't convinced. They smelled stale.

"Where did you get them?"

"I, erm, I borrowed them."

"What if I get asked a question? I can't speak Helmari."

"Don't worry. I'll keep you clear of any other Helmari. Also, it's best if you let me do the talking. If you are asked a question, keep looking down and speak softly, in common. Most Helmari speak common anyway, but it's not unheard of that some don't."

This was stupid. She couldn't really go through with this, could she? What happens if she was caught? Or separated from Kathnell. What would happen if she got lost?

"Having second thoughts?" Kathnell asked.

"Yes!"

"Me too. If this goes the way of the crow, I could lose my job, or worse. Exciting, isn't it?"

Kathnell handed her the clothes. They were simple. Made from linen. She felt their fabric in her fingers. Surprisingly soft. They represented a human culture that Sybelle knew next to nothing about. A tangible link to an entire world beyond her sheltered existence.

She glanced back towards the immaculate quarter. Its gold painted spires and Drellmore blue flags. In the distance, the upper spires of Bennel Palace were visible above the rooftops. She knew that her future lay there, amongst the families of the immaculate. Maybe this was foolish, dangerous even, but this mundane girl had awakened something in her. Something confusing. Sybelle glanced across at Kathnell, who was smiling back at her. She decided she wanted to find out where this led.

"Let's do it!" Sybelle said.

"Saint's piss, all right," Kathnell said, exhaling deeply. "Better put your clothes on then."

The boat was cramped. Sybelle hated the way it swayed. When a larger vessel passed close by, the boat was thrown around in its wake. Surely it will capsize at any moment, she thought. They would all drown! Nobody else seemed to be the slightest bit worried. A sudden gust of wind blew smoke from the boat's stack into her face, making her cough. Her mouth was sour and watery. She stared straight ahead, concentrating on the far shore.

"You doing alright?" Kathnell whispered.

"Yes, fine," she lied.

Kathnell chuckled.

The boat held about twenty other people. Mostly workers and labourers. Heading home for the day, Kathnell said. This was a boat for mundanes, not the luxury yachts or steamers she was used to. The smell of rotting seaweed mixing with stale sweat. It was all she could to do to avoid vomiting.

Kathnell had paid their fare. The thought of payment hadn't even occurred to Sybelle. They tried to sit apart from everyone else. Sybelle's heart almost stopped when someone sat down next to her. A big burly woman, with a large mole on her cheek and greasy looking hair. When they were about halfway across, the woman leaned across towards Sybelle, offering her a small black seed pod.

"Reckon, ya feeling hooting girl. Chewin's? Swears by it me'self."

"Er, sorry, no thank you," Sybelle whispered back.

"Eh? I say ya chew it. Sooth ya gut," the woman said, offering the seed pod to her again.

"No, thank you."

"Suit ya-self gurl. Just helping. Be you hollering ya guts out, not me," the woman said before slumping back in her seat.

Sybelle's heart thumped. She had absolutely no idea what the woman had said. Kathnell stifled another giggle. She stopped when Sybelle administered a sharp elbow to the ribs.

The ferry came alongside the quayside. Ropes were tied. Everyone started to get off. It swayed and bumped against the dockside rhythmically, rising and falling with each wave.

It was too much. Her mouth filled with saliva. She darted to the side and vomited violently. Nobody paid any attention, apart from the woman she'd been seated next to.

"Waste o'me lungs," the woman tutted and walked off.

When Sybelle had recovered enough, they headed into the town.

"Welcome to Elthar district," Kathnell said. "It's not too bad, mostly. My family came here when I was young."

Sybelle looked back across the water to the immaculate district. So very distant.

"You sure there is time to get back across tonight?" Sybelle asked.

"Yes, we've got a few hours yet before the last ferry leaves. Don't worry!"

"Are you coming back with me?"

"Yes. Told you that, didn't I? Not going to let you travel back alone."

"Sorry. Yes. Where are you going to sleep?"

"I'll sleep in our site office, under the house. Done it a few times. I already told mum I wouldn't be home tonight."

"And she's all right with that?"

"Sure, she's used to it."

Sybelle had never spent a single night of her life somewhere other than in the same place as at least one of her parents.

Kathnell led her away from the dockside and deeper into the town. They passed a small Imperial church on one corner, but it didn't look open. Sybelle asked about the church and was a little shocked to discover that Kathnell didn't attend church at all.

"Don't see the point," Kathnell said. "Reckon the Emperor's not got much time for the likes of me."

Sybelle wasn't really sure what she'd meant by that.

"So you don't believe?"

"Not sure what I believe, but that the Emperor watches over us all seems absurd. Seen no sign of divine guidance in this part of town. Nor any sign of Nemesis, either."

"Well, I believe," Sybelle replied quickly.

Kathnell smiled.

"Well, that's up to you, I guess," Kathnell said. "Now, keep your head down, and stay close."

"Why?"

"You wanted to see life in the common quarter, didn't you?"

Sybelle didn't answer. The more she thought about it, coming here with Kathnell had been madness. She had a sudden strong urge to ask Kathnell to take her back to the boat. Back to the safety of home.

Home? The new house wasn't home, she thought. It was just another reminder of how she didn't have any control over her life. She just did what her parents told her to do.

Well, not tonight.

Kathnell smiled at her.

"Well? You coming?" Kathnell asked.

Sybelle smiled back with new found resolve.

The neat streets of the dockside became narrower. Houses smaller, dirtier, and closer together. Roads turned from neat stone, to rough cobblestone, and then dirt.

The place was full of people of all ages and colours. All dressed in drab, inferior quality linens. None of them seemed to smile. They looked miserable. Feeling suddenly self-conscious, she hunched forwards and lowered her head further. Shops mingled with residences. All clustered on top of each other, the definition of the word street became hazy. There was another imperial church here. This one was boarded up and covered in heretical slogans.

"Not going to go any further. Believe it or not, this area isn't so bad. Go further north and you hit the truly desperate districts. Full of refugees from the war. Crime and poverty are the norm there. Definitely not safe for either of us. People go missing there all the time."

"That's terrible. Why don't the authorities do anything about it?"

"You're joking, right? They've tried. Only made it worse. The people there hate both the Hegemony and their own government with equal ferocity. They feel they have been forgotten and abandoned. They're right. Nobody could give four saintly farts about them. Place is run by gangs, mostly. Power moves out. Gangs move in."

"I had no idea."

"No, thought not. Place is strong with the Rebellion as well. Never mind that. There is a pub down this way that I know well. We've got about three hours before we need to get a boat back to the peninsula."

That the rebellion was at work in the area made Sybelle feel even more alone. She moved closer to Kathnell. They turned and started walking back towards the dockside.

They arrived at a place called the Blind Toad. A party

seemed to be going on inside. Music, laughter and tuneless singing spilled out on to the street.

"Is there an occasion tonight?" Sybelle asked.

"What do you mean?"

"All the noise."

"No, it's normal," Kathnell laughed. "This lot doesn't need a lot of encouragement. Remember, let me do all the talking."

"So, I told the fella to sling his fish," the man said, wiping beer froth from his large ginger beard. After a few moments he added, "Told him to take the filthy kitten as well."

The surrounding people erupted into laughter. Kathnell did too.

Sybelle's head swam. She'd been following the conversation as best she could. The joke lost on her. A mix of cheap alcohol, accents, and differences in culture made the conversation almost alien.

She thought she had better laugh along with everyone else. As soon as she started laughing, everyone turned to her, puzzled. She realised with horror that everyone else had already stopped laughing. She'd been laughing on her own like someone deranged. Then everyone burst into laughter again. She along with them. She caught a glimpse of Kathnell. She wasn't laughing, just staring at her. A smile on her face. Sybelle smiled back.

Kathnell leaned across the bar and motioned for the barmaid to come over. A tall, attractive woman called Roz.

"Can we grab two bottles for the walk? It's time I got our visitor here home."

The woman smiled and nodded, returning a few seconds later with a couple of glass bottles. She'd been introduced to Roz when they arrived. Kathnell explained Sybelle was a Helmara engineer from a ship she was helping to repair. Roz had smiled, said hello and then went back to working.

"Just make sure you return the bottles this time, Kath," Roz said, handing over the beer bottles.

Roz turned to Sybelle and smiled, before turning back to Kath and winking. Some kind of secret message passed. Kathnell quickly ushered Sybelle away from the bar. Sybelle noticed her new friend was blushing.

Sybelle staggered after Kathnell, head spinning. The local brew tasted odd. Not at all like the wines she was used to. It was sweeter, with an earthy taste. It wasn't as strong as wine. But then again, she didn't drink wine by the tankard. Several large tankards.

They went through a late night food market. Kathnell introduced her to something called a smoked-porkie. It was the best thing Sybelle had ever tasted! As she bit into the pie, thick gravy ran down her chin. She must look like a mess. She didn't really care.

The place lacked the colours, fine architecture and cleanliness of the immaculate quarter, but it felt so alive!

Her head continued to spin. If anything, it had got worse since they had left the Blind Toad. Kathnell helped her keep upright. They walked towards the dockside. Kathnell said something about getting back. Sybelle took another swig from the bottle. The moon Chandra was low on the horizon, reflecting brightly on the water. Sybelle stopped and stared.

"Hey, Kath, look at the moon."

"I've seen it before."

"Yes, I know, but it's big, isn't it?"

"I think you've had too much to drink. I should have stopped two beers ago. Fuck. Guess you're not used to it."

"Non... sense."

"And I think it's my fault for buying it. Shit."

Kathnell took the bottle from her hand and put in on the ground.

"Hey!" Sybelle said.

There was movement behind Kathnell. Sybelle tried to focus.

"I think you've had eno—"

Someone wrenched Kathnell away from Sybelle and pushed her to the ground. A man she dimly recognised from the pub grabbed Sybelle by the throat and pushed her up against the wall. Her head smacked against the brickwork with a clunk. Pain shot through her skull. Her vision momentarily darkened.

"Helmari witch!" the man shouted, showering her with spittle. His breath stank of alcohol and smoke.

Sybelle struggled to catch her breath. The man's hands tightened around her throat. She grasped at them, trying to break free.

"It's your shit-filthy kind that killed my wife. Been waiting to get my own back. What better than with a sweet little witch like yourself? You should've stayed on your ship!"

Kathnell staggered back upright and turned on the man.

"Get your fucking hands off her," Kathnell screamed.

The man rounded on Kathnell, releasing his grip on Sybelle's throat. He pulled a knife from his waist and thrust it in Kathnell's direction.

"And what are you going to do about it, eh? Maybe once I'm finished with her, I'll take my piece from you too, girl. A friend of a witch might as well be one themselves."

"I'll fucking do you in, that's what," Kathnell shouted back.

"Fuck off," the man said and advanced towards Kathnell, knife held out in front.

Sybelle reached down and picked up her fallen bottle. She raised it high over her head, and with all the power she could muster, brought it down on top of the man's head. It hit with a thud, but didn't break. The man grunted and staggered to one side, clutching his head. Kathnell punched him heavily in the guts, and as he went down, brought her knee up into his face. He slumped facedown in the gutter.

Sybelle stood and stared at the man. Kathnell grabbed her and pulled her along. They went around a corner and towards the docks. Behind them, the man shouted various obscenities and promises of bloody revenge.

They sat together on the boat as it headed back towards the immaculate quarter. There were only a couple of other people heading back with them, so it was easy to find a quiet area towards the back.

Sybelle still felt very drunk, but the fight had sobered her up. She had never been in a fight before. Her pulse still hammered in her chest. She looked across at Kathnell, who smiled back at her. A warm feeling moved through her gut and into her groin. She moved towards Kathnell and kissed her on the cheek.

Kathnell turned towards her, looking surprised. They locked eyes. A deep hunger rushed through Sybelle. Kathnell leant over and started kissing her on the mouth. Sybelle pressed back into her. She felt Kathnell's hand on her thigh.

Hunger blossomed into need.

Part Two

A catalyst. The first turning of wheels that had sat rusting for over fifteen years.

There are moments that separate our memories. Somewhere between fact and myth. Remembrance is not a contiguous line from past to present. History is sectioned into parts. The things that happened before the moment. The things that happened after.

One such moment.

A first fleeting contact with a young woman from a far off land. A startling connection. Someone using my dead friend's lost seer web. All our noble plans had ended with her death.

A full stop on that part of the story.

I didn't know what to make of it. It was fleeting, uncoordinated, a flicker of connection. So brief that I thought it was an illusion, conjured by the trillion things that make me real. A random failing of some ancient device that keeps what I call 'me' alive.

Entropy inexorably calling me towards its inevitable embrace.

The second contact with her had been stronger. This was no hallucinatory decay. I delved into the Whisper. Her thoughts broadcasting like a beacon. Open. Unshackled. A bright lamp in a dark room. Clear for all to see. Reaching out, reaching out. No, not my dead friend. Someone related.

A new puzzle.

A moment in time dividing what came before with what came after.

I tried to warn her to remain silent. Vipers waited in the dark. Drawn to the light. The vipers connected with her first.

Chapter 10

House Tarranis, House Mirala, House Marquilis, and House Atlaris have fallen into chaos.

Pray for their souls, for they have succumbed to the lies of Nemesis and its Heretic followers.

Pray that one day they see the truth again so the Emperor can welcome them back into his arms.

Like we did with House Bargolis, so we shall do with these houses, until once more we are one.

Church sermon, House Drellmore, circa 667 SC

Rust

There was an odd droning sound and a swaying sensation. Rust woke with a start. How long had she been out? The last thing she remembered was being attacked by the demon.

Her own clothes had been replaced with simple grey overalls. At least they were clean. She looked around the small room. No sign of her backpack, her old clothes, or the objects from the ruin. Sindar's breath!

Her body ached, like she was bruised all over. When she moved, her limbs felt sluggish. The wound in her leg had been covered with a poultice and bandage. Other cuts and grazes were dressed with plasters.

There was food and drink on a table, a bed, and a toilet in the corner. Apart from that, the room was empty. Its walls, made from dark polished wood banded with metal. The low droning sound, ever present in the background.

She went to the single window and looked out. At first, the sight was so unfamiliar she didn't comprehend what she was seeing. They were in the sky! She was in the airship. The landscape rolled by far below, at once both familiar and utterly strange. It was odd seeing things from this angle. Everything looked so small. Unreal. Seeing trees, fields, and rivers from above was one thing, but there was something fundamentally wrong with seeing clouds from above. Each one casting its own shadow onto the ground far below.

The window was made from a strange transparent material. Not like the glass that some wealthy houses had in Hammington's Rest. Houses like Indiril's. This was as clear as spring water. Thinking about the glass in Indiril's house reminded her of him. Was he still in danger? What had happened to him?

She tried the door. It was locked. The door had a locked hatch at head height. She banged on it.

"Hey. Hey!"

Nobody came. She banged again. Nothing.

"Fuck."

She slumped on to the hard bed. The noise, she realised, must be coming from the airship's engines. Propelling it towards Sindar-knew-where.

She stared at the ceiling and tried to make some sense out of the last few days. The ceiling's featureless white surface offered her no clues. She rolled over and faced the wall.

The nausea and muscle stiffness gradually subsided. Suddenly extremely hungry, she tried the food. Some kind of loaf and fruit juice. She reckoned that if they were going to kill her, poisoning would be a rather odd way, given her current situation.

This whole thing made no sense. Why had they taken her? She assumed it was all tied to the objects. If so, why had they taken her as well? It all led back to the same questions about Uncle. Whatever the reasons, the Hegemon had launched a raid into Peldaran. A move that would be interpreted as hostile. Indeed, the talk she'd overheard in Nowlton confirmed exactly that. The thought chilled her. Were they now at war because of her?

She tried the door again. A waste of time.

Hours passed. Day turned into night. Here and there the ground was studded with tiny lights. Towns and villages seen from far above. The lights slowly thinned out. Then massive dark shadows passed by, obscuring the sky beyond. Mountains!

She grew restless. Sleep was impossible. She banged on the door again. This time, someone approached. The door was unbolted and a large man entered wearing the body armour of the Hegemony.

"Let me out! Why have you taken me prisoner?" Rust shouted.

"You are to remain in this room for the duration of the voyage," the soldier replied.

"I don't understand. What have I done? Why have you taken me? Why did you kill my uncle?"

She sounded both desperate and pathetic.

"You are to remain inside," the guard repeated.

"What have you done with Indiril?"

Rust tried to push past the man, but he blocked her path. The guard shoved her backwards, stepped out, and shut the door.

"If you insist on banging on the door, you will be sedated again. We will arrive in Lerins in the morning. Until then, shut up."

The footsteps receded.

Lerins?

Rust tried to remember where the place was. Was it the capital of Bennel, the Hegemony puppet state? She lay back on the bed and tried to get some sleep. It was doubtful she would get any.

She woke. Her head spun. No, it was the room that was spinning. It was like the bed was being spun slowly around. When she opened her eyes, however, the room was stationary. Her stomach rolled. She gripped the edge of the bed.

Daylight shone in through the window. Shadows moved around the room. The airship was turning. Something else was different, too. The droning continued, but it had changed in pitch.

Rust walked unsteadily to the window and looked out. They were above a vast city. The largest Rust had ever seen. It sprawled around the shores of an enormous bay. Beyond lay an endless expanse of water. The ocean! She hadn't seen the ocean before. It was impossibly big.

The airship turned and brought a rocky hill into a view, on which an enormous palace sat, festooned with flags. Some of them had a crest she didn't recognise, a red shield on a white background. The others were of a wolf's head. The symbol of House Drellmore.

The airship stopped turning, and the noise changed in pitch again. After a few moments, the airship began moving slowly towards a spire that rose high above one of the palace towers.

The airship had been stationary for some time. She stood looking out of the window, craning to get a better view.

The sound of people approaching. The door was unlocked and several soldiers entered, including the one that she had seen earlier. All carried swords, unsheathed and at the ready. Without a word, the man she had spoken with earlier advanced.

"Hold out your arm," the man commanded.

Rust hesitated.

"Hold out your arm," he repeated.

There was no sense resisting, she thought, she didn't really have a choice. She could make a fuss. It wouldn't make a difference, but at least she could go down with a fight.

With a sigh, she realised she was just too tired. Physically tired of the running. Mentally tired of the confusion. Tired of worrying. Tired of thinking about Indiril. Uncle. Simply, just tired.

She held out her right arm. The man placed a finger sized metal cylinder against it and depressed a button on its side. There was a click and a brief sharp scratch. She felt drowsy and sat down on the edge of the bed. A deeper tiredness ran through her.

Kathnell

Kathnell stared into her empty glass. Her thoughts returned to the boat trip. The kiss had been unexpected. Kathnell had felt Sybelle's mouth pressing back into her. She'd felt the hunger in it. Sybelle's perfume, the alcohol, and her own arousal, all mixed to produce a heady intoxicant. She'd almost lost control.

Then something had stopped her. Being on a public boat hadn't helped. But no, not that. The tiny bit of her mind that had still been rational, the piece that hadn't been utterly consumed by lust, spoke up. She was about to cross a line that led to potentially suicidal territory. This was the fucking Hegemony! Sybelle was immaculate! The very people she had sworn to seek revenge against.

Her meetings with Sybelle had been a bit of fun. A bit of rebellion against the established order. Against the rules. In her own way, Sybelle was rebelling against the same forces as Kathnell. She liked Sybelle too. Sybelle was attractive, and Kathnell enjoyed their conversations.

There was also a part of Kathnell that got satisfaction in watching how this naïve young immaculate girl reacted to the realities of life in the northern quarter.

But there was a line. And she'd been about to cross it.

She'd withdrawn from the kiss. Sybelle moved to re-engage, but Kathnell had stopped her, smiling apologetically and making a plausible excuse for them being on a public boat. Sybelle had looked confused, but after a few moments, smiled back.

Kathnell had taken Sybelle back to her house and told her she wouldn't be able to see her for a few days. Important work. Excuses. Lies. Time to get her head in order.

It hadn't worked.

The last couple of days had been a blur. She'd been to work, but she'd found it hard to concentrate. Now she was trying her good old dependable trick, drink, and drink some more. It wasn't working either. Her mind always finding its way back to Sybelle.

"Can I get you a drink?"

The voice brought her out of her daydream. A middle-aged man with unruly white hair was standing next to her. Great, she thought, just what she needed, another drunk.

"Not interested, pal," she responded, looking him up and down. "You're not my type."

There was something she recognised in him. A nagging itch she'd seen him before. Recollection fluttered away.

"You know it's rude to stare," the man replied.

"Yeah, sorry. But I'm really not interested. Try your luck with the cloth makers in the corner. They'll do a bounce with anyone. I'll get my own drinks, thanks."

She thumbed toward a table filled with old women from the nearby cloth factory. She stood and motioned towards Pelter for another drink. The white-haired man laughed.

"They're not my type," he said. "Anyway, Miss Bilt, has anyone said you're just like your dad? Same crow-sure attitude for sure."

Dad? The itch at the back of her mind intensified. The man had something to do with her father. Had she seen them together when she was young?

She sat back down.

"What did you say?," she replied.

"I said, Miss Bilt, that you remind me of your father. He was a good man. It was tragic what happened to him."

She'd come to the pub intending to forget. Not to be reminded of a time of great pain. A time when her little world had felt like it was about to be shattered.

"What the fuck do you want?" she shot back. "Who the hell are you?"

"Sorry, I didn't mean to upset you. You're quite right. It's rude of me to intrude without at least introducing myself. My name is Chander, and I work for Liberation."

The Liberation?

Pelter had come over and was standing behind Chander. Within earshot.

"Not bothering customers again, are you Chander?" Pelter said.

Chander rose and turned to Pelter. The two embraced like old friends. Slapping each other on the back. Grinning. The action eased Kathnell. If Pelter liked the man, then he couldn't be all bad.

"Get Miss Bilt a drink and put it on our tab," Chander said.

Pelter left, leaving them alone again.

"Now, I'd like to start this again," he said. "My name is Chander Tarn-Alk, and I used to work for your father. For the rebellion. He was my commanding officer."

"The rebellion?", Kathnell replied. "What Nemesis shit are you on about? My father wasn't in the rebellion. He was an innocent man, killed by the Hegemony in cold blood."

"Oh no, he was in the rebellion all right. I'm not surprised they didn't tell you. Best to keep things quiet."

Pelter returned with a drink for them both. Smiling at Kathnell as he approached. Kathnell had the feeling that this was all a setup. Pelter was in on it. The way they had embraced. Not friends. Comrades. The two men looked at her.

"We've had our eye on you for some time, Kathnell," Chander said. "Pelter tells me you're a patriot. Also, tells me you are a brilliant engineer. Talented."

"Why do I feel this is an ambush?"

The two men smiled.

"I'm here to offer you a job," Chander said.

Rust

Rust stirred. Consciousness returned, piece by piece. Senses awakened one by one. A clock chimed. A smell of lavender. Sensation crept back into her limbs. Thankfully, not with the same bruised feeling as before.

She awoke on an enormous bed. Much bigger than the one back home, and significantly more comfortable. Thick feather pillows and spinner moth sheets.

There was a small bandage on her left forearm arm. She peeked underneath and saw a small scab of dried blood. Not where the guard had placed the cylinder thing. No, that had been on her right arm.

She was still dressed in the same plain grey overalls as before. A pile of new clothes lay folded on a chair beside the bed. Neat blue shirt and brown linen trousers.

The room was large and opulent. Ornate patterned rugs covered the polished wooden floor. Impressive paintings of regal looking humans hung from wood-panelled walls. A light smell of lavender perfume mixed with furniture wax.

The bedroom led into an even larger room furnished with leather couches, some tables, and other furniture. Intricate and colourful wallpaper adorned the walls, depicting various outlandish flora and fauna. Several glass-fronted cabinets were filled with books. All of it was ornate, and certainly unbelievably expensive. Two glass doors led onto a balcony overlooking the city and the bay beyond. I must be in the palace, she thought.

Another door led to a small room with a white ceramic privy in the corner, half filled with water. It took her a few minutes to work out how to operate it.

Predictably, the balcony doors were locked. So was the

polished wooden door that led from the rooms. Well, she thought, at least it's an improvement over the little cell on the airship. But she was still a prisoner.

Rust walked over to one table where a selection of fruit, bread, and drink had been left. She tried the door again, shouted for someone to let her out, and then gave up.

Rust sat by the window and gazed out on a different world. The view was wondrous. Baffling. The city was vast!

Grand houses constructed from stone clustered around the nearest quayside. Structures with balconies and tiled roofs. To either side, an expanse of larger buildings, all equally grand. Similar looking to the buildings in the business quarter of Balincross, but far more impressive. Beyond those lay the wider expanse of the city. It stretched for kilometres along the arc of the bay.

The sparkling blue water teemed with boats and ships of every size. All going to and fro. She couldn't believe they weren't constantly colliding. In the distance, a giant ship powered through the water, heading out towards the ocean. Sun glinted off metal structures on the deck. Massive guns festooned the fore and aft. It had no sails, but clouds of white vapour poured from four giant chimneys. The vessel dwarfed anything around it. Far larger than anything she had imagined could float.

Large industrial buildings clustered around the far shore. More water vapour and smoke billowed from tall chimneys.

The vessel, the airship, the knights, the weird demon woman, the tall metal man in the village, this giant city. They represented the vast power of the Hegemony. Despite her dreams of joining the Peldaran forces, she realised now there could be no actual war with the Hegemony. To think otherwise was folly. She wanted to warn the partisans back home. War against the Hegemon meant death.

The thought that somehow she was important to the Hegemony seemed utterly unbelievable. And yet, here she was; their captive.

A jangling of keys. The door lock clicked and opened. Several guards entered. They waited just inside as a man and young woman entered. Rust immediately recognised them both. The man had been with Uncle when he had died. Rust had thought the man had surely died in the blast. His arm had been ripped off. How in Sindar's name was he even alive?

The young woman had the face of the demon that had caught her in Nowlton. She was dressed in a flowing green dress. She was perhaps ten years older than Rust with the same dark skin. All signs of the blackness that had covered her were gone. She smiled at Rust and plonked into a chair. The demon-woman grabbed a glass and poured herself some fruit juice.

The man continued towards Rust. His arm hung limply at his side in a sling, but still very much attached. The skin on his hand was oddly transparent, displaying vaguely disgusting details underneath. One side of his face was pink. The hair on the same side was short. Again, there was the suggestion of slightly transparent skin, exposing veins and hints of muscles.

This was the man that had killed Uncle and ripped her world away. Before this man had arrived, her life had been simple. Safe. Predictable. Replaced with something strange and terrifying. Rust was about to rise and confront him when the demon woman cleared her throat. The demon shook her head slowly. The demon raised her glass towards Rust in toast, and winked.

The man walked up, smiling.

"Hello Rustari. How are you feeling? How is your leg? My name is Trelt Vellorsen. I think you've met Vidyana before."

The woman smiled again. Rust didn't answer. The man indicated the seat across from Rust. Rust ignored him and looked out of the window. He looked like a prick.

"Do you mind if I sit down?"

She didn't answer and continued staring at the distant

ships. The man stood there for a few moments before sighing and sitting.

"You have every right to be angry," he said. "Confused, and frightened. But please believe me, this really wasn't the introduction I was hoping for. And I am really truly sorry for the loss of your—"

The man paused for a second.

"—your uncle," he continued.

At the mention of Uncle, something snapped. All the pent up grief, confusion, frustration, and anger suddenly rose to the surface.

"Sorry!" Rust shouted, pushing away from the chair, "You're sorry!? You invaded my fucking country and killed my uncle, and you're sorry?"

The demon called Vidyana rose and took a step towards them. The man glanced at the demon with the slightest shake of his head. The demon remained standing, but didn't advance.

"Yes, Rust, I am truly sorry, but the actions we took were necessary. We…"

"Invading my country and killing my uncle were necessary?"

"I don't mean to be insensitive, Rust, but we didn't kill your uncle. Your uncle killed himself in a vain attempt to kill me. As you can see from my less than perfect condition, he almost succeeded."

Rust glowered at him. Now she thought about it, he was right. It didn't make her feel any better.

"Look," Trelt continued, "I don't expect you to understand any of this at the moment. Indeed, your reactions are justified, but don't believe everything you've heard about us. The Hegemony. I know this is all confusing, but we are not the enemy you believe us to be, and you are not a prisoner."

"So I can just walk out?"

"Unfortunately, your little game with the artefacts has caused quite a fuss, so regrettably, you must remain here for the time being. It genuinely is for your own protection, and your country's."

"That sounds like felder-shit."

"People have not been honest with you. Your uncle has kept things from you your whole life. We have been looking for you for some time, Rust."

The man smiled.

"What are you talking about?" Rust said.

"I'm sorry, that was too much. You don't need to hear this all just now," he continued. "It's unfair of me to confuse you even more with my excitement. You will be treated well, and you will find these rooms comfortable. If there is anything you would like, please ask the guards when they bring your food. They will get you anything you like, within reason, of course. Over the next few days, I only ask that you cooperate with my colleagues. They would like you to help them with some questions they have. That's all."

"Hopefully," he continued, "with time, you will come to understand that what we do is for the protection of everyone. Now, please get some rest. We will talk more over the coming days. It really is a pleasure to meet you."

With that, the man stood and left, along with his entourage.

"Hey, you need to tell me what's going on!" she shouted at his back. He ignored her.

The woman was last to leave. As she closed the double doors behind her, she smiled and winked again. Rust was alone once more. The strange city outside and her extreme confusion, her only company.

Vidyana

Vidyana hadn't needed her enhanced senses to tell that the young woman was terrified, confused, and angry in equal measure. Her powers just confirmed what was visible on the surface. Minute changes in eye movement, pulse, body temperature, perspiration. Her shade fed back to her the important observations. Some people tried to hide their emotions, her shade usually able to see right through them. She doubted Rustari Parra was anything other than what she appeared to be; a frightened young woman, separated from everything she had ever known.

This was the main reason Trelt had wanted Vidyana there. She was also an excellent deterrent to make sure the young woman tried nothing stupid. Rustari had seen what Vidyana was capable of, so was unlikely to try anything dumb. But anger and fear could make people act stupidly. Best to be prudent.

She found it intriguing that they had gone to all this trouble to extract one person and a handful of artefacts from an irrelevant backwater.

In the hallway, a man that Vidyana didn't recognise was talking to Lord Vellorson. Older. Immaculate. Dark bronze skin. Grey hair and beard. Clothes of a physician. His aspect covering his upper face and forehead. Nervous. The man looked at her as she approached.

"Vidyana," Trelt said, "this is Dr Relshanna. Dr Relshanna, this is Captain Vidyana Baylali."

They shook hands. The Dr's hand was sweaty, his grip light, quick to disengage.

"And there is no doubt?" Trelt asked, turning to the doctor.

The doctor looked nervously at Vidyana.

"What you say to me," Trelt said, "you can say openly to Captain Baylali."

"None, her bloodline is strong," Dr Relshanna said. "The tests confirm it. Very high levels of summoning purity. Exceptional, even. We can't pin it down any more than that at the moment."

"How soon can we be certain of her lineage?"

"A few days at most. We'll need to access the archives back in Ascension City. I will start some tests running in our laboratory. I will need to collect some more blood."

"Of course, just make sure that you keep myself and Captain Baylali informed of any developments," Trelt replied.

"Yes, sir," the doctor said, bowing slightly at them both.

"A Thaumaturge from the West Wind will perform some tests on the young woman over the next few days. Please assist where you can, Doctor," Trelt said. "Now, if you would excuse us."

The doctor nodded and headed off down the corridor. Once he was gone, Trelt turned to Vidyana.

"We will have to wait for the tests to come back, but I'm pretty sure that Rustari is the daughter of The Heretic herself. Yes, you're right to look surprised. The news is potentially explosive. If she fell into the hands of the heretics. Just the propaganda potential alone..."

"Well, that explains a few things," Vidyana said.

"Indeed. She's already shown latent ability to whisper with no training."

"That's impressive. And the artefacts?" Vidyana asked.

"The same. They are being examined on the West Wind, but I'm pretty sure they'll turn out to be Simona's. I recognise the pocket watch from... before. She used to have it on her all the time. Old family heirloom. I've examined it and it contains a memory-well. Gen-locked, as expected. Based on our intel, I'm pretty sure Rustari knows nothing about any of this. That old bastard Harrod didn't tell her a thing."

Vidyana nodded.

"I want you to keep a close eye on everything," Trelt said. "Quietly and covertly. Watch our guest from the shadows, and anyone who comes in to contact with her."

"Yes, sir. If I may ask; How long are we staying here?"

"A while. Maybe two weeks. There are other forces at play, Vidyana. It's safer to keep the young woman here at the moment until we are certain. If we take her back to the capital, a thousand little worms will watch from a thousand little corners. Despite our best efforts, the infection of heresy and rebellion has spread everywhere. Even to our great city."

"However, all this is only delaying the inevitable," he sighed. "Word will get out. I'm certain as the dry middle desert that a delegation from Peldaran is already on the way here to protest. Also, the whisper messages from Rustari that started this whole thing are sure not to remain secret for long. Word will get to the rebels, and the heretics that control them. And maybe other forces too."

That was odd, Vidyana thought. Other forces? Vidyana knew not to ask what those other forces were. If she needed to know, Trelt would tell her. Her faith in Trelt and their divine Emperor were absolute. They were the foundation of her being. They would tell her if she needed to know.

Chapter 11

Behold the deep, and all the wonders within.
    He is their protector.
    He guides the ceph as he guides us.

Book of Union, chapter 4, verse 2

Rust

Rust had been in the palace for two days. She'd spent the time moping around the rooms, thumbing through books in the library, and looking out of the windows.

The view from the window had been a distraction for the first day. Every sight and sound, a novelty. The city itself. The vessels going back and forth across the bay. The smoke from the distant industrial areas. The smell of the ocean.

By the end of the second day, the novelty had waned.

She was constantly hounded by multiple fears. She still didn't know why she had been captured, beyond what Trelt had said. What she was doing here? What did any of this all have to do with Uncle, or the strange objects they'd found? Why was any of it important?

Each evening, just after the guards had brought her food, the man Trelt visited. He was always polite and asked how she was settling in. He often apologised about the situation.

Rust didn't like the man, his politeness seemed too well rehearsed. His words were slippery like a basilisk, squirming and slithering. She didn't trust a word that came out of his mouth. She held him responsible for Uncle's death, despite what he said. If they hadn't invaded, Uncle would still be alive. It was as simple as that.

Her worries went beyond that. She'd always been in search of adventure; always striving to make life in Hammington's Rest more exciting. If she hadn't been so keen to look for adventure, she and Indiril wouldn't have followed Uncle. She would have never found the objects. Would have never —

No, best not to think about it.

Inevitably, the conversations with Trelt always turned to

the same things. What did Rust know about her uncle? What did she know about the ruins where the artefacts had been stored? How did she find out about them? Rust tried her best to obfuscate her answers, but Trelt saw through her responses like someone unpicking a tangled ball of wool. Gradually, strand by strand, Rust's answers unravelled.

It was obvious that Trelt thought Rust, and the objects, were important. Worth going to war for. It was ridiculous. Trelt seemed mostly interested in the objects. Artefacts, he called them. He held a special fascination for the watch. He quizzed Rust repeatedly on what she had seen when she touched it. Rust only gave the vaguest of answers. She hoped it would be enough to make him stop repeating the same questions. It didn't.

"Alright, Rust," Trelt said. "We'll leave it at that for now. Get some rest and we'll pick this up tomorrow. In the meantime, is there anything I can get you?"

"First, you can tell me what in Sindar's fucking name this is all about?"

"I've already told you as much as I can. For now. In time —"

"Bollocks! You haven't told me anything. All you give is vague wormy answers. Why are those fucking objects so damned important? What are they? Why did Uncle have them, and why did he die to protect them?"

Trelt sighed.

"I know you don't trust me," he'd said. "That's perfectly understandable. I wouldn't if the roles were reversed. But in time I think you will come to realise that I only have everyone's best interests in mind. In time, you will have all the answers you need."

Welyne

Welyne Drellmore sat in the study by the window. She leafed through a book she'd purchased in the city yesterday, unable to concentrate on the contents properly.

The view from the window reminded her of Drellgarh, lessening the homesickness that had crept up over the last few days. Just a little. She sighed. Sentimental nonsense she could do without.

It was pleasant to just sit and read. To allow a small part of her to relax. There had been the normal social gatherings since they'd arrived. The things she'd been expected to do. She'd expertly faked her way through them, as she always did. Throughout it, the ball of tension in her gut had grown. A nervousness she'd tried hard to hide from her family. Bartain seemed oblivious. Poor Bartain, she thought, he'd just been happy to have them all here.

Sybelle, on the other hand, looked at her with growing suspicion.

The airship had returned a few days ago. Since then, she'd kept up on the gossip within the immaculate community. Apart from some rumours that a delegation of diplomats from Ascension City had arrived in the airship, and that security around the palace had been stepped up, the local immaculate population knew little else. Pretty useless. Mindless sheep, all of them. Part of the Hegemon machine.

Two days ago, she'd walked as close to the palace as she dared. She'd sat down on a bench and watched. The airship that she had since discovered was the West Wind, hadn't moved since. The Aurumill's flagship. Using a small pair of field glasses, she'd observed several troops wearing Aurumill uniforms, Alexi's not-so-secret elite troops. There were also lots of Jurament too, as well as regular human Hegemon soldiers.

The technology used in the field glasses was on the 'very' forbidden list. Like any item that would allow the world's societies to increase technologically. The Hegemony kept everyone at a rigidly enforced level of technological advancement. Anything to do with electromagnetism was strictly off limits. To everyone but themselves, of course. There were things that were allowed and things that weren't. All part of Alexi's grand plan. Almost entirely nonsense.

She had been considering more direct action, but getting caught would mean death. She was loyal to the cause, but being reckless put her sleeper-cell and family at unnecessary risk.

The world had become more complicated since the early days following Simona. Welyne had been young and idealistic. They would have followed Simona into fire and had literally done so on more than one occasion.

But Simona had been killed by the Hegemony. By Trelt! Most of Simona's loyal followers, captured or killed. Those that survived had fled into hiding, dissolving into the populace to become the Sleepers. Only their rigidly enforced cell structure stopped them from all being discovered. In the years since, they'd been watchful for a time when they might still fulfil Simona's dream. Bring down the Hegemon and return the races to their former glory amongst the stars. Without the needless mass bloodshed that following Liberation would cause. Hard to believe they had all been part of the same group once.

Long years had passed.

She had married. Had children. Her eldest son had become part of their movement. The thought that he may have died as a result would always haunt her. A war raged inside her, on one side, the cause, on the other, family. Logically, the Sleeper cause outweighed the safety of her family. But over time, little by little, the cause had fallen into the shadow of her family. Simona was long dead, and with her maybe the Sleepers' dream. She would always be loyal to Simona's memory, but it was all so long ago. The dream had faded, like the sun bleached photograph of her brother Tomlas by the window back home.

Then Zarl had told her that Simona might have had a child, and she might be about to fall into the hands of the Hegemon. Since then, there had been a constant knot of tension in her guts. Yesterday, that little knot had grown to consume her entire stomach. She'd received a note from Zarl. It was short, simply stating that he had arrived in Lerins. It included a coded message he was contacting a local Sleeper.

She didn't know who the local contact was, but that was how the Sleepers worked. A distributed network, they called it. Contact maintained with only a few individuals. Nobody knew the entire story. It lowered the risk that came with capture and interrogation. Of course, some people had more connections than others. Zarl, being one of them.

Welyne glanced across at Sybelle who sat by the window reading. Her brow creased in concentration. Welyne had noticed a change in Syb the last few days. Unusually happy and distracted. Welyne had thought their move to Lerins would be difficult for Syb, but oddly, she'd seemed happier than she'd been for ages.

There was a knock at the door.

"Come in," Welyne said.

The house butler entered. A local fair skinned human man called Relbert. Or was it Relgor? She kept getting his named muddled up. A sign that she was stressed and distracted. She needed to sharpen up. Details.

"What is it Relbert?"

"A courier just delivered this letter. It is addressed to you, my lady."

Her pulse quickened.

"Thank you. Please leave it on the table."

"Yes, my Lady," he said. No, maybe it was Relgor. He placed the letter on the table and left.

Syb glanced at the letter for a few moments, before returning to her studies. Welyne tried not to seem too eager to open it. Just an inconsequential note. Welyne reached and opened the letter. It was short and cryptic.

W,

Our package has arrived in Lerins. Let's meet.

Z

She placed the letter in her pocket to stop Sybelle snooping. A few minutes later, she rang the bell. When Relgor arrived, she asked him to organise a carriage to take her into the city. She explained to Syb that she needed to go to meet one of her new neighbours. Syb nodded without looking up.

The Lerins Business Exchange was a place for commerce. A building where high-ranking business folk of all types could meet. There were various private rooms that could be hired for meetings, along with several open rooms with seating. Access to immaculate, normal humans, t'kelikt, and even ceph was by strict membership only. On this occasion, she went under a false identity.

The aspect she wore was still the blue of House Drellmore, but it lacked the motifs that marked her out as a member of the ruling family. Today she was simply Mardria Alyanarra, travelling executive for a Drellgarh textiles firm.

The place was busy, filled with immaculate, normal humans, and even a couple of tree-folk. In one corner, a group of t'kelikt were talking to a group of immaculate. There were even facilities for ceph matriarchs to attend in their conveyances, but none were present today.

She went to an empty cubicle and ordered a green tea.

After a few minutes, Zarl joined her and they headed towards a private meeting room that Zarl had booked. They discussed the price of fabrics and other mundane things. Once they were in the meeting room and the door was locked, Zarl placed a small metal disk on the table. He pressed a small button in its centre. There was a brief fizzing sensation in her ears. He turned to embrace Welyne.

"Now we can talk. It's good to see you again, Wel! How's the family?" he said, smiling.

"Skip the spider shit, Zarl," she said. "These last few days have wound my guts into a knot. What's the news? I assume you have some?"

Zarl poured himself a drink of tan brandy from a decanter. He poured another glass and offered it to her. She took it.

"Yeah, my contact confirms that the girl is being held in the palace. Name of Rustari Parra, and as suspected, she was completely unknown to the Hegemony until just over a week ago.

"Also," he continued, "our old 'friend' Trelt Vellorson oversaw the extraction of the girl from Peldaran. Went in with the West Wind. Fired up a whole political shit storm. There is at least one other Aurumill operative there as well. Powerful one, by the sounds of it. A woman. Blessed with quite a few 'gifts' from the Emperor. Might be Trelt's pet, the Baylali's girl. Need to watch out for her."

"Shit. Anything else?" Welyne asked.

"My contact says Trelt and his cronies have also recovered several artefacts, along with the girl Rustari."

That didn't sound good. Any devices of interest to the Hegemony might be dangerous.

"What artefacts?" she asked slowly.

"My contact doesn't know. From the description, one of them is almost certainly going to be Simona's seer web. Makes sense. The others might be anything. They were small, though. A memory-well maybe. As we suspected. Maybe her watch."

That would be bad. A memory-well was very forbidden, capable of recording memories for accurate recall. They were usually tuned to the original user's blood. Gen-locked, they called it. Close blood relatives were often also able to read them. If it was Simona's, and the girl was her daughter, then it was likely only she could read it. A lot of 'ifs' yes, but she didn't like where they pointed.

"There have been several blood tests," Zarl continued. "They confirm she has a very high summoning level. Level nine, at least. My contact says he hasn't seen a level higher. Ever."

Top immaculate summoners scored around a seven. They were rare. Most summoners in the Thaumaturgy scored around a four or five. The immaculate summoning bloodline had diminished in the long centuries after the collapse, mingling with the rest of the human population. Until Alexi had been awoken from his long dream and got things back under control.

The overwhelmingly vast majority of the immaculate population scored around a one or two. Someone scoring above seven would be exceptional. One in a million. Possibly even rarer.

Typically, only Liberation leaders had scores that high, or those that had begun in the heresy and turned away from it. People like Trelt. There was very little doubt in Welyne's mind that at the very least, this young woman, Rust, was the child of a Liberation leader. One that also had access to Simona's long-lost seer web.

Welyne worried how long this could all be kept a secret. If Zarl and the Sleepers knew, then it wouldn't be long before Liberation found out. Then things could turn nasty. Welyne had the feeling that pieces of a giant puzzle, unfinished for years, were moving once more. Slotting in to place and forming unknown and terrifying shapes.

"How does your contact know all this?"

"He works in the palace. Beyond that, I can't really say at this stage. You know how it is."

"Fair enough."

"That's not the end of it," he said. "Before they took the girl from the village, there was an altercation between Trelt and another man. The man detonated a hollow-shell. Injured Trelt and killed himself in the process. It was Harrod."

"Harrod! Are you sure?"

"Yep, afraid so. Trelt addressed him by name."

"Fuck! Then the girl has to be Simona's daughter. Nothing else makes any sense."

"That's my feeling too."

"I always thought that Harrod died when Simona did. Do you think Harrod's been hiding this whole time?"

"That would be my guess. We always wondered what happened to him after the attack. I guess he fled with the girl and got as far away from everyone as he could."

"But if they were hidden, why did the girl contact the Hegemony?"

"All I have is a whole shit-cart load of unknowns. We know nothing of what went on in that village, Wel. We don't know how much the girl knows. What we do know is that she may be the key Alexi needs. They didn't go to all this trouble just for a few weekend laughs. We can't leave her with the Hegemony."

"How do we get this Rustari out?"

"I don't know, Wel," Zarl said. "They will move her at some point. Take her somewhere hidden and remote. Then it's all over."

"It will also be over if Liberation gets her," Welyne said. "When they find out, and they will, they'll make their own grab for her. Can you imagine what might come out? Things Simona tried so hard to keep from them after the split."

Zarl sighed. He looked thoughtful for a moment before refilling his brandy. He downed the fresh glass in one gulp.

"Maybe we are thinking about it all wrong, though," he said.

"How so?"

"Maybe it would be better for everyone if we just killed the girl."

Welyne travelled back to the house in silence. Her mind kept going back to Zarl's comment about the young woman. That it would be better for everyone if she was dead. Some secrets were better off unknown.

But it was not some random stranger Zarl was talking about. The girl was almost certainly Simona's daughter. If she died, then the hope of finishing what Simona had started might finally die as well. They couldn't be sure who the girl's father was, but Welyne was almost certain who it was. Her heart skipped at the thought.

No, she would try to rescue Simona's daughter if she could. She was also almost certainly family. The daughter of Simona, and Welyne's long-dead brother Tomlas.

Rust

Trelt sat across the table from Rust. His skin, slightly less transparent each day. Still, Rust could still make out squeamish details underneath. He scratched the skin on his scalp and hand frequently.

"Let me ask you, do you have a lee back in your village?" Trelt asked. It was the latest in a long line of dumb questions.

He took a bite from a sausage. Rust had to admit, the food looked, and smelled, delicious. She didn't touch hers. Trelt said he had wanted to talk over supper.

"What has that got to do with anything?" she replied.

She continued to stare out of the window at the darkening sky. Despite her best efforts, her stomach rumbled at the smell of the herb sausages, mashed potato, fresh vegetables, and sauce.

"I assume yes then," Trelt replied. "You'll know that it separates your village from the feral. The wild lands beyond. That without it, your village would soon fall back to feral."

She didn't see the point he was trying to make.

"Mmmm, this sausage is really fantastic," Trelt said. "Best on Seendar, they say. You sure you don't want any?"

"I'm fine, thanks."

"As you wish," he said, swallowing down the sausage with a gulp of wine. "We are like the lee, Rustari. The Hegemon. We protect the races from forces that would seek to bring us down. Return the world to chaos. All of us. Not just the Hegemon, but everyone, including the t'kelikt and ceph. The Hegemon is an eternal buffer that separates us all from chaos. A force of balance. Without the Hegemony, and our laws, everything would soon be lost. Like it almost was before."

"The objects you found are dangerous to that balance," he continued. "Their contents falling into the wrong hands could be potentially disastrous. It could bring back Nemesis on us all."

"More shit," Rust snorted. "Nemesis is a joke. It's just a tale. Like the monster under the bed. Something to keep the children in check."

Trelt finished his latest mouthful with another gulp of wine.

"No, it's real," Trelt said, looking out of the window. "I've seen it. I know it is real. Long ago, we accomplished such great things. Marvels! Then Nemesis came and destroyed it all with little more effort than we take to kill a fly. If it returned, it would destroy those of us that remain. The Hegemon protects the entire world by maintaining stability. What we do, we do for everyone, including Peldaran."

It all sounded ridiculous. Some of the wilder divinist tales Indiril told her sounded more plausible.

"You expect me to believe that? I've seen the magic you have. The things you control. You just want to keep all the power for yourselves. The old magic. Easier to keep us all in check if you are the only ones to control it all.

"That's actually very true," he said. "It is easier for us to maintain control like this. But it is a balance. I would imagine you've got access to an apothecary? The medicines and remedies they sell. The methods. The ingredients. The knowledge! Mix this and that in the right way to get anaesthetic, antibiotics, and everything else. It's all in the guild books. The Guild of Alchemy saves more lives through the apothecary each year than you can count. We are the hidden gears that keep the world going."

Trelt tucked into the last of the meal. Rust's plate remained stubbornly untouched.

"What do you do it all for, then? Why keep it all a

secret?"

"To protect us! To stop Nemesis from noticing us and returning. It's the old magic that attracts it. By keeping things stable, we ensure we don't go beyond a certain point. New ideas and changes might seem innocent. A minor change here. A small advance there. More power. More efficient. A new labour-saving device. Better transport. It all leads in one direction. It's in our nature, Rustari. Hubris. As inevitable as the great feral sporing."

"Still sounds like crap to me," Rust replied.

Trelt wiped his face with a napkin and stood.

"That's enough for now," he said. "We always end up arguing and it's not something I want. I'll leave you in peace. Please try the sausages. They are fantastic."

With that, he turned and left.

Rust waited until she heard the click of the lock before turning to the meal.

The morning after, a couple of doctors had taken some more blood samples. One was older with a white beard, the other younger with a red scar on his cheek. The older one looked friendly, whilst the younger one scowled like he had just drank warm feldercow piss. His breath smelled, too. Garlic. She didn't like him.

Both spoke in the same odd accent that all the immaculate she'd seen did. It sounded harsher to her than Trelt's.

Later in the morning, the older doctor had returned, accompanied by a woman wearing black robes. Her aspect was white and covered her full face. The mask's forehead was decorated with a golden embossed triangle. She also wore a black hood and white gloves. It was unnerving looking at her. Apart from her eyes and black hair, nothing of her face was visible.

She had arranged some ornate wooden boxes on the table in front of Rust. Rust was asked to put her hand on top of one and describe any sensations that she had. At first she'd felt nothing, but then there was an odd cold sensation that crept up her arm. She tried to keep the sensations a secret from the woman. There was no point in outright disobedience, but Sindar's Four Arms she would not make it easy.

It was pointless anyway. The sensation had surprised her. She'd obviously given something away in her expression because the woman nodded and asked Rust to withdraw her hand.

Then Rust was asked to put on several rings and bracelets. All had gems that had glowed softly when she had put them on.

Towards the end, Rust noticed that the woman's hands were trembling a little. Whatever she had gleaned from Rust's reaction had either frightened or excited her. Neither seemed like good news.

Then they had left, and Rust was alone again.

Rust spent the rest of the afternoon looking for ways to get out of the rooms. Then she would escape the palace, get out of the city and back to Peldaran. All the windows were locked. She could break one, but someone would surely hear the glass.

The balcony doors were the same. They led onto a tiny balcony that went nowhere. Even if she broke one, then what? The rooms were at least three stories up. The outer palace wall was at least a hundred metres away. The ground below them a wide expanse of courtyards patrolled by soldiers. No, she would not get out that way.

The door was hopeless. It was large, heavy, and secured with a huge iron lock. She'd spent sometime trying to jimmy the lock open with a knife. After an hour, all she had done was scratch the door and bend the knife. She'd even tried the chimney, but that was blocked a few hands up by a hefty-looking metal grate. Sunlight filtered down from above. It wasn't far up, so Rust surmised they were close to the roof.

All she had to do was figure out a way to get up there.

Sybelle

Sybelle held the crumpled note in her fist.

For the last two hours she had paced round the room, either re-reading the cryptic note, or muttering under her breath. She knew Mother had been up to something. Knew it! Mother had been distracted since they'd arrived. When she thought about it, Mother had been acting weirdly before they left. Messages delivered. Odd trips out. Secret meetings.

Another note had come this morning. Sybelle had been lost in her own thoughts about Kathnell. The way her muscles had felt under her clothes. The smell of oil and sweat. She had thought of little else since their kiss on the boat.

The note sat unopened on the table for a few minutes. The longer it sat, the more it burned her to know what was inside. Was Mother having an affair? All the secret messages. Did her lover live in Lerins? Was their entire trip a ruse to continue the liaison?

Finally, Mother had picked up the note and read it. She asked for a carriage to take her into town and came up with a nonsensical reason about meeting a neighbour.

Sybelle watched her go from the window. As she boarded the coach, a little slip of white paper had fluttered from Mother's pocket and fell into the street.

The coach pulled away and receded down the street. Sybelle ran down the stairs, into the street, and picked up the note before the breeze took it away. Only then did she realise she wasn't wearing her aspect. If she was seen in the street without it, word would surely get back to Mother. Too late now. Face covered with her arm, she hurried back inside.

W,

Our package has arrived in Lerins. Meet me today.

Z

What in the saints' holy names did that mean? She could only assume that W was her mother. Who was Z? Must be her lover, she thought. How could she?

Then it was true. Mother was having an affair. All those years of lecturing on how to be a model immaculate citizen. Correct etiquette. The teachings of the Emperor. The church. She had been feeling guilty about keeping her friendship with Kathnell a secret. She'd considered confiding in Mother, but had concluded it would only get them both into trouble. All the time, Mother had her own dirty little secrets. How long had this been going on? Weeks? Months?

Poor father. Enough was enough!

A coach pulled up outside. Mother had returned.

She'd been gone for over four hours. What was she going to say? A thousand scenarios had played out in Sybelle's mind over and over. She would confront Mother, who would reveal everything. That she'd never been in love with her father. It was all a lie. That she'd been trying to get a divorce from her father.

Maybe, it was all a misunderstanding. The odd letters and notes easily explained. Mother would allay her fears and they would laugh together.

In other scenarios, Mother would deny everything and punish Sybelle for prying into her affairs. A thousand scenarios. Most of them ended badly; family in ruins.

Mother was on the stairs. Sybelle heard the telltale noise of shoes on stone steps. The creak of the upper landing. This was it, Sybelle thought. Sybelle stood by the desk, fist clenched in to a tight ball around the crushed note.

Mother walked in.

"Hello Syb, sorry I'm late, but the traffic back from the city was terrible."

Mother stopped. She must have seen the fire in Sybelle's eyes.

"What's wrong Syb?"

Sybelle couldn't find the words. She tried to say something, but nothing came out. She started crying. Mother's expression turned to concern as she approached Sybelle. Sybelle backed away. As Mother drew nearer, Sybelle threw the scrunched note at her. It bounced off Mother's dress and fell to the floor.

Mother went to pick it, but stopped. Her hand moved to her pocket, searching for a note that was no longer there. Mother straightened, leaving the note where it was.

"I'm sorry Syb. I tried to keep this all from you for as long as possible."

Here it came, Sybelle thought. The lies. The excuses.

"Keep what from me?" Sybelle spat out.

"I was always going to tell you," her mother said, "but before I continue, you must promise me that Father must not know about any of this."

"Why should I keep your sordid gutter affair from Father?"

"My affair? I wish it was that simple. I'm not having an affair, Syb."

"You must be! If not, then what?"

"First, you MUST promise me you will mention none of this to Father. I made your brother promise the same thing."

What in the holy saints did Belar have to do with any of this?

"Belar? What are you talking about?" Sybelle stammered.

"Promise me Syb," Mother said.

Her voice was forceful, with an edge of cold metal that Sybelle wasn't used to hearing. Mother wore an expression Sybelle had never seen. Like it was the first time she had seen the real Welyne Drellmore. Almost as though the woman who had been her mother was no more real than the aspect she wore.

"I... I promise," Sybelle replied.

"I can't tell you everything today, Syb. Soon, when the time is right, I will tell you everything. I have always tried to keep you safe. Today, though, you will have to be patient."

"You can't leave it at that," Sybelle said.

"I must! And you will wait!" her mother shot back. "I'm sorry, Sybelle, but you have to trust me with this. I will tell you everything. Soon. Until then, you must tell no one about this. Anyone. Especially not Father. It's more important than you realise. I mean it Sybelle. Anyone."

"Alright."

Mother's face softened. The woman Sybelle had always known returned. The caring, nurturing woman that had always been there for them. The person who always put everyone else first. A caring mother. A loving spouse.

"Now," Mother said, "shall we enquire what is being served for dinner?"

The transition to normality left Sybelle confused. Sybelle nodded, unable to think of anything else to say.

Later that night, Sybelle lay awake, unable to sleep. The conversation with her mother went round and round in her mind. Of all the scenarios she had imaged, there was nothing like this strange non-answer. She remained angry, but the look on Mother's face had scared her. Faced with the note, her mother had changed into someone Sybelle didn't recognise. Someone cold, stern, and ruthless.

She hadn't tried to deny the note or explain it away. Instead, she had acknowledged it, whilst promising that everything would be revealed soon, as if she had always planned on telling her. The comment about her brother had thrown her. How was Belar involved, and did it somehow have something to do with his death?

Sybelle wished she was with Kathnell now. Just to be with her again. To get away from these thoughts. But Kathnell was away and wouldn't be back for a few more

days. Sybelle couldn't wait to see her again.

Rust

Rust stared down at hands that were not her own. An older woman's. Longer fingers. Dark skin; the same as her own. Simultaneously hers, and someone else's.

Like before, the vision seemed almost dreamlike. Focus on any detail and it would blur out like a half forgotten memory. The hands moved along the surface of an impossibly smooth, curved wall. Its surface was white and warm to the touch. She felt a fondness for the thing that was not her own. Like a treasured belonging.

The woman-that-was-not-her stepped back. The thing was like a giant egg, at least six metres long. It sat in the middle of an enormous cavern. A feeling that the thing was asleep, just waiting for something. A command was all it would take. She felt a deep sadness. The woman-that-was-not-her knew this was the last time she would see it for a while. Possibly ever. That it would sit here abandoned until she returned.

Rust had experienced the same vision before, but this time it was much more vivid, overlaid with other senses. There were sounds of water dripping into a nearby pool. The damp, musky smell of the cavern. The warmth of the egg. A breeze brushed against her. The name "cloud-maker" rose from somewhere deep within her mind. She still had absolutely no idea what any of it meant.

The vision cleared. Rust was herself again, back in her room at the palace. Her hands still wrapped around the pocket watch.

Trelt sat across from her. He smiled softly.

"Any luck Rust? Any more detail this time?" he asked.

"Nothing really," she said, setting the watch down on the

table. "Same as last time."

It was a lie, of course. This was the second time that Trelt had asked her to try. She knew she had no proper choice in the matter. She tried to resist the visions, but as soon as she gripped the watch, the visions played through her like she was its instrument. Each time, she saw variations of the same scenes. Each time was a little clearer than the last.

There was the vision where she appeared to be suspended in a black void. Countless stars in all directions. Like the clearest night imaginable. She seemed to move impossibly fast towards what looked like the Earth. How was that even possible? This time, she had seen a little more detail. They didn't seem to head for the Earth itself, but a smaller white circle nearby. Was it the moon Chandra?

Another vision of running through Ascension City. Rain pouring down. The White Citadel in the background. Thunder that was not thunder. Lightning, that was not lightning. A younger version of Uncle. Terrible fear. She knew they had been attacking something. Something had gone terribly wrong with the plan. They were running for their lives. If this truly was a memory, then Uncle had been involved in the attack.

There had been another vision this time. One she hadn't seen before. In it, she was overlooking a campsite in the wilderness, a baby cradled in her arms. She felt a love that was bottomless. Terrifying and absolute.

"You should go inside; The nights are notoriously cold in the desert," another woman's voice said from behind her. Footsteps approaching.

"It's fine Valtha."

"I am monitoring a sand storm approaching from the south-east. A bad one. Probabilistic models predict it will be…"

"You sound like my mother," the woman laughed.

The woman-that-was-not-her turned slowly towards the approaching figure, but the vision faded before she could see details. There was something odd about the other figure. She was completely and flawlessly light grey. Her facial features were out of focus. No, not out of focus, but smoothed out. Missing details. Like a sketch of a person. That was all she had seen.

Of course, she hadn't told Trelt about that one last time either. She'd had to tell her captors something, so she'd sketched out the barest details of the other visions. Trelt had seemed interested in the vision about the giant egg and quizzed her repeatedly on it.

Trelt took the watch and placed it in the metal box from which he had taken it.

"Nothing more about the... egg?"

"No, nothing," Rust said, shaking her head. She would drink week old nax piss before she told him any more.

Trelt insisted the visions were actual memories, recorded somehow inside the pocket watch. It sounded fantastical. Then again, the Hegemony used magic way beyond her understanding. Trelt said the memories belonged to an old friend of his. That they might contain important information. Trelt dismissed her questions about who the memories belonged to. Why couldn't Trelt or someone else read the memories? Why did they need her? What made her so special? She'd tried to ask, but Trelt's answers were always vague and patronising. She would find out soon, he said. It was all for the greater good. Blah, blah, blah.

Rust still had a hard time believing memories could be stored anywhere, let alone in some old trinket.

She'd tried asking the few others that came to her room. The guards. The doctors. But they wouldn't speak to her more than they had to. Only fucking Trelt said over two words.

What she was sure about, however, was that these visions were of interest to the Hegemon. Buried in them was something important. It gave her leverage. She had something they wanted. Trelt tried to hide his excitement when she spoke, but she could tell he was hanging off her every word. Well, fuck him, she thought.

She sat back silently and smiled.

Trelt sighed, locking the metal box with a key. He passed it to a black-robed woman sitting to his left. The same woman that had made her wear the bracelets and rings the day before. The woman shook her head minutely. She knew Rust was lying. She had been staring at Rust the whole time she had been touching the watch. Studying her in minute detail, like someone studying a feldercow at the cattle market. Trelt turned back to Rust.

"You know, Rustari, it really is in everyone's best interest that you cooperate with us."

He paused and looked out of the window for a second or two.

"But... I think we are taking things too fast. We should give you more time to understand what is at stake. I really want to know what you see in the visions and I'm sincerely hoping that you feel confident to tell us... of your own volition. It would be best for everyone."

He nodded to the woman. They rose and headed for the door.

"One day, you'll understand that all this is for a reason."

He stood.

"Now," he said, "it is time you rested. We shall pick this up again tomorrow."

After they left, Rust thought about what Trelt had said. What did he say, 'of your own volition'?. Rust wasn't sure what Trelt meant by that. Was it a threat? She remembered back to when she had put the other device on, back at the secret cache in the ruin. She had connected to something, or someone, that had compelled her to tell the truth. To reveal where she was. She was certain that was what had led them to Hammington's Rest. When that other mind had wrenched the information from her, it had felt like a violation. It was not something she wished to have repeated. No, the more she thought about it, the more she was sure that Trelt's comment was indeed a threat. Tell us what you see, or we will find out, anyway.

She had to find a way out of this place. Then a way to get back to Peldaran and Hammington's Rest.

She fell asleep thinking about her village. The hill with its single ancient oak tree. All the times she and Indiril had climbed it since they had been children. Before all of this. She wept silently and fell asleep thinking of home.

The chimney filled her dreams.

Chapter 12

The Guild of Steam is one of the more powerful guilds. It is influential in almost all areas of immaculate life. The guild masters, members, and apprentices are key members of society. Their employment is vital to the Hegemony. Although the void-stones themselves have to be activated by an immaculate summoner, the systems themselves are maintained by human engineers under the jurisdiction of the Guild of Steam.

As the technology that drives the steam engines requires technical skill, an aptitude for engineering is essential. However, this comes with its own dangers. The very engineering skills themselves could easily evolve into methods and uses forbidden by the Books of Prescription. Members of the Guild are often scrutinised by immaculate guild masters who look for transgressions against the Great Covenant.

Notes on the Guild of Steam, Liberation field notes circa 665 SC

Kathnell

Kathnell threw herself behind the cover of a wooden crate. Her hands shook, and her heart pounded. In the darkness, she could see the shadows of other Liberation rebels crouched around her.

She felt like an impostor. The more time went on, the more she wondered why she was even here. Surely, this was madness.

Two decks below, waves splashed against the wooden sides of the ship. The deck itself was slick with rainwater. The storm, now passed, still flashed with lightning. Thunder rolled in seconds later. Her hair, still dripping wet.

Remember that you are here to do a job, she thought. Concentrate on what you have been told to do. Get to the steam generator. Help to rig it. Then get the thousand hells off before it blew. Maybe she wouldn't have to actually do anything. She was just the backup. The rebels had their own engineer. A man named Ilor. He crouched next to her, his face grey in the moonlight. Stick close to him, they'd said. Follow his lead. He knows what he's doing. The problem was, he looked just as terrified as she felt. Eyes wide. Hands shaking. He'd hardly spoken to her. Not a great boost to her confidence.

There were eight people in the raiding party. Split into two teams. Chander and Ilor were on her team, along with a stern woman she didn't know. She had a nasty scar down her left arm and two of her fingers ended at the first knuckle. Chander and the woman were both armed with weapons. Not crossbows, but guns! Actual fucking guns! Kathnell had heard of the things, but had never seen one. Contraband of the highest order. Beyond illegal. Not even the Hegemon used them. Forbidden by every holy law.

What in the thousand hells was she doing here? Too late now. You're in this up to your tits, she thought.

The church forbade any advancement of technology because they said it would bring back Nemesis; the doom that had supposedly nearly destroyed humanity long in the past. The Liberation said that it was just another method of control. Myths from a forgotten age used to terrify the locals. Keep them in check.

Corric always shut her down for even mentioning making slight adjustments to the guild books. These ugly looking things were way beyond that. Long metal pipes with a wooden stock you could rest into your armpit for support. They smelt of oil. She tried to work out how they functioned from the glimpses she got. Complex and technical. She yearned to take one apart.

They had not been expecting any trouble. Scouts said the ship was unlikely to be guarded. Typically, they had been wrong. Instead, they had found the dockside and deck being patrolled by Hegemon soldiers. They were normal humans, but they couldn't rule out immaculate, or worse, summoners.

They'd had to kill one soldier on the way in. His body dragged quickly out of sight. It was the first time Kathnell had ever seen anyone killed. Strangled with a length of wire. It was so matter of fact. Cold and clean. It made her want to be sick. She tried not to think about the terror in the man's eyes as he'd died.

The two teams had split up. One on each side of the upper deck. They'd got on board with no further problems and were currently crouching behind the crates, waiting for another Hegemon solider to go past.

Yesterday, this had seemed like a much better idea than it did now.

The ship had arrived from Drellmore that afternoon. The Ba'reen Tarat. It carried some kind of secret cargo bound for a distant place called Taldor-Ire. An old Maleth site, recently captured by Bennel forces, shunned and long forgotten by the locals. She'd never heard of it.

Although she'd tried to follow the mission briefing, she didn't get the full gist of it. Apparently, the Hegemon were building something in the mountains. They didn't say what, but it had got the Liberation powers all fired up. The Hegemon's recent proxy war against Bennel's neighbours was apparently really just about them getting control of this Taldor-Ire. She did not know why. She didn't think her fellow Liberation rebels really knew either. Word had come that they must disrupt the construction of whatever-it-was. They'd got word of this shipment and had prepared this raid.

So here she was, crouched behind some crates, soaked to her arse, wiping water from her eyes.

Four days ago, she was ignorant of all of this. Her only worries were about her job and Sybelle. Then she had met Chander in the pub and he had offered her a job. They'd told her engineers were always sought after in the Liberation. They were always looking for more. Why did they need more? What was wrong with the current ones? Probably best not to think about it.

Over several drinks, much had been revealed. By the end, her head had been spinning. How much from the drink and how much from the information, she wasn't sure.

Apparently, Corric used to be part of Liberation. She'd known her father and Corric had been friends, but didn't know they'd both been in the rebellion. That came as a total fucking shock. Corric had always talked about the Liberation negatively. Not outwardly hostile, but definitely not warm and friendly. He had been a Liberation fighter, and a good one too. He'd left the Liberation after her father had died.

Her father had been killed by the Hegemony. That much was true. Everything else she'd been told was feldershit. He'd been a local Liberation commander and had been killed when their group had tried to derail a Hegemon void-train. They'd walked into a trap. Pelter, Corric, Chander and the others had only escaped because her father had sacrificed himself. Corric had wanted to go back and help her father, but the others had knocked him out and made their escape. They said that Corric would have got them all killed. Would have made her father's sacrifice meaningless.

It explained why Corric had always been there for her and her mother. Why he had taken her on as an apprentice. It also explained his outburst about the Liberation leaflet. He wanted nothing to do with them anymore. Chander said it wouldn't be wise to discuss her recruitment with Corric.

Her father had died a hero for the rebellion. A martyr. She'd always been angry at the Hegemony for killing him. That remained, but now pride burned alongside it.

Now, years later, the Liberation was looking to recruit her. Pelter had vouched for her and said they'd been keeping tabs on her for a while. They'd seen her altercation with the drunkard the other night and could see she could handle herself. That had set off a moment of panic. If they saw the fight, then maybe they knew about Sybelle? If they had, surely they would have mentioned it, wouldn't they?

It was pointless to worry. This was too good an opportunity to miss. This was a chance to make a difference, to seek vengeance for the death of her father. Something he would be proud of. To the thousand hells with the Hegemony.

The ship was a beast, several decks high. It was largely wooden, powered by a void-stone boiler. That meant they might have a summoner on the crew.

Her team was huddled behind some wooden crates that littered the flat upper deck. The distant lightning flashes gave occasional glimpses of the rest. The centre of the deck was filled with several large objects, each ten metres long at least. All covered by dark tarps hiding what was underneath. The cargo they had been sent to destroy. The other rebel group was out of sight somewhere on the other side of the deck.

They waited for a guard to pass. Kathnell could hear the guard's footsteps approach. As he passed, the rebel woman with the scar fell quietly into step behind him. They both disappeared around a corner. The woman reappeared a few seconds later, wiping blood from her hands.

Chander turned to Kathnell and the engineer Ilor. He motioned for them to remain. Chander rose and headed after the woman. He was gone for a few minutes before returning. He motioned for them to follow. They went through a door and down a couple of decks, finally emerging into the engine room. The place was lit by oil lanterns. They passed another couple of bodies on the way. One of them was human, the other a t'kelikt soldier. The thing had vicious looking blades attached to several of its long spider-like limbs. A couple of its limbs still twitched. Kathnell wasn't sure if it was dead or just unconscious. Anyway, it was pointless. If their plan was successful, anyone left on the ship would be fish fodder.

At one end of the engine room, were a couple of giant metal hatches in the floor. They were probably access points to a flooded ceph chamber below. Ships of this size sometimes had one or two ceph on the crew. The hatches were closed. Good, it probably meant there weren't any ceph on board.

The void-stone boiler itself lay at the far end of the chamber. A metal sphere about four metres across. An array of pipes, hoses, and gauges festooned its surface. The metal heart of the ship. Pipes snaked away to various tanks, pumps, and other vessels. The main pipes snaked into the next chamber where the pistons that powered the main screws lay. Red pipes for hot outbound water. Blue pipes, return circuit. To the untrained eye, it would be bewildering. To Kathnell, it was familiar. Logical.

"Alright Ilor," Chander said, "tell me if this thing is awake. If so, start your preparations. If it isn't awake, then we move to the backup plan."

The man nodded and went to a bank of gauges in front of the sphere. Kathnell followed. Their plan relied on the void-stone being awake. Void-stones could only be turned on and off by an immaculate summoner. The problem was there were more void-stones than there were summoners. There was a possibility that the ship had its own summoner and it had been turned off when they reached port. Unlikely, but it was possible. If so, they would resort to the backup plan. Cripple the ship with explosives.

Ilor studied the dials and turned a couple of valves, monitoring the changes.

"It's good," Ilor said, nodding to Chander. "The stone's awake and everything looks in range. It's disengaged from the main boiler, as expected, but ready to go."

"Great. Start working," Chander said. "Kathnell, watch what he does, and help if he asks."

They both nodded in reply and turned back to the dials.

Once awakened, Heat-Stones emitted energy no matter what. When not immersed in water, they would radiate their heat into the surrounding air, but with far less efficiency. The hot air was vented into the atmosphere. It was wasteful, but apparently the stones would go on kicking out heat for millennia. Powered by strange ancient magic.

Ilor started to remove the pins that held the valve handles in place on the shaft. Kathnell wondered why.

Afterwards, he started adjusting some valves and levers. Step one would be to isolate the boiler from the rest of the ship. Then, they would jam the safety mechanisms and release valves that prevented overpressure. Finally, they would lower the void-stone into the boiler and get the hell off the ship. Minutes later, it would all go up with a bang.

There was a noise from above. An odd popping sound. Pop, pop, pop-pop-pop. What in the hells was that? Chander immediately took off in the door's direction they had come from. The scowling woman headed towards a door at the other end of the chamber. Both unslinging their guns as they went.

"Keep working," Chander said, "and it might be a good idea to speed up."

"What's going on?" Kathnell asked Ilor.

"That was gunfire," he replied. "Which means the stonie fuckers know we are here. That means trouble. Which means Chander will make sure that none of us are captured. Understand?"

Ilor tapped the boiler for emphasis.

"Shit," Kathnell said.

"Yep. Now shut up and help me."

Chander disappeared through the doorway. The woman crouched next to the other door, aiming down the corridor. Kathnell assisted Ilor, turning handles and reading gauges as he commanded. The popping noise continued. It was getting closer. It was coming from the direction that Chander had gone.

Then there was an unfamiliar noise, a rhythmical thumping. Every second or so. Felt as much as heard. It shook dust loose and sent ripples across a nearby puddle of water. Bright flashes lit up the corridor where Chander had gone, accompanied by much louder popping.

Chander re-appeared with another red-haired man. Between them, they dragged a third, a crossbow bolt sticking from his leg, and another from his arm. Kathnell recognised them from the other team. Two were missing. They fired back down the corridor as they retreated into the boiler room. Hegemon soldiers appeared down the corridor. A few humans and a couple of t'kelikt. Crossbow bolts whistled past Chander and into the boiler room. One struck the console next to Kathnell. The thumping from above continued.

Chander and the other man shut the door behind them and bolted it.

"They have a golem!" Chander shouted across to the woman with the scar.

"Yeah, thought so," she shouted back. "I can hear it. It's gonna rip this thing open to get at us."

"Any soldiers at your end?" Chander shouted back.

"Not yet. Won't be long."

There was a banging at the door they had bolted.

Chander turned towards Kathnell and stopped.

"Shit!" he shouted.

Kathnell followed his gaze to where Ilor lay slumped over the console. He had a crossbow bolt right through the back of his head. Blood trickled down the console and dripped onto the floor, forming a dark pool. Kathnell stared at the man. She'd be talking to him a few moments ago. She hadn't even realised he'd been hit. Chander ran up and pulled Ilor from the console. The bolt emerged from his left eye. Absurdly, he had an almost amused expression.

Over by the locked door, the red-haired rebel was tending to the injured one.

"It's your turn now," Chander said. "Get this bloody boiler rigged. Quickly. Whilst the other corridor is free, we still have a chance."

Kathnell nodded and turned to the console. Chander raced off towards the scarred woman guarding the other corridor.

All that blood! Surely, too much for the wound. It obscured the dials she needed to read. She needed to wipe it away, but just stood there. Just wipe it away, she thought. Try to focus on the what is next. What she had to do. But there was so much blood! Ilor a dead mass. Just dumped on the floor like trash. She willed herself to move, and wiped the blood away with a cloth. It smeared like grease. Her hands shook. A sour metallic taste rose in her throat.

Gunfire erupted from the open doorway. Kathnell looked up for a moment and saw several Hegemon soldiers and a t'kelikt advancing down the corridor. They took cover as Chander fired in their direction. The scarred woman cried out and fell backwards. A crossbow bolt sticking out of her shoulder. She waved Chander away.

"It's just in the armor. I'm fine," she shouted.

They continued to fire back down the corridor, but it was

obvious the Hegemon soldiers were gaining ground. Chander slammed the door and bolted it. They were trapped.

"How long?" Chander called to her.

"Just… Just a couple more minutes. Safety measures are disabled. I just need to prime the stone and submerge it."

"How long do we have before it blows?"

"Three, maybe four, minutes."

There was a terrific crunching noise. Then the entire ship rang. Kathnell fell backwards against the controls. The golem! It was ripping through the hull. It wouldn't be long before it had got down to them. There was no way out. She knew it. They would die in here, Kathnell thought. Her first mission, and that was it. So much for a glorious career bringing down the Hegemony. She locked eyes with Chander. He smiled at her, but she could see the message in his eyes. He knew it too. They were doomed. She realised they would either die in the explosion or they would drown. Either way, she thought, they would end up as ceph fodder.

"Wait!" Kathnell shouted.

"What?," Chander asked.

"The ceph!"

"I don't follow," he said. "If you have something to say, say it bloody quickly!"

"Those are ceph access doors," she said, pointing to the closed hatches in the chamber floor.

Chander nodded and immediately began moving towards them.

"Can we get them open?" he asked.

"Yes, there should be a manual winch to open them, but that will take too long. They should be operated by steam pressure. I'll divert some of the boiler pressure to them. Hang on."

"Will it affect the mission?"

"No, this thing will blow, no matter what."

"Right, everyone," Chander said, "get to the hatches. Whatever Miss Bilt asks you to do, you do. Don't wait for me to repeat it."

Everyone began moving towards the hatches. The red-haired rebel helped the remaining injured one limp over from the other door. Kathnell twisted a couple of levers and opened a valve.

"There should be a lever somewhere, probably painted blue."

A couple of seconds passed. There were bangs at both doors now. The hull shook again as the golem attacked once more.

"I've found it," Chander called.

"It has 'purge' written on it," the female rebel said.

"That's it. Is there a gauge next to it?"

"Yes," the woman said.

"What does it read?"

There was the sound of splintering wood from somewhere above them. The ship shook.

"Twenty-four, no hang on, twenty-five, it's rising."

"Great," Kathnell shouted back, "the second it reaches fifty, let me know."

A few more seconds passed.

"Fifty!" the woman shouted.

If they got out of this, she really was going to have to find out the woman's name. Kathnell pulled another lever and then quickly spun a couple of valves.

"Pull the lever now!!" Kathnell yelled.

The woman pulled down.

Above, the sound of ripping wood and metal got closer. The hammering on the first door was replaced with a loud banging. A bulge appeared on its metal surface. They must have switched to using some kind of battering ram. Maybe it was one of the t'kelikt. They were exceptionally strong.

For a few seconds the ceph hatches remained closed, then slowly rose. Kathnell could see dark water through the gap. She spun another couple of valves. The hatches stopped moving. The master pressure gauge rose.

She stepped back from the console.

"It's done," Kathnell said.

"How long do we have?" Chander asked.

"Three minutes, maybe four."

She realised then why Ilor had removed the pins. She started levering the handles off the valves and tossing them away.

"What are you doing?" Chander asked.

"Removing the handles. If they get in here, they won't be able to turn the boiler off again."

"Great! Good idea."

Thank you Ilor, she thought. She glanced down at his body. It would be destroyed along with the ship. His family would probably never know what happened to him. She knew nothing about him. His reasons for joining. His family. Nothing. Just like father. I'll have a drink for you both!

"Let's go," Chander said.

She turned away from Ilor and headed towards the open hatches.

Trelt

Trelt woke from a dream, a shout on his lips. Sweat soaked his bedsheets.

It had happened a lot recently. This recent bout had started the day after they extracted Rust from Hammington's Rest. Since then, they had come almost nightly. He always awoke with the same sense of foreboding. That disaster would soon befall them all, and he was the only one that could stop it.

He had been standing in a lush park at the centre of a vast city. The buildings were sleek and made from glass. Some so tall they pierced the clouds. Everyone around him was smiling and happy. Children played in a large pool.

Trelt rushed from person to person, desperate to get their attention. They had to leave; they had to get away. Something was coming that would kill them all. Worse than that, it would turn them into ice, to be forever frozen in time.

But, as usual, nobody would listen. Worse, they didn't even seem to notice. They just carried on, laughing, playing games and eating picnics.

Behind him, he sensed a dark cloud. He dared not turn to face it. He stood frozen to the spot as the shadows deepened. He spurred himself into action, rushing to a couple sitting against a tree. He tried to get their attention, but they didn't even notice him.

"Please!!!!!!" he screamed.

The shadows lengthened further, like an accelerated dusk. Now everyone was standing and looking in the same direction. Some pointed, some just stared. Trelt turned to see what they were looking at.

"Oh, please no," Trelt wept.

The sky was full of black shapes. Pyramids, triangles, spheres. Some, no larger than insects, others larger than the tallest building. Some were joined to each other in complex conglomerated forms. Beyond them, faded by the blueness of the sky, were shapes larger still. Things the size of continents.

The smaller shapes whipped around the people, almost too fast to see, dissolving into a dust that passed through them as if they were ghosts. People screamed, but it was too late.

Everyone stopped, completely motionless. Frozen in whatever pose they were in.

They had become memories. Pages in an infinite book. Forever preserved, untouchable by entropy, and unable to move forward. Locked in this moment, forever. Worse than being dead. At least death was an end and not this terrible purgatory.

Trelt had continued to scream a warning, but had woken instead.

He reached for a glass of water. His hands shook, the water spilling on to the covers.

He could command his shade to make it go away. It would dutifully move through his mind and remove the hormones and chemicals that caused his fear. In just moments he could be sharp, shakes banished.

He didn't give the commands. Better to keep the fear real, keep an edge on it. Behind the dreams lay actual memories. Rustari may have the key to stop those that would inadvertently bring about the end. He would stop at nothing to prevent it from happening again.

Last time, they had barely escaped. Countless billions dead. Entire cultures erased. All their dreams, art, history; just gone. Those few that remained had come so far. Far through space. Far through time.

He had thought like Liberation did once. Had actually been one of them. They thought they were doing the right thing. Thought that Nemesis was gone. A thing of the past.

But Alexi had shown him the way. The truth. They must be made to realise that it was better to live this way than to risk the alternative!

Rust was holding back, trying not to let things slip. She didn't trust him. You could hardly blame her. She'd spent her whole life being spoon-fed Harrod's version of the truth. A version that probably didn't cast the Hegemon in a good light. Now she'd been wrenched from her old life and catapulted into a new, confusing world.

He would be patient with Rustari for the time being. His highest priority was to get her to a secure facility where she could be kept safe. Away from Liberation and what remained of the Sleepers. Trelt had already sent word to his closest Aurumill operatives to prepare somewhere that only they knew about. The Emperor and the Aurumill kept a tight ship, but people were people.

As long as Rustari was here, there was a risk, even if it was tiny. Once she was secured, Trelt could work on breaking down her barriers, gain her trust, and find out what she knew. Together, they could find out what was stored in the memory-well. Information that could save them all and prevent disaster.

And, if he failed to get the information voluntarily, he would have to resort to other methods. He hated the thought of it. Trelt knew he had done questionable things in his time. Had ordered the execution of entire families, children included. It wasn't something he took any pleasure in. Every death weighed upon him. But he knew deep down that every one was a sacrifice made to save them all. It was what kept him going. Rustari was no different. He would do what he could to keep her safe, and persuade her to cooperate willingly. But if that failed, he wouldn't flinch from his responsibility. So he let the not quite memory, not quite dream, remain in his mind. Let the fear remain. The fate of everyone depended on it.

Rust

Rust squatted at the back of the fireplace. The area was cramped, with not much room to move. She wiped mortar grit from her eyes, blinking away the resulting tears.

"Fuck," she cursed through clenched teeth.

She continued to chip away at the mortar that held the metal grating in place. It formed a barrier blocking access to the chimney above. Once out, she could scale the inside of the chimney.

Above her, she could see stars. They replaced the rain clouds from earlier. Occasional thunder still rolled in, but the gap between peels had widened.

As children, Indiril and she used to climb the chimney at the abandoned mill. This would be easy by comparison. The memory made her pause. So much had happened since then. Unimaginable things. She'd always dreamed of a glorious adventure just around the corner. Some great excitement that would take her away from Hammington's Rest. A million different daydreams. Reality wasn't as she had imagined.

She chipped again, using a length of metal she'd prised off the underside of a table. Once she was out, she would have to watch out for wyverns. She'd seen a few of them swooping around during the daytime, but she had seen none at night. Still, she would need to be careful.

Each strike threatened to blind her with more grit. She'd been chipping away for several hours. Her eyes were sore and her shoulders burned from holding her arms up for a long time.

There was a noise from the hallway. Footsteps? Rust paused. Was it the guards? They came to check on her every few hours during the day. At night, they left her alone until sunrise. If she couldn't get out tonight, she'd make sure everything was cleaned before sunrise.

The last few days had been the same. Life had almost settled into a dull routine. She knew it wouldn't last. The current situation was only temporary. Whatever they had planned for her, remaining here until she died of old age wasn't it. She'd been visited by Trelt a couple more times, and the older doctor had taken more blood.

She couldn't hear anything else. Probably just a noise the ancient place made occasionally, she thought. Old floors creaked, pipes gurgled, and stone walls groaned with the wind. Almost like the place was alive. She was sure these walls could tell a thousand stories. She wouldn't be sorry to see the back of it.

She chipped again. The grating moved. It was a slight movement at first, but soon she could rock it back and forth. The movement shaking free some larger fragments of mortar.

Then, suddenly, the whole thing came loose. It was heavier than it looked. Rust struggled with the unexpected weight. It slid to the side, striking her on the side of the head. She controlled its descent as best as she could, but it landed with a loud clang.

Rust reached up and touched her head. Just a scratch.

No time to wait. This was it, her chance to escape. If someone had heard the grating fall, then they may come to investigate. If she was going to leave, it was now.

Bracing against the sides of the chimney, she ascended. Within a minute, she was at the top, and out onto the roof. She took a deep breath of air and looked around. The first fresh air for days! No sign of wyverns.

Now what? she thought. The roof was steep. The grey slate tiles, still slippery with water from the storm. Behind her, the palace continued to loom above her. The airship that had brought her was still nestled against the tower. She needed to find a way down. The palace was bigger than she'd thought. Extensive gardens and grounds clustered around a large rocky outcrop. Far below, she could see tiny figures moving along the outer walls.

Even if she found a way down, she was still going to be within the grounds of the palace. Then, even if she got past the outer walls, she would still be stuck in a city that she didn't know. Alone and with no money.

Was this just another dumb fantasy? One more dream of naïve adventure. She slumped against the chimney and touched the side of her head. It was sore, but the bleeding had stopped.

Maybe, she should just give up. Just go back inside and do whatever they wanted. She desperately wanted to find out what this was all about. Why uncle had hidden those things, and why everyone seemed so interested in them. Interested enough for the Hegemony to invade a foreign country. Maybe going back in was the only way to find out.

Maybe Trelt was right. How much did she really know about the Hegemony? She knew that many within Peldaran hated them. But how much of that was just local politics? She knew little of Peldaran's history, and even less about the lands beyond.

She still didn't know the truth about her past. She'd been told they'd arrived in Hammington's Rest when she was little, after her parents had died. Uncle had always avoided the topic. There was always an excuse. He was tired. Not today. When you are older, then I'll tell you everything. Maybe it had all been lies.

What was she thinking? Uncle had always been there for her. Cared for her when she was sick. Fed and clothed her. Encouraged her when she was down. Taught her the ways of the feral. If she was sure of only one thing, it was that Uncle had loved her. Totally and without question. He had died protecting her.

She would be three times damned by Sindar if she was going to just give up now. No, she was going to get out of this place. Get home. Back to Hammington's Rest. And then she would find out what this was all about on her own.

First, however, she needed to get down to ground level.

Straddling the apex, she shuffled towards the end of the roof. There was another roof about ten hands below. She gently lowered herself onto it. Looking down, she could see a long balcony that ran the length of the roof a floor down. Getting to it would be a difficult. About a ten hand drop. She crawled towards the edge, trying to keep purchase on the wet slate tiles.

A bright flash!

The sky lit up. Startled, she turned towards the bay. On the far shore, a giant explosion roared into the sky. Yellow flames, flecked with shots of blue lightning. It roiled and flashed. She felt the warmth on her face. Pieces of debris shot out at all angles. The entire city lit up. The explosion even lighting up the underside of the clouds.

"Saint's shit!"

Then the sound reached her, felt it as much as heard. The roof tiles rattled. She lost her footing and began sliding towards the edge. She scrambled madly for something to hold on to, but the tiles were too slick to hold on to. Her slide sped up. She whipped past a broken tile. She grabbed at it, fingertips trying to get a grip. Her momentum slowed. But then the broken tile was out of reach and she was once again speeding up. Then she was out; over the edge. Falling towards the balcony below.

With horror, she realised that her momentum had taken her too far out from the edge. She was going to miss the balcony completely. There was only empty air between her and the ground several floors below.

She screamed.

Something struck her in the back, and she was moving sideways. A sudden vice-like grip around her chest. Everything was a blur. Arms blacker than the night embraced her torso. Black legs wrapped around her waist. Then she was down, rolling over and over, along the cold stone of the balcony.

The black limbs released her, and she came to a rest on her back.

Once again, she looked into the eyes of the demon. She smiled down at Rust.

"Midnight stroll?" the demon called Vidyana asked.

Kathnell

Kathnell recounted the details for the third time.

She still felt in a daze. The memories felt like they belonged to someone else, but with each retelling, it became more real. It really had happened.

Of all the things, it was the devastation of the dockside that she had the most trouble remembering. Her hands trembled. The shouts and cries for help. The fire! A single crying baby. Had she really been part of that?

The room she had been taken to was small. Drab walls of grey stone. Dark blue-green fronds of some feral weed protruded from the ceiling in one corner. The single wooden door was rough and battered.

Either there were no windows, or the various wooden boxes stacked high against one wall covered them. Each shrouded in a thick layer of dust, labels faded and illegible. They only showed how much this place had been neglected. Forgotten by the outside world. Several hooks hung from a metal beam. Meat hooks maybe? A butcher's cellar?

She sat on a wooden chair facing a long table. Across from her sat Chander, the scowly woman with the scar, and a third man with white hair and a beard she didn't recognise. He had spoken little. He looked friendly and smiled. Like everyone's favourite uncle. Despite this, Kathnell got the impression that he shouldn't be messed with.

She went over everything that had happened.

The initial approach to the ship. The death of the poor engineer. She told them about the ceph pool and how they had rigged the boiler. Their escape through the icy waters. How they had been halfway to the shoreline when the sky above them erupted into yellow and then blue light. The hot wind that had washed over them. The burning heat that forced them back under the water. She left the bit out when she thought she was going to drown. Panicking in cold water, whilst the sky burned. The scowly woman had hauled her to the shore, coughing and spluttering. It was the only time that she had seen the woman smile.

The dock front had been ablaze. Most nearby buildings were in ruins or on fire. Some completely levelled. Flames lept into the dark sky. Cries for help echoed in the darkness. Somewhere a child cried. The ship itself was a ruin. The remnant pieces of its twisted hull steamed as they sank to the quay bottom.

Kathnell stood on the shoreline, mouth open. Horrified at the destruction. Her destruction.

"You did good, girl," the scowly woman had said, "but saint's fucking shit!"

They limped off after the others.

Kathnell had never seen a boiler go up before, but she was sure that they shouldn't burn with blue light. Sink the ship maybe, but not blow it apart and leave the nearby dockside in ruins.

Once away from the burning dockside, Chander approached her. He apologised before proceeding to put a heavy hessian bag over her head. The cloth removed any freshness from the air, replacing it with an unpleasant oily smell. Scowly reassured her she was in no danger. Just normal procedure. She stumbled through a few more streets before she was bundled into a carriage. Several disorienting minutes later, she found herself in this room.

After what seemed like an hour, Chander had returned and removed her blindfold. He joined the other two people across from her before asking her to explain the entire mission.

When she had finished, he'd asked her a ton of questions before asking her to explain it all again. And then, again.

She finished her third retelling.

"Thank you Kathnell," Chander said. "Must seem odd all this, seeing that most of us in this room were with you when it happened, but it's just the way we like to do things. Details are important. Now, please excuse us. I'll be back soon."

With that, the three of them left, leaving her alone. She was tempted to get up and have a nose around the room, see what was in those boxes. She thought better of it and sat where she was. Chander returned after a few minutes. He walked up to her, arm extended. She rose and shook it.

"Welcome to Liberation," Chander said. "Seems like you've made a good impression."

"What was the interrogation all about?"

"Oh that? Don't worry about that. We go through the same with all the new recruits. Need to check out how accurately they remember things. Details really are important. I don't mind admitting it, but you saved our arses back there."

"It's no problem," she said with more casualness than she felt. Inside, she was still a blubbering wreck. For the first time, she realised she was still in her waterlogged clothes. They stank of river mud.

"No problem? I was ready to poop my pants when the engineer died and we were surrounded. I would have died for the cause, but I didn't relish getting blown up for fun. Your quick thinking saved us. You've got my thanks, if no one else's."

"Alright, I was shitting myself too," she laughed.

"However," he said, "things aren't all good. Whatever was on that ship went up with a bigger bang than anyone was expecting. Took the whole quayside out. Killed quite a few. Most of them locals. Bad turn of the wheel."

"Shit…"

"Yeah. Got the stonies in a right state. The streets are now being patrolled by troops from that bloody airship. Nasty buggers, not the normal stonie lovers in armour, but elite troops. Breast fed on Hegemon milk since they were babies.

As fanatical as the stonies themselves. Everyone's gonna have to lie low for a while. Us included."

The wind went from her, and she felt suddenly exhausted. She'd signed up to get back against those that had killed her father, not to kill innocent human civilians. They were common docker folk. People like her. People with families. She wished she'd just ignored all those stupid flyers. She'd often fantasied about killing stonies. Getting revenge on the establishment. Break the chains, as the flyers said. Not this.

Meeting Syb complicated things further. She could no longer convince herself that all stonies were bad. That was just a childish fantasy. When she'd boarded the ship, she half expected that they may have to kill a stonie, or a stonie-loving Hegemon soldier. That was one thing. Killing innocent Bennel folk was something else. She shivered with more than just the cold of her damp clothes.

Chander seemed to sense what she was thinking.

"Hey! That shit back at the dockside wasn't your fault. You did your job, and did it well. If you're going to blame anyone, blame the Drellmore shits who put that magic crap on the ship. It gives me the shivers the stuff the stonies control."

He clapped his hands.

"Now, let's get you some dry clothes," he said, "and a beer!"

Chander came back with a change of clothes and a large pitcher of beer. He left her for a few minutes whilst she changed.

After, she had a couple more drinks with Chander. He explained it was important that she didn't know where they were. In a while, she would be blindfolded once more and taken back home. When required, she would be contacted again. It wouldn't be for a while. He told her to go back to work and her normal life. Continue with everything she had been doing before the mission and not speak to anyone about it. Anyone. She asked if she could speak to Corric about it.

"That would be extremely unwise," he replied. "Corric doesn't see eye-to-eye with us anymore."

The way he had said it left her in no uncertainty that speaking to Corric about it would be a terrible mistake. There was a knock at the door.

"Alright, Miss Bilt," Chander said. "Time to go home."

She stood, and he put the hessian bag over her head again. Once again, the smell of oil filled her nose and lungs.

"One last thing Miss Bilt."

"Yes?"

"If you need to contact us in an emergency, there is a procedure you should follow," he said.

"Yes?"

"It is important that you understand that by emergency, I mean something MORE important than your life being in danger. If you think you are being followed by the stonies, or they are on to you, that's just tough leather, I'm afraid. You'll be on your own. Personally, I'd choose anything other than getting captured. If you know what I mean?"

The implications of his words chilled her. She wondered what she would do if it came to it.

"What I mean," he continued, "is if you discover something of true strategic importance to Liberation through your work, or by some other means. Something you think we could use. Do you understand?"

She went to speak, but her mouth had become dry. She gulped down before croaking out a feeble, "Yes."

"Right. If such a thing should arise, go to the bakery on Wharf Street and wait. If you are approached by someone asking for some tobacco, reply that you only have 'Red Tanner'. Understand?"

"Yes, Red Tanner," she replied.

"Great. Now let's go."

They went out into the hallway. As she was led out, she realised she still didn't know the woman's name. Did not know who the other man was either.

Perhaps that was the way it worked, she thought. The less she knew, the better.

Chapter 13

First, care must be taken to dig the area and remove all feral plants. Feral seedlings must be removed and burned for two entire seasons. Tarn root must be removed entirely to a depth of ten hands. No root must remain.

Thusly prepared, the area must be treated by both mature ground-brew from a local fermenter, and mould-powders to begin growing the mediums and white-mould networks. This shall be done twice a season for three years. Manure and tame plant compost must be dug in twice yearly for the length of treatment.

During the third year, a supply of worms must be added. They should be checked every two months to see if they have taken. It is strongly advised to create and maintain a wormery during this phase.

On taming feral soil, chapter 2, An Introduction

Rust

Rust's back hurt. There wasn't much to see in the darkness of the room she had been taken to. Small and square, barely twenty hands to a side. No windows. No furniture. The walls and floor were made of dark stone. The only source of light came from a slit under the door. The room, as dark as her mood.

There were occasional noises and shifting shadows underneath the door. Guards. She hadn't even bothered to try the door. Instead, she sat slumped against the wall, hugging her knees. The floor and wall felt damp. Maybe it was just the coolness of the stone.

The demon had dragged and shoved her in here. How long ago had that been? More than an hour. A few hours maybe. It must be daytime outside now.

The demon hadn't spoken since she'd hauled Rust onto her feet. She just kept that smile. Her strength had been unbelievable. Rust sensed that it was merely a fraction of what the demon was capable of. The demon had whistled as she'd hauled Rust along. Rust had been too winded and terrified to resist. The demon had saved her from certain death. She'd been about to plummet to a grisly death when the demon had slammed into her mid-air. Her ribs throbbed when she breathed. She wasn't sure if it was from the landing, or where the demon had struck her.

Her bid for freedom had been as brief as it had been well thought out. Stupid, she thought. Had she really thought she was simply going to walk out of the palace? Past all the guards, soldiers and the divines knew what else. And then what would she have done? She was in a city she didn't know. She had no money. Nothing. The furthest she'd ever been was Balincross.

She wished she hadn't bothered and was back in her room. It had a luxury that she had never known. The food they brought her was equally excellent. Sweet pastries and tender meats. No, she thought, it was a lie. It was, at best, a prison. At worst, a cage.

She heard approaching footsteps. There were voices and the sound of the door being unbolted and opened. Light flooded in, overwhelming her eyes. She blinked. A silhouette of a man appeared in the doorway.

"Congratulations, Miss Parra," Trelt said, "you escaped from what my hosts had ensured me was a secure room."

Rust said nothing. Behind Trelt, Rust could see several Hegemon guards.

"Needless to say," Trelt continued, "we will make some changes to your room to ensure your continued safety."

"Fuck off," Rust said, "we all know I'm a prisoner here."

Trelt sighed.

"Things are complicated, it's true," Trelt said. "But your safety IS paramount. If it wasn't for the vigilance and quick reactions of Vidyana you would surely have died. That would have been a sad outcome for everyone."

"Do you expect me to be grateful? To you?"

"Not yet. Maybe in time. Once you have met the Emperor, you will understand. He will make you see the truth. He's eager to meet you."

The Emperor? It was the first time the Emperor had been mentioned. What in the name of Sindar did the Emperor want with someone like her? The bloody Emperor!

"Now," Trelt continued, "whilst your room is being secured, there is someone you should meet."

Trelt led Rust through brightly lit corridors. From glimpses outside, she surmised they must be close to where her rooms were. The view outside was the same. They came to a wooden door that Trelt unlocked. The room beyond was like her own. Maybe slightly smaller.

Rust was surveying it when she heard a gasp from a doorway that led to an adjoining room. She turned to see Indiril, his hand raised to his mouth. He stood there for a couple of seconds and then ran across the room to embrace her.

"Rust!," he said, sobbing. "Thank Sindar you are all right. They said you were, but I didn't believe them."

"Indi!! What are you doing here?" she said. Stupid question.

"They brought me here, after…"

"After the attack?" she said.

Indiril nodded.

Rust had seen someone at the elderuin that might have been Indiril. She hadn't been sure. She'd assumed that they would have left him back at the village. What use was he to them?

"I'm so sorry, Rust. It's all my fault."

"What is?"

"Everything. I'm sorry," Indiril repeated.

"How could it be your fault? It was my stupid idea in the first place. If it's anyone's fault, it's…"

"I told them where to find the secret place," Indiril blurted. "It was me! I did it. I told them everything!."

Rust pushed Indiril away a little. In the days since her flight from Hammington's Rest, Rust hadn't really thought about how they had tracked her to the ruins. The thought occurred to her that if they hadn't tracked her so quickly, she might have got away. She might now be safe in Balincross, or even out of the country.

"I'm sorry," Indiril repeated through sobs. "Please forgive me. You have to understand, I had no choice."

Rust blinked through tears and pulled away completely. She'd been betrayed. Not by a stranger, but by Indiril! Someone she loved and trusted. In her time of most need, he had betrayed her.

Indiril was saying something else, but Rust couldn't really hear. Trelt led Rust silently from the room and shut the door. From the other side, Indiril continued to sob and plead.

Trelt led Rust through the palace corridors. The ever present guards followed several metres behind.

"You really shouldn't be angry with your friend, you know?"

"What do you know about it?" she spat back.

"He really didn't have a choice," Trelt said. "We had to find out where you were before other people came and took you for their own purposes. People that would bring doom to the world. Indiril was made to realise what was at stake and made the only logical choice."

"He betrayed me."

"That is certainly one way to look at it," Trelt nodded, "but you will come to realise as you grow older, that few things are as simple as that."

"Why are you holding him here?"

"Just like you, Indiril is being held for his own protection. To keep him away from those same dark forces. Maybe after you've spoken to him again, you'll understand. It would be such a shame if your long friendship was ruined over something that was really beyond his control."

Rust remained silent as they walked.

She didn't believe any of the crap about Indiril being held for his own protection. It was obvious, really. This was a warning. Why had Rust only been taken to see Indiril now? Why not yesterday? Or before? No, Indiril wasn't being held for his protection. He was being held because of her. To make her do what they wanted.

Welyne

A thunderstorm two nights ago had brought with it an attack on the docks. A loud noise had awoken Welyne from a restless sleep. At first she'd thought that lightning had struck nearby, but there was a quality to the sound that had brought her to full wakefulness. More like an explosion. Going to the window, she'd seen the distant docks ablaze. A cloud roiled upward into the sky. Pieces of lit debris rained down. The fire at the centre burned with an odd blue flame. This was no natural fire. She had known immediately it was an attack.

At first, she'd worried about her husband Bartain. The explosion was close to his shipping warehouses. She had forced herself to be rational and calm. He was fine, and currently a hundred kilometres away.

She would have to wait until morning to find out anything more.

In true form, Sybelle had slept through the whole thing. Welyne had sat on the edge of Sybelle's bed and just watched her. Her daughter snored lightly and smiled in her sleep. Lost in some happy dream.

Tough choices would soon have to be made, she thought. A choice between the Sleepers or her family. Whatever the outcome, her daughter's innocence would soon end. She wasn't sure what would replace it. Anger? Sadness? Confusion? Rebellion? Defiance? Or the usual paradoxical human mix of all. She'd been through this all before with her son. He had initially been angry and defiant. But over time, he had become an important member of the Sleepers.

He had died for a cause that Sybelle knew nothing about. Bartain knew nothing, either. He was oblivious to her double life. Poor, innocent, naïve, lovely Bartain. Sybelle was clever, though. She already knew something was going on and had confronted her. Losing the note had been careless. A sign she wasn't as sharp as she should be. Of course, the note itself meant nothing. Welyne had diffused the situation, but knew it was only a temporary reprieve.

Since their son's death, she kept putting off bringing Sybelle into the fold. She now feared that she'd left it too late. What could have been easily managed over years would now have to be rushed. How Sybelle would take it remained to be seen. But she was strong, just like Welyne.

Welyne could, of course, just leave them. Leave her husband and Sybelle behind, never to return. Change her identity. The Sleepers had some remaining technology that could permanently alter her appearance. Her chest ached at the thought. The plan was just selfishness, anyway. She had to do what was best for the Sleepers and the wishes of Simona. That meant remaining a Drellmore. Staying close enough to the centre to be useful, far enough away to remain hidden.

Sybelle was a strong summoner. They would need her kind in the coming years. Anyway, if Welyne was compromised, and the Hegemony discovered her identity, they would come for her daughter and husband. No, it was better to bring Sybelle into the fold. She'd done it with her son, and she would do it again with her daughter.

She wasn't sure what would happen to Bartain if she was ever caught. The Hegemon would interrogate him using their forbidden technologies. She'd always known the risk. She'd known it when his family had been selected by the Sleepers as being a good blood match. She'd known it when they'd first met, when she had pretended to love him, and then years later when she actually did. He was as innocent as Sybelle.

She'd wiped moisture from her eyes and left her daughter to her untroubled sleep. She would need to stay resolved in the days ahead.

The next morning, she'd gone into town to see what she could find out. The official line was that a ship boiler had exploded. She knew that was crap. Boilers didn't explode with blue flame and take half the docks with them. She'd heard rumours it was an attack by Liberation. These rumours were laughed off as conspiracy theories by the authorities. They had a ring of truth to them, though.

She'd come back home full of worry. The attack on the docks was unlikely to be related to Rustari's capture, but she couldn't be sure. It had indeed been a Carntellis Trading ship that had been destroyed. Many were dead. A couple of them had been at the party a few nights ago.

Bartain's company was bringing in important cargo for secret Hegemon projects up in the mountains. It was the reason he had come to Lerins. Several other similar projects had been started around the globe, all of them at ancient Maleth sites. She wanted to ask Zarl about them. But even if he knew anything, he wouldn't tell her. Just the type of target Liberation would go after. She'd couldn't blame them for that. Whatever Alexi was doing at the sites wouldn't be good for either Liberation or the Sleepers.

Since then, she had been a ball of worry and stress. Of course, nobody noticed. She was a seasoned expert at projecting a perfectly calm exterior.

Welyne shifted in the chair and read the same paragraph for the third time. The words perfectly legible, but all meaning got lost somewhere between her eyes and her brain.

Another thunderstorm had rolled through during the morning, but it had done nothing to clear the oppressive heat. A tension in the air that hadn't been fully released. Outside, wet roads steamed in the noonday sunshine.

She gave up, put down her book, and went to the window. How were they going to get Rustari out? Time was slipping away. They needed to come up with something before Rustari was moved from the city.

Maybe Zarl was right. Maybe it was best if Rustari was dead. Could they kill her off? It sounded horrific, but it was better than her being taken somewhere out of reach, or captured by Liberation. They would bring about their own shade of darkness and bloodshed. There were already accounts of guns on the streets. Welyne shivered at what might come next. This was exactly the type of technological escalation that both Alexi and Simona warned about.

How could they kill Rustari? A direct attack was stupid, and certainly doomed to failure. She had some relics they could use to fight their way in. She had summoning ability, but Zarl didn't. The palace was crawling with Trelt's Aurumill. They weren't to be taken lightly. A direct attack would get them both captured, tortured, or killed.

An explosion? They could find out where in the palace Rust was being held and rig some kind of explosion. A hollow-shell maybe? Even then, how could they get the artefact close enough? No, not viable.

Poison maybe? Welyne let that thought linger. There was something to that. Wasn't Zarl's contact connected to the physician at the palace?

Another option occurred to her. A way out. She got Relgor to send a note.

Sybelle barely reacted when Welyne told her she was going out for the evening. A plausible sounding story about going to see a local musician play. Sybelle tried to hide her reaction, but Welyne knew her daughter didn't believe a word of it.

She would need to sort that out. And soon.

Kathnell

Kathnell sank into the soft embrace of the bed, fluffy covers wrapping her in their warmth. Utterly unlike her own bed, which was little more than wooden slats and thin krell-hemp stuffed mattress.

Sybelle nestled against her, breathing slowly. Kathnell stroked Sybelle's dark plaited hair. It smelt like a summer garden. Flowers and herbs. In comparison, her own hair was like a dry desert.

Kathnell wondered what Sybelle saw in her. She smelled herself. Ripe with sweat, dirt, and grease.

This was the second time they had met since their trip to the human quarter, and the second time they had made love.

Kathnell sighed. This was not at all what she had planned.

Since the raid, Kathnell had a strong feeling that getting close to Syb was a mistake. It would put them both in danger. What would happen if Chander found out? How long had she been under observation before her recruitment? Maybe she was worrying too much. Chander had said nothing about Sybelle. He had mentioned the incident with the drunk, but hadn't said anything more. Surely he would have challenged her if he knew Sybelle was an immaculate?

This whole thing with Sybelle was absurd. She'd spent the best part of her life hating stonies. Thinking of ways to get back at them for her father's death. Now Sybelle had become a lover. Maybe something more.

The entire city was abuzz over the raid on the docks. Kathnell still couldn't believe she'd been part of it. The one responsible for the explosion. Her!

The three versions of herself seemed utterly incompatible. Kathnell the engineer, Kathnell the rebel, and the Kathnell falling in love with an immaculate.

Sybelle wasn't even her type. Petite, slender, privileged, stuck-up, and naïve. They had nothing in common, but there was something that excited her. A feeling deep in her gut that usually left her feeling more than a little distracted. Stupid, like a crush. No, it was too dangerous. Best to stop it now before she did something stupid.

She'd gone to work the day after the raid as normal, still resolved that if she met Syb, she would play it cool. She hadn't seen Sybelle for a few days, and avoided areas where she would most likely be.

It had been early evening, and she'd been sitting on the dockside eating a snack. A shadow fell across her. She'd looked up, straight into Sybelle's beaming face.

"Been trying to avoid me?" Sybelle had said.

"No, of course not."

Remember to play it cool, she had thought. Instead, she just grinned like an idiot and dropped the half eaten pie. It splashed into the water. Her gut fluttered.

"Just... you know... been busy, that's all. Corric's been a slave driver and..." she stammered.

"Nemesis damned, I've missed you," Sybelle said, moving to embrace her.

Kathnell pulled away, looking around.

"Not here, Syb," she said. "Someone might see us."

"Then we'd better get back inside," Sybelle replied before walking off towards the doorway that led to the underbelly of the houses. The one she had given Sybelle a key to.

"Anyway, everyone has left for the day," Sybelle continued.

Kathnell followed her. Kathnell had barely closed the door when Sybelle embraced her, pushing her mouth against Kathnell's. Her rational mind vanished, replaced by something basic and primal. Mind adrift, her hands and mouth, no longer under her control. The sex had been fumbling and basic, Sybelle's lack of experience obvious. It hadn't mattered. Any thought of playing it cool with Sybelle had been forgotten.

They had agreed to meet again the following night, after everyone had gone to bed. Since then, Kathnell couldn't stop thinking about Syb.

Kathnell had waited outside the old kitchen door until Sybelle had knocked three times. The room was relegated to a storeroom now, but shelving still contained several half packed boxes.

Sybelle quietly led Kathnell up the stairs.

"What about your family?," Kathnell whispered.

"Mother has gone out for the evening, and won't be back for ages. Father's away for a few more days. The servants don't stay here overnight. They live in lodgings down the street. We've got the place to ourselves. Now come on."

Sybelle was smiling mischievously. Kathnell smiled back and followed. Kathnell looked at the fine oak panelling and pictures that adorned the walls of the staircase. The rich blue carpet. The House Drellmore coat of arms. What in all the hells was she doing here?

Once in the safety of Sybelle's room, they'd made love again. It was slower and more relaxed than the first time.

Afterwards, they'd talked for a while. Sybelle had told her about her mother's activities. The strange meetings, disappearances and notes. Sybelle had convinced herself her mother was having an affair and confronted her. Her mother denied it. Kathnell admitted it did sound odd, but had nothing to add. Who knew what the privileged stonies got up to?

Kathnell mentioned nothing of her own activities. How could she? By the way, you know that explosion at the docks? That was me. Great, huh?

Instead, she said she'd been busy working. She felt terrible lying to Sybelle, terrified that she would see right through Kathnell's paper thin lies. That Syb had accepted them without question made Kathnell feel worse.

Kathnell asked how long Sybelle would be in Lerins. Sybelle became upset. She thought they would probably leave soon. Her father was away for a few more days, but then they would probably return home, unsure if or when they would come back.

Kathnell had wept as well. What happened to the tough girl she liked to portray? The one that got into fights. The one that drank too much. The one that told vulgar jokes. Kathnell had been with several sexual partners, a few women and a couple of men. None of them had been anything other than a bit of fun. Usually drunken fun. Kathnell wasn't sure what to make of these new versions of herself.

Sybelle stirred, opened her eyes, and smiled.

"Hello," she said, stretching.

Kathnell bent her head down and kissed her on the mouth.

"Hello yourself."

"How long have I been asleep?"

"Just an hour."

Sybelle smiled for a few seconds before a cloud crossed her face. She sighed and focused on somewhere beyond the room.

"What's up?," Kathnell asked.

"This whole thing with Mother. I don't know what to do about it, Kath."

"Don't worry," Kathnell said. "I'm sure it's all got a completely borin' explanation. You're worrying over nothin'. When she tells you, you'll probably laugh at how silly you've been."

"I suppose you're right," Sybelle said.

Sybelle rolled over onto one elbow to face Kathnell.

"You know that explosion the other night?" Sybelle said.

"W-What about it?" Kathnell stammered.

"The ship belonged to the company Father works for."

Shit. Kathnell hadn't known that.

"They say over ten people were killed," Sybelle continued. "One of them was my father's friend. He was at the party the other night. Burned to death in a warehouse, along with a couple of his workers, they say…."

Sybelle continued to talk, but Kathnell didn't hear her.

Instead, Kathnell was elsewhere, surrounded by fire and smoke. Somewhere a child was crying. Mud, blood, and dripping water. The child cried again, louder this time. Shouldn't someone help? Why isn't anyone helping? Kathnell's body was stiff from the cold water. She stared back towards the burning docks. She could feel the heat of the flames on her face. The fire! The fire I made! "You did good, girl," the woman with the scar said. Someone should help the child! All she could see was fire, smoke, blood, and water.

"Kathnell, what's wrong?" Sybelle said, shaking her gently.

"Eh? Wha…" Kathnell replied.

"What's wrong?"

"I'm… fine."

Kathnell felt cold and sweaty. Her heart pounded. Her hands shook uncontrollably.

"I couldn't make you hear," Sybelle said. "I was telling you about the fire at the docks and then you started making a gulping noise. When I turned over, you were just staring off into nothing. I couldn't make you hear. Are you all right?"

Kathnell didn't feel at all well. She needed to get up. Go outside. The room was too small. The roof, too low. A picture on one wall looked down with accusing eyes.

"It's all right. I'm just not feeling very well," Kathnell said. "Probably, just something I ate."

Kathnell started to get up. Sybelle placed a hand on her, pushing her gently back into the covers.

"Maybe you should rest for a bit," Sybelle said. "Especially if you're coming down with something."

"No, it's all right. I think it's just the blasted pie I ate earlier. I was sure it was off when I smelt it. Should have thrown the bloody thing in the river for the ceph earlier. Though I doubt even they would have eaten it."

She raised herself up again, pulling the sheets aside.

"No, probably best if I get home. If I am going to be physically ill, I wouldn't want you to see it and ruin my delightful image."

Sybelle laughed, but was still frowning, not convinced.

Kathnell dressed quickly.

"If you're sure," Sybelle said.

"Yeah. But don't worry, I'll see you again soon."

"How soon?"

"A couple of days at the most. And then we can continue where we left off," Kathnell said and winked.

"Sounds like fun."

Kathnell walked along the dockside towards the ferry.

She took down the fresh air in gulps. It was great to be in the open. The breeze was cool against her damp scalp. She was feeling better, but was still a little lightheaded. At least the trembling had stopped.

When Sybelle had mentioned the dockside explosion, it had knocked the wind out of her. A shock, yes, but when Sybelle had mentioned the death of someone connected to her directly, even if tenuously, Kathnell had been transported right back to the dockside on the night of the raid. Was she going mad?

She stood gazing out into the bay and waited for the next ferry back home.

Zarl

Zarl stroked his beard and drummed his fingers on the wooden tabletop. He looked out at the street below. Full of traffic. Merchants, human, immaculate, a few t'kelikt. All occupied with the ritual actions of a normal working day. Zarl sometimes wished he was one of them. Just an ordinary person in an ordinary world. He wondered what it would be like having normal worries. Income, family, food, sex, relatives, taxes. Forget all about the fucking Sleepers, Liberation, and the Hegemon.

He forced himself back to the present, and Welyne's flamboyant plan.

"Raldir Root?" he said again, not sure if he was asking himself or Welyne.

Could it work? The timing would be extremely tricky. Too many moving parts for his liking. No room for improvisation if the unexpected happened.

"Yes," Welyne replied. "It's perfect. It lowers the blood pressure and induces a temporary coma. The Aldarian don't call it Death's Mask without reason."

"It's just… it's risky Wel. The dosage will have to be precise. Too little and it won't work. Too much and it'll work too well."

"If it works too well, then she'll be dead. Problem solved! Anyway, what choice do we have?"

"I don't know, but time IS running out."

He turned the plan around in his mind like a model, viewing it from different angles. Trying to spot flaws and weaknesses. It would get them Rustari, but what about the artefacts?

"Do you think the rebel attack on the Carntellis Trading

ship had anything to do with any of this?" Welyne asked.

He'd considered that himself, but everything he had discovered led him to believe they weren't connected. The Hegemon had been bringing in some stuff bound for Taldor-Ire. Another of Alexi's schemes. A ripe target for the rebels. More evidence that they had their own network of spies and informants at work within the city.

"No, don't think so. Just bloody Liberation causing trouble. I heard rumour they were going to try something big. All it's done is stir up a wilderbug nest. It has its advantages, though."

"How so?" Welyne asked.

"It's drawn some Aurumill and Jurament forces away from the palace. Security around the place is still tight, but outside it may be lessened. At least for the next few days. Whatever the rebels destroyed riled the Hegemon good."

Zarl took another swig of tan brandy. Not as good as the stuff from Tarranis, but he had seen none of that for years. Not since the Schism when they'd joined the rebels. It wasn't the done thing to drink the stuff anymore. You certainly wouldn't find it somewhere like this. A shame.

"Also," he continued, "I've heard that Trelt is overseeing the bolstering of defences around the docks. Has drawn the slippery bastard out of the palace. For a day or so, at least."

"Well, that settles it then," Welyne said. "Considering everything else you've told me, we don't have the luxury of time. What about Miss Baylali?"

Zarl huffed.

"No idea," he said, "she's not with Trelt. That's all I can say. She could be anywhere. Maybe she's not even in the city anymore. Wouldn't bet on it."

He'd already updated Welyne on everything else he'd discovered. His contact at the palace, Doctor Nortaud, had found out more since they'd last met.

Welyne had been eager to get into the plan's details, but he'd insisted she was informed first. As ever, things had got more complicated. Rust had tried to escape on the same night as the raid on the docks. She'd escaped by removing an iron grate from the chimney and climbing onto the roof. Stupid idiot had nearly died. Apparently, Rust wasn't the only person taken from the village. Doctor Nortaud said there was a second person, a tree-people boy about the same age as Rustari. He didn't know the relationship between the two. A bargaining chip to keep Rust cooperative, maybe? Poor soul, the Empire would use him to get what it wanted. He felt sorry for him, but had to be logical. He was an irrelevant distraction. Rustari was the important one. The tree-boy could rot for all he cared.

The boy had been moved this very morning. He'd been taken to a little office building in the business district. If they'd moved him, then it was likely they were planning to move Rustari as well. Maybe the raid on the docks had spooked Trelt into action.

It was a shame, but they would just have to ignore the tree-boy. Welyne said she would reconnoitre the place, just in case. He thought it was a waste of time, but conceded.

Once Rustari was taken from the city, she'd be taken to some secret Aurumill bunker, and that would be that. Eventually Trelt and his cronies would twist the girl to join them. The Emperor had many techniques, including his dammed visions.

Doctor Nortaud had also told them the girl was definitely a close blood relative of both Simona and Welyne. The doctor couldn't absolutely confirm she is the daughter of Simona and Welyne's brother Tomlas, but few other theories matched the evidence.

"Well?" Welyne asked again.

Zarl raised a hand and took a sip from his brandy.

"Hang on, let me think through the details," Zarl said.

They could trust Nortaud. His sister had been killed by the Aurumill in a raid years ago. The problem was, he wasn't the chief doctor at the palace. The primary doctor was a strict imperialist called Relshanna, by all accounts, a bit of a bastard. Zarl knew the type. All smiles in public, nasty piece of work underneath. They would have to get him out of the way for the evening.

He thought through the plan again. There were several points where things would have to work perfectly or the whole thing would collapse. A hundred questions he would need answers to before they could be certain. He would have to speak to Nortaud again. He knew the layout of the palace, the comings and goings. It would mean asking Nortaud to put his own life at risk. If he was compromised, it would put them all in danger, including Welyne's family.

"I'll need to talk to my contact," Zarl said. "He'll tell me if your plan is more than just dreaming."

"How would he know?"

"He's a doctor at the palace. And, yes, he can be trusted."

"And if he agrees?"

"IF he agrees, we need to move quickly."

"What about the artefacts?" she asked. "The best this does is get us Rustari. If there really is a memory-well, then it will be locked away somewhere safe. I don't see how we can get it."

"We can't. We haven't got time to worry about it, Wel. It's either Rustari or nothing. The memory-well will be useless without her. Its contents, impossible to unlock. The risk of secrets getting into the hands of Trelt and Alexi is the greatest threat."

Welyne stood and let out a big sigh. Zarl looked up at her and placed one of his hands over hers.

"It'll be alright Wel."

She laughed. It was sharp. Devoid of humour.

"We both know that's complete feldershit."

She was right. The plan was paper-thin. He liked plans with as few moving parts as possible, not this cobbled together monstrosity. But he couldn't think of anything better, and time WAS running out.

His shoulders were tight, and his neck ached. He had a pain behind his left eye, blue swirls in his vision, the harbinger of a migraine yet to fully strike. It had been there for a couple of hours, lurking in the background like some unpleasant guest at a party. One that you spent all night avoiding, but who you'd have to speak to at some point. He was sure it would be worse before the day was out.

"Fuck it," he said, and downed the rest of the brandy.

Outside, in the street, life went on like it had done for years.

Chapter 14

The Kalmarnill Redroot is only grown in northern Nemset. Its name originates from the port of Kalmarn that is used to export the plant worldwide.

It takes five years for the root to mature. The roots are dried and crushed. The resulting powder is used extensively in powerful antibiotic solutions. It can also be used as a mild muscle relaxant, although it only has a fraction of the potency of Raldir root for this purpose.

Alchemists Guild. Books of apothecary. Book VII Plants. Chapter 8

Rust

Rust shoved the food knife in to the gap between the window and frame. It bent against the pressure. Her bruised ribs ached with the effort.

There was at least another hour before the guards returned. They had followed the same routine since her escape attempt. They would knock, then if she didn't respond within a few seconds, would enter anyway. It gave her a predictable schedule.

She wasn't sure what she would do, even if she got the window open. Apart from a pleasant view, the balcony led nowhere. She got no pleasure from the view. It just reminded her that her world had shrunk to the size of two rooms. The window glass may as well have been a thick layer of steel. She had to try though, she couldn't just give up. Not now.

The window didn't budge.

It had been a couple of days since her escape attempt. It had ended in absolute and miserable failure. Bruised ribs, her only reward. A doctor had checked her over when Trelt had brought her back. Not the friendly older one, but the scowling one with the scar. He assured her they were just bruised. At first they'd burned like fire, but now they just ached when she breathed too deeply.

Her thoughts constantly returned to Indiril. Initial anger had morphed into guilt and shame. She shouldn't have pushed him away like that. He would be as scared as she was. Just as alone. He was being held because of her. There had been no direct threat to his safety. Indeed, Trelt hadn't directly threatened her either. He maintained his sickeningly manicured friendliness. Slimy fucker.

She might have believed it if it wasn't for Indiril. Why had they waited until she tried to escape before mentioning him? At the time, she had been too blinded by anger to notice. It had since become obvious. No, there was no direct threat, but it was implied.

This morning, a giant ship had sailed into the bay. A vast ocean-crossing cargo ship. Giant steam stacks belched vapour as it went. A low-pitched horn sounded, like the forlorn call of some giant sea leviathan. What would it be like to sail the oceans? With nothing in any direction but unending seas. She wasn't sure why, but the sight and sound had made her weep. Enough was enough, she'd thought. She'd done enough wallowing and started looking for other ways to escape.

She played out the path she and Trelt had taken back to this room after they'd left Indiril. He had to be in the same wing as her, on the same level. Once she had escaped, she would find Indiril, and they would both make a bid for freedom. There were a thousand things they would have to do before they successfully escaped. Deep down she knew it was bordering on fantasy to even consider it.

Don't think about it! Concentrate on getting the window open and then find another way back into the building. Didn't have to be today. Slowly she would build up a plan. She would re-trace her steps, rescue Indiril. Uncle always said that big problems should be broken down into steps. Solve each one. One step at a time.

She pushed the knife further into the gap. It snapped. The tip remained in the gap, but the handle pinged out of her hand.

At the same moment, there was a knock at the door. The guards were an hour early! She couldn't see the knife handle anywhere. The doors opened and two guards entered, followed by the scowling doctor with the scar.

"Hello Rust," the Doctor said as he approached. "Please forgive the intrusion. I have come to give you a light anti-inflammatory for your ribs. I understand they have been quite painful."

His voice was high pitched and soft. It didn't match his face. There was a something about it that grated.

"No," she said, "I'll be fine. I had one yesterday and I'm completely better now."

It was a lie.

"Sorry," he replied, "I insist. It will help with your recovery. You need to be fit and well if you are to travel."

"Travel? Where am I going?"

He ignored the question.

"Please be seated," the Doctor said instead, motioning with his hand to the chair next to the balcony window.

Rust sat.

"Unfortunately, Dr Relshanna has been taken ill, so you'll have to make do with me, I'm afraid."

The doctor placed his bag on the carpet and bent down to retrieve something from it. As he bent down, his eyes shifted to a spot beside Rust's chair. Rust followed his gaze to the knife handle. The doctor was looking directly at it. Her veins filled with ice. It was all over now. The doctor looked directly at her. The man knew!

Without speaking, he shifted his bag so that the knife would be hidden from the guards. He withdrew his instruments from the bag with one hand. With the other, he deftly picked up the knife handle and slipped it in to his bag. He looked at Rust again with the merest flicker of a head shake. Say nothing. Do nothing.

"Now, please give me your arm and I'll make this as quick as possible," the doctor continued, as if everything was normal.

Rust held out her arm as instructed, stunned by the doctor's unexpected act. After the needle went in, there was a slight burning sensation and a warmth spread up her arm. The doctor withdrew the needle and placed a small bandage over the tiny puncture wound.

"There, all done," he said, smiling.

Without another word, he rose and left the room. The

guards followed.

Vidyana

Vidyana smiled as she watched the young woman Rustari. She was trying to prise open the glass door that led onto the balcony. Vidyana's enhanced eyesight allowed her to see the knife clearly. Rust's brow furrowed with the effort.

Vidyana watched from a room that overlooked Rust's apartment. The room Vidyana was in must have been a bedroom once. Maybe a study. Large ornate fireplace. Rectangular patches of brighter wallpaper against a faded background, indications of where paintings had once hung. The room was almost bare now. Just a few pieces of furniture remained. All covered with dust sheets. The place smelled damp. A dull place to watch from, but compared to some places she'd been to in her career, it was almost a luxury. Just another forgotten room in a pointless palace. All these palaces were the same, far too many rooms to be of practical use. All show. Glory days long gone.

Rust had started working on the window earlier. Vidyana could tell by the way Rust moved, her ribs hurt. Not that Vidyana was surprised, Rust had landed pretty hard during her escape attempt. The memory made Vidyana cringe.

Thankfully, Rust hadn't been killed. However, it was a personal failure that Rust had even got as far as she had. Rust was on the roof before Vidyana had realised what she was up to.

Instead of watching Rust, she'd been gawping like an idiot towards the docks where something had been going on. Flashing lights. A crackling sound, muffled by the distance, was unmistakable to her enhanced ears. Gunfire. Here in Lerins! Each year they, and the knowledge of how to construct them, spread like a virulent disease around the world. The fucking heretics, the unholy plague carriers of forbidden knowledge.

Saints be praised, she'd remembered her duties just in time to see Rust emerge onto the roof.

Vidyana had whispered to her shade. Dragon blood coursed through her veins. Time slowed. Each heartbeat felt in entirety. Tiny details snapped into focus. She felt connected to the surrounding room. All the details sharp. Her kavach armour oozed out from tiny holes on either side of her spine. It flowed round her even as she'd fled from the room, slamming open the door with unrestrained force.

She'd passed a guard in the hallway. His face only just registering her presence as she swept past in a blur. Behind her, splinters from the door bounced around the startled guard.

Even with her speed, it had still been a mad scramble to get to Rust in time. She'd got to the an adjacent balcony just moments before an enormous explosion had rocked the distant docks. In her hyper-aware state, she knew to ignore it, her attention now fixed entirely on Rust. Rust, jerked around towards the explosion. Vidyana's shade forewarned her of the approaching shock wave. The shockwave hit. Rust fell backwards and slid towards the roof's edge.

Even as Rust fell, Vidyana's shade was predicting the path the fall would take. The path appeared in her vision like a thread of thin blue silk. It traced out over the edge, before curving downward towards the distant ground below, and certain death. Unless Vidyana intercepted Rust mid fall. A separate red line appeared and traced their course towards the balcony. She had surrendered partial control of her limbs to her shade. She leaped. For a few seconds, her shade moved her muscles with a precision that she could never hope to replicate.

The leap had intercepted Rust perfectly. They'd landed exactly where her shade had predicted. She had rolled, protecting Rust from the worst of the impact. Behind them, the fire from the distant explosion still roiled in to the sky.

It had been close.

Vidyana wouldn't make the same mistake twice. If Rust was even remotely close to getting the windows open, Vidyana would have to pay her a visit. She wanted to avoid that if she could. It was important that Rust felt as comfortable as possible.

Vidyana watched and waited. Rust couldn't see from her point of view, but the balcony doors were secured by iron bands on the outside. She could smash the glass panes all she wanted, but the gaps between the frames were too small.

Rust tried again. The knife buckled and broke. The remnants disappeared out of sight beneath a table near the window. Rust was looking around for the broken knife when something made her stop.

Through another window, Vidyana saw two guards enter. Odd. Unscheduled. One doctor entered. Not Dr Relshanna, but the other one. Dr Nortaud. She glanced down and looked over today's schedule, just to be sure. No, this definitely wasn't on the list. Not that much of a surprise; the doctors lacked the discipline of the military. It was the second time this week that they'd visited without putting it on the schedule.

The doctor's bag and hands were out of sight from her position. After a few seconds, the paraphernalia needed to give an injection came into view. She watched as the doctor administered it and then left. This really was unacceptable. They'd been told after the first failure that all visits must be pre-arranged. Amateurs. She sighed.

Vidyana got up and left the room.

The guards outside Rust's room stood to attention as she approached.

"Do you know what the Doctor was doing?" she asked.

"Just a routine medicine visit he said."

"Where is Dr Relshanna?" she asked.

"He fell ill this morning," the guard replied.

"Ill?"

"Yes, some kind of heart problem, they said."

"Why wasn't I told?" Vidyana barked.

The guard looked towards his female comrade. A look of pleading in his eyes. The other guard looked straight ahead, clearly glad it wasn't her.

"Sorry sir," the guard said, "we only just found out from Dr Nortaud."

Something felt wrong. First the unscheduled visit, then the fact that it was by the subordinate doctor. Now she found out Dr Relshanna had been taken ill. Also, Trelt was away at the docks. Too many anomalies all in neat little line.

Chapter 15

In order of distance from the Sun, the major planets are Agnir, Evenset, Earth, Jewel, Deepset, Mandel and Vinter.

A primer on Navigation, Chapter 2, pt.2
   Guild of Navigation

Sybelle

It had still been light when Sybelle had gone to bed. She opened an eye. Still light. Saints! Just as sleep was about to come, some thought or worry would bring her back to wakefulness.

Thoughts of Kathnell and Mother. The Kathnell parts were fabulous. Wondrous down to the smallest details. The smell of oil on her clothes, and the harsh soap she used to wash her hands. Sybelle wished she could buy a perfume with the same scent. But if the saints demanded balance, thoughts about Mother and her odd activities were the counterpoint.

She tried to think about Kathnell, but her mind always sneaked its way back to Mother. Kathnell was probably right; it was all just a misunderstanding.

That morning, Sybelle and Mother had attended weekly worship at the cathedral. Afterwards, Mother had gone directly into the city on another one of her "errands". Relgor had accompanied Sybelle back to the house in the carriage. If he thought there was anything odd about Mother's behaviour, he said nothing. The journey had been awkwardly silent.

She rolled over again.

There was a noise from downstairs. The clanking of the front door being bolted; Mother home at last. She wasn't alone. Voices on the stairway. Mother, and two other people. Men. She couldn't tell what they were saying, but they sounded agitated. Something was being dragged along the carpet on the landing. Someone made a shushing noise. A door closed. The voices became quieter. Sybelle quickly got dressed and went into the hallway.

The house was in darkness, except for a sliver of light shining from underneath the study door. She padded across to it and listened. What sounded like uncle Zarl, and another she didn't recognise. Incomprehensible babble, muffled and too quiet to make out. The few sentences she heard made little sense.

Something about fishing boats, a submarine, and smuggling. She shuffled closer to the door. A floorboard creaked. The voices fell silent.

Saints! She started back to her room. The door opened.

"Sybelle," Mother said. Sybelle froze. Her voice had the same tone as it had when Sybelle had confronted her. Cold and emotionless. All hints of its normal warmth, gone.

Two other immaculate men stood behind her. Uncle Zarl, and an immaculate man wearing the robes of a doctor. He had a bright red scar down one cheek. None of them were wearing their aspects. A young woman lay either asleep or unconscious on the couch by the window. Unruly hair, common drab clothing. Sybelle stood and stared. Of all the things she had imagined Mother was up to, there had been nothing this... odd.

"Come in Sybelle," Mother gestured to the room. "I think it is time you knew what is really going on."

Zarl smiled.

"Hello Syb, it's good to see you," he said.

"Good... Good to see you too, uncle Zarl," she said.

The calmness of her reply was absurd. Like nothing was wrong. Good old uncle Zarl. Just the usual family gathering. The doctor had retreated to the couch where the young woman lay, checking her pulse.

Sybelle sat heavily in a chair. Mother sat down next to her. Zarl went to join the doctor, who was still fussing by the young woman's side.

"I had hoped that I would have had more time to introduce you to all this when you were older, but things have happened over the last few days that have meant that will not be possible. For that, I am sorry."

"What are you talking about? What things?" Sybelle asked.

Mother raised a hand.

"All in good time, Syb," she said, "but first I want you to understand that your life might be in danger. All our lives. Not through any fault of yours. Indeed, most of it is down to me. My past. In some ways, your life has always been in danger, since even before you were born."

Mother wiped a tear away.

"Your father knows nothing about what I am about to tell you. Your brother knew, before he died. Indeed, he died for the same cause that we follow."

"Died? What… What cause?!" Sybelle said, voice raised.

The two men turned to look, before quickly turning away again. Sybelle's heart raced. An anger rose within her, like the sudden, directionless rage that blossomed when she banged her head.

"Hey, hey. It's all right," Mother said. "This is a lot for you to take in. I remember when I told your brother, and how he reacted. That was under much better circumstances. I'd had time to prepare. You will get your answers, but first I want you to meet someone."

Mother rose and aided Sybelle to her feet. The other two men stood over the young woman. Zarl looked up as they approached. His smile was sincere and warm. The young woman snored softly, deeply asleep.

"Sybelle," Mother said, "this is Rustari Drellmore. My dead brother's daughter. Your cousin."

"My cousin? Your brother? Tomlas?"

"She's a very important person. More so than maybe anyone in this city."

Sybelle looked down at the sleeping figure. The girl didn't look like much. Then she saw it - the painting of her uncle Tomlas in the hallway back home in Drellgarh. Dressed in the smart uniform of an Imperial army captain. She'd often caught her mother standing underneath it, looking up, almost like she was having a conversation with him. He'd died just after Sybelle had been born. The girl's resemblance to the man in the painting was striking. Same cheekbones, nose, and mouth. Her cousin?

Sybelle knew little about her uncle. Mother had always been evasive whenever he was mentioned. Sybelle had always assumed it was because talking about him upset Mother. There had been no mention of a cousin.

The doctor withdrew a slender needle from the young woman's arm and stood.

Rustari. That was a strange name, not at all normal for an immaculate. It was the name a mundane would have, not high house blood.

"My part in this is done," the Doctor said. "Rustari is fine. She'll wake within the next ten to fifteen minutes. A little groggy, but otherwise good."

Zarl handed the doctor an envelope and shook his hand. The doctor looked at its contents and sighed.

"Good luck, Zarl," the doctor said, then turning to Mother, "Welyne, saint's praise your journey."

"You too, Doctor."

The doctor nodded and headed for the door. He stopped and let out a short laugh.

"You know, it's funny," the doctor said. "No matter how much I know about the truth of our past and the so-called saints, or indeed all the other Imperial feldershit, I still use terms like 'saint's praise you' as if they actually mean something. It's good to finally do something worthwhile for the cause."

Without waiting for a response, he was gone. What in Nemesis' name was that all about?

"Now, Sybelle," Mother said, "you have thousands of questions. I understand that."

A thousand questions wouldn't even get halfway, Sybelle thought.

"Rustari will have even more questions than you. She's lost everything she has ever known. She knows even less than you do. She'll wake up confused, and I ask you to wait until she is awake, then I can explain everything to you both at the same time."

"But…" Sybelle went to speak. Mother raised her hand.

"I mean it, Sybelle. You will get your answers. All you have to do is wait a little while longer."

Sybelle felt light-headed. A feeling that her old life was rapidly disappearing. She sat. Something thick and sickly rose at the back of her throat. Mother reached down and took her hand again.

"I can't promise you everything will be all right, Syb," Mother said, "but I will try with my dying breath to make it so."

Trelt

Trelt's arm itched maddeningly. It had grown progressively worse as the day had worn on. What started as an occasional irritation was now a constant annoyance. The skin was still slightly translucent, showing a complex network of veins beneath. It made his stomach churn. It looked better each day, but was still horrifically ugly. He doubted it would ever be the same again. Still, he was lucky the machine had salvaged it at all. He didn't relish the alternative of having to spend months getting the machine to regrow a whole new arm, bit by bit.

The last few days had been chaotic and hectic in equal measure. The heretics had attacked, and successfully destroyed, a critical shipment destined for Taldor-Ire.

He had received instructions from the Emperor via his seers. Whilst the West Wind was here, Trelt was to help track down the rebels responsible for the attack. The local Drellmore and Bennel troops were good, but lacked the expertise, training, and equipment to get fully on top of the rebel situation in the area. House Drellmore had spent the last six months downplaying the strength of the anti-Hegemon sentiment within Lerins. Pride had stopped house Drellmore from telling the full truth. It had become shockingly apparent that the city was awash in anti-Hegemon sentiment fuelled by Liberation cells. Like all the noble houses, Drellmore's doctrine had been honed over centuries and wasn't used to the new guerrilla tactics that had arrived with the rise of Liberation.

Trelt had moved the airship to the docks and had spent the last two days overseeing a crackdown. The heretics had become interwoven into the poorer communities, especially those to the north. Their networks had grown unchecked, festering like an uncleaned wound. It would have to be disrupted. Examples would need to be made. Order restored.

Eventually the Aurumill would set up a network of agents of their own. It would take time, but they would get on top of it.

The Emperor had ordered Lord Drellmore to send more forces to the province, but they were still many days away. Trelt hoped to be out of the area before they arrived. He wanted to get back to figuring out what Rust knew. He suspected the girl knew nothing. Harrod Parra's death had been a deliberate act of denying Trelt more information.

Trelt was headed back to the palace. He'd just come from the building where they were holding the tree-boy Indiril after moving him from the palace. They would soon transport him to another location, away from this festering continent. Trelt would soon take Rustari there as well. The sooner the better.

Trelt's carriage came to a stop outside the palace. Trelt was glad to be back. He couldn't wait to get some rest. He stank and desperately needed a bath. A soak in warm water was just what he needed. That would have to wait. First, he had to check in on Rustari.

He headed for Rustari's apartment. Somewhere else in the palace, the queen of Bennel would be sitting on her throne, ruling her country as best she could. Trelt had met her on a couple of occasions since their arrival. She actually seemed to care for her subjects. It was good to see. The latest in a long linage of Bennel royalty stretching back centuries. Bennel was still technically an independent kingdom and enjoyed a significant amount of autonomy, but it was also a suzerainty of the Hegemony, and since the Schism, House Drellmore had taken more of an active role in its rule.

The Emperor had manipulated Bennel into capturing the territories around Taldor-Ire, one of many projects around the world essential to his plans. But the conflict had caused genuine suffering within the Bennel population and especially within the capital. Suffering that was now being leveraged by the heretics to sow anti-Hegemon sentiment. As the ancient saying went, every action has an equal and opposite reaction.

The doors to the main corridor stood open. Odd. They should have been kept locked at all times. Two guards and a captain stood talking to each other. The captain stiffened and saluted as he approached.

"Lord Vellorson," the captain said.

"What is it? Why are these doors not secure?"

"The prisoner was taken ill and has been taken to the infirmary," the man stammered.

"Ill?"

"My lieutenant went to check on her at the scheduled time. He found her unconscious on the floor. She'd been sick. He immediately called for me. When I got there, the girl looked terrible, pale, and had an extremely weak pulse."

"Where is she now?"

"We called for the doctor and he immediately took her to the infirmary. He said the prisoner had suffered some kind of severe allergic reaction and needed emergency treatment, that it was touch and go if the prisoner would pull through."

"Dr Relshanna thought it was that serious?"

"Sorry Sir, it wasn't Dr Relshanna. It was Dr Nortaud."

Nortaud? That was odd. Where was Relshanna? Also, where the hell was Vidyana? She should have been all over this.

"Where is Dr Relshanna?"

"He was taken ill himself earlier."

Trelt turned and headed for the infirmary. He gestured for the captain to follow. The man quickly fell into step beside him.

"When did all this happen?" Trelt asked.

"About two hours ago, sir."

Two hours! And I've been wasting time checking up on

the fucking tree-boy, he thought. Again, it seemed odd that Vidyana hadn't contacted him about it through the seers.

Two guards stood at attention outside the infirmary doors. They saluted neatly as Trelt and the captain approached. Trelt walked past them and into the infirmary interior. A half a dozen rooms arranged along the corridor. An apothecary, a couple of storerooms, a consultancy room, and two operating rooms. Apart from gurgling water that coursed through overhead pipes, there was no other sound.

"Where is our guest?"

"The doctor told us to take her into the far room," the captain gestured to a room at the end of the corridor. His voice was shaky.

"There are two other guards with them," the captain said, as if to convince himself that everything was all right. That all they needed to do was go through the doors and everything will be fine. You'll see.

Trelt threw open the door. The only person in the room was lying on a table against one wall, covered with a white sheet. The sheet was stained with blood around the mouth area. Both guards were absent.

Trelt lifted the sheet away from the body's head. It wasn't Rustari. Just some unknown middle-aged woman. The captain went through into a back room.

"Fuck!," the captain said.

The two guards lay on the floor. The captain knelt beside them.

"They're unconscious," the captain said. His face was white.

A chute that led down to the laundry room below lay open.

Trelt rushed from the room in the stairway's direction. As he rounded the corner, he nearly collided with a young Aurumill soldier coming the other way.

"Lord Vellorson. Our seers just received this urgent message from Captain Baylali. She took one of our seers with her a couple of hours ago. She said I would find you

either here or in the residence wing."
He saluted and handed Trelt an envelope.

Rust

"Try to be calm", a woman said.

Rust awoke. Her vision was blurry. She could hear her own heartbeat in her ears. Someone was screaming. With a start, Rust realised it was herself and stopped. There were other people in the room, but Rust couldn't make them out through her blurred vision.

When she tried to speak, all that came out was an inaudible mumble. She tried to get up again, but her body just didn't work properly.

"Try to stay calm, Rustari," the woman said again, pressing her gently back down into the couch on which she lay.

Rustari? Nobody called her that.

The woman gradually came into focus. An immaculate. No aspect, but her appearance was a giveaway. Hair neatly plaited. Expensive, colourful fabric waist coat and dress. Who the fuck was she? Where was this? This wasn't her apartment in the palace. She couldn't see any details, but the room was the wrong shape. There were three other people in the background but she couldn't focus on them, they were just vague human sized blurs.

Rust felt exhausted. The world dimmed.

When she woke again, her eyes were working a little better. She still didn't have a clue where she was, or who these three people were. The last she could remember was eating her evening meal and puzzling about why the doctor had not told the guards about the broken knife. She'd always distrusted that doctor, and yet the man had clearly seen the broken knife and said nothing. No, more than that, he had put the evidence in his bag.

A while after the doctor had left, Rust had felt quite ill. She remembered her arms and legs going numb. Then nothing.

"Hello Rustari," the woman said. "Please try not to worry. You are amongst friends here."

"Who, who are you?" she stammered.

"My name is Welyne Drellmore, and this," she said, gesturing towards the young woman sitting behind her, "is my daughter Sybelle."

Drellmore? One of the great imperial houses! Fuck. The ones that controlled the palace. The ones responsible for Bennel's war with its neighbours. Fucking Drellmores!

"Hello," the daughter said.

The daughters' hands trembled. The girl looked grey. Her eyes, wide. She looked as scared as Rust felt.

"And this is my cousin, Zarl Drellmore," Welyne said, looking towards a burly man with white hair and a large beard standing in the corner. The man smiled and nodded.

"What... the fuck... am I doing here?" Rust stammered.

"That," the woman said, "is a good question. The answer is ever so slightly complicated. Some of it is going to be hard to believe, but once we've got you safely out of the city, we will have time to explain everything to you fully."

"Out of the city? What..."

Rust tried to get up, but the woman pushed her gently back down onto the couch. Rust didn't have the strength to resist. She handed Rust a small glass full of a dark liquid.

"You'll need a drop of that before we go on, girl," the man in the corner said, raising his own glass and taking a swig. "Its good stuff. Tan brandy. Unfortunately, not from Tarranis, but still pretty good."

Their accents were strange, similar to the doctors. The words were the same, but spoken in a way that made it difficult to understand. Too quick.

Rust took a swig from the glass. Liquid fire burned her mouth. Her throat immediately spasmed shut. She gagged, and then violently coughed, expelling the remaining liquid. The man laughed.

"Told you it was good stuff," he said.

Rust

It was all fucking nonsense, Rust thought. All of it.

If just a quarter of what they had said was true, and that was a big IF, then Rust's entire life had been a lie. Her mother and father, Uncle, and her Nothari heritage, lies. The supposed 'truth' was utterly ridiculous. But doubt nagged at her. Their stories all tied together and wove around her life, as compelling as it was hard to believe.

These people were strangers. She had no reason to believe them, but they answered many of the questions that she'd had since this whole debacle had started. No, she thought, questions she'd had since she was a child. She was left with the feeling that, although absurd, this new version of her history just might actually be the truth. Each revealed fact raised a thousand new questions. Her head swam with the details. When Rust asked a question, they answered fully and without evasion.

The first revelation had been that her parents weren't Nothari traders. Instead, her father had been a member of house Drellmore. This woman's brother, no less. House-fucking-Drellmore! That made her part Drellmore. Part immaculate. The thought made her feel sick. How could she be part immaculate? The people she'd been brought up to dislike and distrust all her life. Despised by her village. Her country. The very people responsible for the war that Peldaran would almost certainly soon get dragged into.

It turned out that not all immaculate followed the Hegemon and its God-Emperor. It wasn't the unified voice they liked everyone else to think. People like this woman, Welyne, were dissenters.

Not the rebellion, or Liberation, as they liked to call

themselves. No, these people were different. They called themselves the Sleepers. Rust had never heard of them. Hardly anyone had, it seemed, and that was the whole point. An organisation that had worked secretly against the Hegemon since the time of the Schism. What the rebellion tried to do through direct aggression, the Sleepers attempted to do quietly. They both wanted the same thing, however; to overthrow the Hegemon.

The Sleepers had learned of the raid on Hammington's Rest, and through Doctor Nortaud, had arranged her escape from the palace. The same doctor she'd taken a dislike to. The older doctor that she had trusted was the opposite. Fiercely loyal to the Hegemon, and nasty to the core. It reminded her that jumping to conclusions based on initial impressions could be costly. Something Uncle had always taught. There were always two people inside everyone, he used to say. The one you see on the outside, and the genuine person within. Often opposites.

"So, you're part of the bloody rebellion?" the daughter said.

"No, no, Syb," Welyne said. "The Sleepers are different."

"Sound the same to me," Sybelle said, shaking her head. "I can't believe my mother is a heretic."

Welyne sighed.

"The difference is, Syb," Welyne said, "the Sleepers don't want a violent solution. Liberation wishes to overthrow the Hegemon and the Emperor through direct force. By teaching people how to use forbidden things. Things like guns, and worse. The Hegemon has maintained control because they fiercely control access to what we call the 'old magic'. Magic is just very advanced knowledge that nobody else knows. The rebels, however, seek to make everyone equal through the use of the same knowledge. By forcing the Hegemon into submission through war. Guns first, then other things. For them, the aims justify the means. It is doomed to fail. Millions will die. The bloodshed will be awful."

The girl, Sybelle, turned away and shrugged. She looked about as convinced as Rust felt.

"It was Simona, Rustari's mother, that we followed," Welyne continued, "not the Emperor. Not Alexi."

"My mother's name was Simona?"

"Yes Rustari, she was the leader of the Sleepers."

Hearing the name for the first time seemed odd. She'd always thought her mother had been called Sildralla. At least that's what Uncle had said. She felt no connection to this other name.

Welyne said that Simona had been killed by the Hegemon shortly after the Schism. By those working directly for Trelt Vellorson. The same man that had come to Hammington's Rest to find her. Rust's mother and Trelt Vellorson had been friends once, before Trelt had been captured, and turned, by the Emperor.

Uncle hadn't been related to her at all, but a brilliant military commander working for Simona. That at least sounded plausible. Rust had often wondered where Uncle had learned all his hunting and tracking skills. It also explained a lot of what she had found within the elderuin.

Sybelle stood and went to the window. Rust was feeling more awake now, but still shaky from the drug the doctor had given her. She propped herself up and took another sip of the brandy.

"Excellent stuff, eh?" the bearded man said, smiling.

Rust ignored him.

"But why?" Rust asked Welyne.

"Why what, Rustari?" Welyne replied.

"Nobody calls me Rustari. It's Rust."

"Alright, Rust, why what?"

"Why the rebellion? Why the Sleepers? Why any of this?"

"I asked you earlier if you believed in Nemesis. Well, do you?"

Everyone knew about Nemesis, even in the remotest parts

of Peldaran. The Hegemon never stopped bleating on about it. That it waited in the spaces beyond the sky for a sign that mankind had transgressed against it. How, only the wisdom of the Emperor could prevent it. Rust had heard all the stories. Uncle had always said that it was a tale told to frighten people into submission. The tree folk followed their own Divinist religion, but even they had their version of Nemesis, an entity they called the Great Deceiver. The rebels said all of it was feldershit. Not so much a lie, but the Emperor's delusion.

"Of course not," Rust said. "It's just something your priests made up to scare everyone in submission."

"No, Rust. Nemesis is real. That is something that the Hegemon, Liberation, and the Sleepers all agreed on. The problem is that none of us could agree on what to do about it. And that is where all the trouble started."

"You're all mad," Rust said.

This nonsense was making her weary. Or maybe it was the drugs or brandy. She just wanted to be back home. Back in her little village.

Sybelle turned from the window.

"You didn't answer her question," Sybelle said. "Why?"

"Nemesis nearly killed us. Those we now call the immaculate, humans, the tree people, the giants, the t'kelikt, and the ceph. All of us. It was long ago. Only a few escaped."

"Escaped? From where?" Sybelle asked.

"That is going to take some time to explain," Weylne said. "For now, just believe me that Nemesis is real, and it nearly wiped us out. It took a long time for us to even recover. Thousands of years. For a lot of that time, Alexi was asleep. When he awoke, he realised we were well on our way back to discovering the things that had brought Nemesis down on us in the first place."

"The Emperor constructed the Hegemon to make sure that Nemesis didn't come back. He constructed the Hegemon, the Church, and everything else, for one purpose.

To prevent the advancement of technology that would bring Nemesis back. Nemesis was drawn to technology the same way a delann-fly is to rotting fruit. What the Hegemon doesn't control through politics, it controls through manipulation and military domination. It has maintained that balance for many hundreds of years."

"So what changed?" Rust asked.

"Your mother Simona, that's what. The leader of Liberation and people like Trelt Vellorson weren't like the others. It's hard to explain, but they arrived here, on Earth, much later than everyone else. Just before the Schism. They were with a group allied with an entity that had once been the Emperor's sister. An entity called Valtha."

"Wait," Rust blurted. "I've heard that name before."

It had been in one vision she'd had from the pocket watch. The one in the desert with the strangely smooth woman.

"Are you sure?" Welyne asked.

She was about to answer, but stopped. She wasn't sure she trusted these people any more than Trelt. She still didn't know their motives.

"Where?" Welyne prompted. "Was it in the pocket watch? What else have you seen?"

The woman sounded excited and leaned closer to Rust, eagerly waiting for a reply. The same expression on her face as Trelt often wore.

"I can't remember," Rust replied.

Welyne frowned, clearly not convinced.

"Alright. Plenty of time for that later," Welyne said. "What matters is that Valtha and the others brought news to Earth that Nemesis was no longer a threat. It meant that the restrictions the Emperor had put in place no longer needed to be followed."

"What happened?," Sybelle asked.

"The Emperor wouldn't accept this new truth. Simona and Valtha attempted to remove Alexi peacefully by striking at his source of power. The plan failed. However, in the attempt, the Emperor's control over several Hegemon Houses was severed. What we now call the Schism."

"It's important to understand what happened with the Schism," Zarl said.

"You see," he continued, "the Hegemon has access to things that nobody else does. Remnants of technologies that are much more powerful than anything anyone else has. Through them, the Emperor can control the world. You've heard of seers, void-stones, knights, golems and the rest. But he has other things. Things he uses to influence the minds of people all over the world. Controlling them. The Ascended, they call them. These people are in places of power all across the Hegemon. Simona's plan failed, but it severed the Emperor's control over hundreds of Ascended. Mainly within the rebel houses. He lost complete control of several of them. Chaos ensued."

"So what's the difference between you and the heretics?" Sybelle asked.

"After failing to remove Alexi," Zarl said, "Liberation's leader, a man named Patrick Tarvellis, believed that the Hegemon should be confronted head on. Even if the cost was high, it would be worth it in the long run. To Liberation, it's just not acceptable that the races should live in the shadows. He took advantage of the chaos in the immediate aftermath of the Schism. Rust's mother, Simona, and Valtha, believed that it was still possible to convince the Emperor. If that failed, they would find a way to remove him from power without war and unnecessary bloodshed. She had a plan, a way to defeat Alexi without bloodshed. The Sleepers integrated within the Hegemon, quietly spreading influence. Your mother fell in love with Welyne's brother."

"I guess her plan didn't work," Rust said.

"No," Welyne said. "It wasn't ever to come to fruition. Trelt and the Hegemon eventually tracked Simona and her core followers down. My brother amongst them. Simona made sure they wouldn't discover her secrets. She destroyed their entire camp to prevent it. Valtha disappeared. The rest of the Sleepers fled. Some of us have remained undetected ever since. And all the while, Liberation continues to follow their increasingly bloody rebellion."

"But what does the Hegemon want with me?" Rust asked.

"They want what's in your skull, girl," Zarl said, tapping the side of his head. "They know only you can access the memories stored in the memory-well... the pocket watch. Without you, it's just an interesting trinket. Fucking shame we've lost that."

He took another swig from his glass.

Rust understood very little of it. The words flowed over, through, and around her without taking root in her mind. She would have certainly thought they were mad ramblings, but the others in the room looked deadly serious.

Rust thought back to the elderuin. The house Drellmore weapons and armour. The strange devices and objects. It had never made sense why Uncle had been in possession of them and had hidden them away in that remote ruin. Now it did.

The girl, Welyne's daughter, asked just as many questions as Rust did. Apparently, this was all new to her as well. She kept shaking her head. At least Rust wasn't the only one who found this story hard to believe.

Rust asked about Hammington's Rest, and Peldaran. Zarl said that at the moment it looked like Peldaran would enter the war against Bennel, triggered in no small part by the incursion into Hammington's Rest. Zarl said it would be a foolish move by the Peldaran King.

"The problem is Rust," Zarl said, "there were many secrets that were lost when your mother died. Secrets that everyone now thinks you might possess. Things that could potentially bring down the Hegemon. That's what they fear most of all. Like it or not, you have become the centre of a massive shit storm."

"But I know nothing," Rust repeated.

It was almost true. She didn't really know anything.

Uncle had never told her anything about any of this. She'd tried in vain to tell Trelt the same. Should she tell these people more about the visions? No, not for the time being. Keep it to yourself. She needed more answers before she could trust these people any more than the Hegemon.

Rust went to speak again, but Welyne raised a finger.

"I don't expect you to take all this in," she continued. "I know you have a thousand questions. We don't have the time, and you must be tired. But I promise, once we get you to safety, we can go through everything. For now, I want you to look at this."

Welyne stood and retrieved a wooden box from a nearby table, within which were several items.

"These items belong to my brother. Your father. This is his plasma glove. It is a weapon that can hurl fire."

Rust remembered the fight back in Hammington's Rest and the man wielding fire from his palm. She was sure this was something similar. A gold and silver metal gauntlet that covered the wrist. Fastened around the forearm with straps made from an odd blueish cloth.

Welyne removed a piece of paper on which there was an image. A photograph. Rust had only seen a photograph once before, in a shop window back in Balincross. This one was of a smiling man and woman. The man was dressed in fine, immaculate clothing. He wore the insignia of House Drellmore. His smile was lopsided. The woman's clothes were strange, bulky, smooth and functional. Made from a reflective material that looked almost like metal.

"This is my brother, your father," Welyne said, "and this is your Mother, Simona."

Behind them stood another figure, tall and almost greyish-white, contrasting starkly against the others dark skin. The figure had no hair and wore no clothes. It was odd. Simplified, almost like a sketch drawn by a child. Just a thin line for a mouth. Tiny nose and black eyes. The thing from her visions. Valtha?

Welyne noticed her gaze.

"I suspect you already know," she said, "but that is the avatar of Valtha. She was a good woman."

Rust didn't really understand what any of that meant. Instead, she nodded and stared at the picture. The woman had the same jawline and eyebrows as her. Unmistakably family. Until now, it had all seemed so unreal. Disconnected. An interesting story. One without a tangible connection to her. The picture changed it all. Now it was real. For the first time in her life, she looked into the eyes of her mother.

Rust wasn't sure who she was anymore. She felt like she was being swept downstream on a raft towards a waterfall without the ability to alter course. Doomed to be swept over the edge. Her entire life up to this point, a fiction.

It was quite something to realise that your life was a lie. She was alone. Lost. Not only had she thrown her own life into chaos, she had dragged Indiril into it as well. Possibly all of Peldaran. Now Indiril was being held by the Hegemon. She was sure that Indiril would be used as a bargaining chip against her. She had to tell these people, these Sleepers, that if they wanted her help, they would have to get Indiril out as well. She would not do a thing to help them until they did that.

Rust might not be the person she thought she was, but Indiril had nothing to do with it. Since they had been friends, it was always Rust that had got them both into trouble. Indiril was always the sensible one, warning of the consequences of whatever foolish thing she was just about to do. The trip down into the old ruin had seemed like such a great idea. Just an adventure. What would be the harm?

Rust realised that she was sobbing. She didn't know how long she had been crying, but a splash fell onto the picture. Welyne smiled softly and went to remove the photo from her grasp. She tried to resist, but was just so exhausted. She just needed to rest. Just for a few minutes. Try to make some sense out of it all. Her mother. Uncle. The objects. The visions. Hammington's Rest. Sindar, how she wanted to be back there!

"She's still suffering from the effects of the root," someone said. "She'll feel better in the morning."

Rust was swept downstream and onwards towards the waterfall's edge.

Chapter 16

The adult Bittermoth lays its eggs during Redcrown in areas where pollen-spore has settled. The eggs lie dormant until an animal steps on them, at which point the sharp eggs are injected into the foot. After a few days, they hatch and begin feeding on the host. In humans, this can lead to painful swelling of the foot until the larvae have been cut out. If untreated, it will likely end with severe infection and possibly death.

A small type-5 hook knife is best suited to their extraction. The wound should be treated with a suitable antibacterial poultice for three days.

Treatment of minor pests, Book of Surgery IV, Chapter 3, Surgeons Guild

Welyne

Welyne closed the door behind them.

Best to let Rust sleep for now. It was nighttime anyway. The next few days would be rough for the girl. She would go easy on Rust if she could, but her primary mission was to get her away from Trelt and Alexi, and safely into the hands of other Sleepers. Failing that, Rust couldn't be allowed to fall back into the hands of the Hegemon.

Zarl headed off towards the kitchens, mumbling something about pastries and wine. Welyne smiled. Even at a time like this, the man was obsessed with his gut and liver. It was his way of dealing with the stress. They all had coping mechanisms. Her's was to remind herself about what she was doing this all for. Her family, yes, but wider than that, the world. Everyone had the right to know what Alexi was doing, that his obsession with Nemesis was folly.

She walked into the study, Sybelle following silently behind.

Her daughter slumped into a chair, clutching her head. She swallowed repeatedly. The colour drained from her cheeks, and her expression blank. Welyne had been much too slow to bring her daughter into the fold. She wondered if it all stemmed from losing her son. She had always thought she hadn't let that part of her interfere with her Sleeper duties. Of course, that was naïve. How could the death of her only son not have affected her?

Welyne walked over and placed her hand on Sybelle's shoulder.

"Don't worry, our part in this will be over soon," Welyne said.

Sybelle remained expressionless, but nodded slowly.

"Rust will be taken in a couple of days," Welyne continued. "A small ceph submarine loyal to the Sleepers is on its way to collect her from a nearby dock. Zarl has a plan to smuggle her out of the house. Until then, she will remain here. The Hegemon in the palace are going to go crazy when they discover she's gone, but they can't tear the entire city apart looking for her. The doctor will already be well on his way. He's probably already outside the city."

"Then," she continued, "we will return to our normal duties."

"Normal duties? How is anything going to be fucking normal again?"

"It's not. I know. But you'll learn to cope."

"Why didn't you tell me any of... this?"

Welyne poured herself a glass of brandy and took a swig.

"Look Syb," Welyne said, "I've been trying to find the best time to tell you. The death of your brother delayed that. I was trying to protect you. Your reaction to the tests convinced me it was time to act. Then all this happened. I hoped we could get Rust out without you being involved. But you had to poke around. With all your conspiracies about me having an affair."

Welyne poured more brandy into a second glass.

"I'm not sorry," Sybelle said, scowling.

"No, I don't suppose you are," Welyne said. "You're too much like me for that."

There was the faintest flicker of a smile from Sybelle. She passed the other glass to her daughter.

"Here."

Sybelle took a sip from the glass.

There was a clattering noise from somewhere outside. Maybe a cat knocking something over. Then, a faint sound of footsteps.

Danger!

She doused the lamp on the table, crossed to the window, and peeked out through a gap in the curtains. She couldn't see anything obvious. Just an empty moonlit street.

There! A shadow moved in the garden opposite. Now that she looked again, she could see others. Figures trying to stay out of sight across the street.

Shit!

Glancing up the up the street, she saw a couple more shadows cross the road and disappear into the gardens of the houses there. Something dark passed overhead. Large and winged. Silently, it flapped its giant wings and disappeared over the house. Wyvern! Its t'kelikt master harnessed to its back.

Zarl burst through the door.

"We're surrounded!" he hissed, "Fucking Aurumill or Jurament everywhere."

They were trapped! She allowed herself a single second to be terrified. A single second to mourn for her daughter. Then she pushed that part of her deep down to that corner of her mind that she had trained to lock away. Rationally, Welyne knew they would almost certainly all die within the next few minutes. If there was no way out, she would make sure that the Hegemon didn't get hold of Rust, or her daughter.

"What's going on?" Sybelle asked, rising to look through the window.

"Get down! And away from the fucking window," Welyne shouted, pushing her daughter forcibly away. Sybelle staggered backwards and fell against a couch.

"What's going on?" Sybelle asked again, voice high and tight.

Welyne ignored her daughter's question.

"Weapons?" Zarl asked.

"Keepsafe box. In the cupboard," Welyne said, tossing Zarl a key from around her neck. "Whisper-blade, a single hollow-shell and a couple of ship pistols. Throw me the shell."

The hollow-shell was a last ditch thing. She would detonate it if there was no way out. It contained strange forbidden substances. Years ago, Simona had tried to explain it to her. How it was made from the same stuff that made everything else, but twisted somehow, coiled and massively compressed against its will. It had sounded like all the rest of Simona's technology. Incomprehensible. Magic. All that mattered was if she crushed the shell that surrounded it, it would utterly obliterate everything around it for four metres, and cause massive destruction over a much wider area. Gone in a flash, less than the blink of an eye. Not the worst way to go.

Zarl removed the pistols and passed one to her, then the shell. She placed the shell in her pocket and checked the gun. This wasn't one of the crude, oily things the rebels called guns; all metal tubes and springs. With those things, you had a non-zero chance of losing your eyes every time you pulled the trigger. No, these were white and sleek. Old tech. Ancient and forbidden. Each one carried two hundred sliver rounds fired at hypersonic speeds. Accurate and deadly.

"I can't use the whisper-blade," Zarl said, shrugging, throwing it at her as well. She caught it and put it in her pocket as well. In its inactive state, it resembled an ornate white sword handle minus the blade. Carved and embossed with scrolls and swirls. It looked more like a bone than it did a weapon. More ancient magic. Where the blade should have been was a large white pearl. It could only be used by someone with summoning abilities. Zarl didn't have any ability at all. He was a null. A lot of the immaculate were. Welyne had some summoning ability, not enough to get her noticed by the Thaumaturgy, but enough to activate the blade.

Welyne glanced back outside into the street. For a moment, she allowed the panic and the fear to break free. She let out a tiny cry. Feeble and pathetic.

Striding across the street was someone she hadn't seen for many years. Not since she was little more than a baby. Vidyana Baylali. Since then, she'd become Trelt's weapon of choice. The Black Demon, they called her. Ruthless, efficient, and powerful, she was one of the most gifted summoners the Hegemon had. Of course she was. Her parents had been part of Simona's closest allies. Ship's crew.

Behind her, Vidyana dragged Doctor Nortaud. He was bound and gagged, but looked otherwise unharmed. Poor bastard, she thought. They were flanked on both sides by several knights.

"It's Vidyana," she said, looking to Zarl. "She's got Nortaud."

"Fuck."

"Yeah, just about sums it."

Outside in the street, Vidyana forced Nortaud to his feet.

"Welyne Drellmore, you and you family are under arrest for high treason and for harbouring a fugitive of the Hegemon," Vidyana said. "We have your house surrounded. Please surrender immediately."

Enough lingering, she thought.

"Let's go," Welyne said to her daughter. Sybelle didn't budge.

"Get up," she said, hauling her daughter to her feet, "we haven't got time to fuck around."

Her daughter stared wide eyed, looking at her as if she didn't recognise her own mother.

"I'll get the girl," Zarl said, going back out into the corridor. Welyne followed, dragging her daughter behind her.

Outside, Vidyana continued to state her demands.

"We… We have to give ourselves up," Sybelle said.

"Fuck that. That'll be worse than dying. You do not know what they'll do to us," she snapped back. Harsh. She didn't have time to care.

"Don't worry, Syb," she said, "I won't let that happen."

She thought through options. There weren't any. At least none that didn't involve them all dying in a ball of white-hot fire.

It had all been for nothing, Welyne thought. They had

come all this way, but they would go no further. Her journey was at an end. She had tried all she could to keep Simona's dream alive. They had come so close; they were nearly there. Nearly, but not quite. She would not allow Rust to fall into the hands of the Emperor and his sycophant Trelt. Or her daughter. She caressed the hollow-shell within her pocket. Felt its smooth surface.

Zarl returned, half carrying the barely awake Rust and the box containing the old plasma glove. Rust was worse than useless in her state, still half stoned on raldir root. Welyne shot Zarl one last look; a plea for an idea, a single way out. Anything. Zarl shook his head. He had no ideas either. This was it then.

"Wait," Sybelle said, tugging on her arm. Welyne shrugged her off. This wasn't the time.

On the landing they took up position on either side of the balcony, facing down the stairs towards the front door. Welyne toyed again with the shell in her pocket.

She could end it now. Destroy them all in pure fire. Prevent the bastard Hegemon getting Rust again. Prevent them from ruining the mind of her daughter. She just needed to apply pressure to its smooth surface, and that would be it. Just one instant separated them all from silent and painless oblivion. No more struggles. The intense relief that came with that thought was as sudden as it was glorious. Zarl nodded. She started to squeeze.

Her daughter tugged her arm again.

"Wait!" Sybelle shouted. "Will you not listen to me? I know a way out! Through the kitchen."

The kitchen was a dead end, Welyne thought. Nothing there but stoves, cupboards, and a larder.

"There is no way out through the kitchen, Syb," Welyne replied.

She really didn't have time to listen to this.

"Not the new kitchen, the old one. There's a way out. I've used it."

Welyne thought about it for a second. The old kitchens...

On the lowest level at the back of the house. Now that she thought about it, there was that old iron door. To be honest, she hadn't really paid it any attention.

She was about to ask where the door went, but the front doors blew inward, and the world turned to hell.

Zarl

Well, this was a shit ending, Zarl thought. The fucking end.

Zarl aimed his pistol towards the front doors. There was no guarantee that was where the Aurumill would strike, but Vidyana had been in the street and heading straight for the front doors, the poor Dr Nortaud in tow.

He had always clung to the hope that they could pull this off. Get the girl out of the city and into the hands of his contacts. Indeed, things had gone remarkably well. Despite the odds, they'd got the girl out of the palace alive. Welyne's plan had worked. A covert submarine belonging to a ceph matriarch affiliated with the Sleepers had been due to pick the girl up from a fishing boat in a couple of days. They wouldn't show up now they'd been compromised. So bloody close, he thought.

Obviously, Vidyana had tracked the unfortunate Nortaud. Poor bastard. The Aurumill would drain the man's mind dry. Delving, they called it. Whatever was left of Nortaud would spend the rest of its lamentable days sitting in a corner dribbling and mumbling to shadows. He'd seen people who'd been delved. He'd rather be dead. He knew Welyne would destroy them all before she let that happen.

Fortunately, Nortaud knew relatively little. His only contact was Zarl himself. The Sleepers were fragmented for just such reasons, only a few contacts, nobody knowing the complete structure. It was how Simona had structured it. Modelled on underground movements from ancient human history.

Welyne knew the risks. It was a shame about the kid Sybelle; she was a good one. Would have been a great asset. At least with the hollow-shell, she wouldn't feel a thing. The explosion would be so quick that her brain wouldn't even have time to register it before it was reduced to burning dust.

He could hear footsteps and a noise that sounded like something on the roof. It was hopeless; they were surrounded. The Hegemon would burst in, and then it would all end in white fire.

Then Sybelle talked about a way out. Of a door through the kitchens. Welyne dismissed the girl, but she said something that made Welyne stop. Something flickered across his old friend's face. A recognition that something the girl said was true. A flicker of hope.

The conversation didn't have time to finish.

There was a deafening concussion. The doors erupted inwards. They barrelled across the lobby and slammed into the back wall. Splinters of wood and chunks of marble peppered the staircase like bullets. Zarl's ears whistled. Smoke billowed upwards and plaster fell from the decorated ceiling.

Sybelle was screaming; the sound oddly muffled. Zarl wondered if the hearing damage would be permanent. He realised how stupid such a thought was given their situation. Below, through rolling smoke, Zarl saw several Hegemon troopers enter the lobby, crossbows raised towards them. Zarl fired his pistol down into them. Thwack. Thwack. Thwack.

One of them went down. Then a second one.

The rest reached the cover of nearby doorways. A crossbow bolt embedded itself in the wooden banister next to his head. He rolled in to the cover of the nearby hallway.

Sybelle was still screaming. The girl Rust cowered next to her, still half dazed from the drugs. Welyne dragged them both backwards towards the opposite corridor. A couple more Hegemon soldiers entered through the front door.

They were being attacked by normal Hegemon troops, armed with swords and crossbows. At least that was something.

"Is Sybelle correct?" he shouted. "Is there a way out?"

"Might be," Welyne shouted back. She fired her own pistol down the stairs to where the Hegemon were now taking cover.

Then there was still a chance. Still a sliver of hope they could get the girl out alive. Was the risk worth it? Or should they just end it here? At least then the girl wouldn't fall back into the hands of Trelt, and his puppet-master Alexi.

No, if there was a chance, they had to try.

"Can you get there?" he said.

Welyne nodded and pointed down the corridor towards the service stairwell.

There was a crash down the corridor to his left. Splintering glass and wood. A window smashing. So, the Hegemon was on the first floor as well now. A Hegemon soldier appeared in a doorway down the corridor. Zarl fired. Thwack. The man crumpled and was pulled back into the room by another trooper.

Something was wrong. His leg felt numb. He glanced down and noticed a crossbow bolt sticking out of his thigh. He felt no pain. It would come. He tried to move it again. Dead weight. Drug tipped, maybe? Nerve damage? He was fucked.

"Throw me the shell," he shouted.

Welyne hesitated. No doubt going through the same calculations as he was. Weighing the risks.

"Do it, Wel", he said more softly.

She locked eyes with his for a second, then threw the shell over.

"Now, go!" he shouted, "Whilst there is still a chance. Don't fuck this up, Wel, or I'll kill you!"

He smiled. Welyne shot him one last look, and she was gone, Sybelle and Rust following behind.

More crossbow bolts embedded themselves into the surrounding wood. The smoke in the lobby was clearing. Zarl fired again down the stairs towards troopers that were emerging from the doorway they had hidden in. They ducked back.

Two hulking shapes appeared through the smoke. Knights. Zarl fired into them. The bullets bounced off harmlessly. He continued to fire, trying for a lucky hit. None came.

They calmly knelt and raised their right arms. White fire lanced out, tearing through the wood and stone of the balcony. He rolled further into the corridor. Burning splinters fell all around him. Just as he rolled backwards, he glimpsed something moving between them. Something black and impossibly fast. Vidyana.

Before he could prepare, she was on him. She moved with impossible speed, a black figure encased in her kavach armour. Like an obsidian statue come to life. A wonder to behold, really. The ancient technology never ceased to amaze him. He wished he could see more of it. But this was the end. No more adventures. No more brandy. Shame.

She pinned him to the floor with one arm. He tried to wrench her free with his right arm. It was impossible. Her grip was impossibly strong. Bones in his hand cracked under her grip. His other hand closed around the small sphere.

"Stupid old man. Where are the others?" Vidyana asked.

"Go to hell," he spat in to her obsidian-black face.

He squeezed.

Sybelle

Sybelle felt sick, hands shaking violently. She half ran, half staggered, towards the service stairway. Her legs felt numb, about to buckle.

She had barely come to terms with everything Mother had told her, about the girl, about Mother's own past. Before she'd had time to find out, things had gone from bad to hellish. She'd just seen people die. Hegemon soldiers lying in pools of their own blood. She'd never seen a dead person before. She'd wanted to surrender. Mother told her it would be worse than dying. How could anything be worse than that?

Each bizarre moment flowed into the next, all with a strange sense of detachment.

The girl Rust walked, half dazed, beside her. They got to the top of the stairs and Mother descended. The odd little white thing called a gun raised in front of her. In her other hand, she held the odd handle with the ball stuck to the top.

She didn't know what the gun thing was, only that it made a strange noise and killed people. Her mind went back to the dead soldiers at the bottom of the lobby stairs. She'd seen one of them stumble backwards, gore flying from the back of the woman's head. The woman had fallen and lay twitching on the floor, an absurd half smile on her face. Sybelle held onto the doorway. The room started spinning. Bile rose in her throat.

"Come on, Syb!" her mother shouted after her.

There were sounds from behind them, back where they had left Zarl. The thwack, thwack, thwack from Zarl's own gun. She hoped he would follow them soon.

Sybelle swallowed, and followed Mother downstairs and

towards the old kitchen. Rust, more awake now, stumbled on unaided beside her. It was dark and cold in the kitchen, the only illumination came from oil lamps in the hallway. Mother went over to the metal door and tried to open it. It was locked.

"Fuck!" Mother shouted.

"It's all right. I know where the key is." Sybelle said. She went to the shelving, looking for the little blue tin where she had hidden the key.

Mother returned to the doorway into the kitchen and leaned out. Thwack, thwack, thwack. Shouting from the hallway. Crossbow bolts whistled past the doorway, narrowly missing Mother.

"Hurry, Syb!" Mother shouted.

Sybelle found the tin and retrieved the key. She turned the key in the lock, tried the door again, but it still wouldn't budge. It must be bolted from the other side! She slumped against the door and slid down to the floor.

"I'm sorry!" she wept.

There was a rapid clanking noise from the hallway. Something advancing quickly. Her mother aimed the gun down the hallway again. Thwack, thwack, thwack, thwack, thwack. Mother dodged back inside, followed by something massive. A multi-limbed horror, all angles and blades. A t'kelikt. Mother rolled away from it.

Sybelle had seen t'kelikt many times, but never like this. Covered in metal spikes, each leg ending in a nightmarish blade. It darted forwards. Sybelle impotently threw the empty tin at it. It bounced uselessly away. The thing rounded on her. Dark black ichor oozed from a couple of holes in its carapace.

It took a step towards her.

Then it jerked once and slumped to the floor. A large chunk of its torso fell away, exposing dark brown innards. Mother stood over it, holding the odd bone handle. The ball was raised from the handle now, connected to it by an almost invisibly thin glowing blue line. The air surrounding it crackled and fizzed.

Mother strode over and jerked Sybelle away from the door. She swung the blade in an arc towards the door. Sparks flew as the blade sliced into the metal. The lock and part of the door fell away. With a single kick from Mother, the door flew open.

Mother motioned them both through, grabbing a lantern from a shelf. Rust was more awake now, but looked pale. She was trying to speak, but all that came out was mumbled nonsense.

They had barely got through the door when there was a deafening boom. The floor heaved. Dust fell from the ceiling. Behind them, several wooden beams crashed through the ceiling and into the kitchen.

For a second there was silence, then above them the sounds of screaming and shouting.

"Which way?" her mother shouted.

Sybelle pointed down the corridor.

"Down the corridor, then the second door on the left."

Her mother ran off. Sybelle and Rust followed.

They descended a spiral staircase and entered the tunnels that led beneath the house. Her mother looked around, the gun raised in front of her. The place was deserted. Sybelle could hear faint voices from back up the stairwell.

"Where now?"

"Follow me," Sybelle said.

She led them down the corridor and to the thick metal door with the metal locking wheel. Sybelle began spinning the wheel, releasing the mechanism.

"I'm obviously not the only one with secrets," Mother said.

They went through the door, Sybelle closing the door behind them, spinning the wheel once more to secure it. Back down the corridor, she could just make out light coming down the stairwell.

They were now in the large water tank that had once been used by the ceph. Sybelle sprinted along the balcony that circled the space to the other door on the far side. She turned the wheel to open it and they went through. Sybelle spun the wheel to lock it in place. Light appeared at the tiny round window in the other door on the far side, followed by the silhouette of a head. Its wheel started spinning. Shit, she thought, they would be through in a few seconds! Sybelle rushed towards the corridor that would take them back up to the dockside.

Something Kathnell had told her made her stop. What was it? Something to do with the valves next to the door.

"Wait!" Sybelle shouted and headed back towards the door they had just left.

Mounted to the wall were several valves and dials that Kathnell had told her to leave alone. As she got to them, a face appeared at the tiny round window in the metal door. The handle spun. Mother tried to wrench her away.

"We haven't got time Syb. Come on!" Mother said, pointing her gun towards the door.

Sybelle broke free.

"No! Wait. This is important. I can stop them."

"Fuck!"

Her mother released her grip and went to the still spinning handle. She grabbed it and stopped it spinning. Curses came from the other side. A face at the window. Mother gripped the wheel tighter, bracing her foot against the wall for leverage. Another face appeared at the tiny window. Gradually, the handle started to turn again.

"Whatever you've got to do, hurry," Mother said, and turning to Rust said, "Make yourself useful and give me a fucking hand here."

Rust joined her, and together they stopped the wheel from spinning.

Sybelle faced the valves. What was she supposed to do? Kathnell had just said to leave them alone. She'd given no specific instruction. She started turning all the valves in whichever direction they would go. There was the sound of running water through the pipes they were connected to.

Then a muffled thud. A light tremor went through their feet. The handle stopped spinning. Surprised and confused shouts from the other side, which quickly turned to shouts of panic. Fists started pounding on the door. After a few seconds, the noises stopped. Water appeared in the door's window.

Then, the three of them were running again. Sybelle led them up the stairs and towards the dockside. They emerged into the moonlight. Mother threw the lantern into the water. There was nobody around. Where should they go? The dockside? No, too dangerous, too open.

She headed off towards a culvert that Kathnell had mentioned went under the streets. Part of the rainwater drainage system, or something. Sybelle had never been through it, but Kathnell had said you could get out at the other end.

"If we get out of this," Mother said, "and that's a big fucking IF, remind me you and me are going to have a little chat about keeping secrets from each other."

Part Three

A moment separating past from future.

The Hegemon had discovered her! My connection to her broken. My warnings were unheeded. Not my friend. Similar. A variant new but instantly familiar. Daughter!
I knew Alexi would seek her out.

My stupidity! Sulking for years in self-made apathy and pity.
During the Hegemon attack that killed my friend, my last earthly body died as well. Smashed. Buried and lost. Ruined.
But a flicker remained. Ancient things slowly knitting my ruin back together, breathing life once more into its frame. My body clawed its way back to the surface of the living. Reconnected to that other part of me that never sleeps.
I shunned humanity and walked into the desert. Another forgotten relic. Desiccating husk. An oddly disfigured and hooded stranger. Shunned. Little more than a hermit, busying myself with my own arcane projects.

Years that I should have spent preparing! Not delving into ruins.
But in those brief contacts, I knew that there was still hope. If Simona's daughter lived, then there could be a way.

Half a world away, I was powerless to do anything about it.

Chapter 17

House Bargolis was founded in 328SC in the aftermath of the Altaris uprising. House Lunarith, with the support of House Drellmore, pushed back the uprising and recaptured Altaris. The almighty God-Emperor realised that the lawless regions of Northern Leanar had become too powerful to govern from afar, and a marriage between Lord K'Telnar of House Lunarith and Lady Uktollo of House Patrillous formed the start of the new House.

Bargolis has since prospered and now controls a large area of North Eastern Leaner. Sea trade has flourished and Bargolis now forms an important trade hub on the Bargol Sea. The client states now controlled by the Bargolis suzerain include the silvari Kingdom of Gell, which provides some of the best special forces in the Hegemon. Although not immaculate themselves, Gell is staunchly loyal to the God Emperor and the role of the immaculate in the salvation of the races.

A history of the Great Houses, introduction to House Bargolis.

Vidyana

Dark shapes. Blurred outlines. Details coalesced into focus.

Stars shining through a broken roof. The smell of dust. And something else. She knew the scent intimately. Blood.

There was an instant of extreme pain. She screamed. Her shade jumped on it, locking it down.

She coughed up grit and blood. Her breath was shallow.

Her chest hurt. Her left hand felt wrong. She held it in front of her. Two fingers, a mangled mess; sticking out of the black of her kavach armour, bent at useless angles.

She reached up and pulled the two fingers off, tossing them away, useless to her now. The pain crescendoed. She could worry about getting them grown back later. Her kavach armour flowed back around the stumps.

[Warning. You are suffering from a mild concussion. Shock bruising to chest muscles, and left hand function impaired. Automatic triage strictures have been activated.]

Tell me something fucking useful, she thought. The shade whispered in an odd accent she barely understood. It did that when it was overworked.

[I have administered stimulants and pain blockers.]

She looked around.

The explosion had pushed her over the edge of the landing. She lay in the lobby, underneath the remains of a knight. Or at least his lower half. The corpse ended at the waist, a mixture of gore and twisted metal. The top half, nowhere to be seen. Other fallen troops lie scattered around. Mostly dead.

She tried to get up. Her legs and arms gave way. The pain flared again. She collapsed.

Please, saints, give me strength.

[More stimulants], she whispered to her shade.

Everything became pin sharp. Head clear. She pushed herself out from underneath the knight. She was covered in blood. A mixture of her's, the knight's, and Zarl's.

Zarl was nowhere to be seen. Where he had been was now a gaping hole, three metres across. The ceiling and roof above gone. Moonlight shone through. More of the corridor collapsed into the hole. The landing shifted. Bastard had used a hollow shell!

That was twice she'd nearly been killed by one of those things in the last couple of weeks. They were rare. No more could be made. Relics of ancient days.

She was in no doubt that without her kavach armour, she would have been vaporised. She didn't know if it had been damaged. No time to find out.

[Please seek immediate assistance from Aurumill facilities], her shade insisted.

[Not now, please cease your whining,] she said.

The thing shut up.

Where were the others? The doctor had told them that Rustari was with a Sleeper called Welyne Drellmore, her daughter, and Zarl Drellmore.

Surviving Hegemon troopers were getting to their feet. Another knight stomped through the ruined doorway and into the lobby.

"All troopers report. Have you found the fugitive, Rustari?" she shouted.

There were several replies. Far fewer than there should have been.

"No, sir."

"Negative."

"Nothing, sir."

"Down here," someone shouted.

She ran towards the voice. It came from another corridor that led into the servant areas of the house. Downstairs, she found a couple of troopers standing in a ruined room. A twisted metal door led off into darkness.

"Where are they?" she said.

"They went down there," one of the troopers said, "and then down underneath the house."

Underneath the house? She wasn't aware of anything underneath the house. The doctor hadn't mentioned it and there was nothing obvious from the street. If he had known, he would have said. His resistance to the initial delve by her seer had been minimal.

"Why haven't you pursued them?" she asked.

"Some of us did, sir," the taller silvari trooper said, "but water flooded in, and we had to back out. We had to leave four other troopers down there. We think they drowned."

She went down the corridor. A stairwell that led downwards was half full to the top with cold, dark water. Fuck!

She needed to find out where these tunnels went. And quickly. She turned and headed back through the ruined house.

"Get my seer," she shouted to the nearest trooper.

"Yes, sir!"

"And you," she said, "tell the captain to fan out. Search the surrounding streets."

"Yes, sir!"

Fuck. Fuck. Fuck.

She needed to calm down. She was bordering on panic. It would cloud her mind, lead her towards death. She must not let it win. She stopped and knelt. Felt the smoothness of the tiled floor. It's coolness. She breathed deeply. She prayed, and for a few moments thought about the saints, the Emperor, and her dead parents. She slowed her heart rate and stood.

She walked back to the lobby. The house groaned around her. It was dying. Its backbone destroyed. A bit like her fucking plan, she thought.

After she had discovered the Doctor's betrayal, the plan had formed quickly. It had been easy to follow him to his rendezvous with the Drellmores. In hindsight, she should have apprehended them then, but had thought it best to follow them back to their nest. Poor decision in hindsight.

After the doctor had left, they'd captured him and surrounded the property. They'd delved his mind a little. Just on the surface, not enough to do much damage. It was obvious the man knew little outside of his direct involvement. He claimed to work for a group called the "Sleepers". It wasn't even an organisation that she'd heard about, but they had to be connected to the rebels somehow.

She hadn't had the luxury of advanced planning and reconnaissance. They'd moved quickly. Wyverns scouted from the air. The t'kelikt riders had reported good access from either side of the property. They were going to go in all at once. The minutes that followed initially seemed to go well.

There had been no mention of tunnels under the house, but with the luxury of hindsight, it seemed obvious. The house was one part of what had obviously been a much larger building. One side overlooked the docks, and the wyvern riders had mentioned something about what looked like old ceph entrances on the waterfront.

She walked out into the street. Her seer met her. The doctor sat whimpering on the kerbside. A knight stood behind the man. Another couple of knights walked up and down the street.

Other immaculate families were coming out into the street, or gawping from balconies. Pointing and talking amongst themselves. In her mind, they were no different to the mundanes they looked down upon. When it came to it, people were people. Gossip was gossip.

"Get these fucking people off the street," she ordered the nearest knight.

She turned to her seer and sighed.

"Please send a message to Trelt," she said. "Tell him I have temporarily lost contact with the fugitive Rustari Parra."

Rust

Rust looked up as a silent shadow passed overhead. A brief glimpse of black wings in the gap between two buildings. A wyvern. Gone as quickly as it had appeared. The woman, Welyne, pushed them both back into the darkness of the alleyway.

"Come on," Welyne said, quickly crossing the main street and ducking in to a similar alleyway opposite. Rust followed. The daughter, close behind.

The alley was dark. Sensible, Rust thought. The main street ran roughly north-south, the alleys east-west. With both moons high in the south, the main street was well lit, the alley in shadow. She used similar techniques to track game with Uncle. Keep in shadow. Limit silhouettes.

They stood outside the side entrance to some kind of shop. Across the alleyway, she could see the carved circle emblems of the side of a small Divinist temple. Just like the sort you found in Balincross.

The woman busied herself with the locked shop door. It opened with a click. They entered quietly. In the gloom, Rust made out several shelves filled with ornate metalwork. Lamps, candelabras, and the like. The stuff looked expensive. Benches against another wall were full of tools.

She hadn't had time to adjust to all the revelations when she'd woken into this new nightmare. Everything had been dreamlike at first. Nightmarish. Odd flashes of gunfire, explosions, running. Difficult to work out what was a dream and what was real. Of the first few minutes, she could barely remember. Her first clear memory was of going through an iron door that led underneath the house.

They had since escaped into the city, but were still on the

run. Rust had enquired as to the whereabouts of the older man with the beard. Welyne had told her he had sacrificed himself so that Rust could escape. Not so Welyne or her daughter could escape, but her.

She was fully awake now. At least she was out of the Sindar-damned-palace. That had been her plan, even though its execution had been at the hands of others. She still didn't really know their motives any more than she did Trelt's. If the woman Welyne was to be believed, she'd been friends with her mother. That should account for something, shouldn't it? No time to find out now.

Back in Peldaran, she'd been able to use her tracking skills. The land, familiar. Not now. This was an alien world. Their world. Her skills seemed mostly useless. Rust wasn't sure how long it had been since they had escaped the house. Half an hour at most.

"Wait here," Welyne said, and disappeared through another door.

Her daughter leaned against the stone back wall and slumped in on herself. Rust peered out of the window. No signs of the wyvern.

The girl sobbed. Rust couldn't remember her name. Rust sat on a wooden chair facing her.

"Are you all right?" Rust asked. Stupid bloody question, she thought, regretting it instantly.

"What do you fucking think?" the girl snapped.

For a few moments, they both sat in silence. Welyne returned, with a bag full of clothes, and three plain white aspects that would cover just the forehead.

"Here, put these on, and be quick."

"Apprentice trader clothes?" the girl spat.

"Just put them on Syb. Now's not the time."

The three of them got dressed. The woman stripped off without hesitation. The girl disappeared behind some boxes. The clothes were blue and long. Almost like robes. The trousers were baggy.

Rust picked up the aspect and looked at it blankly. How

were you supposed to fasten it? It had straps that went round the head, but she wasn't sure how they went.

"Here let me," Welyne said. She took the aspect from Rust, untangled the straps, and fastened it to her upper face. It covered her forehead only. All three aspects were the same: white, without insignia or emblems.

Welyne closed all the window blinds and put all their old clothes into a hessian bag, which she threw into a metal bin in the corner. She then tossed Rust the golden glove that she had shown her earlier.

"Put it on."

Rust stared at it for a few seconds. The thing was polished to a high golden sheen and inlaid with swirls of a lighter silver metal. It was designed for the left hand. The back of the hand raised into a bulge from which a short metal pipe jutted out over the fingers.

"What, now? Why?"

"Just do it," Welyne said.

Unsteadily, Rust put it on and tightened the straps around her forearm.

"Now," Welyne said, "point your hand into the bin and use it."

"What do you mean? How?"

"The same way you got us all into this fucking mess," she said. "With your mind."

Rust thought back to when she had first put on the circlet, and when she'd touched the pocket watch. That sensation of something warm and cool. She could feel it again now. It was slight, on the border of consciousness. Like a name, not quite remembered. She concentrated on it.

Then, she knew she had a choice. As simple as moving a finger or blinking an eye. If she thought, she knew it would happen. She aimed at the bag in the bin.

[Now!,] she thought.

There was a bright flash. A beam of brilliant white fire erupted from the pipe on the back of her hand. She felt the heat on her face. The hessian bag and its contents instantly erupted into fire.

[Stop,] she thought. The fire stopped. The metal bin glowed a dull red, hessian bag and contents turned almost instantly to fine ash.

Rust was horrified how quickly it had happened. Less than a second?

"That confirms it, at least. Spent bloody years trying to get it to do that. Without so much as a flicker." Welyne said. "For you, just like that. Belar couldn't get it to work either."

Welyne placed a lid over the metal bin, covering the smouldering ashes.

"Confirms what?" Rust asked.

"That you are who we think you are."

Rust went to take the thing off.

"No," Welyne said. "Keep it. It's no use to me, and I doubt Syb either. Might need it. Not out of this yet."

Welyne stood and opened the side door. She looked up into the sky. The girl continued to sob quietly by the window.

"Right," Welyne said. "We need to get out of the city. Our original plan is in tatters, so it won't be easy. Zarl had it all worked out. Damn! The Hegemon will lock the place down tight. Our best bet is to get out tomorrow night. Still not sure how. We can lie low somewhere for the day. Give me time to think."

"What about Father?" Sybelle said.

"I'm sorry Syb," Welyne said. "There's nothing we can do to help him."

"What do yo mean? We have to do something. We can't just LEAVE him."

"He'll be all right Syb. The Hegemon will soon realise he knows nothing. Then, they'll let him go."

Rust knew that was a lie. The man was almost certainly doomed.

But someone else was on Rust's mind. Someone who had been in her thoughts since she'd awoken. Talk of the girl's father and the Divinist temple brought him in to focus.

Indiril. Rust might have been taken from the palace, but Indiril was still there. Alone.

Rust's hopeless plan had been to escape. Hopeless or not, it was a plan that always included Indiril. They would escape the city and return home. Together. Everyone seemed obsessed with Rust. How SHE was important. Nobody thinking for a second about Indiril. Apart from Uncle, he was the only person she'd truly trusted. Uncle. Indiril. Family.

Rust wasn't about to leave him to rot in the palace alone. She was certain they would use Indiril against her, eventually. Welyne and Sybelle continued to argue. The pleading from Sybelle getting more desperate.

Enough. Rust stood.

"I'm not going with you," she said.

The arguing stopped.

"What?" Welyne said.

"I said, I'm not going with you. I am going to get my friend. Indiril."

"Don't be fucking stupid, Rust."

"I know what you are saying about your husband is feldershit. If this Trelt character was willing to invade my country, your husband has no chance. He's a goner. Sorry, but we all know it. I'm not about to leave my friend to the same fate."

"We haven't got time for this! You are the important thing here. Not me, not my husband. Not your friend."

"What about your daughter, eh? Is she expendable like it seems every-fucking-one else is?"

That shut the woman up. Sybelle looked towards her mother.

"Mother?"

Welyne stood silently.

"And what about me? What about what I want to do?" Rust shouted, "Since I got into this fucking mess, everyone has just been interested in what they want to do WITH ME! Move here, move there. Well, I've had enough! You can all fuck off with your talks about destiny."

"Keep you voice down," Welyne said.

Rust raised the gauntlet towards Welyne and backed towards the door. Welyne raised her hands in submission.

"Look," Welyne said, "let's talk this over. I'm sure we can be reasonable."

Rust opened the door and backed out. She ran back down the alleyway. The palace loomed high above the city to the south. Wyverns circled above. The distant sounds of shouting. A breeze from the bay brought with it the droning noise of the airship. Coming and going with the breeze.

Where now, Rust thought?

Behind her, Welyne stepped out into the alley.

"Your friend isn't at the palace, Rust," Welyne called after her.

"He is. I saw him the other night."

"He's not. He's been moved. Close to here, actually. If he was at the Palace, there would be no way of getting him out. Sorry, but that's the truth. You'd be captured, or dead, before you made it to the outer palace walls. You haven't got a fucking chance."

Of course, Welyne was right. She knew nothing about the city, its occupants, or the palace. She was as useless as a ceph on dry land.

"Come on," Welyne said, beckoning back down the alley, "Back this way. If he's still there, we are going to have to act now."

"Why are you helping me now?" she said. "Why have you changed your mind?"

"Because," Welyne said, "you are no use to me dead or captured. And I realise I can't get out of this fucking city without your help, and the prospect of pointing my gun at you, no matter how tempting it is right now, isn't an option either. But realise, once we have your friend, you do exactly as I say. Otherwise, your friend will be just as dead. Understand?"

"I do. Thank you."

"Don't thank me. I think it's a terrible idea," Welyne barked, "but at least we'll have a surprise on our side. There is no way they would expect us to do something this stupid."

Indiril

Indiril imagined walking amongst the trees in his father's plantation. The warmth between his toes, a smell of apple blossom. The scent of home. It made his chest hurt.

He had been trying to lift his spirits, but it just made him feel worse. He'd never felt so alone in his life. Or scared. He wept. He'd cried a lot today, more so than the days leading up to it. Praying to the divines had been useless. Their reply, silence. He'd even tried praying to the Hegemony's Emperor. It left him feeling sullied and ashamed.

When he'd first been taken captive, there had only been raw terror. His last memory of home was being dragged away by a huge Hegemon knight. He'd tried to break free, but it was impossible. The last glimpse was of his father staring back it him, clutching a broken hand. There had been something in his eyes he would never forget. Disappointment. You did this; they said. You've brought this on our family. You and your stupid friend, Rust.

His father had never liked Rust. Indiril didn't know why, but suspected it was because she was Nothari. His father's family had suffered at the hands of a Nothari raiding party. Another old prejudice that ran deep. That look had haunted Indiril more than anything since he'd been taken. He'd spent his entire life trying to impress his father, trying to make him proud. So he wept. In fear. In shame. In loneliness. And last, in anger at Rust for getting him into this.

He just couldn't work out what it was all about. First, he'd been taken to an airship. They'd flown to a palace that he'd later found out was in Bennel. Bennel! He'd been shown great courtesy. Given fine clothes to wear, nice food to eat. The room he was given was bigger than his family's entire house. A man called Trelt had visited occasionally. He had apologised for what happened to his father. Said it was all a misunderstanding. Soon Indiril would be taken home. Indiril asked him about Rust and Trelt said that she was fine too, that she was helping them with something of great importance.

They'd quizzed Indiril about what he knew. Did he ever notice anything strange about Rust? What did he know about her past? What did he know about the elderuin where they had found the things? Relics, Trelt had called them. He'd told them everything he knew.

Then, a few days later, Trelt had brought Rust to see him. She'd looked dirty, tired, and had a nasty scratch on her head. Indiril had thrown himself at her. Apologised for everything he'd done. A blank look had come over his friend, and she'd pushed away from him. He'd tried to explain everything, but she didn't seem to notice. As Rust left, she'd had that same look on her face as his father had. Disappointment. Betrayal. It had broken him.

Yesterday, they'd come for him. Blindfolded, they'd brought him here. Wherever 'here' was. An office of some sort. A small desk by a window. Shelves filled with books and ledgers. The window was boarded from the other side. He didn't even know what time of day it was. The only light came from a single lamp, visible through a hole in the wooden door.

It reminded him of his brother's office in Balincross. His brother had seemed so proud of it. Father was all smiles when they'd gone to visit for the first time. Father was always so proud of Indiril's brother.

The new food was awful. Gone were the sausages and eggs. Replaced with bland soup and stale bread. The guards were even worse. The courteous folk at the palace, replaced with gruff Hegemon soldiers. One of them, a tall man called Ickiwas repeatedly spat in his food. Called him lanky-shanks. There had been no explanation for Indiril's move.

Had he done something wrong? He had pounded on the door to be let out. The guards laughed.

So he now sat with his back to the door, listening to the soldiers outside, thinking of home, descending deeper into despair and depression.

He drifted off to a fitful sleep.

There was a shout. A scream cut short. Sounds of commotion.

Indiril snapped awake. His heart pounded. A loud thwacking sound. Some thumping noises. A muffled cry. Silence.

He backed away from the door.

Someone tried to unlock the door without success. Then again. Finally, the lock clicked. The door opened. Someone stood in the door, aspect clutched in her hand. Someone who Indiril thought he would never see again. Rust!

Behind her stood two immaculate women, one older, the other younger.

Rust ran over and embraced him tightly. Indiril thought his ribs would break. A noise escaped Rust's lips. Half cry, half laugh. She sobbed into his shoulder.

"I'm sorry Rust," Indiril said.

"I know," Rust replied. "I know. So am I. For everything. I'm sorry for dragging your arse into this mess. Sorry for everything."

"What... what are you doing here?" Indiril asked. "I thought you were still in the palace."

Before she could answer, the older woman pulled Rust away from Indiril.

"Let's go. There will be time for this later," she said.

Rust broke away from the woman and turned back to him.

"I'm serious," the woman said. "We have to go."

So many questions. Who were these people? They looked like immaculate. How had Rust got out of the palace? Where were they going? Before Indiril could ask, the woman left.

"Come on," Rust said. "She's right. We need to go. Now."

They followed the older woman into another office. A couple of Hegemon soldiers lay on the floor. Ickiwas lay dead amongst them. His arm, shoulder, and part of his ribcage lay neatly separated to one side. The cut clean and precise. Another had a hole in his chest from which blood still oozed. The air stank. A sick metallic smell. Like the butcher's shop. Indiril stopped and stared.

"Sindar's teeth!" he said.

Rust dragged him away.

"Come on," she said.

Then, they were out of the building and into the street. It was dark, heading towards midnight. The ground ahead rose towards the distant palace. To their left, he heard a familiar droning noise. The massive shape of the airship hung over the city, headed roughly in their direction. The two immaculate women headed off down the road.

"Where are we going? What happened to those guards?" Indiril asked, tugging on Rust's arm.

"No time to explain right now, Indi," Rust said, keeping her voice low. "We've got to hurry. It's a bloody mess. The whole thing."

"Who are these people?"

"Friends… I think."

"You don't sound too sure of that. Can they be trusted?"

"I'm not sure. It's complicated, Indi. We have to hurry. The Hegemon are after us."

"The Hegemon? Aren't these people Hegemon?"

Rust ignored him. They ran down to the next corner after the others. The older immaculate woman put up her hand for them to stop. The woman peered around the corner and then ducked quickly back into cover.

"Fuck," the woman said. "Hegemon Troopers. Two at least. No time to backtrack."

She knelt down and leaned out again, holding a small white thing in her hand. A bright flash accompanied by the thwacking noise again. Someone shouted. Thwack, thwack, thwack. Several crossbow bolts whizzed past the woman's head.

"Rust," the woman shouted, "don't just stand there like a fucking prick. Use the glove! Fire at them."

Indiril stared down at Rust's hand, which was covered in a sleek metallic glove.

"I... I don't think I can," Rust said.

There was another noise. Harsher and louder. Bang, bang, bang. Pieces of brickwork erupted around where the woman crouched.

"Fuck! They've got guns!" the woman shouted.

She ducked back and turned to Rust.

"Right, listen. We haven't got time for you to THINK. Those fuckers want to capture you. Or worse. If we don't get away, you get captured, and the rest of us die. Your friend included. Understand?"

Rust straightened and said, "Alright."

"I'm going to lean out and fire again," the woman said. "When I do, I want you to run to that low wall over there and fire back. Keep low! Understand?"

"I... I...," Rust replied.

"Understand?" the woman shouted back.

"Yes."

The woman leaned out and fired again. This time, she kept firing. Thwack, thwack, thwack...

"Fucking move," the woman shouted.

Rust ran for the wall and then, once into cover, raised her hand over it. A beam of pure white fire erupted from the back of Rust's hand. The woman pointed down the street.

"Aim for the man in the robes," the woman shouted. "He's a seer. He'll be trying to call for help."

Rust fired again. The woman did too. After a few seconds, they both stopped. Indiril blinked away afterimages of the white beam.

Rust stood.

"I... I think we got them. Three of them. I... killed them,"

Rust said. She stared down at her hand.

Down the street, a shopfront was ablaze, along with a cart and a few wooden crates. Several burning forms lie still next to the shop.

"I think I killed them," Rust repeated.

The woman staggered backwards. Blood oozed from a spot on the side of her belly. She gasped and fell against the wall. The young immaculate girl screamed.

"Mother!"

"It's all right," the woman gasped.

Chapter 18

Traveller!
 Do you hear the cindercrow cry?
 Dead of night.
 Light of day.
 Traveller listen!
 Stick to the path, come what may.

Old Seendar Proverb

Sybelle

"We need... to get... out of the city...," Mother gasped, gulping down air between words, gripping her belly. Dark blood soaked her clothes.

They were in a shop. Almost too dark to see. A tailor, or cloth merchant. In the dim light, Sybelle could see Rust rifling through shelves. Sybelle didn't know for what. She felt useless. At least Rust was doing something.

Mother lay against the wall. She'd pulled up her clothes. There was a small hole in the side of her belly about big enough to get your finger in. Thick blood flowed from it and dripped onto the wooden floor.

"First," Mother continued, "we need... to do something about this."

Outside, the droning from the Hegemon airship rose and fell. Louder now. What should I do? She knelt at Mother's side and held her hand.

Rust returned with a length of white cloth and pushed Sybelle out of the way. Rust gently wiped the blood away and probed the area around the wound.

"I've never seen a wound like it before," Rust said.

"It's a... bullet, from the gun... Small metal thing. I think it's still in there. No exit wound," Mother said.

Mother prodded around the wound. "I can feel it. Think it's in the muscle, maybe. Lucky. Must have been a ricochet."

"Do you want us to get it out?" Sybelle asked.

"No! Best to leave it," Rust said. "Most likely we'd do more damage."

"But we can't just leave it! Mother might die. Do something!" Sybelle pleaded.

"Rust is right," Mother said. "The biggest danger... at the moment is blood loss."

The other one, the tree-boy, sat limply on a chair. His eyes were wide open, bright circles of white in the dark room. Terrified. As useless as Sybelle felt.

"It's all right," Rust said calmly. "I've treated wounds before on hunting trips. Not quite like this mind. From crossbows."

Rust lightly probed around the wound with a finger. Mother gasped.

"Sorry. I can feel the... um... bullet. Feels about the size of a marble. It's not deep."

"Are you sure?" Sybelle asked.

"Yes," Mother said. "Let Rust take over... I won't be able to move far like this... I'm losing too much blood."

Rust tore off strips of cloth, rolling two of them up into small wads. She placed the smaller wad against the wound. She handed the larger one to Mother, who put it into her mouth.

Rust and Mother exchanged a look. Mother bit down on the wad in her mouth and nodded. Rust pushed the other wad into the wound. Mother squirmed, her legs locking rigidly. A low moan escaping from her mouth. Rust stopped.

"No... keep going," Mother mumbled through the cloth.

Sybelle felt sick. The panic closer now. She could feel it clawing its way up her spine. She just wanted all this to go away. To be back home in Drellgarh. Or to be with Kathnell again. Rust pushed the wad in a little further. Mother moaned again.

"Good," Mother said, removing the wad from her mouth.

"Is that it?" Sybelle asked.

"No. Need to bandage it. You'll need to help as well, Syb."

"But I don't know what to do."

"It's all right," Rust said. "Just put your fingers on the cloth here and hold it in place. Whilst I secure it."

Sybelle moved her hands towards Mother's belly. They shook as she placed them on the wound. She swallowed sour saliva. Rust tightened the bandage. Mother gasped again.

"Pull the fucking thing tighter," Mother said, "and this time, do it quickly!"

Rust pulled the bandage tighter. Mother spasmed once, and went limp. Her head slumped to one side. They'd killed her! Rust must have seen the look in her eyes.

"It's alright. She's just passed out," Rust said.

Rust tied the bandage and stepped back. The bleeding had slowed considerably. Maybe even stopped.

"Now what do we do?", Sybelle sobbed. She didn't know who she expected an answer from. She just wanted to go home.

"Like your Mother said, we need to get out of the city," Rust said. "Then I'm going back to Peldaran and taking Indiril with me. Away from all this shit."

How were they supposed to do that? She didn't know the city at all, other than what Kathnell had shown her. She was almost as much a stranger here as Rust was. The tree-person still sat limply in the chair. He had done little other than follow them around like a tame chillik. Useless.

Mother coughed. Her eyes opened. She looked down at her abdomen and groaned.

"What do we do, Mother!" Sybelle pleaded.

"Just let me think," Mother replied.

The seconds stretched. Saints! Mother doesn't know what to do either! They should have never listened to Rust and gone after the useless tree-boy. Should have just left him to rot. They could have already been somewhere safe by now. They needed help.

"I know someone that might help," Sybelle said.

"Who?" Mother asked.

"A friend."

"What friend?"

"Just someone I know. She works on the house; on the

heating."

"A mundane?"

"Does that matter right now? Yes, a mundane."

"No. It's not a good idea. We can't trust a mundane. It's too risky."

"What else can we do? Should we just give ourselves up? Maybe we should. I'm sure if we explain the situation, everything will be all right. Just explain…"

"Are you sure you trust this person?" Mother said, cutting her off.

"Yes. She was the one that showed me the vaults under the house. If it wasn't for her, we'd be captured already."

Mother was silent for a few seconds.

"Alright, where do they live?"

"I… I don't know, but I have a pretty good idea where they will be. We can get a ferry. If it's not too late."

Sybelle prised open the cash till and stuffed a few notes into her pocket. She'd gone from respected immaculate to fugitive and thief in just a couple of hours.

Sybelle exhaled when the quayside came into view. She hadn't realised she'd been holding her breath. Thank the saints, the ferry was there!

She'd been half-sure that the last one would be gone, leaving them stranded on this side of the bay. Her fear that they would have to wait on this side until morning, were thankfully unrealised. She wasn't sure Mother would still be alive.

The airship hung in the sky behind them, a black patch against a deep grey sky.

They'd needed to avoid a few Hegemon patrols, but got to the dockside without incident. The Hegemon seemed to be concentrating their efforts around the immaculate districts, and the roads leading out of the city in that direction.

Mother supported herself between Rust and the tree-boy Indiril. She straightened when they rounded the corner and headed for the ferry, trying her best not to look injured. Sybelle walked in front, trying to block the sight of the bloodstained clothing. They'd changed clothes at the tailors, but fresh blood had once again started seeping through.

Thankfully, the ferry master was looking at the airship as they approached. He barely paid them any attention as they boarded the ferry and paid their passage.

"Would'ya look at that," he said in passing, eyes never leaving the airship. "Hellavu thing. What's it all about?"

They ignored him and boarded the ferry. Thankfully, the ferry was almost empty. They took seats away from anyone else. As the ferry pulled away, Sybelle glanced back. Troops in the streets. Both Hegemon and local Bennel soldiers. They were lucky the ferry was still running. It should be calmer when they got to Kathnell's district. Maybe they might get out of this yet.

Kathnell

Kathnell downed the rest of her beer.

"Well, what do you think?" Roz asked.

"Not bad. Tangy. Smoother than I was expecting."

"Liar."

"Yeah, you're right. It's not THAT smooth. Tastes pretty good though."

"Barrowman's Best, they call it."

"It really doesn't taste bad."

It was still made from taptree sap, but they'd added some hops. More expensive than the usual swill. It was also higher in alcohol.

"Reckon we'll sell much of it?" Roz asked.

"Yeah. I'd drink it."

"You'll drink fermented crow piss if it was alcoholic," Roz laughed.

"Fuck you too," Kathnell laughed back.

"Not likely hun."

Roz walked away, smiling. Kathnell looked around the pub. It was getting late and most patrons had left. Just the usual hardcore drunkard locals remained. People like her. She'd had a few drinks already. Should she have another? Just one more wouldn't hurt.

Roz winked at her from across the bar. Kathnell smiled back, but her mind was on other things. Pelter wasn't around. She'd wanted to see him, to quiz him more about his involvement with the rebellion. She couldn't get the dockside attack out of her mind. The flames, the dead bodies. The crying child.

Stray thoughts kept coming to her randomly, with no warning. She'd be in the middle of something and then, slap, she'd be right back at the docks. It seemed like her mind was on a loop, that no matter how hard she tried, her mind kept returning to that same few seconds as they emerged from the water. Legs numb from sea water, body hot from the flames.

Sybelle's news that the dockside belonged to her father's company had snapped something inside her. For the first time in her life, she had a connection to someone within the Hegemon. Someone she'd now shared a bed with. A person connected to the people she killed. Damn the thousand hells, someone she was falling in love with. She just couldn't make the parts of the puzzle fit.

She was about to signal to Roz for another drink, but something caught her eye. Several locals had shuffled over to the windows. They were gesturing towards the dockside.

Curious, she walked over. In the distance, across the bay, the giant airship hung over the city. Several bright search beams shone down into the streets. They swept this way and that. Loitering on one spot for a few seconds before moving on. She'd seen similar beams on Hegemon warships. It figured the airship would also have them.

Occasionally, the silhouette of a large winged animal would pass in front of one beam. Bloody wyverns! What were they doing?

"Hey Roz," she said, "you seen this?"

"What's that?"

"Fucking stonie airship all lit up like a bonfire."

Roz came over and stood beside her.

"Looks like they're looking for something," Roz said.

"Yeah, it does, doesn't it?"

"Maybe they've lost their tits. Always knew they couldn't find them with both hands," Roz chuckled as she returned to the bar.

Kathnell guessed the airship was somewhere near the immaculate quarter. Near to where Sybelle lived. What were they doing? Was Sybelle safe? She reassured herself. Just some weird stonie shit. Nothing to worry about. She decided against another beer.

"I'm off, Roz."

"Take care, lovely."

Kathnell went outside and started walking towards home. After a few paces, a shadow fell into step behind her. Kathnell shot a sideways look at the reflection in a shop window. A hooded figure. Great, another fucking pervert. Just what she needed.

She spun round, fists raised.

"Fuck off, pal," she said.

The figure removed their hood. Fuck. It was Sybelle!

She was crying. The front of her plain tunic splattered with blood. Without a word, Sybelle ran forward and put her arms around Kathnell and hugged her so tightly it hurt. Sybelle's body racked with sobs.

"What's wrong Syb?"

"I... I... We... need your help. It's Mother..."

Sybelle said no more, despite Kathnell's questions. Instead, she led Kathnell by the hand and into a nearby side alley. Slumped on the floor was an immaculate woman Kathnell assumed was Sybelle's mother. The woman was shivering. Blood stained the front of her clothes. She only looked semi-conscious. Two other people stood over her. A young stonie girl with unkept hair she didn't recognise, and a young male tree person.

What in all the nine thousand hells was going on?

Kathnell just stood there with her mouth open.

"We need your help," Sybelle repeated.

Vidyana

Vidyana stood outside the office where the tree-boy had been held. He too had gone. Only one guard had survived. Barely. Medics were currently attending to him. He would live. He was lucky. The rest of them had been sliced up. The place was like an abattoir. From the neat cuts, Vidyana guessed it was a whisper blade. Old tech. Figured.

A carriage rounded the corner and stopped. Trelt got out and walked over to her.

"It seems your little plan has failed Captain Baylali," he said.

She bowed deeply.

"Please forgive me, my Lord." she said. "I have failed."

"That will have to wait until later. I'll be honest, this is a fucking mess. What more do you know?"

"Nothing more than we knew already. The tree-boy has been taken. The surviving guard says that they were attacked by three people. They were led by an immaculate woman. Their descriptions match those of Welyne Drellmore, her daughter, and Rustari. They got into a firefight with some troopers a few roads from here. Three troopers and a seer were killed. One more badly burned."

"Nothing useful then?"

"There is one thing. We think one of them was injured. There is blood from where we think they were fighting. No idea whose it is."

"Any more from the doctor?"

"Nothing. He insists that his only contact was Zarl Drellmore. I'm pretty sure he's telling the truth."

"Well, we can't risk it. I'll have him taken to the airship and fully delved. I hate doing it, but we need every bit of information we can find."

"I've sent orders out to have other members of the close family arrested," Vidyana said, "including the husband."

"Good," Trelt said. "I've ordered the city to be locked down. No traffic, no boats, no trains. I suspect the plans they originally had to get Rust out of the city have been disrupted. They'll still be here. Somewhere."

"What would you like me to do now, my Lord?"

"Come with me. I'm heading back to the West Wind. From there, we can oversee things and drop you to where you are needed far quicker."

"Yes, Lord Vellorson."

She bowed again and followed him back to the carriage.

Chapter 19

And each came to the temple to preach that the Lord was one with all, but each was still replete with pride and hubris.

Divinist proverb

Kathnell

A heavy rain fell in thick streams. Kathnell moved closer to the stone wall, trying in vain to avoid the deluge. What began as light rain had rapidly become a warm summer torrent.

They'd moved away from the main street, avoiding people that had come outside to gawp at the airship. They'd had to half-drag Sybelle's mother. She didn't look good. Face drawn. Eyes unfocused.

Sybelle bumbled through a barely coherent explanation. Kathnell was too stunned to ask anything meaningful. Sybelle had been right to suspect her mother. But for all the wrong reasons. No simple love affair. Conspiracies, secret organisations, and a nonsensical plot involving a girl from a far off country that they had sprung from Bennel palace. A person who they now needed to smuggle out of the city!

Kathnell eyed the rescued girl. Didn't look much. About Kathnell's age. Looked like a stonie, but her hair was unkempt, and she talked with a thick accent. She was kneeling next to Sybelle's mother, trying to stem the flow of blood from a wound in her gut. They'd slowed the bleeding, but the bandages were soaked through.

The girl, the tree-boy, Sybelle, and the mother, wore the plain clothes and simple aspects of low rank stonies. Not that unusual to see in this part of town during the day. Definitely NOT normal at night. They'd drawn a few puzzled glances from the locals before they'd moved into this side street. Kathnell wasn't really sure where the tree-boy fitted into it all. He just stood to one side. Wide eyes looking this way and that.

What the hell would the stonies want with a foreign girl

and a tree-person? Kathnell shook her head and glanced across at Sybelle's mother. The woman was racked by occasional bouts of uncontrollable shivering. Kathnell was no physician, but the woman was in a bad way. Clearly, she must have lost a lot of blood. The woman needed a doctor. Fast.

Across the bay, the beams from the airship's search lights continued to sweep the streets. Closer, from a nearby main road, came the sounds of boots on cobblestone. Shouted orders. Bennel soldiers.

What should she do? It wasn't too late to walk away. Just leave them. Whatever Sybelle was involved in wasn't really Kathnell's problem. As soon as the thought came, Kathnell felt ashamed. She couldn't just leave them. Not Sybelle. Leaving her would haunt her forever.

"Is any of this true?" Kathnell asked the rescued stonie girl.

"Yes, it's true. Or at least I think it is. It's all new to me too. I have no fucking clue what's going on either, to be honest."

"What do they want from you? The stonies?"

"Stonies?" Rust asked.

"The erm... Immaculate"

The girl just shrugged, unwilling to say any more. The rain increased in volume. They all huddled closer to the wall. The alleyway ran with water. Rivulets merging into a central stream.

Realistically, what could Kathnell do? She was no doctor, but Sybelle's mother would be as cold as a shelker within a couple of hours. She'd once seen an engineer's legs crushed by a metal beam. He'd had that same look, like his life was slowly draining away. He'd died hours later, despite the best efforts of a guild surgeon. Even if she survived, how could they escape from the city? It sounded like the whole Hegemon was mobilising. If Sybelle was right, then they were being pursued by not only the Hegemon, but by knights, wyverns, and summoners.

Would Roz be able to help? Or Pelter? Or Corric? No, best not involve them directly. Especially Roz. She didn't need any of this shit. That really only left one option.

"I know some people that might help."

Sybelle looked relieved.

"Thank the saints!" Sybelle said, flinging her arms around Kathnell.

The mother looked up.

"What sort of people?" the mother croaked.

"Just a few people I know. Locals. They'll know what to do."

The mother slumped and let out a bark-like laugh.

"Fucking great," the mother said.

Sybelle looked confused.

"What is it?" Sybelle asked.

"Your friend. She's a fucking rebel," the mother said.

"No, No, she's just an engineer," Sybelle said.

"Ask her then!"

Sybelle looked at Kathnell. Kathnell tried to say something. Some way to explain. Nothing remotely adequate came to mind. The seconds stretched.

"Well?"

She wanted to answer. To tell Sybelle how she had got involved with Liberation. How her family had suffered under the rule of the Hegemon. How her father had been killed. How she barely earned enough to look after herself and her mother. How most people in the city fought for every scrap they could get hold of, whilst their stonie masters got fat at their expense. She didn't say any of that. Sybelle wasn't the same as normal stonies, she told herself. She was different. Sybelle's eyes burrowed into her. Kathnell wanted to look away.

"I'm sorry," was all she could muster.

Sybelle's eyes filled with moisture. Disappointment? Disgust? Kathnell felt her own filling up. The mother coughed out another laugh.

"Great work, Syb. I fucking knew it," she said. "Fucking

rebels."

"Look, Sybelle, I'm sorry," Kathnell said, "It's true. I'm involved with Liberation. But that doesn't change how I feel about you. I know people, and they will help. They are good people. I trust them."

"You trust them? Fuck the rebellion," the mother shouted. She coughed and struggled to get any air down.

"The rebellion," she continued, "are just as bad as the Emperor and his goons. Did you know it was your precious Liberation that introduced the nester plague to Dentor? Killed thousands. Normal people and immaculate alike. Bet they didn't tell you that."

Kathnell had heard the stories of the nester plague in the Drellgarh city of Dentor. A horrifically exotic parasitic disease from the other side of the globe. It turned its victims into mindless drones. Several thousand had been killed before they had eradicated it. Other Hegemon cities had been similarly attacked, but Dentor had been the worst.

"No, thought not," Sybelle's mother said. "I'll take my chances, thanks."

"I do not know what your mother is talking about. I know nothing about any of that."

The mother went to get up, but collapsed. Blood soaked the ground where she lay. It mixed with the water from the rain, streaming away downslope. There was a lot. Kathnell tried to convince herself that water always made blood look worse. Sybelle glanced between her mother and Kathnell.

"Are you sure these people can help?" Sybelle pleaded.

"Sybelle..", the mother began.

"Mother! We don't have a choice!"

They slowly made their way to Wharf Street. Kathnell tried to remember the instructions Chander had given her. She never thought she'd have to use them.

The streets were still mostly empty. A few times, they had to hide from troops. Just groups of local Bennel troops. The sort that she was used to seeing. Lights were coming on in houses. People looked out of windows. The whole fucking city was waking up.

Sybelle warned her about the Wyverns, so they tried to keep to side alleys and places well covered. It was easy in this part of town. The buildings close. She knew the streets to take, the ones that avoided exposing themselves. It took them over an hour to make a journey that would normally have taken ten minutes. Thankfully, the rain had eased off. Kathnell glanced out of the alley and down the street towards the bakery.

"Wait here. I'll be back in a moment," Kathnell said.

The way looked clear. She stepped out into the street. She felt exposed. Any second, a thousand crossbow bolts would fly from the darkness. Nothing came.

She walked across the road and lent against the wall outside the bakery. A minute passed. Two. At any moment, another load of troops could appear. She would have to talk her way out of it. She tried to remind herself that she wasn't doing anything wrong. Three minutes. Four. Fuck.

A man appeared round the corner. He staggered along, holding a bottle of beer in one hand. A drunk. He took a piss against the bakery door. Then he noticed her and cocked his head.

"Got any backo?" he asked.

"What?"

"I said, got any backo?"

That was it. The phrase she had remembered from the Chander's instructions.

"Yes... Yes... But, I've only got Red Tanner."

"That'll do nicely."

Something stung the back of her neck.

She reached her hand up. Something stuck out from her neck. She pulled it out. A little metal needle. The man walked over towards her. He smiled.

The street turned on its side. Her vision filled with a multitude of colours. It was funny. She laughed. She realised it wasn't the street that was turning. It was her. That was funny too. She laughed again.

Why was she laughing? Something was funny, but she couldn't remember what.

Trelt

The doctor squirmed in the metal chair, shouting incomprehensibly at terrors only he could see. His arms bulged in the restraints. He let out a low moan and fell limp. The seer pulled the device away from the doctor's scalp and stepped back.

"Well?," Trelt asked.

"Nothing more," the woman said. "It will be a good few hours before we can try again. Personally, I doubt he has anything left to give. He didn't really try to resist. Probably saved what's left of his sanity."

A few hours might just well have been weeks. A dead end then. They had peeled back the layers of the man's past like an onion. His sister's death during a botched raid by the Aurumill twenty years ago. The series of minor perceived betrayals by the Hegemon in the years since. The befriending by one of the Sleepers. Zarl. His eventual recruitment. A few minor acts of subterfuge and traitorous intelligence gathering. Nothing major. That was until Zarl had arrived a few days ago.

He'd given up a couple of names. They'd be tracked down, of course. But beyond the recent job at the palace, there was nothing more of use. The doctor knew nothing about where Rustari was now or where she would be taken. Fucking sleepers. Simona had been a smart woman.

The West Wind was headed into the bay. They'd been patrolling the streets around the immaculate quarter for a couple of hours but had seen nothing of Rust or the Drellmore women. Nothing. They could be almost anywhere in the city by now.

The city was being locked down. All the roads out,

closed. Trains, boats, ferries, carriages, all banned from travel. Wyverns would patrol the borders with orders to kill anyone that tried to leave. Innocent people would die. The political fallout would be enormous. Trelt sighed.

It would be dawn in a few hours. It would give him time to strengthen his grip on the city. All the troops in the area put onto high alert, both Bennel locals, and Hegemon alike.

Trelt was under no illusions how hard it would be to find Rustari, but they had a lot of resources, and more would soon come. He had already messaged the White Citadel for reinforcements. Every ironclad and troop transport within two thousand kilometres was now heading at full speed towards Lerins. Word had gone out to the seers within each free immaculate battalion within two hundred kilometres, with orders to come to Lerins immediately. Soon they would flood the city and the wider countryside beyond.

All the intel he had on local rebellion members and cells was being acted on. People were being rounded up right now. He would burn this fucking city to ash if he had to.

Sybelle

Sybelle felt drunk. Something covered her eyes. A blindfold? No, some kind of stale cloth bag. Where was she? Where was Mother? Kathnell? Her mouth was gagged. She couldn't move her hands. Tied to a chair. She tried to break free. This was quickly rewarded with a sharp jab to her legs.

"Stop squirming stonie," a woman said. Sybelle stopped.

Voices in the background. The place smelled damp. A faint smell of oil. It reminded her of Kathnell's clothes after she'd been working.

"Someone tell Chander Miss Fancy Pants is awake," the woman said.

A door opened. Someone left.

"Hey Syb, that you?"

Kathnell! Sybelle grunted out a reply through the gag. Another sharp jab to the legs. Harder this time.

"Both of you, shut your kiss holes."

Footsteps approached.

"Take them off", a man said.

The bag was removed from her head. She was in a small room. Some kind of cellar. No windows. Dimly lit by oil lamps. Wooden boxes of various sizes stacked against the walls. A woman with a nasty scar down her arm scowled down at her. Rust and the tree-boy Indiril sat to her side. Both were also tied and gagged. The woman with the scar removed the bags over their heads too. An older man with unkempt, white, curly hair stood beside Kathnell.

Mother lay on a table in the far corner. A man in doctor's robes stood over her. He looked over at Sybelle and smiled gently. His robes were covered in blood. Mother's chest rose and fell slowly. She was breathing, at least.

Several other men and women were clustered around the walls. All armed with a variety of crossbows, swords, and the things they called guns. The man in front of Kathnell removed her gag.

"What the fuck have you done, Kathnell? The entire city has gone mad."

"I can try to explain Chander. I think."

"I was hoping you could. Too much of coincidence, you turning up with two Drellmores in tow, with all the shit going on across the bay. We thought you being in contact with a stonie girl would be useful. But, fuck, not this!"

"You… you knew about Sybelle?"

"Of course we bloody knew. Why do you think you were recruited? Sure, we'd had our eye on you for some time. Maybe in a couple of years you'd have been approached. After you learned to cool your head. Then you turned up with an immaculate girl at the pub. We followed you."

"You bastard."

"I'll admit it was a surprise when we found out she was Drellmore. My colleagues were ready to drop you both like a lead boot. However, I convinced them it might come in useful to have someone on the inside with the Drellmores. Thought you might pick up some useful intel."

"You fucking lied."

Kathnell slumped.

"I didn't lie Kathnell. We just brought forward your recruitment. That's why we gave you the Red Tanner contact. You really think we do that for every recruit? You were a long bet, sure. One that I didn't think would pay off. Now I'm thinking that I should have dropped you like they said."

Kathnell tried to break free.

"You fucker!"

"Come on Kathnell. Let's not get all hot headed again. Just like your father. He was the same. First, let's figure out what the hell has got the stonies so riled up."

The man reached down and untied Kathnell.

"I don't really know," Kathnell said, flexing her wrists. "That's the truth."

"Gotta do better than that, Kathnell. People are dying. Couple of our supposedly 'secret' caches have been raided. Some of our best people have been rounded up. Some killed. Friends of mine. Looks like all the exits from the city are being shut down. Seen nothing like it. Not even after the riots in the Northern districts."

"Alright, alright. All I know is that about an hour ago, Sybelle and her mother came to me with the other two in tow. Sybelle said that the Hegemon had stormed their house looking for the girl. Not sure what they wanted from her. Just that they were trying to get out of the city. The rest sounded crazy."

The man looked across at Sybelle and walked over. He removed her gag.

"So, Miss Drellmore, maybe you can tell me why the fucking hell the Hegemon is tearing up half the city looking for you?"

Sybelle didn't know what she should say. She looked over at Kathnell. Her face streaked with tears. She thought she'd trusted Kathnell, maybe loved her. Now she didn't know what to think. Still stunned that her first lover was part of the rebellion. She felt tricked. Betrayed. Now it seemed as if Kathnell was as much in the dark as she was. She'd been used too.

Kathnell nodded, as if prompting Sybelle to go on. She wasn't sure what the alternative was, anyway.

"They're not after me," Sybelle said. "They're after Rust. The girl in the corner."

The man, Chander, looked over at Rust.

"Why is she so important?"

"You wouldn't believe me if I said."

"You'd be surprised what I'd believe after tonight. And we have little choice, do we? Go on, tell me."

"Apparently, she's my cousin, the daughter of someone called Simona. Some kind of rebel leader from the past."

The room went quiet. Chander took a step back.

"Fuck!" the woman with the scarred arm said.

Chander folded his arms and paced around the room. After a few moments, he left the room, followed by the scarred woman. The name Simona had knocked the wind out of the sails of everyone in the room. Sybelle knew nothing about her, but the name definitely meant something to these people.

"Syb," Kathnell said, "what the fuck have you got me involved in?"

A few minutes later, Chander came back in and removed the gag from Rust.

"So, is this true? That you're Simona's daughter. The Simona?"

Rust shrugged.

"So they tell me," Rust said. "Two weeks ago I was just working Uncle's farm back in Peldaran. I know nothing about any Simona or any of the other fantasies these people have been talking about. I just want to get out of here, and back to my home. The only person who know's more is currently unconscious in the corner."

"That explains the raid in Peldaran as well," the scarred woman said.

"On a normal day," he said. "I'd say this all sounds like shite. But, not today."

Sybelle and Kathnell told Chander as much as they could. Although ungagged, Rust remained silent, glowering from her chair. She answered some questions, but said little to embellish the scant facts they already knew.

A man came in and whispered in Chander's ear. The man's tunic was covered in blood. Chander pinched the bridge of his nose and sighed.

"How many?" Chander asked.

"Thirty at least."

"Any survive?"

The man shook his head.

"Thanks Glarvin," Chander said, before turning to Kathnell. "That was news that an important base of ours has just been stormed. Everyone's been killed. Thirty dead at least."

Chander stood silent for a couple of seconds.

"It's clear to me," Chander continued, "that we need to get you all out of Lerins as soon as possible. If the Hegemon are this desperate to get you back, I'm half inclined to believe your story, as fanciful as it sounds. The problem is, we can't get out of the city by road, and even if we could, we can't outrun their bloody airship."

"Can we get out by boat?" Rust asked.

"No, too slow. I'm betting the airship can outrun any boat we can get our hands on. Unless you're thinking of taking over one of the ironclads?"

"Could we?" Rust asked. "Take one over?"

"Of course not," Chander said, waving the suggestion away.

"Hang on," Kathnell said. "What about by train?"

"Train?" Chander asked.

"Not the normal trains. The big bastards. A void-train. The Hegemon's got several they use for troop transport. There's always one parked up in the northern train yard. They could outrun the airship. Hell, they could outrun a horny fenrir."

"How the fuck do you know so much about them?" Chander asked.

"I've been interested in them since Dad used to talk about them. Been studying to be an engineer, remember? Anyway, I bet they're the only thing faster than that fucking airship. And, as you say, the roads are all closed, so we're not getting out that way."

"They would take too long to fire up. We'd be swarmed before we even got it going."

"That's the thing," Kathnell said. "They're already fired up. Just like the ship we blew up, the military ones are fired by void-stone. Usually, they are kept running so they don't have to have a summoner onboard. And, they can get to pressure real quick."

The ship they blew up? Sybelle realised with a jolt that Kathnell must be talking about the explosion on the docks the other night. Kathnell was involved with that? People had died. Friends of Father.

"It was you that blew up the ship!?" Sybelle screamed.

"Fuck," Kathnell said.

"That was my father's ship! Why? Why Kathnell!?"

"Enough," Chander shouted. "You can continue your little lover's argument later."

Sybelle stared at Kathnell, but she avoided her gaze.

"You really think you can get one going?" Chander asked.

"Sorry, what?", Kathnell said.

"I said. Do really think you can get one of their trains going?"

Half an hour later, a very rough plan had been formed. They would send a group to secure one of the void-trains. Kathnell would get it going. Then Sybelle, Kathnell, Rust, the tree-boy, and a few of Chander's best would leave the city at full speed. Meanwhile, another two groups would raid the track points to route the train west out of the city and then south into the countryside beyond. They would stop the train in the countryside and then head by foot to rendezvous with a rebel cell in a small fishing village.

Shortly before that, a much larger group of volunteers would cause a diversion at the dockyard and steal a steam boat. Hopefully, the Hegemon would think they were trying to escape by sea and chase them down in the airship. With a bit of luck, the void-train would be on its way before they realised what was happening. Sybelle didn't fancy their chances.

"What about Mother?" Sybelle asked.

"She'll have to stay here," Chander said. "Take her chances with those of us left in the city. She ain't going to be much use like she is. Doctor says she's lost a lot of blood. If we move her, she'll die. She'll be asleep for hours as yet. Maybe days. Hopefully, things will calm down once the Hegemon knows you've gone."

Leave Mother here? For the first time in her life, she would be on her own. She glanced across at where Mother lay. The man was right. She'd die if they moved her. The doctor had removed the bullet and had stitched her wound back up. With the right medicines, she would be all right. Her chest rose and fell slowly. She looked so incredibly pale. Sybelle wasn't sure she'd ever really known who Mother was. What about Father? She prayed he would be all right, too. Thinking about him made her feel sick.

Kathnell stood with Chander and Rust. They studied a map of eastern Seendar. Kathnell said something about the train tracks south from Lerins. Chander nodded.

Sybelle wondered if she could ever trust Kathnell again.

Chapter 20

Discovered a village of nesters last week.

The entire village taken by the plague; even the children. Forms twisted and decaying, all spines and cancerous growths. No longer alive, still not dead. Only mindless husks remained, all going to and fro, taking things back to the central nest. They'd made the nest in the village school.

Of course, we reported it at once. Our seer describing the details. Cataloging.

We watched them for a while before purging. Movements oddly synchronised with each other. Almost like as they'd lost their individuality, they'd become something else. Something horrific. Something blasphemous.

Haven't seen any nests since. I pray to the saints that we've finally got this outbreak under control.

They say the nester plague purges you of all your humanity when it takes you, but Emperor save my dreams, the screams as they'd burned!

Private diary of Hegemon Captain - Near Dentor - SC 670

Rust

Rust took another sip of water and a bite of bread. Stale and dry. The palace food had been the best she'd ever tasted, soft, sweet and spiced. This meal was basic. Absurdly, it reminded her of home.

The rebels had given them all new clothes. Basic shirts and trousers. It was good to be in something that wasn't covered in blood.

They still sat in the same room they'd been taken to. Although they were free to move around, but it was clear they couldn't leave. She'd been escorted to the toilet blindfolded. Several times, they heard people moving about upstairs. The man Chander insisted they would be safe. The looks on the faces, the whispered conversations, told a different story.

It was the first time she'd been able to talk to Indiril properly since they'd rescued him. If rescued was the right way to describe their current situation. She wasn't entirely convinced this was any better than being back at the palace. No, not true, the man Trelt was a snake.

Not that Rust really trusted these people any more than she had anyone else in the last couple of weeks. She suspected if the opportunity arose, the rebels would use her just like Trelt would.

At least the woman, Welyne, had tried to tell her the truth. That was something. But she was gone too now, taken away unconscious. The table she'd been on, still covered in bloody bandages. The rebels assured Sybelle her mother was going to get better.

Rust had tried to explain it all to Indiril as best she could. But in telling it, it just became more confusing. His legitimate questions, unanswerable. Indiril nodded through it all, but it was clear he was having a hard time believing any of it either.

"So, you think this plan will work?" Indiril asked.

The plan sounded like the sort of stupid daydream she and Indiril used to play act as children. The two of them against the Hegemon! Back then it was fought with sticks and hay bales, now it was with airships, terrifying things called guns, and the prospect of a very real death.

"Of course," Rust replied. Now it was her turn to lie. "We'll soon be out of this city and on our way back to Peldaran!"

"Do you really think that?" Indiril said.

"Yes, they can't watch the whole city."

"No, not the city. About Peldaran. You really think we can get back there?"

"Yes," she replied, trying to convince herself as much as her friend.

"And these people," Indiril said, nodding toward the rebels. "You trust them?"

A group of rebels stood around the table discussing the plan. The girl, Kathnell, sat to one side. She was trying to engage the girl Sybelle in conversation, but she turned away and took a bite of her own bread. How much did Rust know about any of these people? Any of them. All the various factions.

"I'm not sure Indiril. I don't know who to trust. Apart from you."

Indiril reached over and took her hand and squeezed it.

"It'll be all right," Indiril said. "You'll see."

Rust laughed.

"What's so funny?"

"You trying to convince me it will be fine? I thought I was the one trying to convince you!"

They both laughed. Absurd that anything should be funny right now.

"You know there's no going back, don't you?" Rust said,

"To Peldaran I mean."

It was only as she spoke the words that she acknowledged their reality. All this time she had wanted nothing more to escape and go back to Peldaran. To Hammington's Rest. Lone Oak. The river. Uncle… That somehow, when they got home, everything would be back to normal. Before everything had fallen apart.

The Hegemon was after her, not Peldaran. If by some crow-granted wish she returned home, all it would do is put everyone she had ever known into more danger. They could never really go back, not in the ways that mattered. Time had moved on, impossible to undo, dragging them both into an uncertain future. Rust looked over at Indiril. He smiled, but there were tears in his eyes.

"I know," he said.

"I really am sorry, Indi." Rust said. She started to sob. "About all of this. I wish I'd never followed Uncle. Never gone in to that stupid ruin. You tried to warn me. But, no, I thought it would be an adventure."

She sobbed uncontrollably for the first time since Uncle had died. Indiril put a long arm around her and pulled her close.

"I know," he said. "It's all right."

But it wasn't all right, and never would be again. The world had changed. The time of childhood fantasies was at an end.

They sat in silence for a few minutes. Just silent in each other's company. If she closed her eyes, Rust could almost imagine they were back in Hammington's Rest. Just taking five minutes to rest on the river bank and have a bite to eat. Nothing fancy, just stale bread and warm water. Just her and Indiril. Fishing. The bread tasted great. The water, refreshing.

Someone opened the door. Rust opened her eyes. Reality flood back in.

"Come on," Chander said. "Time to go."

Kathnell

Kathnell peered over the low wall separating them from the train yard. Damp and dirty bricks, their original red colour diminished to almost black by age, grime, and pre-dawn shadows. The rain had stopped, but the ground was sodden. A thick fog had descended, obscuring everything beyond a couple of hundred metres. She squatted to avoid getting her legs wet. Her thighs beginning to burn from the effort.

The place looked deserted. Still too dark to see much detail through the thick grey murk.

"This is taking too bloody long," the woman with the scarred arm said. Kathnell had finally learned that her name was Albea.

"It's gonna be mid-fucking-day before we get the train running at this rate," Albea continued.

The woman glanced around. She looked twitchy. Not surprising, considering they were about to steal a military void-train from the Hegemon on the assumption that Kathnell could get it going. Albea might be nervous, but Kathnell was almost shitting herself.

Sybelle crouched to Kathnell's left. Rust and the tree-boy to her right. The two of them in whispered conversation.

They were accompanied by a couple dozen other rebels. All armed. A combination of swords, crossbows, and guns. One man had a belt equipped with little apple-sized metal spheres he'd called 'nades'. When Kathnell had asked what they were, he's just mouthed "boom" as if she was supposed to know what that meant. It didn't sound good.

They were waiting for a couple of scouts to return from a reconnaissance. The train they were going to steal was about a hundred metres away, separated from them by an expanse of open ground covered in tracks, points, and a few other conventional steam engines. The military train dwarfed the others. A faint haze of steam rose from a vent on its top. A great sign. Its heart was burning hot.

"Where in the saint's hole, are they?" Albea asked. Nobody replied.

The train was long. Eight carriages at least. Void engine at the front. Behind it, storage carriages, and then the troop carriages. The troop carriages were two stories high. The whole thing must weigh as much as a mountain. Getting the entire thing moving would take too long. It would take an age to get up to speed, pulling all that weight. Any pursuers could simply walk up and step on. Their plan hinged on separating the front of the train from the rear. Cut most of the weight, increase the acceleration. Could she really get the thing started? It would be an embarrassing way to die if she couldn't.

Rust was fiddling with some sort of metal glove. She tightened, loosened, then re-tightened its straps repeatedly. Rust mumbled something to the tree-boy about not wanting to use it again.

Sybelle held a sleek silver thing that looked like a gun, clearly of superior design to the metal ones the rebels had. She also held something that looked like a white bone. Kathnell had no clue what it was.

They had spoken little since they'd left the rebel cell. Something had broken between them. Understandable. Kathnell had fucked the relationship right up. Just like all her others. *Oh, by the way, as well as being your lover, I'm also a rebel.* Great work Kathnell, just great.

"What in the all-the-hells are those things anyway, Syb?" Kathnell asked, trying to strike up a conversation.

"What these? I didn't know if they would even work for me. They belong to Mother. I'd never seen them before yesterday."

Sybelle stared at them for a few seconds, as if seeing them for the first time. Must be a lot to take in, Kathnell thought. What with her mother, the girl Rust, and now Kathnell.

"So?" Kathnell prompted.

Sybelle picked up the bone thing.

"This one is some kind of sword. When you think about wanting it to, this ball thing rises and the space between it and the handle becomes a blade. I tried it earlier. Seems to work. Mother cut right through a steel door with it when we…"

She didn't go on.

"What about the other one?"

"It's one of those gun things. Haven't tried it."

Sybelle shuddered and stopped talking. Kathnell was trying to think of something else to say when she noticed movement to her right. The two scouts appeared, keeping low as they vaulted the wall.

"The Hegemon seems to be concentrated around the station itself. About a dozen actual Hege troopers," the male scout motioned to the large formless grey building emerging out of the fog a few hundred metres away to their right.

The female scout pointed to the area in front of them.

"There's a second group," the female scout said, "patrolling the actual yard. Only about a dozen troops. All armed with crossbows. Locals. Not Hege's. Might be more, but couldn't see them. Not through this damned fog. The two groups don't seem to mix."

Albea nodded.

"Well," Albea said, "the Hegemon in the station will soon join the fun when the hammer hits the shit. I was hoping to wait for the diversion, but it's getting lighter by the minute. Maybe another ten minutes at most, can't afford to…"

She stopped and raised her hand.

"Shhh," she said.

In the distance, Kathnell could hear a popping noise. Looking South the sky lit up with flashes, followed once by a much brighter flash. More popping and then a loud crunch.

The diversion! The noise and flashes continued. Albea waited for another minute.

"Right," Albea said. "Time to haul. Remember the plan. Keep low. Stay a few metres apart. Keep moving. You four, stay here and pick off anyone you see. Fog's gonna make it difficult. I don't care if you think you see your own mother out there. If it moves and it ain't us, shoot it. When we get to the train, follow up. We'll cover. The rest, let's go."

Most of the rebels rose, climbed over the wall and headed off in the train's direction. For the first time, Kathnell realised she and the tree-boy were the only ones that didn't have weapons.

Albea turned to Kathnell.

"Alright, my new red-headed friend. Time to see if you can pull off another magic show. Less weird blue explosion shit this time, eh? Let's go!"

Vidyana

Vidyana paced around the flight deck, glancing out of the curved windows. The bay area spread out below, the industrial and human areas to the north, the richer areas to the south.

The pre-dawn sky was getting lighter by the minute. Each minute that passed, another failure. She'd fucked up. She thought that by following the doctor and being smart, she could get a jump on these 'sleepers'.

Hubris. The underestimated foe is the deadliest foe. The teachings of Saint Za'wella mocked her from memory. Silently, she said a prayer for forgiveness.

The city was shrouded in a dense fog that had swept in from the ocean after the storm. It clung to the ground in patches, thicker out to sea and near the shores. A confusing mass of maze like streets. A vast area to find one small group of people.

The city was being shut down. It was extremely unlikely they had left the city yet. Each minute, the noose tightened. It was a race between the fugitives escaping and the lockdown.

Trelt stood impassively, arms behind his back. Waiting. He remained confident the fugitives would be caught. That they would try something drastic. Vidyana felt less confident. An Aurumill seer entered and saluted.

"Lord Vellorson, I have received communications from a unit near the northern docks. They observed a large group of armed figures heading for the docks. Rebels, along with a couple of immaculate. They have guns. Our unit is in pursuit."

Might be just a group of desperate rebels making for the

port, Vidyana thought. They'd been rounding up as many known rebels as they could. Word had got out. Vidyana wasn't so sure it had been a wise move. It could cause so much confusion that the fugitives might get out in the chaos.

"Captain," Trelt said, "Move the West Wind to the docks and prepare a landing party."

"Aye, Lord Vellorson."

Almost immediately, the pitch of the engines changed, and the deck sloped subtly under their feet. The view shifted to the right.

"Vidyana, go with them."

"Are you sure, my Lord? It could be just some rebels. They…"

"No. These are armed with guns. Which means they are in with the central group. Not just your normal organised crime sympathisers. And the report of immaculate can't be ignored."

"Yes, Lord Vellorson."

Vidyana left and headed down to the troop debarking area. A long room. Metal doors along each side. The others were already strapped into their harnesses. Cables attached them to winches. A few shock troopers and a combat seer. All covered in the best lightweight bone armour the Aurumill had. They were checking over their gear as she entered.

It would be a combat drop, of course. She would drop with the others. Twenty seconds from stepping out to being on the ground. A thin cable all that separated them from falling to their deaths. Still, it was far quicker than taking the passenger basket down.

Vidyana fitted her own harness and made sure the cable was secure. The drop captain checked her over, to be sure. He nodded.

Metal doors along each side opened out and upwards. Wind rushed in. The drop captain looked out and shouted.

"Forty seconds!"

Rust

Rust kept low, like she was told. They moved quickly towards the train, leaving the cover of the wall behind. The fog cleared a little, leaving her feeling exposed. Every part of her wanted to turn around and head back towards the wall. She willed herself onwards, Indiril behind her.

Rust followed Kathnell and Albea towards the void-train. She fiddled with the gauntlet again, making sure it was tight.

As they got nearer, Rust realised the train was nothing like the trains in Balincross. This thing was huge. Sleeker. More advanced than anything Peldaran possessed.

They had covered about half the distance when a rebel close to Rust crumpled and fell.

"Crossbows! Bennel troopers!" someone shouted. A couple of silhouettes appeared beside the train.

Almost immediately, the fog lit up with flashes and loud cracking noises from behind them. Crack. Crack. Crack. Rust flung herself at the ground and held her hands over her head. Indiril followed her down.

Someone grabbed her by the shoulder. It was Albea.

"Get up, you fucking tit. It's our cover team firing back. Move!"

Rust got up and propelled herself forward. The ground was uneven. Indiril close on her heels. The silhouettes by the train had retreated into cover.

"Right behind you," Indiril said.

The fallen rebel lay motionless, quickly left behind in the fog. Stride by stride, the train got closer. A silhouette appeared next to one of the other carriages. It raised something towards them. Rust was about to raise her glove towards it when a rebel beside to her fired his gun. There was another flash and an accompanying crack. The figure next to the train fell over. A wave of relief went through Rust; she hadn't had to fire. More crossbow bolts whistled past in the fog.

The group split up as planned. About half headed right. Their job was to unbuckle the rear carriages from the essential parts at the front. Something about power and weight ratios. It meant nothing to her. The rest of them, Kathnell, Sybelle, Indiril, Albea, and about a dozen rebels, headed for the front of the train.

Another four Bennel soldiers stepped out right in front of them from between two carriages. Albea almost barrelling into them. One of them struck Albea with a sword as she passed. Albea made an "oomph" noise and went down. Another was aiming straight at Sybelle with a crossbow. Sybelle ducked to one side and raised her own gun towards them. Sybelle fired. Blue flash. Thwack! Missed. However, it was enough to make the soldier flinch and step backwards. A few more Bennel soldiers appeared ahead. Crossbow bolts whizzed past.

One of the other rebels fired into them, hitting one in the chest. The soldier jerked and fell back between the carriages. Bright blood splattered up the carriage exterior.

Rust stopped. She was staring right at a Bennel soldier. A woman. Two metres away at most. Her crossbow rising towards Rust. Rust flicked her gloved hand out and closed her eyes.

[Do it,] she commanded.

There was a whooshing noise. White light shone brightly through her eyelids. She was expecting a scream. Nothing.

[Stop]

She opened her eyes. The woman soldier was still standing. Dead. The white fire had burned right through her almost instantly, leaving a fist-sized hole right through her chest. Her clothes burned. The soldier stood silently for a second, then toppled over backwards. Rust's nostrils filled with a sickly smell of burned meat.

Other rebels had taken position behind a rusted water tank and were firing towards the Bennel soldiers. Rust, Indiril, and Sybelle joined them. A couple more Bennel soldiers went down. The rest now retreating backwards. The noise from the guns was deafening. Sybelle fired after them as well. The Bennel soldiers continued their retreat. Their crossbows, no match for the rebel guns. The fog swallowed them up.

Sudden silence. As soon as it had begun, it was over. Rust heaved and vomited onto the ground. Kathnell was helping Albea back to her feet.

"It's alright. Sword glanced off. Bruised shoulder at worst."

Albea turned to Rust, looking at her hand.

"Don't point that fucking thing at me!"

Rust realised her arm was still raised. Now pointing towards Albea and Kathnell. Shakily, Rust lowered her arm.

She'd just killed someone. This wasn't like the fight after they'd rescued Indiril. Then, the people she had seen had been at a distance. This time, she saw the person close up. Saw the woman raise her crossbow towards Rust. The puzzled expression in her eyes as Rust had raised her glove towards her. Rust wondered if closing her eyes made her a coward.

"What about the soldiers?" one rebel asked.

"Leave em, no time." Albea said. "Kathnell, it's all up to you now. Get this fucking thing moving."

Indiril picked up the dead soldier's crossbow and ammunition, trying not to look at the hole in her chest.

They boarded the train engine through a side doorway. There was more room inside than Rust was expecting. The trains back in Peldaran had tiny little compartments with room for just a couple of people. You could get twenty in here, at least.

Kathnell headed for a waist high console towards the front of the room. Banks of dials, valves and gauges. A bunch of polished copper pipes ran from the console and disappeared through holes underneath a pair of small windows overlooking the train's sleek nose. The walls of the room were lined with metal tables and cabinets.

Kathnell stood at the console and pulled a couple of levers.

"Great, void-stone is awake. Not slotted though."

She tapped a gauge.

"Water levels are good. That's great. Pressure vessels are at ambient, but shouldn't take long to pressurise. Filling the pre-chambers now."

Kathnell started turning handles and levers. Checking gauges as she went.

"This going to take long?" Albea said. "I thought it took hours to get a train going."

"Not these fellas," Kathnell said. "Don't build up steam like a regular train. These use the void-stone to heat water to high pressures almost instantly. Inject it directly, see. Sure, there are pressure vessels, capacitors really, but—"

"Stop the lecture Red," Albea said, "I ain't interested. Just want to know how long it's going to take."

Kathnell studied a couple more gauges.

"Should be moving within the next couple of minutes."

"Great, because we've got trouble."

"What?" Kathnell asked.

Albea stood in the open side doorway, looking back towards the station. Rust leaned out and followed her gaze. Figures emerged from the mist.

"Couple of dozen soldiers. Hegemon, might be Jurament," Albea said.

A rhythmic tremor went through the train. A gigantic shadow appeared in the mist. Six metres high. Rust had seen a shape like this before back at Hammington's Rest. Monstrous and metallic.

"Oh no," Rust said.

"Golem!" Albea shouted.

Chapter 21

Rejoice, for I bring tidings from Ventarso.
 The war has ended. Ventarso is free!
 The seers sing of victory.
 But Lament! For the mighty Porlain has fallen.
 The sky weeps countless tears.
 The best of us slain. Woman no more.
 Passed into memory. Ensuring immortal remembrance.
 We will remember her.

Remembrance for Saint Porlain: Books of lamentation and remembrance

Vidyana

Vidyana's descent was rapid. Cool night air rushed past. Her skin tingled. It felt like she was stationary, and it was the ground that was rushing up to meet her. Exhilarating! She was tempted to use the dragon blood to drink in her senses, each fragment of a second at a time. She didn't. She needed to be sharp in the minutes ahead. Needed to keep her reserves. Her hand and chest still hurt from Zarl's suicidal attack. Her shade constantly nagging for her to go easy. She still didn't know how much damage her kavach armour had taken.

White flashes lit up the fog below. Gunfire. A couple of streets over. She looked around at the troopers going with her. All Aurumill. The Hegemon's finest.

The thin wire that attached them to the airship sang with increased tension. Their descent slowed. The street took form. Buildings. Tiled roofs. Shops. Wet cobblestone pavement.

They landed and immediately released their harnesses. Wires disappeared up into the sky.

The flashing in the fog continued, accompanied by the snap of gunfire. She was disgusted by how many guns she'd seen in the last few days. A blasphemy! A blight upon the world that threatened to bring the old evil back. The Destroyer. Nemesis. Now, in response, the Hegemon would be forced to use them as well. Each of the troopers she was with had them. Instruments of death, long banned, had been taken from storage and distributed. All because of the heretics and their rebellion. The Hegemon would have to make more. It was inevitable.

She carried her own firearm. Not like the metal things the

rank and file troops carried. Hers was much older. A relic of ancient ages. Long, sleek, and white. She could trace its ownership back to Saint Porlain herself. Some two hundred years ago!

A Hegemon captain was waiting for them as they approached the dockside.

"Well?" Vidyana asked.

"A couple of dozen. Most are armed with guns. About half have taken up position in a warehouse, overlooking the wharf. They are suppressing any attempt we make to approach. The rest are preparing a boat to leave. Three people dressed in immaculate clothes are with them."

"Do you know they are actual immaculate?" she asked.

"No actual confirmation."

Vidyana followed him to a low wall overlooking the dockside. Several Hegemon troops, a seer, and a few armoured t'kelikt crouched behind it.

"That's the warehouse," the captain said, indicating a brick and wood building sitting between them and the nearest wharf.

The position the rebels had taken up was excellent. It gave them clear sight in every direction. Two Hegemon troopers and a t'kelikt lay dead in the street between.

Wyverns circled overhead, not able to do anything other than observe. The buildings too close for them to get any lower.

"And the boat?" she asked.

"On the other side of the warehouse. Fast clipper, we think. Steam. It was already fired up when they got here. Had just dropped off its cargo."

They had little time to waste. Normally, it wouldn't have been a problem. The West Wind could outrun it. But this damn fog...

[Let me see heat]

Her view shifted. In the warehouse, she could just make out five red splotches behind the wooden wall of the first floor.

"Five on the upper deck. Looks like the lower level is clear."

"You sure?" the captain said, glancing towards the warehouse. He sounded sceptical.

"I'm going to draw their fire. When you see me reach the building at that corner, have your men approach and lay down fire from behind those crates to the right."

"How are you going to get over there without being shot?" the captain asked.

She didn't reply.

"The same goes for you," she said to her squad.

"Yes, sir!" they said in unison.

She expanded her kavach armour all the way. It flowed up her neck and around her face.

"Be ready. I am about to move."

[Dragon Blood.]

The world slowed. The captain said something. By the time the first word left his mouth, Vidyana was already on her feet. Over the barricade. Into the street.

She brought the bone white gun up and aimed at the first red shape in the warehouse. A figure crouching beneath a window. Thwack. Wooden splinters erupted from the spot she was aiming at. She moved across the road, zigzagging as she went.

The cobblestone road beside her erupted as a bullet slammed into it. The sound followed. Missed, you fucker. Her shade projected lines on her vision; tracking the shot back to another red blob. She let her shade take partial control of her arms. Felt muscles tighten. Her aim shifted. Thwack. She aimed again. Third target. Thwack.

Another bullet landed in front of her. Change direction. Her leg muscles strained. Zigzag. Pause. Aim. Fourth target. Thwack. Move. Aim.

A bullet hit the road to her left. Pieces of fractured cobble bounced off her leg. Her shade registered pain. Not much. It would have to wait.

Fifth target. Thwack. Move. Zigzag.

She reached the corner of the warehouse. A few seconds later the Hegemon troopers opened up with their own guns. They blasted the front of the warehouse. Splinters of wood and chunks of brickwork flew in all directions.

She went inside.

A rebel came down the stairs in front of her. Blood from a shoulder wound. No older than eighteen. Handsome. Shame. Thwack. He arched backward. Blood and brain shooting from the back of his head. She paused. One second. Two. No more came. Three. Four…

[Stop]

The world resumed its usual speed. Her legs and arms ached from the brief exertion. The speed and stress more than a normal human body could endure. More than a few minutes of such strain would kill her. A few seconds were fine.

She heard a chugging noise. The boat! She looked out of the window and could see the clipper pulling away from the quayside.

"Secure the fucking warehouse," she shouted. "I'm going after the boat."

[Again. Give me speed.]

The world slowed again. She sprinted. The boat had almost reached the end of the wharf.

[More speed!]

She sped up. Her shade warning about imminent muscle tissue damage. She ignored it and jumped.

Vidyana stood on the deck, surrounded by several dead rebels.

The usual mix of retired along with a few fresh faces. She didn't really care about the older ones. They'd most likely been criminals before the schism. Just looking for another way to get back at "them". Already bitter about something. Same the world over.

It was the young ones she felt sorry for. The ones her age or younger. Almost only ever recruited from the poor.

Those without hope. Given a chance to belong to something bigger than they were. Even if it was heresy. It wasn't their fault. Each of their deaths was a reminder that it could have been her. They'd been indoctrinated into the heretics. Their minds twisted towards an ideology that didn't really care about them or their families.

They had put up a fight. She killed several of them. The rest decided that they would rather face the cold water of the bay and had jumped overboard.

Her leg throbbed from where the fragment of cobblestone had pierced through her kavach armour. A sign that the kavach armour wasn't working at optimal.

There was no sign of the girl, Rustari, or her companions. Three people dressed as immaculate were hoaxes. A total waste of time. A coincidence maybe. Just some rebels that thought it best to get out of the city. She doubted it. This stank of diversion.

She brought the boat under control and came to a stop next to the wharf. The West Wind was hovering above the wharf-side and had already lowered several tethers.

She met the captain on the wharf.

"You are to come immediately," the man said. "Lord Vellorson wants you back on the West Wind. This was just a diversion."

"Yeah, worked that out myself."

Kathnell

The train shuddered. Kathnell felt the vibration through her feet. A loud squealing noise came from underneath the floor. The sound jarred her teeth. Metal on metal. Wheels against track. The train shuddered for a second time.

"We're moving, Red!" Albea shouted. "You bloody did it!"

Kathnell glanced out of the low window at the front. Very slowly, they started moving. Kathnell tried not to think about what was following them.

Thump. Thump. Thump. She could feel it. The rhythmic thumping of the golem's walk.

Albea lent out of the open doorway and fired her gun. Flash. Crack. Kathnell jerked at the sound. Crack. Crack. For a moment, she was back at the docks. Covered in water. The sound of a child crying.

She shook her head. Need to concentrate, she thought.

Trying to distract herself, she studied the dials. Everything looked good. The pressures. The temperature. The vacuums. All, fine. Speed gauge. Hang on, that wasn't right. Too slow. They were barely crawling. The train was hardly accelerating. Slower than walking pace.

Alba fired again. Kathnell couldn't think. Another tremor went through her feet. More violent this time. The train lurched sideways. Sybelle was now leaning out of the train as well. Firing back towards the rear with her own gun. Albea swore. The sound of the golem's walk continued.

Why weren't they speeding up? The dials all checked out. With the carriages decoupled, they should be going faster. IF the carriages had been decoupled, that was.

"Are the carriages uncoupled?" she shouted over to

Albea.

"What?"

"I said, are the fucking carriages uncoupled?"

"No! Heges were approaching the train. Our troops engaged. Thought it best to get going."

Shit, they were still attached to all the carriages behind them! Dragging all that dead weight. That plan depended on the other squad getting the rear carriages uncoupled before they started moving. They would get up to speed eventually, but there was a kilometre long slope up out of the train yard. They would be at barely running speed before they were halfway out of the city. It would be possible for the whole Hegemon to just step onboard. They needed to get up to speed quickly. The plan depended on it. She'd bloody told them as much back at the rebel hideout! Make sure you get it uncoupled before we move, she'd said. Insisted on it. She'd told them!

"Why didn't you bloody say before we started moving!?"

"Thought getting moving was more important. There's a fucking golem! A golem! Thought we could decouple once we're moving."

"Not that simple. Once there's strain though the couplings, it's going to be hard to pull the lever. Very hard. Maybe impossible. We cannot outrun a lame feldercow like this!"

"Shit!" Albea said.

"Yes, shit!"

The train lurched again. There was a momentary hiccup, as if the train had paused for a split second. A terrific screeching noise came from behind.

Kathnell leaned out of the nearest door to look for herself. And there it was, the whole bloody train following behind them. She couldn't see any Hegemon troopers. Just flashes lighting up one carriage. Clearly a fight going on inside. She had no idea who was winning. The golem was trotting beside the carriages, trying to grab the train with massive steel hands. As she watched, it tore big sheets of metal off the last carriage. The rear carriages wobbled dangerously.

Fuck! If the golem derailed the rear carriages, it would bring the whole thing to a halt.

"We need to decouple the carriages," Kathnell said. "If we don't, we're fucked."

Albea looked back towards the golem.

"Right! Janno, Killen, Frelda," Albea said, pointing to three of the rebels. "Come with me. The rest, stay here."

"It's going to be bloody difficult to uncouple the train when there is strain," Kathnell said. "I'll ease up on the power for a few minutes. It might make it easier to pull the lever. Might!"

"Where is it? The lever."

"Not sure," Kathnell said. "Not on this thing. Normally between the carriages. Looks like a long pole with a handle. It'll be connected to the joint that links the carriages."

"Do you think a grenade will do the trick?" Albea asked.

"A what?"

"Never mind. Guess we'll find out. Right, got it," Albea said, moving towards the door in the back of the carriage. Rust got up and followed.

"Out of the fucking question," Albea said. "Apparently, you're the top-prize they're after. You're staying here."

"No way," Rust said. "Look, if the train stops, we're all dead. Anyway, I've got this."

Rust taped the glove with her other hand.

"Your funeral. I'm done babysitting." Albea said.

Albea nodded once and went through the door. Rust followed, Indiril close in tow. A couple of seconds later, Sybelle got up and went after them.

"Be careful Syb!" Kathnell said.

Sybelle didn't reply, and disappeared through the door, leaving Kathnell with the remaining rebels. She waited a minute and eased back on the throttle.

Rust

Rust followed Albea and the other rebels through the carriage. Indiril and Sybelle close behind.

The smell of burnt flesh still filled her nostrils. She couldn't get the look on the young Bennel soldier's face out of her mind. Confused, almost amused, as she stared at Rust's pathetic and harmless gloved hand. Two seconds later, she was dead. Just like that.

A crackle of gunfire came from ahead. The constant thump, thump, thump, of the thing they called a golem. Felt through her feet as much as heard. She'd seen one back at Hammington's Rest and had hoped to never see one again.

The first carriage they passed through was essentially just a corridor bordered by storage rooms and water tanks. She passed one room that was full of weapons. Swords, crossbows, shields.

The carriage lurched violently. She steadied herself against the wall. For a moment, Rust could detect a noticeable tilt to the floor. It settled back with a thump and squealing of metal. Albea reached the door at the far end.

They passed into the space between the carriages. A rush of cool air. Dawn light illuminated warehouses and stationary trains. They weren't even out of the train yard! The pace was barely faster than a slow jog.

The second carriage was like the last one, except for a large workshop in the middle.

Another blast of cool air as they passed into the next carriage. This one was much taller. Back at the rebel base, they'd said these were the troop carriages. Two stories high. It was empty. The sound of gunfire grew louder. They passed quickly through its lower level and outside again.

Albea opened the door to the second troop carriage. Flashes illuminated the interior. The gunfire grew immensely louder. Smoke filled the carriage. The air stank. An odd smell, like fireworks. Something whistled past her. Splintered wood stung her face.

"Take cover," Albea shouted.

Rust dived behind a row of wooden seats. Indiril and Sybelle followed her. The sound was deafening.

She peered out. Further down the carriage, a fierce fight was going on between a group of rebels and some Hegemon soldiers. The rebels had taken position behind a waist high partition that separated the carriage into two, where a set of spiral stairs led to the upper level. The Hegemon had taken a position at the other end of the carriage. Bullets from the Hegemon's guns pinged off the partition. Thankfully, it appeared to be made of metal. More flashes came from the upper floor. One rebel was attending to a wounded comrade. His arm hung limp, clothes stained red with blood.

In between the two groups, lay several bodies. A mixture of both rebels and Hegemon.

"We have to push them back," Albea said.

Albea rose to her feet and started firing towards the far end. The other troopers with her began firing as well. Sybelle was firing her own gun. Thwack, Thwack, Thwack.

Rust wanted nothing more than to stay behind the door. It was safe there. Let Albea and her troopers do what they were good at. They knew what they were doing. They were fighters. She wasn't. She would only get in the way. Then she noticed Indiril had also stood. He had cocked his crossbow. He fired.

Indiril, the boy who jumped at his own shadow. The first to run in the other direction when a fight broke out. Indiril, who always had his money stolen by the big human teenagers. He shouted wordlessly into the maelstrom. He fired again. Stupid bastard was going to get himself killed!

Rust willed her legs to move. She stood and took aim with her gauntlet down the corridor. Nothing happened. All

I need to do is think, she thought. Just think, and it will happen.

[*Now*]

She kept her eyes open this time.

Fire, bright as the sun, shot out from the gauntlet, passed over the heads of the rebels and slammed into the back wall at the far end carriage. She arced it from one side to side, and then up and down, drawing a flaming line across the back wall and into the ceiling. One second. Two. Wood cracked and erupted into fire. Metal walls glowed red at its touch. Three. Chunks of the ceiling fell in flaming ruin onto the floor, followed by parts of the upper level. Dense black smoke now obscured the far end of the carriage.

Then, suddenly, it shut off without her instruction. Silence fell over the carriage.

A Hegemon trooper staggered out, clutching his head. He crumpled and fell, smoke billowing from his body.

"Fuck me," someone to her left said.

Rust tried to make the fire start again.

[Again!]

The gauntlet whispered to her. Something about heat and void capacitance levels. She didn't understand it, but innately knew to continue would be dangerous. She would have to wait before she could do that again.

Albea moved. The rest followed. They were halfway to the partition when the Hegemon started firing back from within the smoke. They weren't all dead then. The group ducked back behind cover.

"Can you do that again?" Albea asked.

"I… I don't think so. I think I need to wait a couple of minutes."

Something rolled out of the smoke towards them. A ball. Grey metal. About the size of an apple.

"Nade!" someone shouted.

A bright flash. A noise that was more physical than actual sound. A punch to her whole body. Rust fell backwards. Her ears rang.

She blinked away after images. Several rebels lay still. Several more moved slowly. A few retreated towards them, pulling the wounded as they came.

Sybelle fired her gun into the smoke. Rust tried her gauntlet again. It whispered to her. She needed to wait.

"We have to pull back," Albea said. She pointed back towards the carriage from which they'd come. "We can decouple there."

The rebels nodded. Rust looked towards the partition. The wounded troopers still lay in the corridor. Two troopers with Albea started moving towards the wounded.

"Leave them," Albea shouted. "We have to continue with the mission!"

The rebels hesitated.

"I said leave them," she said.

They nodded and fell back towards the door.

Albea pulled one of the grey metal balls from her waist belt, did something to it, and tossed it in to the smoke at the far end. They continued to retreat towards the door. An explosion lit up the smoke at the far end, sending bits of debris flying in all directions.

Then, through the smoke, the Hegemon started firing at them again. Another rebel was hit. She fell in the aisle. Hole in her chest. Dead. They bundled through the open door and into the space between the carriages. Rushing air and dawn skies.

"You'd better be worth this!" Albea said to Rust.

Rust looked over at her. Tears streaked the woman's face. A face that Rust had thought could only ever look angry, now looked grief stricken. Rust didn't know who the dead rebels were. Or the wounded ones they had left behind. This woman did. Her people. Friends and comrades.

The remaining rebels took up positions on either side of the door and fired back through the smoke towards the other end. There was barely enough room for them all on the walkway.

"This must be it, right?", Albea said.

Rust looked over at a lever that sat on one side of the walkway between the carriages.

"I guess so," Rust said.

Albea tried to pull it. It didn't budge.

"Help me! It won't fucking budge."

A couple of rebels went to assist. Nothing. It was stuck.

"Shit!" Albea said.

The Hegemon continued firing. Rust could hear the bullets ping off the wall of the carriage. One rebel was hit in the shoulder. The man stumbled backwards, lost his balance, and fell over the edge of the walkway. Gone.

Rust ran over and tried to help. It wouldn't budge. Not even the slightest movement.

"Hegemon are advancing!" a rebel shouted.

Something whispered to Rust. Not a voice. A thought. The glove. It was ready to fire again.

"Stand back," Rust said.

She raised her glove and pointed at the joint that connected them to the rear carriages.

[Fire!]

White fire struck the joint. The metal glowed red. Orange. White. Globules of molten metal dripped away. There was a snapping noise. The fire shut off again. Another whisper about safety limits and capacitors. The gap between the carriages was growing. Slowly at first, but widening with each second.

"We're free!", Sybelle said.

Albea stepped onto the other side. She offered her hand to Rust. Rust stepped over as well. The others followed. The gap continued to widen between them and the rear carriages. The last of the rebels had to jump.

They entered the first troop carriage. They'd done it, Rust thought. She collapsed inside the door and breathed out. The rest took a moment to check their weapons.

"That was too bloody close," Albea said.

There was a loud ripping sound. Metal strained. Someone screamed. The whole back wall of the carriage tore away.

Wind rushed in. The silhouette of a giant metal figure appeared through the ruined hole that moments ago had been the rear wall of the carriage.

"Golem!" someone bellowed.

The golem trotted behind the carriage. Then a fist the size of a person appeared in the gap. It held a rebel in its grip. The golem tossed the man away like he was a child's toy. A giant two metre long sword thrust into the jagged gap.

Chapter 22

Gone is their smell/mark/name!
　The air/sky has called it home/family
　Sorrow/loss!
　Remembrance/knowledge remains
　They are blessed/revered
　Another must follow/replace
　Colours/status changes/becomes
　As all must change/become

Translation of t'kelikt ascension rite of village Elder becoming Savant - Notes on t'kelikt social hierarchy

Sybelle

Sybelle scrambled on all fours away from the gaping ruin that moments ago had been the back wall of the carriage. Details blurred by confusion, panic, and gloom. The golem gripped the twisted edges of the hole with one hand. With the other, it swung a massive metal sword into the gap. Each concussive strike sent more of the carriage spiralling off into the dawn sky. The golem's thrashing movements silhouetted black against the dawn sky.

Around her, the others also retreated further into the carriage. The giant sword crashed into the bench seats in front of her. Its metal frame crumpled on to her ankle. Not enough to crush it, but enough to trap her foot. She tried to move her leg. Nothing. The golem loomed closer. It's sword crashed down into the floor just a couple of hands away from her head. The impact jarred her skull and sent splinters of wood flying. She thrashed around, desperately trying to free her foot. Oblivious to her plight, the others continued their retreat.

"Help!" she screamed. "I'm stuck!"

The woman, Albea, stopped and looked at her. Something flickered across the woman's face. Sorry, it said, but you're going to die here. Then, the expression was gone. The woman hesitated and started back towards Sybelle.

"Fuck," Albea shouted.

The golem swung its sword again. More of the carriage came away. A whole chunk of roof peeled back in the thing's grasp, flying off behind them.

Beyond, the outside world swept past. They were beyond the train yard now, into the wider city beyond. The northern district, close streets, houses all crammed together.

Although they were now gaining speed, the thing was still easily able to keep pace. In the background, she could hear a familiar low droning noise growing louder.

She strained at her foot. It was stuck fast. The golem's other hand penetrated further into the carriage. She stared into the thing's head. Massive. Smooth. Eyeless. Metallic. She really was going to die here.

Then Albea and Rust were with her. They both strained at the crushed seat. It didn't budge. Albea and Rust ducked as the sword flashed over their heads. The tree boy Indiril fired his crossbow at the thing's head, bolt bouncing impotently off.

They heaved again. Nothing.

Then, the golem's fist was around Albea. The woman looked surprised. Eyes wide. Then she was gone.

Moments later the giant hand returned, empty, clawing its way towards her and Rust.

The other rebels fired at it with their guns. Bullets pinging off as harmlessly as Indiril's crossbow bolt. The ricochets threatening to do more damage to them than the golem. Rust shouted wordlessly and shook her glove. Cursing it like she was arguing with it. The train gained speed. The golem was having to jog to keep up now.

Sybelle fired her own gun at it. Maybe her bullets would do more damage. No, they bounced off as uselessly as the others.

The bone sword!

She reached down and found the handle at her waist. Rust ducked back as the golem made another grab.

"Get back! I'm going to try something!" she shouted to Rust.

Rust moved behind her. She flicked the little switch on the side of the handle. The little white stub rose, the crackling blue thread appearing behind it. The golem's hand moved towards them. She swung her arm towards it, slashing downwards. Catching the seat as well. There was a flash. A portion of the seat flew away. The golem's wrist erupted with blue arcs. The giant hand spasmed and fell, landing in the middle of the carriage with a thump.

The golem withdrew its truncated wrist. Exposed cables twitched and sparked. Severed pipes spewed green fluid onto the floor, covering her and Rust. She swung again, chopping off another section of wrist.

The golem reeled backwards. For the first time, the thing made a loud, low-pitched noise. Almost like a moan. Sybelle knew that behind each golem was an operator. A talented seer that could use the golem as if it was their own body. Somewhere close by, a seer was reliving the pain of having their hand and lower arm chopped off. The thing stumbled, tripped, and went down. The ground shook. It rolled twice and smashed into the side of a house. Rubble fell on top of it.

The train continued to pick up speed. Each second, the acceleration increased. She swung her sword at the remains of the seat. Her ankle came free. The other rebels were with her now. They fired backwards towards where the thing was stirring from the ruins of the building.

She was free, but Albea was gone. The remaining five rebels without leader. Just five left! They stopped firing and turned towards Rust. The low droning noise continued. Louder now. It changed in pitch. Sybelle looked up through the ruined roof into the sky. Rust followed her gaze.

In the gaps between the low cloud, something enormous hung in the sky. The airship!

Even as she watched, black shapes descended from it on cables. One looked human. The rest were different. Too many legs. T'kelikt. They were all rapidly descending towards the front of the train.

Flashes appeared from the sides of the airship. Bullets whizzed around them. The carriage floor erupted with each strike. Two of the rebels were hit multiple times. They crumpled to the floor, bullets still slamming into their bodies. Blood splashed Sybelle's face. Someone shouted wordlessly.

A hand on her shoulder. Pulling her. Rust. She mouthed something to Sybelle. They needed to move. The rest began retreating towards the front of the carriage and the relative safety of an intact roof. Sybelle, Rust and the boy Indiril followed.

The roof of the carriage clinked with bullets. Some punched through and bounced dangerously around inside. They would all die if they stayed here.

A rebel opened the door that led to the gap between their carriage and the engineering one ahead. She was immediately struck on the shoulder. She stumbled and fell onto the walkway. Bullets continued to clink off the surrounding metal. Rust rushed over to the fallen rebel.

The bullets ceased. It was as if the airship knew they shouldn't fire at Rust. They still wanted her alive! Rust looked up at the airship. She screamed fury into the air and aimed her gauntlet upwards towards the airship.

White fire shot upwards from her hand. It roared, painfully bright, into the sky. Sybelle had to cover her eyes with her hands. Before, Rust's glove had stopped after a second or so. This time the fire continued, lancing upwards into the sky. Three seconds, four, five.

The bullets started again. They bounced around Rust. Splinters of wood flew into the air. Sybelle was amazed Rust wasn't hit. She just stood there, firing into the sky. Screaming wordlessly. The fire continued. Six seconds. The stubby barrel on the back of the gauntlet glowed red. The incoming bullets stopped. Steam rose from the gauntlet now. Seven. Rust continued to scream.

The white fire stopped. Rust collapsed onto the walkway, clutching the gauntlet to her chest. Steam, or maybe smoke, rising from it.

Something was different. The sound. The droning noise had stopped.

Sybelle rushed over to Rust and looked up. Above, the sky was on fire! One whole side of the airship was ablaze. The thing veered to the side, away from the train. It rapidly lost altitude as it vanished out of sight behind the rooftops.

Rust checked the woman over. The shoulder wound looked nasty, but most likely survivable.

It wasn't over. Ahead of them, from the front of the train, came sounds of gunfire, muffled by the wind. Then screams.

Kathnell!

Sybelle forgot everything else. She pushed past Rust and ran through the rear engineering carriage towards to the front of the train.

A t'kelikt warrior appeared in front of her. It rushed at her. Armoured carapace and sharp blades flashing. Clicking and whistling as it came. Sybelle ducked left and swung her sword at it. Missed! It sliced harmlessly into the wall. The blade flickered and switched off. The tiny pearl fell to the floor and rolled away. She flicked the switch again. Nothing. Come on, saints damn it! Maybe it didn't work without the pearl, she thought.

The t'kelikt barrelled into her. She fell backwards, knocking the wind out of her. She tried to gulp down a breath.

An armoured leg smashed into her chest. She fell backwards. Then the thing's forearms were slashing at her. A finger's distance away. She backed up, trying to reach the pearl, holding the t'kelikt off with her other hand. Its other legs reached around her. Squeezing. Squeezing. She gasped for air. It was going to kill her!

Bang! Bang! Something warm splashed her face.

The t'kelikt fell sideways, twitching. A rebel appeared behind her, gun in hand. Rust and the others, just behind.

The rebel fired three more times into the thing's carapace.

Sybelle shook herself loose of the t'kelikt's grasp and picked the pearl up from the floor. It attached to the top of the bone sword with a click. She shoved the sword into her belt. Then, without a word, ran towards the front of the train.

Kathnell!

Vidyana

Vidyana readied her equipment, checking everything again. Harness, armour, gun, and sword. Her shade whispered that her heart rate was slightly elevated. Good. She savoured the knot in her gut. Part excitement. Part fear. She welcomed it. It would keep her sharp. Alive!

This would be the second time today she'd dropped from the airship. This time, she was about to land on top of a moving train. Straight into combat.

Somehow, Rust and her new friends had stolen a train. Not just a train, a fucking Hegemon void-train! She had to give them credit. It wasn't something she had expected. Trelt neither.

A good amount of effort had gone into providing a well-timed diversion at the docks. Lives had been sacrificed. Despite her hatred for all the heretics stood for, she respected their tenacity.

Of course, it confirmed that Rust was now with the damned heretics. A massive complication. If it was just these elusive Sleepers, that was one thing. Now, the very people that Trelt had feared would get hold of Rust had done so.

Trelt was genuinely afraid of what the heretics could extract from the girl. Secrets that once freed into the world would be hard to re-bind. New technologies loose upon the lips of the races once more. The Covenant warned them. The way of Nemesis. It taught them that there were secrets that should remain forever quiet. Little things. Things that over time would lead inexorably towards a future that would bring back the great enemy. A minor improvement to a woodworking tool here, a change to farming equipment there. A path to ingenuity and increasing complexity. Guns were one such secret. Another wrung on the ladder towards inevitable doom. Vidyana had never seen Nemesis. The Emperor had, and if some were to be believed, so had Trelt.

She checked the harness again. This time, she wouldn't be going with human troopers. Behind her, six t'kelikt soldiers also readied themselves. All were armoured in steel. Formidable, agile, fast. Ideally suited to landing on the moving train. Five of them had greyish blue fur of normal adults. The one at the front was slightly larger than the others, its fur black. An elder. The leader of the group.

"Ready?" she asked it.

It waved its forelimbs and emitted a string of whistles and clicks.

[This individual indicates that readiness is optimal. The grasslands sing with commitment and softness underfoot. The herd/prey will be hunted!]

Vidyana nodded back.

The pitch of the engines changed. The floor tilted. She grabbed an overhead bar to steady herself and looked down out of a window in the floor.

They were above the train now. The rear carriages had been discarded and were dropping behind. Just four parts of the train left now. The engine, two engineering carriages, and a single troop carriage. Shed of most of its weight, the train was speeding up rapidly. Another five minutes and it would be at the city's edge and fast enough that the West Wind wouldn't be able to keep up.

Vidyana's attention shifted to the troop carriage. Flashes from within. Gunfire. The roof was partly gone, torn away by the golem that trotted behind it. It continued smashing it with fist and sword. As she watched, the golem plucked someone from the carriage and tossed them aside. The figure hit a nearby wall and lay still. Vidyana prayed for yet another lost soul. Killed by ignorance and lies.

Back at the train yard, the summoner controlling the golem would have to be quick. Each moment took the metal monster and its master further from each other. At some point, the connection between them would be broken. Then, the golem would become several tons of useless metal. Hopefully, Vidyana would be on the train by then.

The golem reached inside the train. Blue flashes. The golem reeled back, lower arm missing. It tripped and fell, tumbling into a nearby house.

Saints!

Vidyana reached for the nearest speaking tube.

"Get us lower. We need to get on that train now! Go towards the front! Put us down on the front engineering carriage!"

The engine noise changed pitch again. The floor tilted forwards. She wasn't sure what had brought down the golem. It had to be an immaculate relic. You couldn't cut off a golem's arm that easily. Something belonging to one of the sleeper women.

She looked down again. This was it. They were right above the forward engineering carriage. Just behind the engine.

"Five seconds!," she shouted.

The t'kelikt bowed in unison. The doors swung up and back. Cables spooled out. They jumped. For the second time in a day, she experienced the rush of falling at not quite terminal speed.

They were halfway down when gunfire started from the airship. It peppered the carriage at the rear. A risk, she thought. They could just as easily kill Rustari as the rebels. She had no clue if the girl was even on the train. Don't worry about that for now. First, stop the train and neutralise anyone that wasn't Rustari.

The roof of the train rushed up to meet them. Her muscles readied themselves. She landed heavily, rolled, and came to a stop. The t'kelikt had no such problems; they landed sure footed.

They all immediately moved backwards, towards the gap between the front and rear engineering carriages. They approached slowly. A couple of heretics were waiting for them. Guns braced and aimed up at them from below. The heretics opened fire immediately. One of the t'kelikt troopers was caught in the torso. It skidded and fell over the side. Pray for it later. The others went prone on the rooftop.

Then something flashed into the sky ahead of her. Her augmented eyes automatically dimmed down the brightness. A white beam of intense light shot up from the gap between the rear carriages, piercing the sky. Towards the airship!

The beam struck the gondola, fire immediately erupting at its touch. A series of explosions tore a hole in the gondola's underside. The beam moved slowly left and up the side of the airship's outer envelope. The skin peeled away like the hide of some enormous animal. Flaming ribbons fell away. Vidyana could see into the heart of the ship and the gas bags that kept it afloat. One ripped open, gas venting into the air. The engines increased in pitch, desperately trying to fight against the mortal wounds the beast was suffering.

The beam shut off, but the damage was already done. The airship was tilting to one side. The engine noise stopped. Its rear dropped as it veered off course. She quickly lost sight of it behind the speeding rooftops. Holy saints! Trelt!

Push down your fear, Vidyana. Remember your training. It is not your immediate concern. Her thoughts threatened to shift back to Trelt. The man that had rescued her from the heretics when she was young. The closest thing to a father she had. Was he alive? Or lying dead in the airship's wreckage? Concentrate on your mission. May the saints inspire you. You are the will of the Emperor made manifest!

One of the t'kelikt was clicking a question. Asking her what to do. She didn't know. The airship was gone! Trelt likely dead.

The heretics would pay for what they had done. And Rust, she would pay as well. Vidyana rose.

[Full dragon blood][Remove all limiters!][Kavach

armour now]

Her shade didn't even respond. She could almost feel its own anger overlaid on top of hers. It fizzed with its own type of fury. Together, they would be glorious!

She welcomed the rush through her veins. The holy gifts she had been given. The pain she would feel over the next few days would be awesome. She would drink it. Bath in it. Relish it. For it would remind her of the power she was about to wield.

"Follow me," she shouted. "Long live the Emperor!"

The t'kelikt whistled and clicked, waving their armoured forelimbs in front of them.

[The herd/prey shall fall under our forelimbs]

Time slowed. Her kavach armour flowed from the ridges on either side of her spine. It slid round her body, up her face, across her eyes, into her mouth.

To most others, the buildings would be speeding past. To her, they moved past with glacial slowness. She moved, somersaulting down between the two carriages.

Two rebels. Guns raised. Only just beginning to register her presence. She fired into the heretic nearest to her. Felt the gun's bone white handle tremble in her hand. Bullets hit. One in the head, two in the chest. Surgical. Precise.

The second heretic turned towards her. Surprise, fucker! Vidyana landed in front of them. A woman, maybe mid-twenties. Another brainwashed fool. Each of their deaths was unnecessary. A crime for which the heretic's leaders would eventually be held responsible. She vowed to find them one day and make them pay for every one of the deaths on their hands.

Vidyana ducked towards the heretic and sliced with her sword. The woman flew back, slamming into the closed door of the forward engineering carriage. The woman crumpled and lay still.

The door was closed. The t'kelikt scuttled beside her. She signalled for the elder and two others to take cover on either side of the door. The other two headed back towards the rear of the train.

Vidyana did not know who or what was waiting for them on the other side of the door. No, that wasn't quite right. It was death that awaited. Whether it was hers or the heretics remained to be seen.

"Saints forgive us all," she said.

She punched the door with all her augmented strength. Her kavach armour stiffened, protecting her strengthened bones from the worst of the impact. The door flew inwards.

A group of rebels. Already in position. Guns raised and aimed at the door. They opened fire.

Vidyana ducked and danced towards them. She moved too quick for them to track. They fired. She felt bullets speed past her, tearing up the air. Several hit her. Left leg, shoulder, right arm. Her kavach armour shrugged off most of the impact. Not all of it. She knew she was injured. Her shade calmly relayed the damage in calm detail. The kavach armour was failing. She ignored it all.

Later. She would deal with it all later.

For now, she had become a demon. Death manifested. Divine instrument of the God Emperor.

Kathnell

Kathnell stared at the dials. All looked good. Speed was climbing. Steam pressure, optimal. Water reserve was near-full. They were free of the dead weight now. She'd felt the tremor. The dials confirmed it.

Two rebels were arguing about something. Kathnell tried to listen in.

A bright light bloomed behind her. Dawn gloom flashed into bright daylight. It lit up the control room interior. Her own shadow cast onto the console. She jerked around.

"Saint's arse! The airship's hit!" one rebel shouted.

The man was leaning out a side door, looking towards the back of the train.

"You sure?" Kathnell asked.

"Yeah, looked like that glove thing that stonie had. Ripped right into the fucker. It's lit up like a cheap Emperor's Day firework. Holy piss, the things going down."

The other rebels cheered. Kathnell smiled too. They were making good ground. Speed increased rapidly now. They would hit the incline out of the city soon. That would slow them a bit, but with all the dead weight gone, it wouldn't stop them.

More noises came from behind them. Muffled bangs and cracks.

"Shit," the rebel said. He ducked back inside.

"What is it?"

"Something's going on further down the train. Sounded like gunfire. Some remaining Hegemon, I guess."

"See!" one of the other rebels said. A woman in her fifties. "Told you I saw something land on the train."

"Don't be crazy Shaleen," another said. "Just Albea and the others mopping up the last of 'em."

More noises. Closer now. Kathnell heard it this time. The unmistakable pop-popping of gunfire. The door to the carriage slid open. A head poked through.

"Gunfire! At the rear of this carriage!" the man shouted.

Some rebels had gone through into the carriage a few minutes ago to secure it. Shit! This didn't sound like Albea mopping up. Someone was advancing. Towards them.

Shaleen and the other rebels exchanged glances. She and another of the rebels went through the door to investigate. Leaving Kathnell with four remaining rebels.

Kathnell stiffened. What if this Shaleen was right? What if someone, or something, had landed on the moving train? Only someone idiotic would do such a thing. Or someone very dangerous.

Something cold and dark clawed its way up her spine. She wasn't on the train. She was back at the dockside. Cold from the water. Heat and light of a fire on her face. Someone was screaming. A child. She tried to concentrate, but the sounds of gunfire dragged her back to the dockside.

Not now!

"We have to protect the consoles!" Kathnell said.

"Eh?"

"We are under attack. They will come here. Here! If they disable the controls, it's all over. Everything."

"It's nothing, just some remaining Hege's."

"What about what Shaleen saw?"

"Ah. Woman's half blind. Too much hee-haw if you ask me."

"No, I don't like it," Kathnell said.

She moved to one of the large metal tables fastened to the walls. She swept the tools off and unfastened it. She pulled. It was bloody heavy. At least it meant it was solid.

"Give me a bloody hand," Kathnell asked. The rebels looked at her like she was mad.

Light flashed through the open doorway. More sounds of

gunfire. A scream.

"Give me a fucking hand," she shouted. "We need to make some cover in front of the console."

The rebels rushed over to join her.

Within half a minute, they had tipped over three of the tables and arranged them between the console and the rear doors.

Signs of battle were closer now. Shouting. Each pop of gunfire, louder by the second.

"Maybe we should go to help!"

"No, whatever it is, it's coming this way," Kathnell said.

It went quiet. Just the rhythmic clattering of the train on the rails. Either it was all over, or they were about to get fucked.

The four rebels took up positions behind the overturned tables and aimed their guns at the open doorway into the engineering carriage. They knew it too.

Kathnell had no gun. Instead, she clutched a big metal wrench she'd found in a toolbox. Her knuckles, white. The seconds dragged. Kathnell thought she saw movement through the doorway.

Then something erupted from the open side doorway. All legs and knives. It jumped across the carriage towards the first set of rebels.

"T'kelikt! From the roof!" she screamed.

It was already on the first rebel. Pinning him to the floor. It tore into him with bladed arms. It looked injured already. One leg missing, another twisted at an odd angle. Black ichor covered one side of its head. Still, it fought like a monster.

The other rebels fired into it. A few stray shots hitting their fallen comrade. He twitched from the impact, but he was already dead. Most of the bullets bounced harmlessly off the t'kelikt, but a few penetrated the armour.

Cold gripped Kathnell. Cold water. A distant crying of a baby. She edged back towards the console. Legs numb.

Another t'kelikt entered through the opposite side door.

This one was larger. Its fur was black. It ignored the rebels and jumped towards the table where Kathnell was standing.

It was after the console! They were trying to stop the train.

The thing slammed into the table in front of Kathnell, pushing it towards her. The t'kelikt clicked loudly, like rapid barks. Then it was over the table. She tried to move, but her body was frozen rigid. Back against the console.

It swung an arm at her. A barb slashed across her arm, ripping away fabric. A few fingers closer and it would have ripped her arm off.

The rebel to her left fired into the thing's side. It hissed and turned away from Kathnell, towards the rebel woman. It launched at the rebel. Kathnell had a chance to strike, to hit the thing with her wrench. Instead, she did nothing. She just stood rooted to the spot.

A fire. Cold water. A crying child. She couldn't move.

The black t'kelikt struck the rebel. The poor woman didn't stand a chance. Her gun spun away and landed at Kathnell's feet.

Just pick it up!

Reach down and pick it up!

Move!

Her hands were shaking violently, but she managed to pick up the gun. She pulled the trigger. The gun jerked, most shots missing, but a couple hit the t'kelikt. It wheeled back around to face her.

The two remaining rebels had killed the other t'kelikt. They started firing into the black t'kelikt as well. It jerked under the impact, crumpled and fell. Silence again. Was it over?

For a moment she felt the beginnings of hope that it might be over, but something inexplicable was moving through the carriage.

A figure. Impossibly quick. Featureless. Black as space. It moved like a dancer. Precise. It carried a sword in one hand, and something white in the other. A melding of gun and bone. Kathnell wanted to shout, to warn the two remaining rebels. A warning. All that came out was a formless cry.

The first rebel was under attack before the sound left Kathnell's lungs. The gun the figure held flashed three times. Thwack, thwack, thwack. Two holes in the rebel's chest and one in his head. Dead before he hit the floor.

Kathnell raised her own gun, impossibly slow compared to the speed of this new black nightmare. Her time was up. She knew it. There would be no getting away from this. For all the stupid risks she'd taken in her life, all the mistakes, all the gambles, getting killed by a demon hadn't seemed a likely end. It was a shame, really; they were nearly out of the city. The houses flashed past outside. Wider streets. Suburbs.

The other rebel was turning now, towards the new threat. Too slow. Too late. The thing's sword cleaved the man across the chest.

Kathnell fired. Held down the trigger. The gun jerked. Bullets hit the thing. Square in the torso. Crack. Crack. Crack.

It stumbled backwards. Kathnell continued to fire.

But there were no more bullets. She continued to pull the trigger. The gun clicked uselessly.

Kathnell pressed up against the console, staring down at the demon. Her hands reached behind her to steady herself. She thought of the cold water and the crying baby. She hadn't meant to cause that explosion. She'd just wanted to get back at the Hegemon for killing her father. She'd thought it would feel good. She hadn't meant to hurt innocent people. People with names.

She thought of her father, and how she'd only wished she could speak to him again. She wondered if his last moments had been like this?

What about Mum? She would be left alone without Kathnell's income. When Corric found out what she'd done, he would be ashamed. The thought stung. Stupid

Kathnell, he'd say. Bloody stupid. An odd thing to think of before you died.

The figure walked slowly towards her. A woman, cut from the blackest marble.

She felt the controls, the dials, the levers that she had spent her life learning about. All would be for nothing.

The thing advanced, a hint of a smile on its smooth black face.

Kathnell felt over the smooth controls. Searching.

It slowly raised its sword. Now the other rebels were gone. It was taking its time.

Kathnell's hand slammed down on the button she had been seeking.

A scream of brakes. The carriage lurched. The overturned tables slid violently forward. Kathnell fell backwards against the console.

The black thing stumbled towards her, overbalanced. It slammed into the overturned table in front of Kathnell. The thing went down. Another table slammed into the first, pinning the nightmare between them. The thing howled.

Both tables continued to slide forwards, slamming into Kathnell.

Something sharp hit Kathnell in the face. The back of her head impacted on the metal of the console. The vision in her left eye went red.

For a second, the demon lay limp. Kathnell pushed herself away from it. She spat blood. Then the demon stirred. With one hand, it casually pushed the table violently away.

With her one good eye, Kathnell looked up into the face of the nightmare. It raised its bone white gun towards her.

"Nice try," the thing said.

Rust

Rust's hand burned. Raw pain. Skin red and swollen. Like when Uncle had been brewing, and she'd accidentally put her hand in the hot liquor.

Just like then, it was her fault. The gauntlet had tried to shut itself down, but she'd forced it to continue. It whispered of the danger. Incomprehensible images in her mind. A small gem deep inside the complex mechanisms of the gauntlet. A conduit for vast and limitless energies elsewhere. It tried to warn her it was being damaged. She'd ignored it. Whispered warnings turned into pleas until it was screaming into her mind. Pure rage had forced it to continue.

As the airship had burst into flames, something coursed through her. Something dark, exciting. Like the relic had long been asleep, and had found its purpose again. More than that, though, she'd felt powerful. Almost intoxicated. She hadn't even felt the pain at the time.

She did now. Red blisters already forming on the back of her hand. She forced the gauntlet back on, ignoring the pain.

She stepped over the fallen t'kelikt and ran to keep up with Sybelle and one rebel. They were a good ten metres in front. Half way through the carriage already. Indiril and the remaining rebel followed. That was all that was left now. Just the five of them. Two rebels, Indiril, Rust, and Sybelle. They'd left an injured rebel back in the last carriage. The one that had been hit in the shoulder. She'd live, but her fight was over for now. Rust had taken her gun.

"Sybelle!" Rust called. "For Sindar's sake, slow down."

The immaculate girl ignored her, continuing to run towards the front of the train.

"Syb.."

Something dark flashed into the corridor. Whirling limbs and blades. Another t'kelikt!

It hit Sybelle hard with an armoured arm, sending her reeling into the wall. The t'kelikt immediately launched itself at the nearest rebel. The woman fired a couple of shots before a bladed forearm struck her across the face. She crumpled and fell. The t'kelikt ignored her and focused its attention on Rust.

The rebel next to Rust fired. At this range, the sound was deafening. Smoke. Smell of fireworks. Most shots bounced harmlessly off. A few connected. The noise stopped, gun spent. The man began backing off towards the rear of the train, reloading.

Rust knew the gauntlet would be of no use. It would be quite some time before it would work again. Days maybe. It was damaged, but would somehow heal, given time. All these things she knew, without understanding why. Facts whispered into her mind.

Indiril raised his crossbow and fired. The bolt bounced off the armour covering the thing's head. It clicked and whistled loudly as it advanced towards them. Indiril started reloading his crossbow.

Rust raised the gun she'd picked off the fallen rebel. The t'kelikt picked up speed, legs churning at the smooth floor. She pulled the trigger. The gun jerked violently. The first couple of bullets were on target, the rest woefully inaccurate.

The beast was almost on her. Moments away. Its mouth open. Fore limbs raised to attack. All spines and blades. Then it fell, sliding along the floor towards her. It came to rest a few hands away. Black ichor oozing from an open mouth, from which a lone crossbow bolt protruded.

"Holy Nemesis Indiril!," Rust shouted.

"Did you see that!?" Indiril said.

A single, cold-hell in a million shot, Rust thought! The fallen rebel was trying to get up. A cut across her cheek and scalp. Sybelle stood, gulping down air. Rust ran over to her.

"Are you all right?" Rust asked.

"I... I think so," she said, looking around.

"It's all right," Rust said. "We killed it."

The uninjured rebel helped his fallen colleague to her feet. The gash on the woman's face didn't look as bad as Rust had feared.

"I'll be fine," the woman said, touching the wound. "Let's get this over with."

Outside, the train continued to pick up speed. The sound of gunfire from up ahead began again.

Sybelle's eyes went wide as if remembering where she was for the first time. She turned around, clutching her white gun.

"Kathnell," Sybelle shouted. "We have to get to Kathnell!"

The five of them entered the forward engineering carriage. The place was a hell-scape. Blood and dark ichor splattered the corridor. The floor was slick with both. Many rebels and a t'kelikt lay scattered about. Parts of them, at least. All looked dead. Very dead.

They ran towards the open door to the engine carriage. The train lurched. Wheels squealed. Sybelle held on, but Rust and Indiril fell forwards. The two rebels only just avoided falling into the spikes of the dead t'kelikt's armour. The noise ceased. The sudden braking ended.

Rust and Sybelle were the first through the door.

Another two t'kelikt, and more rebels, lay dead on the floor. Several makeshift barricades scattered between the door and forward console.

Kathnell lay slumped on the floor next to the forward control console. Unconscious, or possibly dead. Blood streaming from her head.

Something terrible stood over her. Smooth black. The demon. The one called Vidyana. It pointed a gun at Kathnell, similar to the one Sybelle had. In the other hand, it held a bone white sword.

"Kathnell!," Sybelle screamed.

The demon turned towards them. Sybelle fired her white gun at the demon's chest. Thwack, thwack, thwack. The shots slammed into the black flesh, sending up spurts of black oil. The demon grunted and fell backwards, disappearing over the console.

Gun raised, Rust stepped over the fallen bodies and gingerly advanced towards the first barricade. She didn't take her eyes off where the thing had disappeared. The two remaining rebels and Indiril followed.

Sybelle ran over towards Kathnell.

"Wait," Rust shouted. She'd seen the thing in action before. Seen how they could move. Sybelle ignored the warning.

"Kathnell!"

A black shape darted from behind the console. It moved fast, jumping whilst aiming its gun at the injured rebel woman. It fired three times, striking the rebel woman twice in the chest and once in the head. Inhumanly fast and accurate.

The last rebel fired his own gun. Bullets, wide of the mark, struck a wall console. Hot water vapour erupted from where they hit, billowing into the carriage.

The demon landed. Fast, but not uninjured, left arm hanging limply. Sword missing. Sybelle's gun had done actual damage! Blood trailed behind it. Clouds of water vapour continued to spew from the broken console, filling the carriage with white mist.

Rust fired her own gun. It fired twice, then clicked, bullets bouncing uselessly off the thing's black skin. Rust pulled the trigger again. Nothing. Sybelle tried to raise her own gun. The demon was quicker. It fired at Sybelle.

It missed! The thing missed!

It jumped at Sybelle, landing a heavy kick to her chest. The impact lifted Sybelle off her feet and sent her crashing into the wall dangerously close to one of the open external doors. She landed with a crunch and went limp. Sybelle's gun spun uselessly away down the carriage, disappearing into clouds of vapour.

Indiril fired his crossbow at the thing, hitting it in the chest. The bolt snapped on impact, falling to the floor.

The demon laughed.

The remaining rebel dropped his gun. He knelt, praying silently. Indiril backed off towards the rear of the compartment. Out of options. The demon turned towards Rust and started walking calmly over.

"Time to stop playing Rustari!" the demon said.

Rust backed towards the open doorway where Sybelle had fallen. The demon, partly lost in clouds of valour. The city flashed past. No, not the city. Countryside! The demon dropped its gun.

"See all the trouble you've caused," the demon mocked. "All the needless death. This is all on you."

"Feldershit!"

Rust reached the open doorway. She bent over Sybelle, keeping an eye on the demon at all times. Sybelle was out cold, her leg twisted at an odd angle. She was breathing. That was something, at least. Rust reached down to the girl's waist. Rust plucked something from Sybelle's belt, holding it out of sight behind her back.

The thing outstretched its right hand. Blue sparks arcing between the thing's fingers.

"Time to end this," the demon said.

"I'm not coming back!" Rust shouted, standing and taking a side step towards the doorway. Cool morning air rippled the fabric on her back.

"I didn't really expect you to. Maybe I should let you die here. For what you did to Trelt! Just a little accident. I don't care now. You've caused enough trouble."

The demon took another step. The blue sparks increased in intensity. So sure of her victory. So arrogant. The black oil flowed back away from its face, exposing the woman underneath.

"What I did? You're the ones that invaded my country.

My home. Hurt my friends. My village!"

Rust edged closer to the doorway.

"Ha! Poor little farm girl. You don't have a fucking clue, do you? You think these people are on your side? Any of them? You have no idea what the larger picture is. The trouble these people have caused. You should be thanking us for saving your worthless village from people like these."

The demon was just a couple of feet away now, hand reached out towards her. Surely, Rust was still worth more to them alive than dead?

"So, this is your new plan? To kill me? I thought Trelt said I was important. Well, I'd sooner throw myself off this thing than go back!"

Rust edged backwards. Feet dangerously close to the edge. The ground shot past underneath. Just one unexpected jolt and she really would be gone.

"Alas, I would love you to die, but I have my orders."

Rust stepped backwards. One foot in midair. The wind threatened to tear her away. The demon darted forward, gripping Rust's shoulder and pulling her back towards safety. Eye to eye.

"Fuck you!" Rust spat in the demon's face. Behind her back, Rust gripped the magic sword she'd taken from Sybelle. She wasn't even sure it would work. Her thumb found and pressed the little button on its side. The blade shot out, glowing bright blue.

Rust swung her arm up and around in an arc. Slicing into the demon's left side. The demon gasped, took a step forward, and fell against her. Eyes locked with Rust's. Surprise. Shock. Hate.

The demon was missing her left forearm and part of her lower left leg. Black fluid bubbled and spat where the leg and elbow ended. It frothed and fizzed. Black tar quickly flowed back up over the demon's face, bubbling as it did so.

The bubbles tried to reform around the missing arm and leg, almost as if unaware they were missing. The bubbles expanded, spreading all over the demon's body. They pushed against Rust like large black blisters. Popping and reforming. Threatening to merge into Rust's own clothing. Nearby metal surfaces arced with sparks. The hair on Rust's arms stood on end. The air stank of something metallic.

Rust stepped sideways and shoved, pushing the now shapeless black thing through the open train door. The demon fell out, landed heavily, rolled twice, and came to rest in a field. The train quickly took it out of sight behind them.

The only sounds now, the rhythmic noise of the tracks and the incomprehensible praying that came from the surviving rebel.

Rust turned and collapsed beside Sybelle. Indiril rushed over and threw his arms around Rust.

"Thank Sindar! Sindar's fucking breath. You did it!"

"Stop swearing, Indiril," Rust laughed.

Sybelle moaned softly. The rebel soldier continued to just kneel and pray. He didn't even seem to notice that the fighting was over.

"Help Sybelle," Rust said, "I need to check on Kathnell."

Rust staggered over to where the young rebel woman had fallen. She, too, was breathing. Blood streamed from a very swollen left eye socket where a sliver of metal stuck out. She wasn't sure if her eye was damaged or not. Not sure what was best to do, Rust pulled the metal out. Rust tore a piece of cloth off her own shirt and wrapped it around Kathnell's eye.

The girl moaned, reaching her hand up towards her face.

"Leave it. It's all right, it's all right," Rust said.

"Sybelle, where is Sybelle?"

Rust looked over at Indiril, who was tending to Sybelle. The girl was awake.

"I'm... I'm here Kath!" came a weak reply.

Kathnell visibly relaxed. She tried to reach up to her eye again.

"Don't worry about that for the minute," Rust said.

"Did we do it? Are we safe?"

The rebel had stopped praying now. He'd at last realised that the fighting had stopped. Now he just sat in the middle of the floor weeping, surrounded by his fallen comrades.

The morning sunlight streamed in through the open doorway. Trees and open fields.

"Yes," Rust said, "I think we are."

Chapter 23

I see no more of them, for their kind has passed forever into nothing.

All their great works, like dust.

A million glorious histories, no more.

Only he remembers. And that shall be his greatest burden.

Books of Maleth - Lamentations - Twenty nine

Indiril

Indiril stood on the quayside and gazed out to sea, worn paving stones cold against his bare feet.

He couldn't imagine so much water! Vast. Limitless. Filled with Sindar-knew-what. He shivered. They would go OUT THERE soon.

Waves crashed onto the steps below them. Fine spray reached his face. How long had the steps been there? Hundreds of years at least, judging by how they'd been worn down by an immeasurable number of footsteps. History, as vast as the ocean.

The weather had turned from high summer heat to unseasonably cold and windy.

The vessel that would take them was small and wooden. It bobbed up and down in the water. A toy! Surely, a joke to suggest it could cross THAT. He failed so see how anything so small could survive a journey of a day, let alone the expected week.

Indiril feared the sea. It seemed so large compared to anything he'd ever seen. They said it was common for his people; the Silvar.

He looked over at Rust. She was talking to Kathnell and Sybelle. Rust's hand was bound in white bandages. The blisters underneath looked terrible. It seemed almost impossible that just over two weeks ago, they had both been back in Hammington's Rest. Before all this happened. Two weeks!

Only two rebels from the train had survived. A man called Krishpell that had been with them during the last fight, and the woman who'd been hit in the shoulder. The rest of them, including their leader Albea, were dead. All of them sacrificed just to get Rust out.

Kathnell wore a bandage across her left eye. According to the local doctor, she would be permanently blind in that eye. The metal shard had penetrated through to the nerve. The biggest risk now was infection. Thankfully, the doctor had access to a local apothecary, which had prescribed some poultices and salves.

Sybelle sat, her leg in splints. There were times over the last couple of days that Indiril thought she wouldn't make it. They'd carried her for kilometres through dense woodland. Her leg held limply.

The rebel, Krishpell, had tried to set her leg as best he could. She needed a proper doctor, he said. Sybelle hadn't been able to bear any weight on it. Indiril could see the pain etched on her face, the sweat glistening on her forehead. She'd never complained once. Kathnell, always at her side. At night, she heard Sybelle whimpering, tended to by Kathnell.

They'd abandoned the train about two hours after they left the city. Krishpell said he and Albea had some rebel contacts in a small fishing village called Cappel, but it was many kilometres by land away from the railway. Before they'd left the train, Kathnell had rigged the controls so it would continue without them. She was unsure how far it would get, but it would at least give them a head start.

The trek through the woods had taken three days. Days in which they'd had nothing to eat other than what Rust had foraged. Without her, they would have surely perished. Sybelle had grown increasingly weak with each passing kilometre. By the last day, she had to be carried by them all. Barely awake and delirious. Ranting about her mother, her father, and her brother. She cried out for her brother most of all.

Kathnell's eye continued to close up, oozing blood. They'd run out of bandages, but Rust had found some local leaves that would act in their place. The rebel woman's shoulder had become infected, and she started getting feverish. Regardless, she trudged on with the rest of them.

Despite the hardships, Indiril had found the journey fascinating. He'd heard there were lands like this, places where the feral had been pushed so far back that there was no need for the Winnowing, no need for a lee. They walked through kilometre after kilometre of woodland without fear. Oak, ash, birch. No spikes, no spines. Even so, in the deep woods, they'd found scattered pockets of feral growing unchecked.

They were physically exhausted by the time they reached Cappel. Krispell had left them at the edge of the village to get help. He didn't return for several hours. Indiril had fretted that Krispell had left them, or worse, betrayed them. But he returned and had brought help. Some locals with food and medicine.

The local rebel cell issued them with new clothing. The rebel cell was composed of three people. Two farmers and a fisherman. All looked over sixty. They were all saddened by the loss of Albea. Indiril got the impression she originated from nearby. This wasn't the same organised militia as they had back in Lerins. These three didn't even have guns. But they knew Krispell and promised to help get them away from the area. Away from Lerins and the island of Seendar altogether. They were headed for a place called Vidash, on the northern tip of the mainland. From there, they would be taken somewhere else.

He had never been at sea. It wasn't something he was even in the remotest sense looking forward to. He realised he was staring at the group. An odd bunch. United by events. Rust smiled and walked over to where he stood.

For a few minutes, they both just stood and looked out at sea together. Indiril sighed. Rust cocked her head in question.

"We'll never see the Lone Oak again, will we?" Indiril said.

"I don't know, Indiril, I really don't. One day, I hope so."

"As do I."

It was certain they wouldn't be going back soon. Not to Hammington's Rest, Lerins, or anywhere any of them called home.

Indiril wasn't sure what they'd do when they got to their destination. It was likely the rebels would try to use Rust the same way Trelt and the Hegemon had. The Hegemon still had the pocket watch, but it was useless to them now without Rust to unlock it. Rust said she didn't trust the rebels any more than he did the Hegemon. For the time being at least, they had little choice but to go along with them. They'd talked of little else since their escape on the train. They would decide once they were away from the current situation and things had calmed down. Maybe get away from the rebels and make their own plans. Only time would tell what Sindar had in store for them next.

Kathnell was worried about her mother, alone back in the city. But she took comfort that someone called Corric would look after her.

Sybelle's fever had broken, but she continued to worry about her mother and father. Especially her father, who knew nothing about any of this. Of her brother, she said nothing more.

Rust stood silently for a few moments.

"I'm remembering things from those visions," Rust said. "Little details. Things that seem to come more into focus now than they did at the time."

"Things like?"

"I have one vision of a tall mountain, with clouds on top. Streaming away to the east. I can see it clearer every day. Almost smell it. I think it is called Cloud Maker. I think it's important. No, I know it's important. There are answers there."

"Then I'll help you find it! Together, we'll track down this bloody Cloud Master, or whatever it's called. Like we've always done. Together."

Rust turned to look at him before hugging him tightly. At last, she pulled away. Together, they turned once more to the sea and watched in silence as the waves continued to crash against the ancient quayside.

Everything else could wait until tomorrow.

Trelt

The sky was dark. The air, cold. Colder than it should be. Just the height, Trelt told himself. It made the air thin. He took another breath from his oxygen mask.

Far below, Ascension City spread out towards the horizon. It was nearing midnight. A patchwork of districts sketched out by countless streetlamps. Few got to see the city like this.

He stood on a small balcony high up the side of the White Citadel. There was no railing. Thankfully, the elderstone around the doorway was illuminated from within. He didn't relish standing here in complete darkness. He wasn't afraid of heights, but it was an awfully long way to fall because of a misstep.

A steam powered elevator had brought him most of the way. He'd had to climb the last couple of hundred metres himself. He breathed deeply, taking the cold air down. It felt good.

He waited as he'd been instructed.

Why here?

He gazed down at the city. Soon it would rest for another night, but it would never sleep. Like Alexi, it would remain eternally awake, the beating heart of their necessary empire.

The climb had been tough. His broken legs and pelvis had only just healed. He'd been in the restoraleum for two weeks! Two entire weeks, immobile and unconscious as the thing knitted his broken body back together. He'd never have made this climb without the oxygen mask. He had no memory of anything after the airship had been struck. His first memory was of waking up from the restoraleum.

He was lucky. Many others had died in the West Wind

when it had crash-landed in the city. No, not luck, he decided. It was because of who he was. It gave him access to rare technologies that others could not access. Technology only available to a privileged few. It was privilege, he decided, not luck. No shame in it. It was necessary. Then again, at some point, he'd been in the right place at the right time to even find himself in this position. Destiny then?

He didn't believe in destiny. Luck then!

He laughed.

"Something funny, my friend?" came a voice from the steps behind him.

Soft footfalls approached. He didn't turn. He knew the voice. Alexi. Spoken through one of his Avatars.

"Oh, just trying to work out if I'm lucky, privileged, cursed, or if this is all destiny. Usual existential shit."

The Avatar walked up and stood beside him. Grey and perfectly smooth.

"Probably all four, if you ask me. Before they put me in this thing I remember wondering if I was about to die. I have that memory. A memory of the fear. The unknown. Is it my memory? Or did the flesh and blood of Alexi perish when they put his mind in here? I THINK I feel the same. I have all his memories. Immortal now. Or nearly. Certainly, it was a privilege that afforded me this opportunity long ago, before we left. I was born into the right family. Our wealth was unrivalled in all of known space. But am I alive, or just a ghost that doesn't realise it died? Am I lucky, cursed, or privileged?"

"I don't know Alexi."

"Of course you don't! Nobody does. Neither do I. Not even with all my power. I have access to billions of pieces of information. All I have to do is think, and the answer it there. I am here, looking at you. At the same time, I am down there, talking to an envoy from the other side of the world. He wants more trade concessions. We'll grant them, for a price calculated precisely long before he even arrived.

Across the harbour, another part of me is talking to a ceph matriarch from House Tiama. I hold all these conversations simultaneously without error, all whilst controlling the beating heart of this city. I plan for contingencies tens of years into the future. And yet, I have no answer. So go on, ask the universe your questions. If it responds, and you get your answer, be sure to tell me."

Trelt laughed again. The avatar joined in.

"Splendid view, isn't it?", Alexi asked.

"Yes, magnificent."

"Good! I knew you'd like it," Alexi said. "Did you bring it?"

Trelt reached into his pocket and withdrew the box.

The Avatar took it, gently removed the object within, and held it up to eye level. It glittered in the light from the doorway. Simona's pocket watch. The object that had caused them so much trouble.

"How is Miss Baylali?" Alexi asked.

Trelt sighed.

"Making progress, but she was badly injured. Her kavach armour protected her, but still she nearly died. She hasn't woken yet. She doesn't know how much of her they've had to regrow. I want to be there when she wakes."

"I know she means a lot to you, Trelt. "

"Yes, she does. I try to protect her as best I can."

"And yet, you put her continually at risk. She's one of the few pure navigator lineages left from the ship. I worry you forget that sometimes."

"I don't forget Alexi. What she does, she does willingly. She is too stubborn to be held back."

The avatar smiled and nodded.

"No news on the Rustari girl?" Alexi said.

"None. They have certainly left Seendar by now."

"No matter. We still have this!"

"But we can't unlock it without Rustari."

"But we have her blood. There are ways and means we can crack these things without the individuals themselves.

If our hands can't access its secrets, we will forge ourselves a set of hands that can."

Alexi handed the pocket watch back to Trelt. He looked at the watch-face. Twelve hours, instead of the usual ten. Two full revolutions marking twenty-four hours.

The twenty-four hours of the distant and long-dead Earth.

Acknowledgements

The first person I would like to thank is you, the reader. Thank you for reading Hegemon Reign, the first book in the Shadows of Nemesis series. I hope you have enjoyed it. Without you, the places, ideas, and characters would remain mere words. With your reading, they transcend into existence. Thank you.

I would not have been able to write this novel without the continued support of my wife Samantha. You have been my ever-present source of encouragement whenever self-doubt and anxiety threatened to derail my writing. This book would never have been written without you.

I would also like to thank my beta-readers for their invaluable feedback and advice. Thank you, Sandra, Paul, Ines, David, Alex, Andrea, and Elaine. Without your invaluable feedback, some of my more embarrassing mistakes would have gone unnoticed. Thanks also go to Adam and Dean who spotted some additional mistakes and inconsistencies in the first version that I have since rectified.

Lastly, I would like to thank all the sci-fi writers that over the years whom have inspired my imagination. To name but a small few, Arthur C. Clarke, Larry Niven, Carl Sagan, Frank Herbert, Peter F. Hamilton, Alastair Reynolds, Isaac Asimov, Hugh Howey, and Iain M. Banks. The entire list is too long to mention here. Thank you for the stories and characters that have transported me to places unseen and the infinite landscape of futures that might be. Without you, the future is nothing but death and taxes.

About the author

S. J. Halls is a software engineer, writer, and author of the novel Hegemon Reign, the first book in the Shadows of Nemesis series.

He spent his early years roaming the Suffolk countryside around the village in which he grew up, most often on his battered bicycle. Growing up, he became fascinated with all things space, science fiction, and computer related. Having taken in interest in pens-and-paper role-playing games as a teenager, he has always enjoyed creating new worlds and characters for others to enjoy.

After an education in computer science, he now works as a software engineer within the environmental and energy-saving sector, topics which he remains passionate about.

S. J. Halls relaxes by helping his wife create their wildlife garden, taking astro-photographs of the night sky, walking the family dog, playing role-playing games with his friends (yes, he's still playing them now), and reading.

He is a self proclaimed nerd, and encourages everyone to "embrace your inner nerd".

For more information, visit his website sjhalls.com

Printed in Great Britain
by Amazon